D0293566

THEATRICAL

THEATRICAL

Maggie Harcourt

USBORNE

For Clare and Alex:

we'll always have the Ustinov.

First published in the UK in 2018 by Usborne Publishing Ltd., Usborne House, 83-85 Saffron Hill, London EC1N 8RT, England. www.usborne.com

Text © Maggie Harcourt, 2018

Cover illustration by Helen Crawford-White, studiohelen

Cover illustration © Usborne Publishing, 2018

Author photo © Lou Abercrombie

The right of Maggie Harcourt to be identified as the author of this work has been asserted by her in accordance with the Copyright, Designs and Patents Act, 1988.

The name Usborne and the devices ♀ 🜨 **USBORNE** are Trade Marks of Usborne Publishing Ltd.

A CIP catalogue record for this book is available from the British Library.

ISBN 9781474940689 JFMA JJASOND/18 04701/1

Printed in the UK.

Because everybody knows the
real drama happens backstage…

ACT ONE

Audition

ACT ONE, SCENE ONE

Fifteen minutes.

That's only...what, nine hundred seconds – right?

Nine hundred seconds late feels so much better than *quarter of an hour late*. Doesn't it?

Okay, so no. I'm fifteen minutes late.

And what that makes me is screwed.

My umbrella turns itself inside out thanks to the March mini-hurricane blowing round the corner of the building. Funnelled between the long, low warehouses of the industrial estate, the gusts are even stronger here than they were on the main road. At least back there the rain just fell downwards; now it's going every possible kind of sideways... and I swear some of it's actually coming back up at me. I ditch the umbrella. It's blatantly not helping.

Unit thirty-two, unit thirty-two...

Come on, come on, come on...

Unit eighty-seven.

And a dead end.

You have got to be *kidding* me.

I turn around and swim back up the road to the sign that lists all the businesses and companies on the estate with their unit numbers, looking for anything that even remotely resembles *Earl's Theatre Rehearsal Room*. Or *Theatre*. Or even *Room*.

Basically, at this point I'll take anything that's legible.

Five minutes later, I shove open a battered metal door in a red, two-storey unit – the mythical unit thirty-two, which turned out to be on a completely different road and in between unit number forty-one and unit number ninety-three (although perhaps that's only on Thursdays – maybe on Wednesdays and alternate Sundays it's next to unit thirty-three, just for fun). I peel off my soaked coat. Inside is…not quite what I was expecting. The front section of the unit has been divided off to make an entrance space; there's an empty clothes rack nailed to the side wall, so I hang my coat on one of the pegs, where it drips gently. The reception area is deserted, and the only furniture is a sagging, slightly grubby sofa and a little glass table next to it, piled with crumpled back-issues of *The Stage* and an old dog-eared copy of the Spotlight *Contacts* book.

This is not even close to how I imagined the entrance to the rehearsal room of a theatre like the Earl's would look. I think I'd pictured…I don't know, maybe something a little cleaner? A plush velvet sofa, maybe. Gleaming floor-to-ceiling windows with natural light streaming in and a waxed wooden floor.

Wrong on all counts.

"Umm…hello?"

My voice bounces off the dingy grey walls, coming straight back to me. *This is how horror films start*, says a small voice that belongs to a bit of me I almost certainly don't want to listen to. *It really is.*

Beyond the sofa is another door – a blue one this time, with a small, neatly-printed card taped to it.

INTERVIEWS.
(Knock & enter.)

I wonder whether whoever typed it meant to make it as passive-aggressive as they have by adding the full stops. Who adds punctuation to a sign like that?

I squeeze as much rainwater out of my hair as I can, and I knock. Full stops or not.

The room on the other side is much, much larger – it's actually kind of like my school's gym hall. It even has the same floor tiles, but with dozens of little black-and-yellow taped crosses and Ls stuck to them. The main difference, though, is the back wall – the whole thing here is taken up by a huge pinboard, where hundreds of sketches, colour printouts and pages of notes flutter in a draught. And in front of it all, smack in the middle of the hall, is a table where three men and one woman are sitting – looking incredibly bored and *not a little* annoyed.

"Uh, hi?" I raise a hand, hoping they didn't spot the water that just dripped off my elbow. "Hope Parker. I'm here for the internship interview? I'm really sorry, I got…"

"Drowned?" says one of the line-up, barely glancing up from the book he's reading. He smirks at his own joke, then arches an eyebrow at me and drops the paperback – the novel about magicians that everyone seems to be reading lately, dog-eared and thick with Post-it notes poking out – on the floor with a bang. I recognize him almost immediately and want to curl myself into a ball in the middle of the floor and never speak or move or do *anything* again. Because it's Rick Hillier. I finally get to meet Rick Hillier, my favourite actor, my favourite director, my favourite everything…and I'm late and approximately ninety-seven per cent rain. Excellent.

"Is it still raining?" The woman – she must be Amy, the Earl's Theatre deputy stage manager who rang me about this interview – looks up at the ceiling as though she's worried the water will start pouring through any second.

I push my hair back behind my ear again. I've had showers that have left me drier than this. One of my trainers sprang a leak outside unit fifteen and I can still feel the water swooshing around my toes.

"A bit."

"That explains why you're late, I suppose. We'd almost given up on you," says another of the men. Sitting at the end of the table, he's older than the others – even older than my dad, I'd guess – and he's got a folder open in front of him, which he keeps tapping with the end of a pen. I decide that it's probably not the best idea to say that I'm actually late because I was practising – rehearsing – for this so hard that I completely forgot to check the time. I should have checked the time. But if they want to go with the rain story, let's run with that.

"Yes. The rain, and the bus…" I shrug and a drop of water very slowly trickles down between my shoulder blades.

"Well, now you're here you'd better sit down." He points to the cushioned chair in front of the table – then looks straight over my shoulder. "Or perhaps one of those would be more practical…?"

I follow his gaze to the stack of hard plastic chairs beside the door. I drip back across the floor to the door, drip a chair out of the stack and drip all the way back to the table, sitting down across from the four of them. As one, they stare back at me. This is brutal.

"Here." Amy has been rummaging in the rucksack at her feet and pulls out a towel, holding it out to me across the table.

I shake my head. "I'm fine, really. Thanks."

I sneeze.

"On second thoughts…" I take the towel and sit there with it in my lap like I've somehow forgotten what towels are for.

This is going well.

"So. Hope. You're seventeen, and you're from Marshfield School – is that right?" Folder Man looks down at his papers, then carries on without waiting for an answer. "You've applied for the stage management placement with us, haven't you?"

"Umm…yes?"

"We've got your form, but we'd like you to tell us a little about yourself – starting with why you want to work in a role like this."

I practised this. I did. I've got a whole spiel about close readings of a script and bringing a theatre company together as a family, looking after them and making sure they have what they need. I can talk about a theatre as a living, breathing machine where everyone is a cog and it's only when the cogs are all turning together that the whole thing comes to life. I have stuff about finding props, about tech week; about schedules and supporting the director and problem-solving and *everything*. I've practised it in front of my mirror every night this week. I wrote it on cue cards, just to be sure.

The ones I realized on the way over that I'd left under my bed. And now I can't remember any of it.

Superb.

Four pairs of eyes look at me expectantly.

I've got nothing. Nothing but wet hair and wet shoes and wet jeans.

It's Amy who takes pity on me. "Wow, Charlie. Big question to hit her with when she's only just sat down!" She looks along the table at him. "Maybe we could start with something a bit gentler?"

He shrugs, and she takes this as an *okay*, turning to smile at me. "You said on your form that you've got some experience of backstage work. Talk to us about that a bit, Hope."

"Umm…"

I know this is the bit where, according to the form, I'm supposed to have the chance to *demonstrate a passion for practical theatre.*

For two years, I've volunteered at the Square Globe Community Theatre in my free time as an assistant stage manager – aka the dogsbody, errand-runner, gluer-and-stapler of broken scenery, and the wielder of the safety pin and iron-on webbing that sticks anything to *anything* (trust me, I've tried). Two years of first-night applause and last-minute adrenalin rushes, end-of-run parties and those in-jokes that are only funny if you were in the room when something happened – which I usually was. Two years in which I've helped actors learn their lines, hissed their lines from the side of the stage when they forgot them, and listened to them complaining when lines they *had* learned got cut before they had the chance to forget them. I've learned how to get mic tape off someone's neck without making them cry, and I have even carried a pantomime cow costume to the dry-cleaner's in an unseasonal heatwave. (Tip: it's not too difficult if you actually wear the back half to walk in, but you do get some funny looks.)

And I've loved every minute of it.

Being in a theatre – any theatre – is like walking into an enormous hug. To me, standing at the back of an auditorium and looking at the stage feels like a pair of velvet-covered arms are wrapping around me and pulling me close. It's where I'm meant to be. Give me a headset and I'm happy – even one of the crappy old ones at the Square Globe which were fished out of a skip behind the Earl's. The first time I put one on, I realized it still had the red-and-gold Earl's logo stamped on it, and I promised myself that one day I'd be putting a headset on in the Earl's itself. Preferably one that hadn't come out of a skip.

This is my only chance to talk about all that, really. Not just because if I don't I can forget the placement, but because even though my mum loves the theatre, she belongs to another part of it. She's confident and so sure that she knows what she's talking about, and when she's working she can always say what she means and it makes sense. She just *does* it. She could talk about costumes all day (and people literally pay her to do that sometimes) but the stuff she cares about is always *meant* to be seen. It's the swooshing silks and swirling capes, beads and glitter and things shining in the light. And that's the opposite of what I am. The opposite of where I think *I'm* meant to be. And she'll never get that: how can she? People see her work and they know it's hers – she's famous for it. As for Dad and my sisters, well, they've had so many years of Mum's theatre-related dramas that the thought of me bringing even more of them home wouldn't go down well. The community theatre stuff's one thing, but as far as they're concerned, one theatre professional in the family's quite enough.

Which is why nobody knows I'm here.

This is *my* dream, that *I* need to make happen. *On my own.*

At least, that's partly why, anyway…

Four pairs of eyes are still looking at me expectantly, and everything I have to say – everything I *want* to say – turns to dust in my mouth and my voice evaporates. All the passion, all the enthusiasm, all the…whatever else I'm supposed to show them I have? Dust, smoke and ashes.

I have, to borrow a phrase from the actors, *dried*.

Amy rescues me again, clearing her throat and pointedly looking at my form on the table in front of her.

"Just one thing before we go any further. Would you be

willing to sign an NDA for us?" She pulls a printed sheet of paper out of one of her folders, holding it out to me.

"A non-disclosure agreement?" My fingers close around the form.

"We can see that you've got good experience of script reading, prop management and rehearsal notes, which is great. We're hoping to bring our intern in on our next... well, our *current* production. It's finishing out its rehearsal-room time and moving into the theatre for technical rehearsals. We've got some stage magic designed by Katie Khan we'll need to be on-site to really get working and that might be a bit of a challenge...but let's not get ahead of ourselves. I have to say, though, that looking at your background, I think this show would be a good fit for you."

I nod. Enthusiastically. I can't actually make any sound, but nodding I *can* manage.

Current production.

Amy is still talking.

"...And between protecting the magic and the fact we're expecting it to be a high-profile show, the NDA is standard. It's not just you, I promise," she adds.

I know this. I know I know it.

I know what they're rehearsing now, but suddenly my mind's gone blank and all I can do is nod like an idiot. My whole brain is blacked-out by panic.

So I nod some more. What have I got to lose?

"Obviously, we're aware of your school commitments, but if we were to offer you the place, we would like to have you with us for the next few weeks. So that's next week, and then into the Easter break for the end of rehearsal, tech, and – of course – opening night. Can you confirm you'd be available for the whole period? Your school will have to be on board, and sign off your absence."

I keep nodding. This seems to be enough.

"Okay. Great. The internship is focused on the deputy stage manager role – from your application I imagine you know a lot of this already – and you would be required to work across all the different aspects of stage management. At the end, we can provide you with a reference should you wish to apply for a formal stage qualification." She pauses, checks something written in her notebook. "The pro-rata pay isn't particularly good, I'm afraid – but at least it's something. Nobody goes into theatre to get rich, do they? What else? The actors have just about got their lines down and are largely off-book, but they'll need the odd bit of prompting. You'll be supporting Rick here –" she nods at Rick, who nods back even though he now looks like he actually hates me – "with rehearsal notes and blocking out the actors' movements across the stage ready for when we move into the theatre." She flips through her notebook again. "You say you've done a little of that?"

It finally hits me.

Piecekeepers.

That's the show. The stage adaptation of *Piecekeepers* – the magic book with all the spells trapped in paintings; the one Rick was reading. It gets a six-week run at the Earl's before it transfers out to the West End.

And the lead?

The lead is Tommy Knight.

Actual *movie star* Tommy Knight.

Oh god.

This show is a huge deal. And they're saying I might get to work on it.

"A bit." My voice comes out wobblier than I'd like. I sound exactly as nervous as I feel, and that's not good.

"Great. Mostly you'd be shadowing me, especially through the technical rehearsals, as well as looking after the props. Oh, and we would also need you to work with our wardrobe intern…" She glances at my form. "But you don't need me to tell you about wardrobe, do you?"

No. Please no.

I wait for someone to say it. They always do.

"Parker? You don't mean…not as in Miriam Parker? You don't happen to be related, do you?"

Hope Parker-as-in-Miriam-Parker. Yes, *that* Miriam Parker: legendary theatrical costume designer Miriam Parker. When I get talking to anyone in theatre, it always comes back to my mum eventually.

"How many Olivier Awards does she have now? Is it five or seven?" (It's eight, actually, and thanks for asking.)

"And what about the Craft BAFTAs?" (One – and a near-miss three years ago. We still don't mention that one.)

"Oh, and didn't she make the dress that What's-Her-Name wore to that premiere…?" (Probably.)

But not this time. I keep waiting, and it simply doesn't come. Nobody says the M-word. Instead, Rick makes a sound halfway between a grunt and a sigh…and that's it. I'm in the clear.

I could have put her name down on my form, of course; nothing would have made her happier than if she thought I wanted to follow in her footsteps. She'd probably have exploded with joy, collapsing into one last pile of spangles and bugle beads… But then I'd be the girl who got an internship at the Earl's because of her mum, which is the last thing I want after everything I've done to get here. Everything I've done by myself – without dropping my mother's name to do it.

I want to do this on my own, not to follow someone else. To know I got it because I worked for it, and because I earned it.

Amy looks at me for a long, long time and jots something down on my form, and Rick folds his arms across his chest, stretching his feet out underneath the table. "So you've done two years at the Square Globe. What does that mean

– weekends?" He fixes me with a look that makes me feel like a bug pinned to a board in a museum.

"Whenever I could get over there. Weekends, holidays, evenings after school…"

"And they won't miss you?"

"Umm…" I fidget with the edge of my damp sleeve, squeezing out a drop of water. "I've…" *What is it people say?* "I've stepped back from the Square Globe a bit."

Something that looks almost like a smirk flits across his face. "Stepped back?" He studies me carefully, searching for more. Well, he's not going to find it – not here, not now. Not Rick Hillier.

After a silence long enough to stage an opera, he nods and moves on. "What about theatre you've seen? Can you tell us about something you watched recently?"

"Oh…I went to the Royal Court. The Almeida, and the Old Vic."

"London or Bristol?"

"Both."

"Did you indeed?"

"I saw you. You were really good. *Really* good." I hear it from somewhere outside my body. I can't stop it – it just *comes out* of me – and now I definitely, definitely want to curl up in a ball and die. Or possibly have the ground open up and swallow me and then this will be *over*.

"Well, thank you. That's very kind."

The lines at the corners of his eyes crinkle slightly, and… he's almost smiling. Rick Hillier. Actual actor/director/ general-all-round-theatre-rock-star Rick Hillier, sitting in front of me and smiling. At me. Or at least smiling *near* me.

When I saw him onstage at the London Old Vic six months ago, he'd shaved off all his hair for the role and – from where I was sitting, at least – he looked like he was three metres tall and made of nothing but solid muscle. Now he's just a guy who's…what, almost forty…with a grey-speckled, trimmed beard, close-cropped dark hair and a slightly tatty jumper with holes near the ends of the sleeves. Holes which he's hooked his thumbs through.

And despite that and the (almost) smile, he's still *terrifying*.

"I, umm…I don't get to see that much live theatre. School. Trains. The show times and the cost, you know? But sometimes I get cheap tickets…" (By which I mean I haul myself on an early train on a Saturday and schlep to the West End and queue for day seats and returns and those weird sort-of-standing tickets right at the back…) "And I go to loads of the cinema theatre screenings." (Like I could forget the time I was going into the screen showing *Richard III* live from the Barbican with all the little old ladies on their social outing, while everyone from my year in school was going into the next screen to see…I don't know, *Exploding Monkeys With Shotguns IV* or something. It was weird. Maybe *I'm* just weird.)

A thick, heavy silence has fallen around me.

Did I say *all* of that out loud?

Amy is nodding and Rick is still half-smiling and sort of narrowing his eyes, and Folder Man – Charlie? – is looking at me thoughtfully, and I wish I knew how to make myself sound calm, collected and competent; maybe sound a bit like a seventeen-year-old interviewing for an internship at a real theatre and less like…well, me?

"Do you have any particular deputy stage managers whose style you would hope to emulate?" Charlie Folder Man comes back with a low blow, and honestly, I preferred his first question. Particularly seeing as this one's a trick. I shuffle in my seat. My jeans squelch.

Is it a trick?

The seconds crawl by like weeks.

No, it's a trick. It's definitely a trick.

I think.

"I read something – ages ago – that said the best DSMs are like ninjas. Kind of invisible. They hold everything together – but unless you actually know what they do, you never see them. You wouldn't even know they exist, never mind realizing they were running around behind the stage and the set the entire time you were watching a show. They're like…" Another drip runs down between my shoulder blades, making me completely lose the thread of my thought.

"I…the, um…sorry – what was I saying?"

"Stage managers are ninjas, I think it was?"

"Oh. Yes. Well, kind of. Maybe they're more like wizards? Either way, that's the kind of DSM I'd like to be. A wizard ninja. Wizinja. Winja. Yes."

I make myself stop.

It was better when I couldn't actually talk. Anything would be better than this. I just compared the deputy stage manager of an actual theatre to a wizard ninja.

I did that.

Out of the corner of my eye, I see Amy smile – a real smile – although at a stern look from Charlie, her face almost immediately blanks and she shuffles the papers in front of her.

"Okay, let's go back to the original question," she says, looking right at me. "Why stage management, specifically? It's not the easiest job in the theatre. You're involved in every aspect of a production, right from pre-production and rehearsals all the way to get-out when the show closes. The hours are long and they're unsociable. It's not the most straightforward career to balance a life with."

And this time I don't need cue cards.

"When I was little, my mum…" I stop myself. I start again. "I got to go backstage at the Earl's when I was a kid. There was an opera company in." I remember it so clearly. Back then, Mum was working in theatre full-time – it was right before she started doing freelance TV and the odd wedding, before she properly started her own business.

The last interviewer – the third man, who's been fiddling with his phone since I walked in and hasn't said a word – suddenly sits straight up and looks at me. His eyes are very small and a very bright shade of green. It's a little like being watched by a cat. "At the Earl's, you say? You must have been quite young – there hasn't been an opera company through the theatre in ten years."

"Nine." I probably shouldn't have corrected him – especially seeing as I'm not entirely sure who he is. "It was nine years ago. It was my eighth birthday – that's why I remember it, I guess. The chorus sang 'Happy Birthday' to me."

Like anyone could forget that. Ever.

"And that was what made you want to work in theatre? Why?" Amy asks.

"I was waiting in the corner of the production office. I think the stage team were having a meeting, and it was just…the way they talked. How they knew everything about what was going on in the theatre and everyone in it…like it was part of them and they were part of it and you couldn't separate them. Like they belonged there. And listening to them, I suddenly couldn't imagine wanting to do anything else or be anywhere else, and I haven't, ever since. Walking around all the little corridors backstage, the corners the audience can't see – even at the Square Globe – it's like you're being let into a secret. Like everything that happens on the stage is just a reflection – or the tip of an iceberg, the tiny bit that most people see. The only bit most people *ever* see. Backstage – that's the rest of it."

I can't stop it. The words, the ideas, come fizzing out of me like fireworks.

"People come to the theatre to be shown things. To experience things. They want to be taken somewhere else, somewhere they can never really go. They want a journey – and you, everybody backstage…you're their passport."

Charlie scribbles something on the page in front of him – probably a huge *NO* across my name, if the expression on his face is anything to go by – and closes the file.

At least I tried.

I *tried*.

"Well," he says, "thanks for coming in, Hope. We're running short of time so we'll have to leave it there – but we'll be in touch."

So that's that.

I look at the clock, and it's exactly fifteen minutes since I walked in.

This has been the longest nine hundred seconds of my life.

* * *

"How was…what on earth happened to you?" Mum stops halfway across the tiles of the hall floor, her teacup midway to her lips.

"It's raining." I kick the front door shut behind me.

"Is it?" She actually walks to the window, puts the cup and saucer down on the sill and peers out. Like I've somehow made the whole thing up and I'm soaking wet because pneumonia is fun. "It is, isn't it?" She turns around, and she's already forgotten that I'm behind her: I see her jump. "Well, don't just stand there. You're dripping all over the floor!"

With that warm welcome, she heads back into the kitchen and I can hear her rummaging around in a cupboard for a cloth. If it was, say, Faith who'd come in soaking wet, she might get offered a towel to dry her perfect, perfect self off – but I get a cloth to clear up the mess I've made. The joy of being the youngest sister of three, right there. Mind you, it goes both ways: if it's a choice between being overlooked or in the centre of the full, blinding glare of maternal attention, give me Mum's benign neglect any day. At least I get to stay a lot further under her radar than Faith and Grace do on the (thankfully) rare occasions they come home for the weekend. Then it's all, "Grace has done this marvellous thing…" and, "Did I tell you? Faith has single-handedly cured the common cold and brought about world peace, and she didn't even chip her perfectly-manicured nails in the process."

I think that kind of attention would make me shrivel up on the spot. Just as well I don't get it.

Mum comes padding back down the hall on bare feet, balancing her cup and saucer in one hand, her phone jammed in between her shoulder and ear as she hands me a floor cloth with the other.

"Sorry, darling. I have to talk to my supplier about that silk they sent me last week – it was completely the wrong... Yes, I'm still here," she adds into the phone, then back to me: "You can tell me all about your day over dinner."

She gives me an apologetic smile as she nudges her studio door shut behind her, disappearing between brightly coloured bolts of cloth and boxes of pins – and the first thing I feel (other than wet, because there's really no escaping it) is relief. I'm in the clear – she still thinks I was at the Square Globe. And I guess from her point of view, that's a pretty safe assumption... But even if I had told her where I was really going, I wouldn't want to go over the interview right now. Not when the wound is still fresh.

Wizard ninjas. Good job, Hope. There was so much I wanted to say; so much I could have – *should* have – said about why I'd be good...and what did I end up sounding passionate about? Eavesdropping on a conversation when I was a kid. Stupid Hope. Stupid, stupid, stupid.

But at least I don't have to talk about the mess I made of the interview...because she doesn't know anything about it.

I could have told her everything – right from the minute I saw the piece about the internships in the paper…but I didn't.

I didn't because, actually, I *couldn't*. I don't want Mum stroking my hair and telling me I should be louder and brighter – like I can somehow wrap myself in the patterned fabric she buys by the metre and be someone else. I don't want her to tell me I should make more noise about myself. What I *want* is to not have to talk about me.

And that's exactly what I'm going to do. Not talk about myself, or the internship at the Earl's. Not at all. Let everyone think it's just another normal day in HopeWorld.

Like talking to Rick Hillier about theatre is a normal day.

I was just in a room with Rick Hillier, talking to him.

Talking at him. Like an idiot.

"You were really good…"

Yeah, well done. Like he cares what you think, Hope.

In the safety of my room, I rummage under my bed for my cue cards – which are right where I left them, along with the letter inviting me to the interview which asks me to please be prompt. Ha. I open it out and reread it four times – and every time I find some new way I've managed to cock the whole thing up. Like how Charlie Folder Man was the Earl's front-of-house manager, and the other guy – the one I corrected – was none other than Franklin Hamilton, the owner of the Earl's, and the one responsible for setting up the new internships and outreach programme I was applying for. So I totally just told him he was wrong about his own theatre.

Brilliant.

I screw the letter into a perfect ball and throw both it and my useless cue cards at the bin by my desk. They miss. Of course they do. The cards scatter around it like giant confetti, and the letter bounces into the middle of the black-box model I made of the Old Vic's stage last month, which sits alongside my bookcase. The paper ball knocks over the tiny scale figure of a man with a shaved head standing in the centre of the stage. I pick him up and straighten him out, putting him back on the little black X that marks the centre of the spotlight, and then I scoop up the cue cards and the letter and drop them into the rubbish.

Layer by layer, I peel off my wet clothes and let them fall on the floor, trying to ignore the creeping halo of damp that spreads out from underneath the pile, turning the pink of my rug to crimson. (It looks like a bloodstain. Here lies the body of Hope Parker's dreams. RIP.) I pull on my pyjamas and my favourite old jumper and wrap a towel around my hair, and with every piece of clothing I play back another question in my head. Of course I have the perfect answers now.

I kick the theatre model across the room.

It skids across the carpet and glides to a halt in front of my wardrobe, and we eye each other resentfully.

And then I give in and go pick it up, straightening the

now-dented proscenium arch and putting it back on the floor by my shelves…and all the while, the miniature model of Rick Hillier watches me from his cardboard stage.

Somewhere under my soggy clothes, my phone rings.

My phone never rings.

It can only be Priya. I had to tell her about the interview, especially as she was going to cover for me if I needed it, and now I haven't messaged her the second I got out, she wants to know how it went. Is it okay to answer with "Not well" and hang up?

She'll give up in a minute. I'll message her later.

My phone keeps ringing.

And then it stops.

And starts up again almost immediately.

That's not Priya. She knows that if she calls and I don't answer, I don't want to talk.

So who's calling me?

I scrabble through the damp pile and yank my phone out of what are quite possibly the wettest jeans that have ever existed. The screen's a bit…misty, showing a mobile number I don't recognize.

"Hello?"

"Hello! Hope?" A woman's voice, familiar but barely audible over a loud clattering sound. "Sorry about the noise – can you hear me? It's Amy. From the Earl's. You came to the rehearsal room earlier and I wanted to say…"

You wanted to say thanks for your time, but we've decided to give it to someone else. Someone who didn't make a complete arse of themselves; who looks like they're half-together. Who turned up on time.

"…I wanted to say thanks for coming in. It was great to meet you…"

Mmm-hmmm.

"…And I've had a chat with my colleagues, and I thought I'd call and confirm we'd like you to come in and start on Monday if you're able to?"

I…what?

"Hope? Are you there? Sorry – can you hear me all right?"

"You're giving me the placement? You're sure?" The words come from someone else – whoever it is they're giving the place to. They aren't mine. It isn't me. It can't be.

"That's what I said. We're giving you the place, if you still want it?"

"Of course I want it! Yes! But…but why me?"

Why me? Why am I even asking? Why am I giving them a chance to realize they've made a mistake and change their minds?

She laughs, and it's a nice sound. "You had it the minute I read your application, Hope. I just wanted to meet you in person first to make sure you knew what you were getting into. You're perfect for it – you're passionate and ambitious and you've got more experience than anyone else who applied, but more than that, you understand the job. Anyone can learn the skills but you understand what theatre *is*, and you understand what it needs to be."

"I do?"

"You do. I guessed that much from your form, but I wanted to be sure. And I could hear it in the way you talked."

"Right."

I'm not even sure I understand what it is I'm supposed to have understood.

"Do you need any kind of confirmation letter from us for the time off school? I know the break covers most of it, but if we can help…?"

"The drama teacher already spoke to the head for me, and I've given them a reference letter from the Square Globe, but I'll ask if they need something from you too."

"Great. Let me know on Monday – and please bring that NDA with you. We'll see you then, ten o'clock at the Earl's rehearsal rooms."

It's really happening. She means it.

I have the place. I'm going to work at the Earl's Theatre.

Me.

An actual theatre.

A professional theatre.

"Wear something comfortable. I don't need to tell you how much movement there can be in stage management, so nothing restrictive."

"Okay. Yes. Absolutely." And then, before I can stop it... "And I promise I won't be late this time."

There's the shortest of silences at the other end of the phone line, and then: "See you Monday."

ACT ONE, SCENE TWO

The second the bell rings for lunch at school the next day, I grab my bag and run for the "performance space". They did try to call it "the auditorium" for a while, but as it's basically the same as the gym hall, just with a little platform for a stage at one end and a couple of speakers on the walls, that didn't stick. It only gets used for prize-givings, parents' evenings and open days, and – once a year – a school show, so "performance space" it is. Today it's as empty as usual… except for one person sitting in the middle of the platform.

Priya.

As usual.

She beams at me when I walk through the door, then holds up the piece of paper she's obviously been reading. "Look what I've got!"

"A free pass from PE?"

"The notes from Miss Bartlett."

"For the DramSoc Spotlight Show?" I try not to pull a face. Every year, Miss Bartlett and the school drama society put on a spring show, entirely written, directed, performed and produced by them – but not crewed by them. For that, they need us. "Is it any good?"

Priya's expression makes her thoughts clearer than words ever could, as I fold myself down to sit beside her on the platform.

"Ah." I rummage in my bag for my lunch.

"So?"

I look up from my bag. Priya is staring at me. I start unwrapping my sandwich, pretending I don't know what she's waiting for. Of course it doesn't work.

"Are you going to tell me then?"

"Tell you what?" I gulp down a large bite of chicken and lettuce sandwich; Priya rolls her eyes.

"Okay, so I get *one* lousy message from you saying you got the place and you'll tell me about it tomorrow – which is today – and then you avoid me all morning—"

"I did not!"

"You sat next to Kemal in chemistry."

"He's better at titration than you are!" (This is true.)

"Yeah. But *he* doesn't let you copy his notes, does he?" (This is also true.)

I shrug.

"Sooooo? You got the place? Tell me!"

"I got the place." And even though I told myself I was going to be cool about it, that I wasn't going to make it a *thing*, my heart swells inside my chest…because I did. *I got the place.*

"I knew you would!" She nudges me happily, and I try not to feel guilty. Priya could have applied for it too – she's been at the Square just as long as I have. But when I asked if she was going to, all she did was shrug and say, "I don't think I want it like you do. It's fun, but it's not my *life*." Which, given we're here talking about theatre while she's working on two different shows, is kind of ironic. She nudges me again.

"And was *he* there?"

"I told you – yes, he was there, and yes, he is exactly as terrifying as I thought he'd be."

Priya snorts with laughter. If anyone is ever going to understand the way I feel about Rick Hillier, it's her. Mostly because it was Priya I dragged along with me to stand outside the stage door of the Bristol Old Vic, waiting in the pouring rain for forty-five minutes…only to completely lose my nerve and run away right before Rick came out. I still remember hiding around the corner, watching his back disappear off down the street while Priya poked my arm and hissed "What did you just do?" at me until he was out of sight. She still brings it up, which is why I have absolutely no intention of telling her about the whole wizard-ninja thing.

"And what did your mum say when you told her you'd

got it?" When I don't answer, Priya's eyes narrow. "You *did* tell her, didn't you?"

"Nooooo?"

"Hope! Why not? I thought it was only a secret in case you didn't get it!"

"I…was never going to tell her. Them. At all."

"You're joking." She stares at me. "You're really not? What the hell?"

"Come on – you've met my mum. She'll be all…*her* about it. And I just want to get on with it, you know?"

"But what are you going to tell your parents about school?"

"I told them I've been offered some work experience in the back office at the Square Globe. Marketing, mostly."

"And they believed that?"

"Mum's so busy, she's on her own planet right now, and Dad couldn't be happier at the thought of me working in an office like Grace. If they ask any questions, I'll just… improvise."

"You? Improvise?" Priya makes her snorting sound again. "Sure thing. But she's going to find out. Not from me," she adds, "but she will. You can't hide this – not from *your* mum." She shakes her head. "What are you going to be working on? Is it what I think it is? Because it *has* to be, right? Rick Hillier's working on *Piecekeepers*, so you must be too?"

She beams at me, and I'm halfway to saying that yes, it *is*

Piecekeepers, when my mouth snaps shut. If they want me to sign an NDA and I blab everything to Priya straight away, I'll have wrecked any chances I have of being taken seriously before I even set foot through the door. I shrug enigmatically. It's Priya. She'll figure it out – and then I won't have actually told her. I lean over and grab the notes from her hand. "Talking of shows, what is it this time?"

"You know Bronwen in Year Eight? The one with the dark hair and the glasses?"

"Oh no."

"Oh yes."

"The one who thinks she can act?"

"Guess what…?"

"Don't."

"She thinks she can sing, too."

Priya runs through the notes like a pro – of course she does. But even though I want to listen, I can't seem to focus on her voice. Her words keep fading out like an old car radio, and instead – cutting through the static – there's the echo of Rick Hillier, of Amy, of the whole interview playing back in my head; of Mum, and how I told her I'd be at the Square Globe.

Of how I lied.

But what else could I do?

This is where everything starts – everything I've ever wanted.

And if that's not worth one teeny tiny little white lie, then what is?

Second time around, it doesn't take me long to track down unit thirty-two – not even on a Monday morning. Although I am slightly surprised to find it where I left it on Thursday: I was half-expecting it to have moved, just to spite me. But there it is, and I am dry and (despite having spent an hour getting dressed, changing my mind, getting undressed again, and trying to find an outfit that says "serious, reliable, *totally* belongs here") I am on time.

Early, in fact.

Yes. I, Hope Parker of the Perpetual Tardiness, am ten minutes early.

Which is why my heart sinks when I turn the corner and spot Amy sitting on the pavement outside the rehearsal room unit.

Is she waiting for me? No. She can't be. Why would she be? She did say ten o'clock, didn't she? I can't be late. Not today.

Casually, I fiddle with the sleeve of my coat and check my watch as I get closer. Definitely ten to ten.

Amy glances up as I reach her. "Don't worry – you're not late. I needed some…air." She glances over her shoulder in a way that instantly makes me feel I'm missing something.

But then she looks back at me and grins, flicking her blonde ponytail behind her as she clambers to her feet. Even though it still feels like the depths of winter rather than spring, she's wearing knee-length shorts with pockets all over them – most of which seem to be full to bursting point – and boots with socks scrunched down around her ankles. The black fleece which completes the outfit looks like it's two sizes too big, and has bits of sawdust stuck to it.

"So, then. Are you ready?" she asks, and there's something about her voice that tells me whatever I say, and whatever I think, I'm probably not and never will be.

"Definitely!" I say, following her into the reception area, where the shabby sofa is piled high with jackets and scarves and the coat hooks have overflowed onto the floor. In the middle of the glass table – on top of all the old papers and sitting in pride of place like it's some kind of art installation – is a gold-painted motorcycle helmet, while dumped on the floor in front are a pair of expensive-looking motorcycle boots. "Ready for anything!"

And then she pulls the blue door open – and wow, am I not even *close* to ready.

Part of the room is taken up by what must be the end of a warm-up: ten actors are standing on yoga mats with their hands in the air and their eyes closed, sticking out their tongues and making loud "Aaaahhhh" noises.

Picking her way around them, Amy waves towards the

mats. "They're just finishing up, but you're welcome to join them other mornings if you want to. Some of the technical crew find it helps, especially when you're on your feet all day."

"Mmm."

They've started shouting "Ha! Ha! Hooooo!" now. All of them.

Beyond the shouting yoga there's another knot of actors, who look like they're working on a scene. Five of them stand in a loose semicircle, scripts folded over in their hands. Another two are perched on chairs outside the group, obviously sitting this section out. Amy points apparently randomly around the room, reeling off name after name. I almost immediately forget them all – except for Nina, the assistant director, who is sitting at a table piled high with papers and files, making notes on a script. She looks like she might be in her early twenties – younger than a lot of people in here, but definitely older than me, with tightly braided dark hair and an expression of serious concentration. Standing next to her, his sleeves rolled up, his arms folded across his chest and shaking his head furiously, is Rick.

I am definitely the youngest person here. No pressure then.

"We're just waiting for Tommy. You'll have seen some of his film work, I'm guessing," says Amy quietly as she tucks my signed NDA form into one of her pockets.

Oh god.

Tommy. Knight.

I'd completely forgotten. How? How could I forget?

I was so stuck on the idea of being in the same room as Rick that I forgot Tommy Knight.

Tommy Knight with his hair and his eyes and his...him.

If Rick Hillier is a theatre god, Tommy Knight comes direct from the cloud where they make movie stars. In his case, tall and slender RADA superstars, fresh from playing the villain in a string of Hollywood blockbusters. And now he's making his triumphant stage debut – *here*, of all places. This is supposedly his way of proving himself as a "serious" actor – whatever that means.

"I should warn you that he and Rick are not getting along at the moment," Amy whispers. "Tommy's been a real pain, missing early rehearsals and skipping out when he's supposed to be here. He was meant to have his hair cut for the role yesterday, and he didn't even turn up. I know he's around, though – that was his bike outside. Could you have a quick look and see if he's on his phone somewhere?" She points me back towards the door.

"Me? Sure!" If it comes out a little too fast to be cool (or even remotely normal), it's because I have just been given My First Job. Go talk to the cast, like a human. Okay. I stride across to the blue door, trying to keep my heart from exploding. This is really it. I'm here and I'm part of the company. And I'm looking for *world-famous actor* Tommy Knight. Obviously.

Sitting at the side of the room, a guy with dirty-blond hair glances up from the script he's annotating, his feet up on another chair as he peers over at me. He's young, too – maybe my age, maybe a year or two older, and kind of cute – but the most striking thing about him is his eyes, which are the most astonishing shade of blue: really, really *blue-blue*. The kind of blue you only normally see in adverts for Caribbean cruises. But realizing I'm not coming for him, his eyes soon flick back down to his script. I take it as a sign I look like I should be here, that I fit right in.

I confidently push the door to the reception area open and…

There's a loud thunk as it hits something on the other side and bounces right back at me.

And then a loud "Ow! Jesus!" from the something on the other side.

Oh god. I recognize that voice. It's a Hollywood voice, and it can only belong to one person.

What if I've just broken Tommy Knight's nose?

A little more carefully this time, I push the door open and peer around it. In the foyer on the other side, our lead actor is doubled over, his hands cupped around his nose and his jaw-length black hair falling across his face.

"Oh my god. I'm so sorry. Are you okay? I'm so, so,

so sorry. Can I get you something? Do you need help?" I take a step closer to my victim.

Still hunched over, he shakes his head (cautiously) and takes an equal-sized step in the opposite direction. Away from me.

"I think you've done quite enough already."

"Really, I'm so sorry – I had no idea you were on the other side…"

"How fortunate for me, otherwise you might really have put your back into it."

I don't know what to do. Should I call for Amy? Should I get an ice pack or an ambulance, or…?

And then Tommy Knight straightens up and slowly, carefully, lowers his hands. He pulls a face, stretching his jaw and touches the end of his nose with his fingertips.

"And you would be *whom*, exactly?"

"Hope. Hope Parker. I'm the stage management intern."

"I see."

Dressed in skintight black jeans, a baggy white T-shirt that somehow clings to him in enough places to make it very hard to look away (I mean, I know for a fact he's thirty-one this year which should seem ancient, but he doesn't look it at *all*), and black studio trainers, he has a dozen woven leather bracelets tangled around his wrists. They slide up and down his arms as he examines his nose. Deciding there's no permanent damage, he looks straight through me, and I jump out of his way as he storms through the door and into the rehearsal room.

I freeze. Should I even bother going back in there? Should I just walk straight across to the front door, open it and keep on walking until my feet wear out? I just (nearly) wounded our star. How can I go back in there?

Because you have to, says a small voice in my head. *Get a grip.*

I mean, it could have happened to anyone – couldn't it?

I take a deep breath and walk back into the rehearsal room.

Standing next to Rick and the assistant director, Tommy looks fine enough, his hair bobbing as he gestures wildly at something on the sheet of paper Rick's holding. Never mind not getting on – judging by the look on Rick's face, these two are moments from going toe-to-toe with each other in a ring. As if on cue, Rick shuts his eyes in frustration and, without any more warning, slams the flat of his palm down on the tabletop. The legs of the flimsy folding table promptly collapse, sending paper and pencils scattering across the floor.

For a second, Rick looks embarrassed – "Sorry. Sorry, Nina. Sorry…" – and rubs at his eyes as Nina immediately ducks down and starts gathering bundles of pages into her arms. He props the table back up, and it looks like he's about to kneel down and start helping her when he stops to glower at Tommy…who is standing with his hands on his hips, and one foot on a piece of paper.

A piece of paper that Nina is trying to pick up.

He's actually stopping her from picking it up.

What an absolute *bell-end*. So much for all those interviews that bang on about how charming he is.

Rick fixes him with a look like a thunderclap and every actor is suddenly edging a step or two further away, as subtly as they can. Every actor except Tommy.

Giving him a hard shove, Rick grabs Tommy by the shoulder and half-drags, half-steers him to the far side of the room and through an open door marked *Kitchen*. The door slams shut behind them, so hard that everything in the rehearsal room rattles. Including my teeth.

I probably ought to help Nina pick up the scripts and the notes, but I can't move. I've never seen a director treat… anyone like that, let alone the lead actor in their production – even if they are being a dick. It's totally out of line, and nobody – not the assistant director, not Amy as the DSM, nobody – is stepping in to stop it. It's not right.

"But this…he…that's not…"

I feel Amy's hand settle on my shoulder, patting reassuringly.

"Piece of professional advice, Hope. Don't get in the middle of an ego battle between two brothers. Especially not those two."

"They're *brothers*?"

This is news to me – although it definitely goes some

way to explaining the look that Rick gave Tommy. I know that look. Anyone with a sibling or two knows *that* look.

"But…but…"

Amy has obviously had to do this more than once: she's ready. She's probably got cue cards somewhere.

"Rick finished at RADA first, and broke out right away with that role at the Donmar. When Tommy started working and registered with Equity, he picked a different professional name – probably just as much to annoy Rick as to make sure he didn't get labelled 'Rick Hillier's brother'. They…don't get along."

"Why are they both working on this then?"

"Because whatever he might think, Rick's not God. No, this is down to the producers – but they didn't actually mention Tommy until Rick was already under contract to direct." She sighs the deep sigh of somebody who is very, very tired of this. Then she spots my expression. "Don't worry. Keeping the two of them from actually throttling each other isn't your responsibility. Not your circus, not your monkeys. I just wish they weren't mine…"

The sound of shouting, muffled by the door, filters through from the kitchen, along with a noise like a cupboard being slammed repeatedly.

"I don't suppose it's too much to hope that's Rick banging Tommy's head against a wall, is it?" Amy mutters, then pulls a face. "You didn't hear me say that, by the way."

"Hear you say what?" I ask in my most innocent voice.

"I knew I liked you," she laughs. "First thing you need to know about stage management? Hear everything, say nothing unless you need to. Knowledge is power, and discretion is everything."

I think back to Friday, and how I nearly told Priya *everything* as Amy leads me around the scattering of papers, smiling at Nina the AD as she passes. "All right?"

"I think we'd better get some teas in, my lovely. Unless you've got a bottle of Scotch handy?"

"I'm already on it."

Nina gives me a smile and a nod as I'm led away towards a row of chairs on the far side of the yoga mats.

"Second thing about stage management? Know everybody – cast, creatives and crew."

We have stopped in front of an occupied chair – two, if you count the massive handbag taking up a second. The first is taken by an East Asian guy who is *definitely* my age; his hair is swept back from his forehead and he's wearing a long black waistcoat over a red T-shirt and skinny jeans, along with the most enormous white trainers I've ever seen. He beams at me with a big smile that's almost too wide for his face. I give him a pathetic half-wave of hello.

"George, this is Hope. Hope, I'll be back with you in a sec. I'd better go and make sure our director and our lead haven't murdered each other."

I think she's only half-kidding.

One of us has got to say something, so in the spirit of not being the only person under twenty in the room any more, it might as well be me. I point to the handbag on the chair.

"Do you know whose bag this is?"

"Oh, that's mine," says George in a broad Newcastle accent, grabbing the handles and swinging it onto his lap, then down to the floor. It makes an alarmingly loud thud when he drops it. "Sorry – I just chucked it anywhere. I brought every bit of make-up I own with me, just in case. I didn't know whether I'd need it today." He looks me up and down. "I'm the hair and make-up intern, by the way. And the wardrobe intern too. I think. It's all a bit muddled, really. George Soo. Like Peggy, only...not."

"Huh?" He's lost me.

"Peggy. Peggy Sue? Like the musical?"

I've got nothing, and he laughs. It's a warm, open laugh, and he waves a hand as if to say *forget it*. "I know. Feeble joke. You were Hope...?"

"Hope. Yes." In no way did I almost forget my name there. No way. "Hope, stage management."

"Nice to meet you, Hope Stagemanagement."

I should have seen that coming.

He laughs quietly. "Sorry. Bad joke. My family's Korean, so there's a whole surname thing. So what's your actual name, then?"

"Hope *Parker*. I'm the stage management intern. Probably."

"Probably?"

"If they don't immediately chuck me for opening a door straight into Tommy Knight's face." I flop down on the seat next to him and pretend not to notice him stifling another laugh. I guess it is *almost* funny. He looks familiar somehow, in a way I can't quite place. "Okay, weird question – but have you done anything at the Square Globe?"

His whole face lights up. "I knew I knew you! *Merchant of Venice* last year. I helped with make-up when Stevie got the flu!"

I remember. Stevie called and said a friend of a friend would cover her – and he did. He was good, too. "That's where I know you from!"

And that's all it takes to break the ice – one short, shared production where we didn't even meet properly, and here we are. Fellow travellers on the Good Ship Theatre.

Across the room, I spot Amy heading back towards us, her eyes only just visible over the stack of folders she's carrying.

All of which have my name on them. Literally.

I shoot a glance at George's giant handbag. "Any chance I could maybe borrow that later?" I ask feebly – and he looks up at Amy's payload and winces.

"I don't think they'd fit…" he whispers.

I think he's right. This lot'll barely fit in a suitcase, never mind a handbag.

I've only been here half an hour, but suddenly trying to copy Kemal's chemistry notes is starting to look a *lot* more appealing.

ACT ONE, SCENE THREE

Amy pulls up another chair as George gazes open-mouthed at the pile of ring binders. "I've got a few bits and pieces for you, Hope. Now seems as good a time as any to have a quick look through, before we really get stuck in with the rehearsal." She risks a quick glance over her shoulder towards the kitchen, where there's still shouting. The door opens a fraction and is slammed shut again – but not before the words "I'm not done with you yet, you selfish little sh—" seep out. When she looks back round, Amy's smile is rictus-like, and her eyes look like she's about to kill.

"As I said in the interview, your role involves a lot of script and rehearsal notes – here, at least – and supporting Rick, Nina and the cast, particularly Tommy. Yes, I know," she adds, then carries on without even pausing for breath. "In the theatre, it'll be more of the same. Lots of prompting and cueing. If you're comfortable with that, we'll get you running the crew cues and making stage calls. Sound good?" She hands me the first, fullest folder. "There's your copy of the script. You'll want to read that through and make whatever notes you need, but you can do that in your own time. For today, we'll put you on the book – here's your pencil."

My fingers take the pencil of their own accord. I know how this goes: follow the script and prompt anyone who forgets their lines, or goes left when they're supposed to go right. Keep track of any changes with the pencil.

Folder after folder comes at me. "Here's everyone's Contact pages – have a good look at those. It'll help you get to know the company. And this is the rehearsal and call schedule until opening night – I'll be handling most of this so you won't need it all, but it's good to have… And here's a copy of Rick's prep notes."

She piles them into my hands – and I was wrong about the first one being the fullest. The last one, Rick's notes, is so full that it has a fat elastic band wrapped around it to stop it from exploding outwards.

"Mmm." I know that stage management means paperwork – endless fiddly lists and call sheets and needing to make seventy-four copies of everything, blown up to 144 per cent (the magic number that makes book-size pages into A4 pages) – but this is a *lot* of paperwork. The Square Globe has always been…well, to be perfectly honest, a bit rubbish at this sort of thing, so these folders are a whole new world. The noise I make is small and high-pitched and panicked –

and (I hope) easy to miss. However, Amy doesn't miss anything.

"You'll pick it up soon enough, don't worry. I've marked up the lighting and sound cues on your copy already, so you've only got line prompts to worry about for the moment." She flips a couple of pages and points to a pencil squiggle in a margin, then, with one practised motion, Amy slaps the folder shut, twists it round in her hand and shoves it at me, landing it on top of the pile in my lap. Beside me, George is still staring at Mount Ring-binder in shock.

"Oh my god. I thought the sketchbooks they gave me were bad enough. Is there more?" George whispers, tucking his trainers even more tightly under his chair.

Amy doesn't bat an eyelid. I guess this is all just an average day for her, but I'm starting to feel seriously out of my depth – this is *not* how things happen at the Square Globe. She points to a battered little-old-lady shopping trolley in the far corner of the room, one that's more hole than filthy tartan fabric. I can almost smell it from here. "I dug that out of the stores for you to carry the files home. You'll probably want to look through them away from rehearsals, and things tend to wander here. Mostly because Rick keeps picking them up if he forgets his own notes – keep an eye out for that. The trolley's not glamorous, I know, but it'll do."

I stare at it in horror. I have to use *that*? How the hell am I going to get it past Mum?

Meanwhile, Amy carries on as though giving someone a trolley that looks like you stole it from outside a bingo hall then left it in a field for six months is a perfectly normal thing to do. "I'll talk you through the call schedule tomorrow, but it's fairly self-explanatory – just the list of everyone who needs to be at each rehearsal. We don't need all of them every day, but of course when we get to tech week, we'll start to need more people. Then we'll have to have the full company in for the technical and dress rehearsals. The one you've got to watch," she says in a conspiratorial voice, making George lean that little bit closer, "is Tommy. Supporting the cast is part of the job, but I particularly need you to be available for anything he wants help with – errands, that kind of thing. Keep his head in the theatre as much as you can. We can't afford to let him get distracted. You do understand, don't you?"

"What happened to 'not my monkey'?" I ask.

"Hope, when it comes to getting Tommy to rehearsals, he very definitely *is* your monkey."

With note-perfect timing, the kitchen door bangs open and Rick storms out. He walks straight over to the table – where Nina has reassembled their collection of notes, scripts, pencils, highlighters and a large tub of menthol chewing gum – without meeting anybody's eye, then throws himself into his seat and starts chewing furiously; head down, eyes shut. Nina raises an eyebrow at him, then turns to the actors, who have suddenly appeared in their places again.

"Sorry for the delay, everybody. We'll start in a moment, if you're ready."

Rick nods to nobody in particular, then without raising his chin from his chest: "Amy?"

"Yep." Amy is on her feet and halfway across to him before I can even breathe. She pulls a pencil and battered notebook from one of her bulging pockets. How the hell does she move so fast?

"Set up a time to get Tommy's hair taken care of, would you?"

"What does he need?"

"Jamie's hair is – and I quote…" Rick picks up his script and looks directly at his brother, who has just sidled out of the kitchen and is glaring at him. "Short, wavy, blond. *Blond*, Tommy. You hear that, or did you forget the conversation where everybody agreed a wig wouldn't work for this one?"

"I didn't forget, darling. I just didn't think blond was my colour." Even though I've heard it so many times – in his films, over the radio, in interviews…just now – it's still a shock to be in the same room as that voice.

"Did you actually read the script? I mean, I assume it's far too much to expect you to have read the book like the rest of us. Your character's hair is blond, and that's an end to it."

"When –" Amy slides herself between them, pencil poised over her book – "do you need it done?"

"I don't know – yesterday?" Rick snaps back – but it's not aimed at Amy. It passes right through her to Tommy, who bats the barb away with a roll of his eyes.

"Leave it with me." Amy's notebook disappears back into one of her many pockets. "Hope? I think we'd better get that tea for everyone. Have to keep the troops happy."

I risk a glance at Rick, who has settled down with his legs stretched straight out in front of him, his chin resting in one hand and a scowl plastered across his face. He taps his upper lip thoughtfully with one finger.

Happy is not necessarily the first word that springs to mind.

As though she's read my thoughts, Amy nudges me. "Tea and biscuits usually goes a long way…" She stops. "Oh, god. Biscuits. I forgot to pick them up on the way. You make a start with the first round of teas, I'll nip out and get some. There's a tea list in the folder."

Walking over to the kitchen, I casually (at least I hope it's casual) look over at the guy with the script and the blue eyes again. It's a copy of *The History Boys* he's working on. He's completely absorbed in the notes he's making, and spinning his pencil between his fingers. Suddenly, he frowns and shuffles in his seat, his lips moving around words I can't hear – then he freezes, and I dart through the door into the kitchen before he can notice me watching him.

In the relative safety beyond the door, waiting for the kettle to boil, I skim through Amy's tea list. There's a note at the top about always checking for allergies, intolerances and just plain old fad diets, and to always keep it up-to-date because it saves interrupting the flow of a rehearsal – something I imagine would make Rick even *less* happy. I read through the list again, and one more time to be sure. I have to get this right. It's all very well telling myself it's just a few cups of tea, but right now this is the most important tea I or anyone in the world has ever made.

I pull two of the Earl's Theatre mugs out of the cupboard, one for Rick and one for Nina, as director and AD always get the first teas at the Square Globe, and then I spot Rick's tea note. Three sugars? Three?! No wonder he looks so angry – he's probably got permanent toothache.

Three.

And…I can't find the sugar.

I look in the cupboard.

I look under the sink. Behind the bin. On the window sill.

I look in the cupboard again. Just in case.

There is no sugar.

How can there be no sugar?

No sugar. Right. Okay.

Is Rick likely to notice if there isn't any in his tea?

Maybe I can make it a bit…milkier? And if I don't leave the teabag in too long…?

Rocking back on my heels, I peer around the door. I could always ask someone?

Still no sign of Amy, and everybody else is completely lost to the rehearsal: absorbed in watching Tommy, his script rolled up and tucked into the back pocket of his jeans, his hands held out in a plea to somebody only he can see. It's hard to look away – like he's turned a dial inside himself and made it impossible not to watch him. Nearly impossible, anyway – because however entrancing he might be, I still find myself looking at something else. Some*one* else. The guy with the blue eyes by the door, who has put down his script and is following Tommy's every move with diamond-sharp focus.

But as far as I can tell, I'm the only one not watching Tommy. Even George, sitting on the other side of the room, is entranced.

The spell is broken as Tommy finishes his line and steps aside, while another actor takes his place. He turns too suddenly in the middle of a speech, crashing into one of the others, and Rick growls.

"Do you think you could possibly try that again? Perhaps while maintaining some grasp of the space around you, Dom?"

There's a bit of shuffling and some flicking of script pages at the table, and they start up again. I can see Tommy's smirk from here as he leans back against a wall to watch, and I wonder whether it's meant for his brother or for poor Dom who just got his head bitten off. Beside Rick, Nina glances at her watch and then over her shoulder at the kitchen door – right at me. I do the first thing that comes into my head…and I give her a little wave.

Nina drops her hands out of Rick's eyeline and makes a very clear T symbol with her forefingers, followed by a sharp jerk of her head back towards the director.

Milky, weak and sugarless it is.

A few minutes later I carry the mugs over to the table, trying not to get in anyone's way, and slide them in front of Nina. She raises an eyebrow at the off-white colour of Rick's tea but I shrug and run away as fast as I can, retreating to the relative safety of the kitchen. I'm almost there when I hear a loud snort, followed by a sort of cough behind me. Something mug-like bangs onto a tabletop – and I duck out of sight as fast as my legs will carry me, with only the quickest glance back into the room.

Which is when I see something out of the corner of my eye.

Tommy Knight is watching his brother intently from his spot behind the other actors, his doomed black hair falling to his chin. And as he does, he reaches into a plastic bag he's holding screwed up in one fist, then pops something from it straight into his mouth. Realizing he's being watched, he looks over at me and grins – opening his lips just enough that I can see what he's holding between his teeth before he crunches it.

It's a sugar cube.

"How's it going? Keeping up all right, are you?"

I'm so focused on my notes, making sure I've blocked out all the movements the actors are trying, that I don't hear Amy walk up – so when her voice comes from behind me, I jump. She peers over my shoulder at the catastrophe that is my script folder, running her finger down line after line and glancing at the mocked-up stage area marked out with tape in front of us.

"The sofa needs to be a little bit more…here." She reaches around me and scrubs out my wonkily-drawn sofa rectangle and redraws it in almost exactly the same place. She studies it, then nods. "Better."

I must look blank, because she taps the sketch with her pencil. "Three millimetres makes a big difference when you scale up to the size of the stage – especially if you've got a lighting crew about to go into overtime, and who want to know why the spot isn't hitting the sofa like it's supposed to. Get it bang-on now and your life will be easier later. Get it wrong and…" She screws up her face. I don't actually need her to finish the sentence – I get the idea.

"The rest of it looks great, though – good job, Hope." She nods approvingly and vanishes again. I'm not sure how she does it – perhaps that's the "ninja" part of stage management, moving stealthily and silently and completely hidden until you strike. I hope I get the chance to pick it up because *there's* a skill that would come in handy for sneaking into class late without getting detention.

I risk a glance back over my shoulder, but as far as I can tell, Amy has basically evaporated.

"Hope?"

My name.

That's my name, isn't it?

And that was…that was…

Rick.

Rick said my name.

Rick Hillier said my…

Everyone is looking at me.

Everyone.

"Umm?"

Rick does not look impressed. He's looking right at me, leaning back in his seat to see past Nina.

"Sorry. I missed…"

"Yes. Yes, well, I think that's spectacularly apparent."

"Sorry."

"Whenever you're ready – and if you don't have more important things on your mind – could you check whether Jamie moves to kick the chair before or after his line?"

Tommy rests his hands on his hips and scuffs the soft toe of his trainer against the floor. "It's before, Rick," he sighs. "Before."

"Let's just check, shall we?" Rick's voice sounds like it could dissolve steel…and with a sinking feeling, I realize that I can't answer.

I don't know.

I've written down the movement…but I've written it literally alongside the line. I can't tell whether he's supposed to kick the chair before he speaks, after he speaks…or even while he's doing it.

Everyone is watching me and everyone is waiting.

Don't panic, Hope. Don't panic.

I look at the line again. It's short – very short. If he kicks the chair beforehand, he'll risk the sound of the chair falling drowning out his voice, and that's not a decision Tommy would ever make. But if he kicks it after, it changes the read of the line – instead of it being angry, it's a bit…helpless.

I make up my mind.

"During the line," I say – and my voice is clearer and sharper than I expected. I actually sound like I know what I'm talking about. "He kicks it mid-line."

Rick purses his lips and looks down at his script, checking

his own notes, then leans over and looks at Nina's. She nods, and he waves a hand at Tommy.

"There you are then. Let's go again, from 'tomorrow won't matter', please."

Nina gives me a small wink, then a thumbs up. "Good call," she whispers – and I think she means it. I nod and shuffle a couple of script pages, trying to look cool about it, but really I want to scream with joy. I got it right. My first day, and I made a *good call*. It makes me happy, right until I look up and see Tommy staring at me. His eyes are two icy-cold searchlights, boring straight into me, and I can *feel* the chill creeping across my skin.

Rick might well be terrifying…but something tells me *this* is the brother you don't want to cross.

And I think I just did.

ACT ONE, SCENE FOUR

By the time we get to the end of the day, it feels like I've been there for years. I don't quite understand how the clock on the rehearsal room wall can only say 4.30 p.m.: I would have guessed closer to midnight. I'm knackered from the sheer fear of messing up – everything is so *intense*, so much *more* than I was expecting. Or ready for. On top of that, my fingers ache from making note after note after note on the script; from sketching arrows around little pencil boxes, rubbing them out and then redrawing as Rick and the actors work out the movements of characters. I've lost count of the cups of tea I've made – but somehow, I've not managed to drink a single one.

George obviously feels the same; when I look over to the table I saw him at earlier with the head of wardrobe at the Earl's, he's slumped forward over a stack of fabric samples. It looks like he may be trying to drown himself in them. Or possibly eat them. Mum would love to hear all about that…but *no*. A tiny warning flare goes off inside my brain.

No telling Mum, because that will require Explanations. No telling Mum *anything*.

"How was that?" Amy straightens the last chair around the makeshift stage as I gather up the last batch of mugs.

"It was…" I stop. It was what, exactly? Exhausting? Draining? Harder work than I ever imagined during all those times sitting in my folding chair on the floor of the Square Globe, dreaming about what a *real* rehearsal room must be like?

It was.

And it was incredible.

Amy smiles, spiriting a roll of bright green gaffer tape away into one of her many pockets. "I know that look." She pushes a strand of hair behind her ear and folds her arms, studying me as I stand there with my hands full of other people's tea mugs. "You're wondering what you've got yourself into."

"No, no. Not at all." Although I kind of am, a bit. Not that I'm going to actually say that out loud.

"Hope?"

"Yes?"

"Can I give you a piece of advice?"

"Sure." I shift my grip on the mugs and they rattle alarmingly.

"Don't pretend, okay?"

"Pretend?"

"Doing this, you're surrounded by people who pretend for a living. It's their job. Leave it to them. *Your* job is to tell the truth, and make them better."

I stand there with my mugs, staring at her. What does that even mean?

Across the room, George seems to have collected both himself and his stuff together, and he gives me a wave as he heads for the door. I half-wave the mugs back, and Amy nods at him before turning back to me. "You don't have to pretend it's not hard," she says, holding out a hand for one batch of mugs. "It *is* hard. It's a hard job, and not everyone can do it. That's why *you* got it and not someone else. Because I know you've got what it takes."

We're the only people left in the rehearsal room – everyone else has drifted away to catch buses or run lines or…do whatever they do. At the Square, we'd all clear up together and then pile out of the side door into the coffee shop across the road to pick over the minor triumphs and tragedies of every rehearsal. I wonder what they're doing right now. Priya's probably just arriving there after school with all the others – Orson and Amelie and Matt and Riz – everybody I know. I could always go over there on my way home…

But then they'll all ask me, won't they?

Priya knows what I'm doing because she needs to. She's the only one of my friends who Mum really knows, and if

I can trust anyone to cover for me, it's Priya. Just because Mum doesn't know any of the others, however, doesn't mean that what I'm actually doing couldn't get back to her if I told them…so I'm not telling anyone. Not unless I *have* to. I'm just going to keep my head down and hope. It's not like I'm doing anything *wrong*, anyway. I just want to do this my own way.

Outside, I hear the roar of a motorbike starting up.

Tommy. My whole scalp goes cold just thinking about him. I thought I'd be excited, working with someone like him, but it turns out *excited* isn't quite the right word – unless, of course, you'd be *excited* to be juggling a live hand grenade, a shark and a very expensive crystal vase. Because everything about Tommy Knight feels like an unexploded bomb.

"You can head out if you like. I'll load this lot into the dishwasher and switch off."

"Okay." I nod, grateful to be relieved of duty.

"You did well, you know. That was one hell of a first day."

I meet her gaze and she smiles. "Thanks."

"See you tomorrow. Can you be here for nine in the morning? I want to take you through a few things before we start the run-through… Although," she adds with a sigh, "judging by today's performance it'll be more of a stumble-through. We're having some trouble getting the timings for one of the stage illusions right, so it looks like we'll need to work on that some more before we move into the theatre for the last few rehearsals. Still, at least we've got *plenty* of time to get it down."

I try not to laugh – and she sees it.

"It's okay to laugh. You're right to. Time is never a theatre crew's friend. Besides, it's not life and death. It's only theatre…"

Only theatre? How can she say that? How could *anyone?*

"And we'll get it done. It'll all come together in the end. That's the real magic." She nudges the kitchen door open with her foot – then stops partway through. "Don't tell anyone I said that, though. If you do, they'll all start to relax, and then where will we be?" She winks and slips through the door, letting it swing shut behind her and leaving me alone in the main room.

"You did well, you know. That was one hell of a first day."

In the empty rehearsal space, I hear her voice in my head as clearly as though she's right next to me and saying it again – only this time, I don't even try to hide my smile.

I chuck my script into the top of the hideous granny-trolley – now stuffed with all the papers and folders Amy gave me earlier – and tip it forward, wheeling it behind me. It squeaks, and even on wheels it still weighs a ton. I have so much reading to do – but all I can think about now is getting home and lying face down on my bed until morning.

Perhaps if I open a couple of the folders and lie on those, the information will somehow...sink in by osmosis or something?

On my way out, something on the floor catches my eye. Or the wheel of my elegant trolley, at least.

It's a book. A script.

I lean over and pick it up. *The History Boys*. That guy must have dropped it. I flip through the pages, skimming for a name – anything. There's a slip of paper with a scribbled note about preparing a scene; something about an assignment. Whoever owns this takes their script prep seriously – alongside the lines are careful pencil annotations: symbols, mostly, and markers for breaths and emphasis or the occasional query. I read a couple of the lines again, following the notes, rather than the way I'd read it.

It sounds like someone else's voice, someone just over my shoulder, talking to me. It feels like a conversation between the two of us, private and quiet. I can hear them in my head, even if I can't see them – and even if I don't know what their name is, I know who they *are*.

And they have the bluest eyes I've ever seen.

I close the book, and I'm about to leave it on the nearest chair, but...it's got all those notes in it. If it were me, I'd hate to lose them.

I look back at the trolley. If only my notes were as easily portable as the script.

In the end, I slip the book into the trolley and wrangle it out of the rehearsal room, down the street to the bus stop – it's only when I'm suddenly disappointed not to see the script's owner that I even realize I was sort of hoping he'd be there. A different, older man already waiting stares at me, which makes me mildly paranoid until I see it's my glamorous travelling companion he's looking at. I don't blame him – it's the kind of thing that *should* be stared at. Preferably in a museum.

Sitting on the bench at the bus stop, I send a photo of the trolley to Priya with the caption *New Best Friend*. It feels strange to be doing this without her – although I'm not really doing it without her, because straight away she pings back a whole row of question marks, and then:

Nice. Meet any actual humans, or is it an all-trolley production?

A few. Make-up & wardrobe intern, George. Filled in at Merchant of Venice?

FAMOUS humans. As in famous actor-y sort of humans? Plus: assume you didn't run away from RH this time?

What was it Amy said? Knowledge is power...and discretion is everything. Discretion and a signed non-disclosure agreement.

Funny. RH super-intimidating, but no other famous humans today.

Another little white lie. Great. Somehow fibbing to Priya

feels worse than doing it to Mum – maybe because she already knows so much. I'll be able to tell her properly about Tommy another time, but for now she'll just have to wait.

But when the bus finally trundles around the corner and I scramble on with my phone and my trolley, it's not Priya or Tommy on my mind – it's still blue eyes and dirty-blond hair, and wondering who he is.

Mum is in her studio when I get in, so I shove the trolley under the stairs and stick my head around her half-open door. My mother has apparently been eaten by several metres of red silk, which cover the floor, the worktable and finish off draped around the wooden dressmaking mannequin in the corner. All I can see of her is the top of her head and a hand.

"Are you winning?" I ask.

"You're home!" The top of the silk is yanked down, and her face appears over the top of it. It's really, *really* unsettling. "How was it?"

"How was what?"

"Your work experience at the office." She blinks at me. "Honestly, if you wanted to get some experience, why didn't you just ask me? You could have worked for me…"

"Uh, no thanks. And I'm an intern, not a work experience…experiencer."

"Or – as I was about to say – I could have spoken to someone for you. An editor – or if you really wanted marketing, I could have called Demet at the Royal Opera House…"

She would have, too. She would have, because she wants to help. It would never once occur to her that whatever I did after that phone call, however good I was, to everyone I met or spoke to or worked with, I would always just be "Miriam's kid". I shake my head. It's never going to happen. Not since a director at the Square Globe heard my mother's name, looked me up and down, narrowed his eyes and said, "Well, we all know why *you're* here, don't we?"

Of course I knew why I was there – because I didn't want to be anywhere else – and I didn't understand why he sneered when I told him that. It wasn't until later that I realized what he really meant.

Mum's awards gleam on the shelf at the back of the room, propping up a stack of fashion magazines. "No, it's fine. Really. This is good – they needed help in the back office anyway," I say.

But she's already gone back under the silk – I can hear her humming. I pull the door shut after me and turn back to the stairs where my trolley, stuffed with rehearsal notes, schedules, list templates, profiles and script sheets is waiting. I eye it warily, and it eyes me right back.

"All right then. Let's do this."

* * *

The trolley does not make the return trip to the rehearsal room in the morning. Instead, I've sorted all my piles of paperwork, taken photos of the non-essential ones on my phone and reorganized the most important ones into a single lever-arch folder which is safely tucked into my backpack – along with an emergency supply of sugar. I never want to hand Rick Hillier a sugarless tea again as long as I live, not after the withering look he gave me. The trolley, meanwhile, has retired. By which I mean I shoved it to the back of the hall cupboard and hid it under a bunch of my sisters' ancient, abandoned sports kit.

As it turns out, Tuesday is much like Monday, only with more tea-making, more note-taking and a lot more rubbing out. After one particularly *heated* scene run-through, there's so much crossing-out and so many rubbed holes in the paper that I give up on three pages of script I've been using and just go to photocopy new ones at the machine in the lobby. It's the only time I get to see the outside of the rehearsal room, through slightly grubby glass.

George, when I catch him over lunch, isn't doing much better.

"I spent two hours last night making up one of these shoulder-bag things to impress Jonna, who's in charge of wardrobe – and when I finished, guess what…? Half of it was inside out."

"Is that part of the internship, making stuff? And how can only *half* of it be inside out?" I gulp down a segment of orange, trying not to dribble juice down my chin…because even though I'm mostly listening to George's tales of sewing woe, I've also spotted Blond Guy – and he keeps glancing over at us. It's only for a second: a quick flick of those blue eyes, a shift of his shoulders and then he looks away again before he thinks I notice.

But I do notice.

Just like I notice that he chooses the exact moment I'm drooling juice at George and wiping my chin to look again.

When I sneak another glance back over at him, he's already staring into his script. Because the thing is, I keep looking at him, too.

"You aren't really listening, are you?"

"What? No. Yes. I am absolutely listening."

"You're not. You're looking at what's-his-face over there. I'm looking at you looking at him…looking at you."

I fold my orange peel together and squeeze it between my fingers. The air suddenly smells like Christmas.

"He's not looking at me."

Except, when I take a chance at one more look, he is. Our eyes meet and they hold for the length of a single breath…and then he breaks away. I want to kick myself for not smiling at him.

"Tell me who he is and I'll give you his inside leg

measurement," George whispers, fanning himself suggestively with his notebook. I pull a face at him, and toss my orange peel into the bin.

"Oh, come on. You must have looked him up. Haven't you got all the casting files in that monster heap of paperwork?"

"I wouldn't do that!" I try to look offended. "It would be so unprofessional to look through everyone's details just to—"

"You couldn't find him, could you?" George cuts me off with a melodramatic roll of his eyes.

I shake my head. "Nope. There's a couple that don't have headshot photos attached – the ones who haven't been in anything professional before, mostly. He must be one of them."

I run through the shortlist of faceless names in my head. He doesn't *look* like a Tony, or an Orran. I suppose he could be a Harry, or maybe a Luke…but right now, I kind of like the mystery. The Mystery History Boy.

Whatever his name is, I haven't seen him run any lines yet – not that it's a surprise really. Today's focus is still Tommy, and I've heard more than one actor mutter about whether they were actually *needed* for another day of Tommy-watching. Needed or not, it was Amy who signed them all in – so I have no clue about who this guy is playing, or even what his name is. But I do have his *History Boys* script in my bag, don't I? I just need to find the right time to give it back to him, and try actually *speaking* to him…

which might take a bit of a run-up, considering I couldn't even manage to smile at him a minute ago.

I shake my head thoughtfully – and even if George isn't listening, I say it anyway. "I don't know his name. Not yet."

"And then, right, Bronwen goes for this big note – and I'm talking proper jazz hands. No idea where she got that idea from…"

"Uh-huh." I roll over on my bed, shifting the pencil from behind my ear and pulling the script with me. Priya's voice sounds tinny down the phone.

"And then…" There's a sound midway between a snort and a giggle. "She opens her mouth, takes a deep breath… and sneezes. Right in the middle of the note."

"Uh-huh." I doodle a row of footlights across the bottom of my page. It's not that I don't want to listen to Priya's blow-by-blow update of the show – I do – but she isn't really calling to tell me about her day. She's calling to hear about mine – and I can't tell her.

It makes our conversations a little…one-sided, to say the least. Worse, it means that she feels she's got to tell me literally everything about the school show to justify her call – including those moments that every show has in rehearsals, the ones that were funny at the time but afterwards just feel a bit *mean*. Priya isn't mean, she's just trading gossip. Except

I have nothing to trade. While she's busy with the school show, I'm busy chasing lunches and making tea – and even those seem stupidly hard. I feel like the stuff I *have* got right has just been a fluke, like I've somehow tricked my way in there, or that Amy mixed my form up with somebody else's, and at any moment she's going to turn around and tell me there's been a mistake: they wanted someone more confident, someone who knew what they were doing – and that's clearly not me. I've been lucky so far – but surely my luck has to run out soon. And when it does, they'll see…and that will be that.

The fact I can't tell anyone any of this – not even Priya – because of that NDA and my own idiocy in trying to keep this whole thing a secret, makes it even worse.

There's a break in the chatter down the phone.

"You're not really listening, are you?"

"Sorry, Pree."

"What's up?"

I want to tell her about the fact I'm spending my days (my blissfully anonymous days) in a room with Rick Hillier and Tommy Knight, and that they're *brothers*; that I'm watching a show, which I know is going to be massive, being built from the ground up. I want to tell her how it feels to sit in that room and listen to the cast sharing all their stories and gossip about the shows they've been in before… But I can't. All I can tell her is that I've made a lot of tea.

Except…there is one thing I can talk about, isn't there?

"It's not so much about the placement, but…"

"But what? Go on." I can hear her on the other end of the line, sitting a little more upright and holding her phone a little more tightly.

"Okay. So, there's this guy…"

ACT TWO

Rehearsal

ACT TWO, SCENE ONE

I wake from a dream full of mini-Tommys chasing me around while an impossibly huge Rick stands on a stage, telling me I'm wasting his time and to get out before he calls my parents to come and fetch me.

And frogs. There are lots of frogs. Which I'm trying to collect in a bucket.

My bucket has a hole in it.

Wondering what my subconscious is trying to tell me, I shake off the remnants of the dream and tell myself that no, Rick is not going to call my mother and ask her to come and take me home. He doesn't even know her... Does he? Mind you, unless I do something about the paperwork and rehearsal notes scattered all over my bedroom, nobody's going to need to tell her anything – she'll be able to figure out exactly what I'm doing just by looking at my floor. So I shove everything under my bed.

Better.

I mean, you can just about see them, a few sheets

here and there, but they kind of blend in with everything else.

The poster I got when we went to the RSC.

The tickets from shows stuck to my pinboard.

The collage of columns I cut from *The Stage*.

The faded photo of me, little me, outside the stage door of the Earl's, with its glowing light above the entrance shining like a tiny sun. I used to try and see inside every time we walked past when I was a kid, because I knew there was magic in there.

There still is. I know there is.

I get dressed.

When I get to the rehearsal room, the foyer is less cluttered than it has been – there are a few coats, but most of the company clearly aren't in yet, and despite the fact I spent ages staring at the sheet last night I have no idea who's on the schedule for today. I'll have to look when I sit down.

Thankfully there's no sign of a motorbike helmet.

I slip into the rehearsal room to find Amy sitting with Rick and Nina at the director's table, chairs arranged in rows behind them. Hearing the door, Rick's head snaps around to check who has come in. He's holding a whole red apple in his mouth; it reminds me for a second of those illustrations of whole roast piglets you see in history books.

Amy laughs, and he remembers it's there, biting off a chunk and putting the rest of it down on the desk.

"Good morning, Hope. Ready for another day?"

Rick Hillier said my name.

I have *got* to get over this.

"What do you need me to do?"

Amy sets her mug on the table. "I've got a checklist for you – let me get it out of my bag." She rummages in the pile of things under the desk, and behind me the door opens again as George, immaculate in black jeans and a scarlet and silver T-shirt, walks in with a portfolio and waves it at me. I'm about to wave back when I spot the figure right behind him in the doorway.

Mr Blue Eyes.

He takes in the room, and I swear his eyes rest on me a moment longer than they need to. Then, head down, he walks straight past me over to the table and says something to Rick – who nods, makes a note on one of the sheets in front of him, then tucks his pencil behind his ear.

I have made up my mind. I am going to talk to him and give him his book back. I *am*. Definitely. Yes. Probably. Almost certainly... Because if I don't, Priya will never let me live it down.

Amy reappears and flaps yet another piece of paper at me. "Today's schedule," she says.

As I take it, I nod over at the guy. "Sorry – who's he?

I've seen him around, but I don't actually know what he does."

He passes me again on his way back across the room, stopping to peer under the chairs, pulling what looks like another script book out of his pocket.

"Luke, you mean? He's a drama student. Funnily enough, he works part-time as one of our front-of-house staff too – a lot of them do, because the staff get free seats for the shows. We're lucky to have him, though – he's good. You'll see when we run some of his scenes today."

A drama student. I guess that explains the script.

"I didn't see his picture in the files. What's his role?"

"You should know that already, Hope," she says. "Picture or not."

I should? *How?*

"Here. He's on the call sheet I gave you yesterday." Amy flicks through the schedule in her hand to the copy of today's call sheet. "Do you want to start ticking the names off as they come in?"

My eyes slide down the list, looking for a Luke. And there he is in black-and-white: Mr Luke Withakay. *Lancelot.* The second-in-command of the Piecekeepers, and the Magister's right-hand man. Not the biggest role in the show – that's Jamie, and then maybe Lizzie – but an important one. Not bad for a student. On the line below his name, there's something else written in smaller italic text.

THEATRICAL

Jamie (U)

He's not just Lancelot. He's Tommy Knight's understudy.

I take the sheet.

"Hi there." I stop beside the seat he's looking under. "You're Lancelot, right?"

He straightens up and adjusts his beanie hat. "Uh…" He seems to be looking at the sheet, the floor, over my shoulder – anywhere, in fact, but at *me*. His gaze darts about the room like a bright fish, flitting this way then that.

"I mean you're playing Lancelot. And understudying Jamie? You're Luke?"

He relaxes – his posture softens and suddenly his eyes lock onto mine, and I can feel the warmth of his gaze. "That's me," he murmurs. His voice is unexpectedly deep.

Also, this is awkward, because now we're both just standing here. And I should leave. Or he should. One of us should, anyway – or at least say something. But my feet don't want to move…

In the end, it's me who cracks first. "I think I have something for you," I blurt at him. "Wait here?"

I dash for my bag before I can second-guess myself and pull out the copy (slightly more dog-eared than it was) of *The History Boys*.

"Here." I hold it out, before spotting the bent corner. "Oh. Sorry about that." I try to fold it flat and press it down against my leg.

Seeing the book, his face lights up. "Thanks – uh…?"

"Hope. I'm Hope."

"Hope." He makes my name sound full. "Thanks. I was looking for that – I thought I might have lost it or…" He tails off, staring at the book in my hands. "It's got my notes in it," he adds – and I understand. Losing your notes is never just about losing your *notes*. It's about losing your connection with a play, with a character. A connection you've made by letting them become a part of *you*. But he can't know that when I started flicking through his script, I couldn't stop. I've spent time reading his notes, poring over them, turning over the different line readings of each scene he's annotated. Too much time – time I should have spent on our own play, on my own script – but I couldn't help myself. This felt like a window I couldn't pass without looking in; a door left ajar with a golden globe of light above it.

He reaches for the script, takes it…and as he does, his hand brushes against mine, just for an instant, just the slightest touch…

His skin is warm and soft.

Warm like his voice.

"Thanks," he says again, quieter this time.

"You're welcome."

I just stand there like a total muppet.

And then I remember what I'm supposed to be doing.

"Right. Well. So, you're clearly here, so I guess I'd better tick you off on the call sheet. There you go." I put a little tick next to his name.

The door opens, and a couple more actors dressed in their rehearsal uniforms – tracksuits and trainers for most of them – stroll in carrying their bags. They head off to the far corner of the room and start doing some warm-up stretches.

I roll up my little register sheet. "Duty calls, I guess. Nice to meet you, Luke."

I try to walk away, cool and professional – but I can't.

I have to look back – and I do, quickly: a fast glance over my shoulder, letting my gaze slide across the room. I could be looking for anyone, at anyone. But I'm not.

He's still holding the script in his hand, his face turned down towards it. What would I do if he looked up and saw me now?

Do I want him to?

Dodging round a couple of chairs, I tick off a few more names as I spot new company arrivals coming through in a steady trickle. And when I take one last look over, Luke is leaning back in his chair, ruffling his hair with his fingers… and this time he *is* looking right back at me. I snap my eyes away from him and over to the other side of the room, pretending to be concentrating very hard on the first thing I see. Which happens to be George, who instantly panics and starts mouthing "What?" at me.

The rehearsal room has filled with a buzz of energy – not quite noise, but something between sound and excitement. Today's the deadline Rick gave them to be completely off-book. With the actors (hopefully) knowing their lines and not needing their scripts, the creative team gets to see what they do when their hands and their minds are free and their bodies have settled into who they're meant to become. Words, movements, feelings: it's the first time the production breathes.

It also means that I need to concentrate more than ever. With the cast off-book, there's bound to be a few times they forget their lines, and my job is to prompt them, which means I've got to follow the script line by line…all while checking we've got the movements and cues marked on the prompt copy. On a smooth scene, it's all right – but on a bad one, it's a little like jumping on a trampoline while wearing stilts and drinking a glass of water, blindfolded.

It'll be *fine*.

I carry on ticking off the last few names until there's only two left: Juliet, our Lizzie, and – surprise – Tommy. Well, we can't start without him, can we?

George has settled down with his iPad on his lap and is flicking through what looks like a Pinterest page full of hairstyles, making notes in an A4 pad alongside him and occasionally looking up to study the actors as they mill about, warming up.

I lean on the back of the chair next to him. "Morning!"

"Hey you!" he says brightly, half-turning in his seat and holding up the tablet. "What do you think about this for her?" He points to a tightly braided style on the screen and then at Ruby, the understudy for Lizzie as well as one of Jamie's friends, currently wriggling her way out of a sweater across the room. "I have to find three different styles for her wig, research them and write a pro and con thing for each one, then Jonna and Nathalie said I can do the wig fitting for the one they all choose." He glows with excitement. "Me! They're letting me help choose her style!"

"That's amazing!" I peer at the screen. "Have you got the other two there as well?"

He nods and proudly flicks through another couple of near-identical hairstyles. "What do you think? I don't want to get it wrong and look like a total idiot."

I make a vaguely approving, thoughtful sound, even though I can't actually see any difference between them. But what do I know?

George is still looking at me expectantly. "What do *you* think?" I ask, hoping that'll do.

"I like this one." He taps the second of the identikit hair-triplets. "But I don't know where I'd put the mic…"

I've checked enough costumes in the moments before an actor steps out onstage to know about the perils of mic tape. "You could try there?" I point at the middle of the front edge of the hairstyle, where a parting would sit.

George purses his lips and zooms in. "Interesting..."

I don't get to find out whether that's a good "interesting" or a bad "interesting" because the door is thrown open and Tommy sails in. I guess I should be impressed that he's not actually *last*. He sashays across the room, dropping an insanely expensive-looking leather backpack on the floor and draping himself over a chair. Rick spots him and folds his arms expectantly.

"Are we all here?" His voice creaks with barely-contained irritation.

Tommy ignores him.

The silence in the room is deafening – and then George catches my attention. He's making a rolling gesture with his hands, widening his eyes at me.

Oh. Right.

Me.

"Umm...we're just waiting for Juliet..." I brandish my register of ticked-off names, just as Juliet comes barrelling through the door.

"Sorry. Sorry. My cat got out. I'm so sorry if I've held everyone up." She's been running – she's out of breath and her words tumble out one after another, piling up in the middle of the floor along with her bag and her coat. This is obviously good enough for Rick, who nods and claps his hands together.

"All right then. Two minutes, everyone!" He folds a new stick of chewing gum into his mouth.

From his seat, Tommy snorts and mutters something inaudible.

I'd better go put the kettle on...

We break for lunch at noon and Tommy immediately snaps his fingers at me from the back of the room. Charming. Luke is sitting at the end of a row of chairs, his head buried in his show script, a spiral-bound notebook on the chair next to him where he's been making notes about Tommy's performance. The tricky thing about being an understudy is making sure that if you ever get to play the role, your performance is yours...but not so different from the lead actor's that it throws the rest of the cast off-balance. I give him a smile as I pass, but he's so absorbed in his work that he doesn't notice me. Tommy, on the other hand, watches me every step of the way.

"Good. I need you to fetch me something."

Hello to you, too...

It's part of the job. It's fine. It's *fine*. "Sure, what can I get for you?"

Support the cast, be there for Tommy, keep his head in the theatre; keep putting one foot in front of the other along the tightrope across the burning pit of Fired...

"My phone. I need my phone."

"Right...?" I wait. Unless he's expecting me to magic it out of the air, he'll have to give me at least a little more information.

"It's probably in my room at the Grand."

"You're still in the hotel?" I thought he would be in digs or a flat or something, the way most actors would be...but then I guess it's different when you're *Hollywood*.

"Yes, obviously I'm in the hotel. Unless you know something I don't?" Somehow he manages both to roll his eyes in disgust and close them in pain at my stupidity all at once. "Well? Off you go. The penthouse. Tell the concierge 'crème de menthe', and he'll be happy to help."

"Crème de menthe?" I repeat back at him.

He blinks at me, and even though I can't believe he's asking me – *telling* me – to spend my lunch break on some stupid errand, even though I can almost feel my blood boiling in my veins...his eyes are fixed on me, and suddenly he's Tommy Knight the movie star, and I am standing right next to him and...

"Yes. It's a password. I set one up with the staff at every hotel I stay in – it lets them know you work for me."

Oh, do I?

"And Hope?" He gives me a dazzling, million-watt Hollywood smile. Perhaps he's going to say how grateful he'll be; how he knows it's a lot to ask.

"Mmm?"

"The sooner you go, the sooner you'll be back – yes?"

I hate him – and I don't even get the chance to tell him so, because apparently satisfied that he's messed up my day enough, he spins on his heel and walks away.

I shoot a stricken look at Amy, but she's busy doing something complicated with gaffer tape.

Tommy glances round, realizes I've not gone anywhere and makes a small shooing gesture with his hand.

I look at the clock on the wall. Ten past twelve. There's a minicab office three units down, isn't there? If I go now, I might actually make it back for some of my break.

Right.

I grab my bag and I'm gone. Do I call the hotel? What do I even say to them, other than "crème de menthe" and hope that Tommy's not setting me up for some elaborate prank?

Why didn't I get Tommy to speak to them on my phone before I left?

Why didn't I tell Tommy to go fetch his own stupid phone?

Tightrope of Fired. That's why.

I half-walk, half-run along the pavement in the direction of the cab office. Luckily, there are three cars out front – and even from the road I can see the drivers sitting in the waiting room.

I completely forgot to ask Amy for money. There's a petty

cash box, isn't there? Why didn't I just *think*? I decide to sort it out when I get back, and ask for a car to the Grand.

I slide into the back seat of the cab; the driver clears his throat loudly, slamming the car door.

It's fine. It's fine. I'll just get a receipt and—

"So where are we going?" The voice comes from right next to me, and it's all I can do not to shriek.

George. Bundling himself into the back seat with an expectant look on his face.

"What are you doing?" I hiss at him. I'm about to tell him to go away, but we're already moving.

"What are *you* doing?" he asks, looking out of the window. "Are we off on an adventure?"

"Tommy's forgotten his phone, so naturally I'm fetching it. Because that's my point and purpose in life, you know. Why are you here?"

"Followed you. Why's Tommy need his phone so badly?"

"Hang on – you *followed* me?"

"I saw you talking to Mr Hollywood. Thought you might be on some exciting secret mission."

"Apparently Tommy must be contactable at *all* times, and it can't possibly wait until the end of the day."

"Oh." George ponders this. "Why's that then?"

"Maybe he's waiting for the call to tell him he's won Dickhead of the Year."

"Sounds likely. So where are we going?"

"His hotel."

"His actual *room*?"

"Easy, tiger. They'll never let us up there."

"Then how…"

"Shhhh." I shut my eyes and rest my head against the seat.

The hotel concierge is, as I predicted, not having any of this "going up to the room" business. Not even my offer to call Amy and get Tommy on the phone seems to be enough.

"His room?" He studies us carefully: me, trying to look at least slightly together, and pretending that yes I absolutely knew I had a pencil stuck in my hair when I walked up to the desk and I definitely and completely meant for it to be there…and George, who is trying to take a selfie in front of the enormous vase of flowers in the middle of the lobby.

"George!" I hiss at him under my breath.

I'm sure I can see a vein bulging in the concierge's forehead that wasn't there a moment ago.

I sigh. There's no way I'm getting out of this, is there? "Crème de menthe," I mutter.

"I beg your pardon?"

"He said…Mr Knight said to tell you 'crème de menthe', and you'd know it was really him. Or me. You'd know that I was here for him."

"Wait here, please." His raised hand is as immovable and unavoidable as a granite cliff as he picks up the phone handset with his other. "Housekeeping? Who am I speaking with? Zelda. Perfect. How are you, my darling? Yes. Yes. Listen – a guest believes he has left his mobile phone in his room? Mmm. Mmm-hmm. Mr Knight, in the penthouse. Yes. His assistant is waiting in the lobby to collect… Could you? Perfect. Wonderful. Thank you, my darling. Yes, yes. You'll know her. Mmm." He hangs up and fixes me with a stern look. "Wait. Here."

So I do. And I picture telling Tommy exactly where he can stick his phone.

"… and so they cast Tommy," says George, his voice breaking through my thoughts. "Apparently, he didn't even have to audition. Can you imagine?"

"Sorry – what?"

"You're in a world of your own, aren't you?" He shakes his head. "Calm down. It'll be fine."

"This is such a waste of time. I'm *not* his assistant."

"You're meant to be keeping him happy, and if this is what keeps him happy then it's what you've got to do. Stop stressing."

Said like that, with his Geordie accent, it's almost impossible to argue. "What were you saying about the show?"

"Just something I read online this morning. Gossip pages on the *SixGuns* website."

"*SixGuns* is pretty trashy, George."

"So you don't read it, then?"

I open my mouth, realize I have no answer, and close it. George takes this as his cue to continue.

"Tommy was spitting feathers over missing out on the award nominations again this year. Apparently he wanted to be taken 'seriously' so he told his agent he needed to do some theatre. The producers demanded a star – and voila! Tommy Knight, on a stage near you!"

"No, I know that. But I thought the whole point of him doing theatre was to not be…Hollywood-y? He wanted to do something that got away from all that star stuff, didn't he?" Not that you'd know it from the way he's behaving so far.

At that moment, a woman wearing a housekeeping uniform and carrying a phone appears from a side door. She hesitates, scans the lobby…and then spots me and starts walking over. I give her a less-than-enthusiastic wave. Obviously that's what "You'll know her" meant.

"Mr Knight's phone?"

I thank her and practically snatch it out of her hands.

"Watch it," George mutters, jumping out of the way as I swing around.

We bundle back into the taxi with the precious cargo.

"Did you see that?" George leans over me to look out of the window as we pull away. "I could've sworn that guy just came out of the hotel and took our photo."

"You what?"

"He had a camera."

"It's just a tourist, George. Why would anyone want to take a photo of *us*?" Turning Tommy's phone over in my hands, I elbow George onto his half of the back seat. "Anyway, I get that if you're *going* to have a big name in the play then Tommy's perfect."

"He is, isn't he?" George sighs.

I elbow him harder. "Yeah, all right. But what I don't get is why they even needed a name for *Piecekeepers*. Have you seen how many copies the book has sold since it came out? And all the fan stuff online?" I have. I looked. I wasn't exactly crazy about the book, personally, but plenty of people are.

George snorts. "Doesn't mean anyone will come and see it though, does it? You know how it goes. You can't guarantee anything in theatre – it's why so many telly actors are getting cast in things they've got no business being in, just because they're a *name*."

"Wow. Bit harsh."

"No it isn't. Besides, the Earl's doesn't exactly have a reputation for the most cutting-edge productions, does it? Maybe they wanted to show what they can do if they have the chance? Prove themselves or something."

It's why the news that *Piecekeepers* would open here

before going to the West End has caught everybody by surprise. Shows like this don't open all the way down here in the south-west, an hour (and then some) out of Paddington. This kind of theatre happens in London. Okay, maybe after a few years it would tour here – but opening? No way. Suddenly, the Earl's has become the little regional theatre that could, and is punching well above its weight. And people are watching; not all of them friendly.

And what that means is that nobody on this show can afford to mess up.

Nobody.

Paying for the cab leaves me completely broke. George didn't think to bring his wallet on this so-called exciting secret mission, so it's down to me. The cab driver reluctantly hands over a receipt so I can claim the money back from Amy, muttering the whole time about the traffic like that's my fault. Mind you, thanks to the traffic, it's also taken much longer than I was hoping – the lunch break is almost over, and it's already quarter to one by the time I walk through the rehearsal room door, brandishing my prize…

Only to see Tommy, handing Amy's phone back to her.

I walk over to him and hold out his precious, precious handset; he stares at me like I've tried to hand him half a potato.

ACT TWO, SCENE ONE

"What do I need that for? I've just made my call."

And with that, he sashays off to pick up the rehearsal where we left it.

ACT TWO, SCENE TWO

I sit at the creative team desk, making notes with one hand, popping the last few crisps from the lunch table into my mouth with the other. Seeing as I spent my entire lunch break fetching and carrying for Tommy, I didn't get time to eat – and all that was left on the food trays by the time I got back were a few packs of crisps and a couple of sad-looking cheese and pickle sandwiches which George leaped at and shoved in his mouth as fast as he could.

I keep an eye on the script as I chew, just in case someone forgets their line, but everything seems to be running pretty smoothly – if you ignore the stage illusion, which has now reduced Amy to sullen silence and which Rick has announced he's not wasting any more time on until we can try it out on the actual stage. And Tommy might be a bit (a lot) of a dick – but he's good. He's really good. When he steps into the rehearsal stage area, everyone's attention is drawn to him every single time. His voice is like a saw wrapped in silk: soft and quiet one second, sharp and cutting the next. Each word his character Jamie says, each move he makes, feels like it was always meant for him. Even Rick nods along thoughtfully, only occasionally taking his eyes off his brother to scribble something in the margins of his script. We're flying through this rehearsal, and just like Amy said, things are starting to pull together into what feels like a whole play; with nearly two weeks before opening night, there might even be time to—

Somewhere at the back of the room, a phone rings. Loudly.

Rick rolls his eyes. "Whose is that?"

The spell is broken, and everyone drops out of character. Postures change and the actors' faces shift back to their everyday expressions. And then Tommy bounds out of the taped-off area, heading for the ringing mobile.

"That's my manager's ringtone. I need to take this."

Maybe it was better when he didn't have it…

No apology, no suggestion of letting it go to voicemail. Nothing. He grabs his phone from his chair and swishes out through the door into the foyer. "Hello? Yes. Yes, I'm…"

The door closes behind him and cuts us off from the conversation.

Everyone in the room looks at one another, and at Rick – who is tapping the end of his pencil irritably against his teeth.

"Luke?"

Luke's head snaps up from his notebook.

"It doesn't look like we're going to make it to your scene today, I'm afraid. Fancy switching roles and taking a run at this one while we wait for Mr Knight to grace us with his presence once more?"

Luke nods. "If you're sure?"

"If nobody has any objections, I think it would be good to keep things moving. I like the energy we're getting from this run-through." Rick glances at the actors, who mumble and shrug and nod and gradually slide back into their characters, dropping their usual selves like discarded coats. "Let's back up a little – can we take it from Lizzie's entrance? Whenever you're ready…"

There's some shuffling as the cast find their positions and reset their rehearsal props – someone picks up a mug from the table at the back of the stage area and tosses it to another actor offstage, while someone else grabs a chair and turns it the right way round.

And then they start.

At first, it's just the same: Juliet, playing Lizzie, does her thing, and all the while Luke is waiting at the side of the stage area. Rick is nodding and chewing and nodding, and Amy and Nina are both studying Juliet's performance. And then Luke comes on…except he's not Luke any more. The guy I was talking to earlier, the one who's been sitting there all morning quietly reading and taking notes – he's gone. Just…gone.

In his place on the stage is someone else. Jamie. Every bit as real and magnetic as he was when Tommy was embodying him – but somehow different. Luke is following Tommy's blocking, keeping to the same points on the stage like we all need him to, but the lines spin out of his mouth with different meanings. He leans in closer to Juliet's Lizzie, whispering softly to her where Tommy used a barely-controlled growl…and I can't be the only one who sees the blush creeping up her cheek.

She didn't do that when Tommy said the line.

But looking at Luke standing there, only a breath away from her, I don't blame her at all.

Because that – what Luke's doing – that's the closest thing to magic I've ever seen. It's a vanishing act: he's still wearing the same clothes, still has the same colour hair, same colour eyes, but everything else about him is gone. His voice is different. He moves differently. The way he carries himself is different… He's someone completely new.

Never mind that he's playing Lancelot – how is he only the understudy for this part? He's better than *Tommy*.

Every single person in the rehearsal room is focused entirely and completely on the stage, on the way Luke's hand is resting on Juliet's shoulder. It feels weird, like we're watching something real – like we're spying on something private. He moves closer to her, his hand sliding down her side, his arm wrapping around her waist and drawing her in…his lips almost brushing her cheek…and the whole rehearsal room is holding its breath…

And then the slow-clapping starts from the back of the room.

Tommy has slipped back in, unnoticed, and is leaning against the wall beside the door, watching with a sardonic expression.

"Oh, bravo. Well done." He stops clapping and sniffs. "And there was I, worried about holding up the rehearsal."

Rick leans back in his seat, turning his head towards his brother. "That's not what it looked like from here. We're on the clock – and I thought it would be good for Luke to stretch his wings a little." He grins darkly, and no one in the room could miss the threat. "He's not at all bad as Jamie."

"Yes, well. He isn't me, is he? He'd do better concentrating on his own part." Tommy bats Rick's words away – and he's right. After all, it's his name on the posters, isn't it? His face.

As he steps over the tape marking the front of the "stage", Luke becomes himself again. I see it happen, and Jamie dissolves as he walks over to Rick for notes on his performance. The feedback he gets is quick and to the point – and good. Very good. Nina adds a comment from her notes, and Amy says something about watching his shadow crossing Juliet's face…and then they all turn to me.

"Hope. Any thoughts?" Amy asks.

"Ummm…." I look at my prompt script. I have no idea why – I know I didn't write anything down the whole time Luke was onstage. I was too busy staring at him, wasn't I?

I peer at the pages, hoping it at least vaguely looks like I'm reading something very interesting and important. "No, no, I think that was great. Really…yes. Awesome."

Luke smiles. "That'll do me," he says – and for a second it looks like *he* might actually be blushing. Trick of the light, probably.

Amy raises an eyebrow at me, and I can actually hear George sniggering into his notes behind me. I turn around and glare at him, but it only makes him snort and huddle down behind his iPad.

Even Rick looks like he's in danger of breaking into a smile. Great. A chance to dazzle him with my insight and attention…and I'm an idiot.

I stand up, pushing my chair under the table and not even caring that the legs squeal against the floor. I can't be in here with everyone looking at me one minute longer. "Does anyone want tea?"

"Great idea, Hope. Ten minutes, everyone."

I hold my head up as I walk to the kitchen, right the way through the door…and as soon as I've checked nobody followed me, I start banging my forehead against the mug cupboard.

"Stupid. Stupid. Stupid. 'Really awesome.' Hey, Hope, here's your chance to do something other than take notes on whether the lamp's supposed to be on the left-hand side of the table or the right-hand side of the table…and you come up with 'awesome' like some stupid kid."

I lean my forehead on the cupboard door. I just wasn't expecting that, and it caught me completely off guard. He was *so* quiet, and *so* awkward…and then so *good*.

"Don't take it to heart. It wasn't that bad," says a voice behind me. I roll around, not quite taking my face off the Door of Shame. Nina is standing just inside the kitchen, her arms folded across her chest.

"No," I mutter. "It was definitely worse. I sounded like an idiot." I sigh, and she cocks her head to one side.

"You didn't, not at all. Not having notes is fine – it means you've been invested in the performance. That's the goal." She picks up the kettle. "Need a hand?"

I start pulling mugs out of the cupboard and doling out teabags, spoons of instant coffee, Juliet's weird green-tea granules and something one of the other actors apparently brought back from a silent retreat in Spain. I don't know what it is, but it's gloopy and dark orange and smells like… well, something *bad*.

We stand there, waiting for the first kettleful of water to boil. "What's it like working with Rick?" I ask.

Nina shrugs, but there's a longer pause than I was

expecting before she actually answers. "Oh, you know. He's a perfectionist. Amazing, but he likes things done his way – which is fair enough. It does mean a lot of research, though, because that's how he works. Even by the usual standards, you could say he's an over-preparer. It drives my girlfriend crazy when we're in pre-production. She says it's like living in an old archive."

I picture the heap of papers I shovelled under my bed – the notes and printouts of actors' headshots and half-crossed-through lists of props. "I know what you mean."

I load a tray up with mugs and the giant carton of milk (and the selection of smaller non-dairy milk cartons that seem to be breeding in the fridge at the moment: almond, soya, oat…and apparently this new one is hemp – who knew?) and nudge it towards her.

"Can you take this one out? I'll bring out the next lot."

As she heads back into the rehearsal room, I start lining up the second batch of mugs. Waiting for the kettle to reboil, I keep thinking back to Luke on that stage. It's incredible the way actors can do that. It's not like when you *see* them "acting" – and believe me, I've seen plenty of that at the Square Globe – but when they completely disappear and you forget they have another name, another life. You forget that they exist at all outside that time and space, and you tell yourself that you know them; that if you met them in the street you could be friends with them…and then they come offstage and the mask drops and they put on their own names again, take back their real lives, and you realize that you never knew them at all. You only saw what they wanted you to see.

Tommy spends the rest of the day snarling at everyone. Not only is he sulking about Luke stepping in for him earlier, but according to George (who, like all wardrobe and make-up crew, knows *everything*), the phone call with his manager was yet another bit of bad news: a meeting he had with the head of a studio about getting into producing didn't go as well as he'd thought, apparently. This hasn't helped his mood, so along with everyone else I make a point of keeping out of his way as much as possible.

And Luke? He leaves as quietly as he slipped in and out of Tommy's shoes, and when I turn around midway through a scene, he's vanished. But while I'm straightening the room ready for the morning, I spot something on the floor under his chair. It's Luke's script. What is it with this guy and keeping hold of his stuff? I flick through it, even though I have my own well-thumbed copy that I can probably see with my eyes shut by now. Like *The History Boys*, it's full of pencil annotations in the margins; here and there words are underlined and circled. He's studying it – picking it apart and working out how to fold it back together again.

"He's not forgotten that one too, has he? Fabulous actor,

especially for a first-year, but you can tell he's a student – he'd forget his skull if it wasn't attached." Amy nods at the script as she passes my bag across. She looks as tired as I feel…or maybe I look as tired as she feels. It's hard to say but, either way, I'm tired.

"Last day in the rehearsal room tomorrow," she says. "And then we're into the Earl's."

Already my mind is picturing the narrow corridor I've walked along so many times in my dreams since that birthday. This is a problem, because Amy is actually still talking to me. I haul my brain back into the rehearsal room and try to focus on what she's saying.

"…lot more to do after the get-in, when we've got access to the whole theatre. I'll need you to familiarize yourself with the layout as quickly as you can – I know that's a lot to ask, because it's a bit of a warren backstage, but you'll get the hang of it. It's the same kind of thing you've done plenty of times before. Just…bigger."

I nod. It's a theatre, and I know theatre all the way down to my bones. How hard can it be?

Instead of heading home at the end of the day, I peel George away from his wig catalogues. "Enough hair. Come on, we're going."

"Going where?" He frowns at me.

"Cinema. I'm meeting a couple of friends from the Square Globe, and you're coming."

"I am?"

"Yes. Stop looking at the hair, George."

"I just…"

"You're *coming*."

He doesn't put up a fight as we head for the bus stop.

Just for once, I don't have to worry about whether Mum's going to pop her head out of her studio when I get home and ask how I'm doing: a couple of her RCD (Red Carpet Dress) commissions are almost finished and have, over the last forty-eight hours, gradually taken over the entire house. Every flat surface is covered in lace or gold braid, and Dad complained he actually found bugle beads in his porridge yesterday morning. So even if I was ready to go home, I don't think home is quite ready for me yet – not unless I want to be handed a pair of pinking shears or asked to help pin fifteen metres of silver and black netting together. Which means I'm free. For a bit, anyway.

Tommy's face stares out at me from the poster on the side of the bus stop. *The Earl's Theatre is proud to present Tommy Knight in his stage debut…*

"Like you've not had enough of looking at that face for one day," George says as the bus pulls in.

"Quite."

* * *

112

"Hey! Hope! Over here!"

I look down the street and see a group of familiar faces waiting for us: the backstage crew from the Square. It's so good to see them that, at first, I almost wonder whether they're actually some weird kind of Tommy-induced stress hallucination, but no – they really are there.

"Come on!" Priya stamps her feet impatiently. "We'll miss the start – you've taken ages!"

"Sorry. Bus."

"You always say that when you're late, and I know for a *fact* it's only true half the time." She gives me a gentle shove, then leans around me to smile at George. "Hi!"

"You remember George? *Merchant of Venice?*"

It turns out almost all of them remember George – particularly Priya, who keeps smiling at him when she thinks nobody's looking.

We pile into the tiny cinema lobby with its old-fashioned box-office window, get our tickets and scramble up the spiral chrome staircase to the second screen on the top floor. Funnily enough, this used to be a theatre too, built in the 1930s. Even though it's been a cinema since the sixties, it still feels theatre-y inside, like the magic hasn't quite worn off and never will – which is probably why it's one of my favourite places outside an *actual* theatre.

At the front of the group, Orson mutters something about popcorn and Priya groans.

"Can you not?"

"We've still got two minutes – I'll go," I say. I'm already at the back – and by the time Orson squeezes down the narrow stairs past everybody, we'll *all* have missed the beginning.

Orson peers around the others. "Are you sure?"

"Yeah. It's fine – just don't ask for anything difficult."

"Can you get a large bucket of salted?"

"Are you dreaming?" Priya shakes her head. "Sweet."

It's an old argument, and there's only one solution.

"How about I get a mixed one? Sweet *and* salty."

Orson grumbles, but Priya shushes him, and as I duck back down the stairs to the lobby, I hear her telling him to live dangerously once in a while. Seeing as Orson is normally the one in charge of hauling on ropes at the Square Globe – and more than once has nearly got dragged across the stage when he wasn't paying attention – that's more than a little ironic.

There are only a few people ahead of me in the queue, which is good. I don't really want to miss the start either – but if I've picked up anything from two years of backstage work at the Square, it's that nobody gets anywhere unless they're part of the team. The actors would be standing on an empty stage in the dark, the costume department would be making clothes nobody will ever wear and the lighting department might as well be flashing an SOS in Morse code into the night sky. So this is me taking one for the team. Especially as the queue doesn't seem to be moving along anywhere near as quickly as it should be…

The problem is the guy at the front, who's got the concession seller looking seriously confused. Like the person in front of me, and the woman who has just joined the queue behind me, I crane my neck as discreetly as possible to listen in on the conversation.

"…Mix them up?" the girl behind the till is saying. She's holding a large empty popcorn box in one hand, and something else I can't see in the other. "But what would you do that for?" she asks. The guy says something I don't hear, but she laughs and shakes her head, then dunks the box into the popcorn, pulling it out three-quarters full. She rests it on the glass counter while she opens a large bag of Maltesers which she shakes into the box. To finish the whole thing off, she sprinkles another scoop of popcorn over the top and hands the abomination over. As one, the queue gasp. Oblivious, the guy walks off with his popcorn in the direction of the stairs. But just before he disappears behind the banners and posters that decorate the outside of the spiral, I catch sight of a familiar profile: a straight nose, lowered towards the popcorn he's carrying and trying not to spill. Narrow shoulders and dirty blond hair. My heart skips. *Luke.*

No. I must be imagining it.

"Who would do that to a tub of popcorn?" whispers the woman behind me.

"Someone with no soul," I hiss back.

By the time I get my family-sized bucket of mixed salted and sweet popcorn and scramble back up the stairs, there's no sign of Luke and the trailers are almost finished. I pick my way along the narrow row of seats and drop into an empty space next to George.

"Took you long enough," he whispers, carefully lifting the popcorn out of my hands and passing it down the row to Orson, who is busy making excited *gimme gimme* noises.

"Some weirdo in the queue was getting fancy with his snack choices."

As Orson passes out handfuls of popcorn, I sink back into my seat and let myself fall into the film on the screen.

Outside, we all pull on coats and make promises to meet up soon. A thick mist has come up from the river while we were inside and there's a damp chill in the air. Priya puts her hands on my shoulders and looks me in the eyes. "I know you can't tell me much, but it's going okay, right?"

"Yes." I nod vigorously. "It. Is. Great."

"And what about your mystery script guy – how's that—"

I cut her off by suddenly discovering I have popcorn stuck in my throat and coughing loudly.

She rolls her eyes but smiles anyway. "Oh, riiiiiight. I get it."

"We miss you!" Orson bellows into my ear, and the whole bunch of them take this as an excuse to mob me, crowding round and laughing.

When I fight my way out, George slings a tentative arm around me in a half-hug and says he'll see me tomorrow. As I head up the road towards the bus stop, I see yet another poster of Tommy's glowering face (he really is everywhere) and my stomach churns… It only stops when I spot the back of Luke's head further along the road, his hair catching the light of every street lamp he passes under. I quicken my pace. It has to be him. *Has* to be. There can't be many people who look like him wandering around – not in a town like this. Also, I want to ask: quite apart from what kind of monster really could do that to popcorn, was it sweet or salted?

But before I can get very far, he turns down a side street and disappears into the mist. And even though I walk a little faster, peering into the fog, by the time I get to the street lamp where the alley joins another road, there's no sign of him. I pull my coat a little tighter around me and walk home.

Mum's studio door is ajar and opera seeps out into the hall, competing with the radio in the kitchen.

"I'm home – I'm just going up to my room!"

I wait at the bottom of the stairs for a second, but both my parents are absorbed in their own worlds. That's no bad thing right now: I'm suddenly so tired that the insides of my bones hurt and every time I blink it feels like someone's thrown a handful of grit into my eyes. I need to have a lie down for a few minutes, quarter of an hour or something, and get my head together.

And even though I don't actually mean to, even though I haven't had dinner yet (unless a shared bucket of popcorn counts) and there's the schoolwork I've missed that Priya's been emailing over, and *stuff* to do…my eyes are too heavy. Not just my eyes, either, my whole body's too heavy, and my bed is too comfortable.

As my eyes close, I see one last flash of tropical blue eyes and a smiling face, turned half-away from me to whisper into Juliet's ear.

And as everything slides into the dark, Luke's eyes look up and lock onto mine.

ACT TWO, SCENE THREE

No sooner have I walked into the rehearsal room on Thursday than Amy, "just for fun", gives me a section of the script to mark up with some new light and sound cues based on a meeting Rick had with the head techs yesterday evening.

Amy's idea of fun and mine do not overlap.

After watching me scratch my head for a while, she drops into a crouch beside my chair, lowering her voice to a whisper so she doesn't disturb the rhythm of the rehearsal behind her. "How are you getting on?"

"Not great," I sigh, holding up the book so she can see it.

She runs a finger down the page and stops. "What's this one?" she asks, tapping the horrific tangle of pencil scribbles midway down.

"I don't know?"

"Hope."

"I can't do it."

She purses her lips. "Yes, you can. Take it one cue at a time."

"But there's so many, and they're all happening at…"

The room has gone very quiet.

Too quiet.

I look round, and realize the rehearsal has stopped – and Tommy is staring at me. I smile back at him. Nothing happens – and then he sighs. "Line?"

He's forgotten his line and needs a prompt. Not surprising, really – the first thing Rick announced this morning was that this scene needs completely reworking. So between the new blocking and everything else they're tinkering with, it's a miracle no one's needed prompting until now. It was a complicated enough scene as it was…

I flick back to the current page.

"Line!" Standing in the middle of the taped-off stage area, he looks like he's about to stamp his foot.

"No," I call back – and I can actually see the shocked look on his face.

He tries again. "Line, please?"

Something weird is happening. "No."

"Line. Please."

"No!"

From where I'm sitting, I can see the back of Rick's shoulders trembling.

Tommy walks right off the imaginary stage and marches over to me, standing with one hand on his hip, every bit of him the star. "Do you think this is a game? Do you? Because let me tell you – it isn't. This is a professional working environment, not somewhere you get to…to…to play at being a grown-up. And while you think you're being clever, you're holding everyone up."

Rick has put his face in his hands and is making a peculiar snorting noise, shoulders now shaking so hard it's a wonder his arms don't drop off. Next to him, Nina is focusing very, very hard on her notepad – but even I can see her smiling.

When I finally manage to get enough of a grip to speak, my voice comes out loud and clear, carrying right across the rehearsal room.

"The line, Tommy, is 'No'."

Absolute silence descends. Nobody moves, nobody speaks, nobody even breathes. All eyes are on Tommy (and me), waiting to see how he'll respond to this.

He opens his mouth once, then closes it again. His eyes narrow and he tips his head ever so slightly to one side… and I can't help but remember the look he gave me on my first day, when he stole the sugar from the kitchen.

"Right. Of *course*."

And without warning, his face cracks into that enormous bright smile, and he nods at me and spins on his heel, striding back over to the stage and rubbing his hands together with a quick "Shall we pick it up?" to Rick as he passes.

All I can do is sit there, blinking at him.

"What was *that*?"

George has slipped quietly into the chair behind mine, and his whisper is both so dramatic and so sudden that I actually twitch. The cues I'm holding on my lap flop to the floor and papers scatter around my feet.

"Jesus. Don't *do* that!"

"Sorry." He is clearly not even slightly sorry. "But what happened there?"

"I gave him his line." I shrug, scrabbling for the pages. One seems to have wedged itself under the leg of my chair; I'm not quite sure how that's physically possible, but it's managed to do it anyway. I stand up and scoot it along the floor with my toe.

"You didn't just give him his line. You gave him a spanking in front of the whole company."

"I think that's a *bit* of an exaggeration, don't you?"

Somewhere in the middle of the fading terror of telling Tommy Knight he's wrong, a glimmer of triumph shines brightly out at me. Because I got it right.

"No," he says. "You just schooled Tommy Knight in theatre."

Someone had to, I think – and then wonder where the hell that came from… Right before I see who's standing just inside the door, talking to Amy, and wonder where *he* came from. We're due to finally run his Lancelot scene today but I just wasn't ready.

ACT TWO, SCENE THREE

George turns in his seat to follow my gaze.

"Oh, *reeeeeeeally*…?" He draws out the "really" so it lasts until Luke has covered most of the distance between us and arrives to find me hissing at George to piss off.

He stops, waiting to see if we've finished talking. "Sorry, am I interrupting, or…?"

"No. No, George was just going, *weren't* you, George?"

George beams at me. "I was?"

"Yes. You were. Going. Right?"

"Oh. Oh. Ohhhhh. Yes, I was going. Hair charts to study. And Tommy's hair! I get to help touch up his roots!"

"GOODBYE, GEORGE."

He takes the hint and wanders off, humming a song from *Matilda*.

Luke is still standing there, one hand tucked into the pocket of his ripped jeans. "So. Hi."

"Hi."

"Look, I can't quite believe I'm this dense, but I think I left my script behind. Again. My actual script, I mean."

"You did."

"I was hoping maybe you'd found it? Seeing as you found the last one, I mean." He stops abruptly.

I lean over and fish his script out of my bag, holding it out to him.

He takes it, almost hesitantly. "Thanks." Maybe I'm imagining it, but this time when our fingers touch as he takes it, his skin seems to rest against mine just a little longer than it did before.

My cheeks feel hot in the cool of the room; under the warmth of his blue, blue gaze.

The gaze that I couldn't stop picturing as I drifted off into sleep last night.

I'm still holding the script. I'm making this weird.

It shouldn't be weird. It's not weird.

I let go of the script – and somehow, at the exact same moment, his grip on it loosens and it falls to the floor between us.

"Ooops – sorry…" And he bends to pick it up – at exactly the same time I do. Our heads collide halfway down with a tooth-rattling thud. "Wow, is Tommy so threatened that he's paying you to put me out of commission?" He takes the script again – properly this time – as I rub my throbbing head.

"I think I probably came out of that one worse."

He doesn't walk off. I was expecting him to walk off, but he hasn't. "Do you…do…do you act?" At first it's hard to tell whether he's talking to me or to himself, as he's looking at the floor – but he waits, and when I don't answer, he looks up and it's obvious he meant me.

On the stage, he moves closer to her, his hand sliding down her side, his arm wrapping around her waist and drawing her in…his lips almost brushing her cheek…

Was that only two days ago? Because since then, I seriously haven't been able to get him out of my head, and it feels like he's been in there for ever. I keep seeing him inside my mind, keep hearing his voice speaking Jamie's lines over and over and over. It's so stupid because I barely know him…but I *feel* like I do.

"I…? Do…act?"

I have lost the ability to form sentences that make sense.

"You know, theatre. Do you act?"

"Ha!" My laugh is so loud that half the company look round to see what's going on.

He looks at me weirdly. "Everything okay?"

"Yes. Sorry. I was…I had something stuck in my throat there. No. Not an actor. No way. I just…really like theatre. I like seeing how it fits together."

"Me too," he says quietly.

I try to be very interested in the order of my sheets, shuffling them busily.

I look up.

Luke is still there. Still waiting.

"I was wondering," he says…and now I really do have something stuck in my throat and I *think* it might be my heart. I have to swallow really hard to make sure it doesn't climb any higher and end up in my actual mouth.

"Mmm-hmm?"

"Have you got a minute?"

I stick the end of my pencil in my mouth, hoping I look thoughtful.

"Mmm-hmm." It comes out a full octave higher than the last one.

"There's a section I just can't seem to get right – there's a phrase in the middle and it's throwing the rest of the line out. I'm worried the more times I go over it, the worse it's getting."

The inside of my mouth tastes like pencil sharpenings. I take the pencil out of my mouth and pretend not to notice the toothmarks I've left in it.

"Sure – no problem. When do you want me to…um… help?"

There's a cackle from the row of seats behind Luke. George. Luke doesn't seem to hear, and screws up his nose. "Well, if you've got time now, that would be great. I really want to nail it before Rick sees."

"Sure. Sure, sure, sure. Yep. Can do, can doooo…" I make myself stop before George – who I am confident is hiding behind a chair and listening gleefully to every single word – has some kind of accident. "What scene was it again?" I reach for my folder, but instead he simply hands his script to me. The pages are warm from his touch.

"It's the scene between Lancelot and Lizzie right before Lancelot's fight with Jamie."

Of course it is. Flipping through the pages and nodding, I wonder exactly how I'm going to manage this – there is only one scene between just Lancelot and Lizzie in the entire production. And it's the one where he tells her he loves her. Which does not make this awkward at *all*.

"Okay. Got it. Great." I put on my serious script-face, the one Priya says always makes me look like I'm about to sneeze. "Ready when you are."

He takes a deep breath and closes his eyes as he starts, feeling his way into the lines. He's right: he hasn't got them yet – not quite. It's not that he doesn't know the words, more that they *sound* like a script, like something he's learned rather than something he's saying for the very first time, something he's saying because he needs to. He stumbles in the middle of a sentence; hesitates, corrects himself and frowns as he picks up the thread again.

There's a faint line through one of his eyebrows – it looks like a scar. How did he get it, and when? Climbing a tree when he was a kid? In a football match or falling off a bike? In a fight? In a stage fight? Five different images of him flicker through my mind, one after another. Five possible versions of him – and all the while, his voice is there and...

His voice is not there.

His voice has, in fact, stopped.

Ah.

I blink.

He's looking straight at me, both eyebrows (scarred and unscarred) raised expectantly.

Is everyone's bone structure as symmetrical as that? Because his cheekbones are really, really balanced.

And pretty.

Really pretty.

"Hope?"

"Yes I am right here, hello. Right here."

"Are you okay? Your face is all flushed. Do you need to sit down? I can get you some water?"

I give him a look. Over in his usual corner again – safely out of Luke's sight line – George waves at me, then holds up his iPad. He's drawn a pink heart on the screen. Checking that I'm still watching, he holds up a finger and taps it on the screen. The heart flashes on and off, as do the red CRUSH letters he's written underneath. I hate him.

Luke has spotted me looking right past him and is halfway to turning around and seeing when I grab his shoulder and stab my pencil wildly at the diary sitting in front of me.

"That was all good. Really good. I actually think you've got it, more or less. And, ummm…just to check…you know, the schedule? And you're all good with that? All set? Because…yes. Of course you are. You know. Great. Great. Great. Yes. Okay then! Awesome!" I flourish the pencil at him a little too hard, and smile a little too widely…but at least George has put his stupid iPad away and nobody's the wiser about any of it.

Except...

There, taking a long swig from his water bottle at the side of the stage and looking from me to George to Luke and seeing everything?

Tommy.

Oh, goody.

ACT THREE

Get-in

ACT THREE, SCENE ONE

The stage door.

The Earl's stage door.

I stand on the pavement like an idiot, staring at it.

A *late* idiot, staring at the stage door she should be walking through in a hurry…but I can't. I feel like I have to remember this. Every last detail of it matters.

The door is hooked open, waiting. The inside panel, swung outward and visible from the street, is painted red. A large white sign with thick red lettering reads:

STAGE DOOR
Wait here for autographs

Underneath it, a smaller sign says: *No public admittance. Authorized visitors only beyond this point.*

And today, that means me.

Beyond the door, a small flight of painted concrete stairs leads up and turns sharp right – and I can't count the number of times I've walked up them in my dreams, just like I did on my birthday all those years ago.

Over it all, lighting the way, is the globe light, and it feels like it's shining just for me.

The rehearsal room was fine…but this is why I'm here.

And I'm *here*.

Throwing a quick glance over my shoulder in case anyone happens to be passing by, I step through the stage door and – wanting to make myself remember; wanting to imprint the feel of the treads under my shoes, the coldness of the handrail under my fingers – I walk up and round the turn in the stairs to sign in at the desk…

…And find myself face-to-face with a small ginger cat who is sitting on the sign-in book, blinking at me.

"Umm…hello?"

The cat studies me for a long moment, then starts washing behind one ear.

Right.

I try again.

"Hello?"

There's a faint rustling sound, and a cupboard door slams somewhere nearby before a woman with huge curly black and silver-streaked hair appears from behind me, edging around the desk. The cat stops washing and makes a chirping sound as she comes near. It's more than I got.

Gently tipping the (reluctant) cat off the sign-in book,

the doorkeeper looks me up and down. "Stage management intern. Yes. You're on my list."

"Is that good?"

"I should think so." She scans down a printed sheet of paper. "Hope?"

"Yes. That's me. I'm Hope."

I can stop talking now.

"I'm Roly," she says, pushing the sign-in book and a pen towards me. "You sign in here." She points to a column already full of names. Amy's is – predictably – at the top, followed by Rick's. On the other side of the page is the actors' sign-in, and instinctively I find myself scanning it for Luke.

"Go on through," she says, waving the pen in the direction of the second door on the right and snatching the list away before I get the chance to look for any other names.

Not that I can really think too much about anyone or anything else right now, because the *door*…

THE STAGE
Silence in this area during performances please

Through the little glass pane in the door I can see the lights are all on…and I can hear Rick calling out to someone.

Everything's waiting, just on the other side.

So I walk through.

* * *

The door leads straight into the wings of the Earl's stage. I can see it stretching out in front of me between the flat panels that shield the backstage area from the audience. I have no idea how anyone could ever want to step out there. What if you walked out into the spotlight and could remember the name of every teacher you've ever had, the birthday of everyone you've ever been friends with – but not one word of your lines, and it's so obvious you've dried that everybody in the building could tell? What if you went left when you were meant to go right and crashed into one of the other actors, or your costume ripped, or your wig somehow got caught on a piece of the set? What if you broke a prop? What if you *fell off the edge of the stage*?

"Hope? Is that you back there?"

Rick's voice carries across the auditorium, over the stage and into the wings. I've got so used to the idea of "Rick the director" that I'd almost forgotten about "Rick the actor", trained to make himself heard across a theatre even when he whispers.

I shuffle my bag onto my shoulder and stick my head out through the side of the flats.

"I'm here! Sorry, I got—"

"No, no. That's fine." He waves my apology away. "We're still sorting some things out. Do you want to take some time to have a look around downstairs and backstage? We'll need you to get a feel for the place, and it's rather a maze back there. There's a press event a few of the team need to attend – we'll find you when we need you after that."

Do I want to? Obviously. It's what I've wanted since I was a kid – to be allowed to poke around back here.

"Oh. Okay. Sure. I'll just…"

I can barely see him, sitting somewhere in the middle of the stalls – even with the house lights fully up, the spots on the stage are blinding. And hot. I can already feel sweat starting to prickle against my scalp. *How* do actors do this every night? *Why?* Shielding my eyes with my hand, I finally pick him out – and Nina, and three or four others I don't recognize. They're huddled around a couple of laptops on a table set up across several seats in the stalls, and even though I'm on the stage, even though I'm in the actual spotlight, I'm forgotten.

Invisible.

I try to stop the smile, but I can't.

I'm here.

The Earl's Theatre, with its rows of plush red seats; its gold-painted cornices and gilded columns. Empty, the auditorium looks huge. It *is* huge. Does it look bigger or smaller from here when it's full, I wonder? In just over a week, I'll find out, I guess…

The more I look, the more I see – not just the red and the gold and the gleaming, glittering magic of it all, but the things that make the magic work. There, at the back, there's a sound tech desk. And there, in the box stage-left, are the bank of speakers and a follow-spot to track the actors as they move. The same on the other side of the stage. Beside the doors are the seats for the front-of-house staff: narrow flip-down perches upholstered in the same red velvet as all the others but with far less padding.

And the thought drops into my mind easily, like it's coming home: *Which one of those is Luke's? Where does he sit when he works here?*

I can picture him folded into one of the seats, watching the stage, or standing inside the door, checking tickets and smiling people to their places. I can picture him everywhere. Instinctively I look down at the bare boards under my feet. Where will he stand when he's onstage? Here, where I am? A little to the left? I imagine his feet in the same spot as mine, the two of us overlapping like shadows cast by different spotlights.

And there in the wings is the reason I'm here, sitting there unnoticed by everyone but me: the prompt desk, the desk I've wanted ever since I can remember. Tucked right up against the wall, it's a tall, narrow thing on castors with an equally narrow little stool tucked beside it, bearing a pair of monitors, a row of switches and buttons on the front and a little light with a blue bulb. A sheet taped to the side is the script for the auditorium announcements. *Good evening, ladies and gentlemen…* There's a headset sitting on the desk, and even from here I can see the gold of the Earl's crest glinting on the side.

I'm here.

"Hope! You're here – good. Hold this a minute, would you?"

Amy hands me something as she marches past. I take it automatically.

It's a hammer.

"Come on, with me!" She doesn't even break her stride.

I look at the hammer.

It has no answers for me.

So I follow her through a door, down another set of concrete steps to the lower level of the theatre and into a labyrinth of tight corridors that smell of glue and sawdust. It smells of things being made, things being built; magic being stapled and sawn into shape. It smells of *backstage*.

"I need to speak to the guys down in the workshop – you might as well come and see it while I'm there."

Amy's voice bounces off the walls as I trail after her. At least it's well-lit down here – the lights don't get turned off during a performance like they do in the wings so there's no need to learn the exact whereabouts of every single piece of set, equipment or rope in case you trip over them in the twilight at the edges of the stage. It's only the stage team who need to be part-bat, navigating by dim blue torches. And luck.

The corridor turns almost completely back on itself and ends in two battered steel swing doors with loud banging coming from behind them.

The workshop.

There's sawdust on the floor and a workbench covered in tools and tubs of varnish. A large pinboard papered with sketches and technical drawings takes up most of the wall above it, alongside a row of hooks. One of them holds a pair of heavy-duty work gloves, another has a hard hat. The hard hat has been covered with leopard-print fake-fur and has the word *Musher* painted on it in glitter.

Leaning against the far wall is a row of framed paintings that could have come straight from a museum – but even from here, I can see that they're still drying. Priceless antique pictures that were made the day-before-yesterday… Everything is deadly serious here – but it isn't. Nothing and everything is play. It's false and it's fact and it's real and it's imagined and it's perfect.

Amy has launched into a long, involved discussion with a tall guy wearing dodgy cut-off denims and a black vest (also covered in sawdust). He keeps waving a spirit level around for emphasis while Amy peers at a sketch pinned to the wall: a drawing of a huge wooden throne. It must be the Magister's seat for the Piecekeepers' headquarters set. It's just as fantastical as I'd imagined it to be – especially as that's meant to be a huge manor house in the middle of nowhere, full of paintings with magic trapped inside them. It looks ancient and solid and – to be honest – a bit *haunted*. When it's all assembled onstage and lit, ready for the first time Jamie sees it… I can picture it already. It'll look incredible.

The varnish fumes make the air feel buzzy – warm and woody, a little like the inside of a violin must smell – and somewhere a radio is playing. There's a rack of short scaffolding poles stuffed into a corner, and a crowd of coloured buckets full of clamps, clips and mysterious lumps of metal. And as far as everyone who sits in the auditorium upstairs knows, none of this even exists.

Amy remembers she has a shadow and turns to me.

"Duty calls, I'm afraid. Can I leave you to find your own way around and familiarize yourself with backstage? You'll need the production office, wardrobe…George is up there somewhere, I think. The dressing rooms, green room… Oh, and can you let Roly know I've ordered some lunch for the company and crew? It'll need to come through the back."

"Lunch. Dressing rooms. Wardrobe. Got it."

"Great. I'll come and find you later." She pulls a tape measure out of her pocket and turns her attention back to the drawing on the wall.

"Right. Show me…"

Ducking back out of the workshop, I retrace my steps to a junction in the corridor where, helpfully, there is a sign pointing to *Wardrobe, Dressing Rooms, Toilets, Showers* in one direction, and *Prod Off, Stage, Green Room* in the other.

Production office or wardrobe.

Which way?

George.

I turn right for wardrobe and follow the corridor along, stopping outside a white door with a blue plastic sign screwed to it.

Make-Up/Hair/Wardrobe

I knock several times, listen…then open the door. The familiar waxy smell of stage make-up and hairspray wafts out – as does what sounds like a very loud swear word disguised as a cough. There's a scuffling noise and there, sitting in a revolving chair in front of a row of mirrors framed by white bulbs, is George.

"Helloooooooo!" The chair spins him away from me, then back again, then away, then back…

I wait for him to stop spinning.

"Hi, George. Why are you holding that hairbrush like that?"

"Like what?" He tries to stuff the hairbrush down the back of the chair so I won't realize that he's been singing into it – and forgets there's a gap in the chair back. The hairbrush drops to the floor with a clatter and rolls over to my feet. We both look at it. "Never mind. Anyway, why are *you* holding a hammer?"

I look at the hammer. I'd actually forgotten I still had it – was I supposed to give it back to Amy or leave it in the workshop or…?

"Never mind." I check the room for somewhere inconspicuous I could leave it, but there's nothing inconspicuous about a whacking great hammer in the middle of all the mic tape, wig pins and sponges, so I give up and shove it into my rucksack as best I can. "It's Amy's, and if she passes me something I just kind of…take it?"

This is good enough for George. "Look at this place, Hope. Look at it!" He leaps out of the chair and bounds forward, throwing his arms around me in a quick hug. "Just look at this!" He grabs the top folder from a pile of paperwork by the mirror and flicks it open. Pages of make-up reference sketches – blush, eyeliner, special-effect placements like latex or wax – flip past, along with A4 photos of make-up-less cast members. I see a flash of blue below blond hair and my heart jumps – I almost rip the folder out of his hands. Meanwhile he's chattering about the make-up trial run he's helping Nathalie with tomorrow, and what wigs he's looking after and how they've asked him to help assemble the costumes. He grabs a rolling rack and wheels it out from its spot against the wall. It's filled with identical garment bags, each one labelled for their actor and character. There at the front is *TOMMY: JAMIE (1)*. Behind it is another hanger and bag marked *LUKE: JAMIE (1)*.

Luke's costume.

Luke.

Luke on the stage, leaning in to Juliet…

"You've gone all flushed again. You keep doing that, you know." He shoves the rack back into its space with a rattle.

"Me? Oh, sure. It's a bit…stuffy in here, that's all." I pull at the neck of my top for emphasis and concentrate on a bag further back: *JULIET: LIZZIE (3)*. It looks like Lizzie's torn coat from the end of Act One. No danger there. Not for me, anyway.

George arches an eyebrow at me. "I won't tell anyone. Promise."

"Tell anyone what?"

"If you wanted to just be a bit excited." He starts stroking the first Tommy garment bag. It's a little creepy. And I know as well as he does that's not what he actually means.

"I am excited. I just wear my excitement on the inside. Unlike some of us."

George sniffs loudly and turns away to pick up his hairbrush.

I leave him where he's happiest, singing along to the radio, and find my way past the dressing rooms, through the maze of stairwells and passageways in the back half of the Earl's: upstairs, downstairs, out to the loading dock and back again. It's an old building that has had extensions built onto its extensions over the last two hundred years, and nothing leads quite where you expect it to. No wonder they wanted me to get used to finding my way around. The corridors are lined with framed programmes from productions that have been staged here: plays, musicals, ballets, every kind of show. At regular intervals, there are photos mounted on the walls too – pictures from rehearsals or first nights, curtain calls with the boards strewn with flowers; shots of whole companies collected on the stage, their arms around each other's shoulders and broad smiles on their faces. Being here, being *this*, is being part of something bigger.

I push through wide doors, narrow doors and double doors – and suddenly find myself front of house several floors up, outside the Scott private bar in the upstairs foyer. The main staircase twists its way down in a wide square in front of me, the sounds of voices drifting up from the dress circle bar two floors below, where they're holding the press reception Rick mentioned. I lean on the gleaming wooden banister rail and listen to the chatter, following the lines of little white bulbs strung onto silk-wrapped wires that dangle straight down the centre of the stairwell – the famous "Earl's chandelier". Every bulb is in a tiny metal cage, hanging there, just out of reach.

I look down over the rail, my eyes following the red

cables all the way to the red-carpeted floor of the main lobby and there, right in the centre, is a familiar figure. I don't understand why he's there at first – but of course, he works here when he's not acting too, doesn't he? There's not exactly much rehearsing going on today, not with the get-in. He's not wearing his usual jeans and T-shirt, but what must be his theatre front-of-house uniform: a black waistcoat and trousers, and a black tie. His hair is combed back away from his face, his hands folded together behind his back.

And suddenly, he looks up.

Right at me.

The whole staircase shifts beneath me. The whole *building* shifts – stage and stalls, dressing rooms and bars – and I find myself curling my fingers around the rail, holding onto it as though it will keep me from falling all the way down into his eyes. The lights in their little gold cages are blinding tiny suns and I can feel the heat from every single one of them. They're so bright…

I blink and shake my head like that's going to help.

He looked up; I saw him.

And he saw me.

But when I look back down to the foyer, he's gone.

* * *

THEATRICAL

Amy, when I finally track her down again, is pacing up and down the middle of the stage and having a heated phone conversation about…something, with…somebody. And while I'd love to get closer and listen in, my survival instinct is stronger than my curiosity. She paces some more, and pinches the bridge of her nose as she listens, tipping her head back to stare at the roof. The dividing line between auditorium and backstage, the exact point between performance and private space, runs directly above my head. One side, the auditorium side, is gold and white and decorative plaster. The other – the stage side – is black and white and metal: the grid of bars that fly backdrops and scenery up and down from the tower, the lighting rigs with their spots bolted on. From here, even the curtain looks different – all I can see of it, high above me, is a dangling line of gold fringing. It looks like some kind of sea monster floating by on a current.

Sighing, Amy finishes her call and drops her phone into one of her seventy-odd pockets.

"I'm glad you're here – could you take a look at the crew timesheets for me? I've got a nasty feeling we'll go into overtime, and there's always a couple of them who forget to mark their hours at the end."

The *timesheets*? I try to hide the look of panic that must, surely, be obvious on my face. Signing people in and out is one thing, but this is people's actual *pay*. Something I've never dealt with before. She notices me looking stricken and adds: "It's part of the job, I'm afraid. They're in a folder on my desk. Roly will help you – you'll need to cross-check with her, and you can let her know about lunch while you're there."

Somewhere, deep in her pockets, her phone starts ringing again and she strides off into the darkness at the other side of the stage.

"Hello?"

ACT THREE, SCENE TWO

The corridor to the production office, down on the lowest level of the building, is bare concrete lit by a series of strip lights that would turn even the healthiest tan grey. But this is the corridor I remember so vividly that, when I finally push the door open, I half-expect to see a little girl with frizzy hair, wearing her favourite dress and shoes and sitting in a chair in the corner. But she isn't there, because she's me.

The production office is small, and dark and full of... stuff. There are more framed pictures on the walls here – and letters, too. Some are little more than one-line notes or autographs scribbled on napkins from the bar, others are written in neat, flowing handwriting on beautiful headed paper. All of them are from actors who've been the lead in something here, and each of them is carefully, proudly hung on the wall. The rest of the room, of course, is More Stuff. Folders, scripts, boxes of pencils, stacks of books, plastic tubs full of tape in every imaginable colour for marking out the stage, Sharpies, screws and spare bulbs for Amy's kit.

Sitting on one of the desks is a tiny plastic tray with a bottle of perfume, a tube of hand cream, a red MAC lipstick and an almost-finished eyeliner pencil. It looks almost absurdly out of place amongst all the theatre clutter, but it's Amy's other kit. The kit for when she's not striding through the gloom running the show. The actors all put make-up on to do their jobs and take it off when they're finished; backstage, through the looking glass, it's the other way around.

I nudge the tray back against the wall and sit in the desk chair – giving it a quick spin because it looked kind of fun when George did it – and set to work rummaging through piles of neatly stacked papers for everybody's timesheets. Everything is eerily quiet. I try very hard not to, but I can't help remembering the story about the theatre's ghost. All theatres supposedly have ghosts, and here it's meant to be the spirit of a former general manager who likes to check everything's running to plan. She rearranges paperwork, turns off lights and resets any script on the prompt desk to the front page – but she's supposed to smell like flowers and all I can smell right now is damp plaster, so I'm probably on my own.

Having found what looks like all the timesheets, I push the chair away from the desk and spin it right across the room, bumping against the shelf on the far side. The scale model theatre sitting there rattles, and something falls over on the stage: a tiny but elaborately decorated miniature

Piecekeeper throne, just like the drawing on the wall in the workshop.

Just by being there, the model theatre makes me feel more at home, more sure of myself – it's so like the one I have in my room. Carefully, I reach into the theatre box and pick the throne up, setting it back in the middle of the miniature stage. Better. Something fidgets at the base of my spine, because tucked into the edge of the box, prompt-side in the wings, there's a little scale figure looking out at the stage – just like I would be. Maybe it's only a coincidence, but it feels like a welcome present from the theatre.

With every step I take along the corridors, I keep expecting someone to shout at me; to ask what the hell I think I'm doing or who I am and where I'm going… But it never happens. Anyway, I guess all I'd need to do is tell them I'm meant to be here. Who knows – if I keep telling myself that, I might even start really believing it.

The maze of corridors and stairs and doors feels like it goes on for ever, but at last I end up at the bottom of yet another flight of stairs. The noises of the theatre get louder fast as I go up them…and when I come to a door closing off the top of the stairs, I can *feel* the crashes and thuds on the far side of it. I thought this was a shortcut back up from the office – but it doesn't sound like I'm where I thought I'd be.

Carefully, I open the door and peer out.

A giant stone urn is hurtling towards me from the other side of the stage.

"Watch out, love!"

I pull my head back into the safety of the stairwell, and slam the door shut.

Someone shouts something on the other side, and I'm glad the door's thick enough to muffle their actual words. My phone, buried in my pocket, realizes it suddenly has reception and pings at me. It's a voicemail…from Mum. From ten minutes ago. Uh-oh.

Perhaps if I can get up to the walkway above the stage, it'll be quieter?

I try again, making a break for it, deeper into the wings towards the steep ladder to the fly-floor. Tucking the timesheets behind a cardboard box at the bottom of the ladder, I swing myself onto the first rung and climb.

I fumble with my phone.

"Hey, sorry. I didn't have reception – you called me?"

"So you *can* bear to speak to your mother!" She sounds odd – like she's a long way from the phone. Or…she's outdoors.

"I'm just a bit busy today, that's all."

"I know, I know. I'm teasing you, darling."

Loud hooting in the background.

"Are you out?"

"Hmmm?"

A cold puddle forms in the pit of my stomach. Mum's out and about – and she calls me? I know my mother, and this can't be good.

"I'm just running into town on a couple of errands and as I'm passing I thought I'd pop in and—"

"No!" My voice is loud enough to echo around the fly-floor. Below me, everything stops as the crew look around for whoever just shouted – and why. But thankfully none of them even think about checking up on the intern standing on the fly-floor. They give a collective shrug and return to what they were doing. I lean back against the ladder and close my eyes. My mum is on her way to the Square Globe, where she is expecting to find her daughter working in the marketing office.

My mum is about to be:

a) disappointed, because I've lied to her and I'm not there,

b) confused, because I've lied to her and I'm not there,

c) furious, because I've lied to her and I'm not there,

d) all of the above. Because lying. Not there.

Unless, that is, I can stop her.

What is it the actors always say? Find an element of truth in every role, no matter how small? Okay. Small truth time.

I open my eyes. "No – there's no point. I'm not there."

"You're not there?"

"No."

"Well, where are you then?"

"I'm…" *(In the loo. In a shop. In a storage unit. In Spain…?)* "I'm picking some stuff up for the office. From the printer's. Because that's where I am. At the printer's." I gulp down panic. "Yes. There was a bunch of…of leaflets and they came out all wrong so I said I'd take care of it and that's what I'm doing right now which is why I'm not at the theatre and there's no point you coming by because I won't be back for ages and I know you're busy and—"

"Hope?"

"Yes."

"Breathe, dear. I've told you before – don't run all your words together. It makes you terribly difficult to understand. So I take it you don't want me to come and see you?"

"No, it's not that. I promise. I'm just…not *there*."

(Which is true. I guess this does work.)

Unfortunately, I forgot that I was talking to my mother, because suddenly: "Which printer is it? I thought they did all their printing in-house?"

"It's a new thing. New printer, I mean. For programmes. This is basically a trial run and—"

Somewhere below me there's a crash as a trolley runs into a wall, and I desperately hope it doesn't carry down the phone line. Luckily for me, Mum seems too preoccupied with the printer idea to notice.

"Are they any good? I've been thinking about getting some new business cards made up – what did you say they were called?"

I didn't. Because I made them up, didn't I? It seemed like such a good idea at the time…

"Uhh…" Frantically, I look around me for inspiration. "Wall and…grid…ly? Yes. Wall and Gridley."

"Wall and Gridley?"

"Yup. Mmm-hmm. They're new."

"I see. Well, let me know if they're…oh, sorry, darling. My other line's going, and it's probably the Oliviers again."

"Okay. Yep. Sure, no problem. You go. Love you – bye!" I jab the disconnect button on my phone before she has a chance to say anything else, then lean my head back against the wall and listen to the pounding of my heart. Because *that* was close.

I've never been on a fly-floor before. The Square Globe doesn't have a proper grid or a fly tower for the crew to bring backdrops down from – not surprising, as it has a grand total of five ropes, and it's usually Orson working them all in between doing his science homework. This, though, is a whole different ball game, and standing here feels a little like I've climbed inside an enormous piano. Dozens and dozens of ropes are tightly stretched over the side wall of the theatre, disappearing straight up into the tower or down the wall below me, their counterweights stacked in neat piles in their cradles.

"Wow."

It's *exactly* like being inside an enormous piano. Or maybe a bell tower.

I stand there and stare at them, and it's just me and the ropes. If I touched them, they would sing. How could they not?

I'm barely aware of my hand moving, reaching for the nearest...

"Oi!"

A strange voice snaps me out of my trance, and I drop my hand. Glaring at me from the other end of the fly-floor is a guy in a black T-shirt and jeans, his arms folded across his chest and a pair of thick gloves tucked into his belt.

"Sorry, I was... I'm Hope. I'm one of the interns. Sorry. Rick told me to look around..." I manage to shut myself up before *I'm allowed to be here, honest!* comes out and completely and eternally blows any hope I might have of appearing professional.

His face relaxes. "*You're* the intern?"

I'm not quite sure how to take this, so I settle for nodding.

"Fair enough." His head moves in something that's half-nod and half-shake. I get the feeling he's examining me. "First day in the theatre?"

"Here? Yes. I've been at the Square Globe, and I've been in the rehearsal room..." I tail off. "Is it that obvious?"

He laughs, and this time it's *definitely* a nod. "You'll get the hang of it soon enough. First lesson of the fly-floor? Don't touch the ropes unless someone's told you to."

I'm not sure whether I'm in trouble. It wasn't like I was going to do anything with them – I'm not that daft...

I should probably get back to the timesheets. Before I can move, he sucks in a long breath, then sighs. "Well, Hope. Seeing as you're here, you can make yourself useful. I need to do a bit of maintenance, but just as I was coming up the stairs, I realized I've forgotten part of my kit." He pats the tool belt at his waist. "Pop down to the tech storage room and tell Rav you need a long weight. He'll know what you mean."

"Right. Long weight. Okay." Relieved to have been dismissed, I turn on the spot – and then turn right back. "Where is tech storage, out of interest?"

He points at the ladder. "Down, down again, past the production office, left and second on the right."

"Right."

"That's what I said." He turns his back on me and runs a hand up and down one of the ropes, tugging experimentally on the knot. It's only as I'm halfway down the rungs (which are terrifying on the way down – no way were they this steep going up) that it clicks that he's checking I didn't mess anything up.

Grabbing the timesheets, I dodge another piece of

walking scenery and dive back through the door to the basement, heading past the production office and finally winding up at the very end of the corridor and in front of a grey door marked TECH STORE. I've walked so far along the corridors that I may well be under my own house at this point, but I've been given a job, so I'm going to do it. Being useful. That's what deputy stage managers are supposed to do. Keep things running.

I knock. Another guy – again, in head-to-toe black, but this time with short, spiky hair – opens the door.

"Hi. Rav?"

"What do you need?"

So much for being friendly. "I'm Hope, one of the…" I stop. I try again. "I'm the stage management intern. I was sent, by…ummm…actually, I don't know. But he was up on the fly-floor and said he'd forgotten something?"

Rav studies me. He raises an eyebrow.

I wait.

He waits.

I'm supposed to be talking. "Right. Yes. So, he sent me down for a long weight? He said you'd know what he meant?"

"Chris sent you?"

"If that's his name, then yes."

"And he said I'd know what to give you?"

"Yes."

Rav purses his lips, then nods slowly. "As it happens, I do. I think I have the very thing."

He disappears back into the store, pulling the door shut behind him and leaving me in the corridor. I lean back against the wall.

This is good, actually. It feels like I'm part of the crew already – like this is completely normal, what I do every day. Maybe when I take the weight up to…whatever his name was – Chris – he'll show me what he was going to do…

I stretch out my legs, one at a time. Bend my ankles back and forth. Peer at the soles of my trainers.

Reach up towards the ceiling and lock my fingers together, turning my palms up.

Drop my arms; shake out my wrists.

Check my phone. No signal down here.

Rav is taking an awfully long time.

I wonder how much stuff there is in the tech store? It must be pretty full, I mean, to…

To…

He sent me down here for a long weight.

A long weight.

A long wait.

A. Long. Wait.

Oh my god, they're hazing me.

Unbelievable.

I yank open the door. Rav is settled in an old armchair

with a wad of stuffing poking out of the top, a screwdriver and an old plug in his hands. He looks up at me. "Not bad. It usually takes them at least five minutes. Tell Amy she picked a smart one." He grins and a hot ball of embarrassment forms in my chest, spinning round and round. I can feel it boiling inside me – and then suddenly, it's washed away by a rising laugh.

George.

I need George.

Now.

There's no sign of George in wardrobe – just a lot of wigs sitting on their stands, hair neatly pinned in place to set, and a couple of racks of half-assembled costumes in front of the bulb-framed mirrors. He must be on his break. So I duck back out to the corridor. Where would he go?

At the far end of the passage, a door – left ajar – moves in a draught.

STUDIO THEATRE BACKSTAGE ACCESS.
PLEASE BE QUIET AS ANY NOISE BEYOND THIS POINT
MAY BE HEARD ONSTAGE.

The much smaller studio theatre. It's not being used at the moment. Bingo.

But there's no sign of him at all. Not on the narrow stage, not in any of the seats, not even in the little tech booth at the back… Although, there is – if I hold my breath – a noise. Very, very quiet music. It sounds like it's coming from the middle of the auditorium…

I clamber over the front three rows of seats and look over the back of them – to find George lying on the floor, headphones plugged into his iPad and completely absorbed in a make-up tutorial video.

"Hi!" I lean over and tap him on the top of his head. "Whatcha doing?"

"OHGODWHATTHEHELLWHATAREYOUDOING?" He lets out a high-pitched burst of panic, rips his headphones off and manages to both drop and catch his iPad all at once.

"Hey." I give him a little wave.

"You nearly gave me a heart attack." He sits up and slides the tablet into his bag. "Aren't you supposed to be running around being busy?"

"Aren't you?"

"I'm on my break – and let me tell you, I've earned it. I've been pinning wigs all morning and I had no idea how much it makes your fingers ache when there's thirty of them. And then there's the other thing." George shuffles on the floor in the gap between the rows and crosses his legs, looking around like he's checking nobody else can hear him. "A couple of days ago, Nathalie – have you met her? She's the wardrobe assistant – asked me to order in some supplies from Screenface to be here for this morning, so I rang them up with the list she sent me. This morning, the courier drops off the package and I'm getting it all out, checking it off, and – get this – one of the things isn't there. So I call them up again, and I'm having a real go, and they start laughing down the phone. 'What's so funny?' I ask, and they tell me to check again and hang up on me."

"Seriously? But that's—"

He holds up his hand. "Wait for it. So I find Nathalie, and I tell her that we've got everything except the invisible concealer, but they've accidentally included an empty pot in there and—"

I groan. "You too?"

He blinks at me. "*You* figured it out?"

"The empty pot. Invisible concealer."

He looks so distraught that I can barely stop myself laughing. "If it's any consolation, they got me as well. I got sent to the tech stores for a long weight."

This perks him up. "What happened?"

"They left me there."

"Oh, a long *wait*!" He snorts.

I'm just glad it wasn't only me. It means it's not personal – it's a hazing, a ritual. A way of checking that someone belongs – and even though we clearly both fell for it, it kind of means that we've passed their test too. I drape myself over the back of the seat and he pulls a sandwich wrapped in a paper napkin out of his shirt pocket, gulping it down in one enormous bite without dropping so much as a single crumb.

"How do you do that?"

"Hungry," is all I get back as he wipes his mouth and fingers with the napkin.

"Hang on…is that…lunch? Already?"

He side-eyes me, confused. "Yes?"

"I mean, theatre lunch." I jab a finger at the napkin. "Was that the food delivery?"

"Yeah, it arrived ages ago. Didn't you know?"

"I must have missed it." My stomach growls so loudly that George's eyes widen. "Think there'll be any left?"

"Maybe?" He sounds doubtful. "But when I was coming out of there, I passed most of the build team in the corridor on their way in. You should go now, or it'll all be gone."

I push my hair out of my eyes. "I promised Amy I'd get the timesheets done after I'd looked round backstage, maybe I'll run out and get a sandwich after that."

George nods at the bundle of paperwork. "Well, if you ask me, it looks like you need to have lunch first." He flaps a hand to shoo me away. "They were in the stalls bar," he says. "Go get 'em."

Maybe he's right – it's not like I can't eat while I'm doing them, is it? Multitasking. I can do that. "Thanks."

I slide off the seat and give him a goodbye salute. He's already plugged himself back into his headphones and is focusing very hard on blending.

The stalls bar is on the other side of the theatre. I pile the staff list, my folder and timesheets into my arms along with a pen. I'm almost at the top of the stairs, and I've just about figured out what the little +*ht* note on one timesheet means, when, without warning, the top folder slips from my pile and hits the steps with a loud thump. Sheets of paper cascade down the stairs like a waterfall.

I make a grab for another stack of sheets that's starting to slip, but I'm too late. Down they go…and for a heart-stopping second they take me with them.

But suddenly there's a hand on the top of my arm, steadying me. I look round into those blue, blue eyes which eclipse everything else and my heart bangs hard against the inside of my ribs, because he is both the best and worst person to save me from plummeting head first down the steps.

"Hello there," he says, and it takes me far longer than it should to realize that Luke isn't looking down at me, but across at me. He's crouching on the step beside me, sitting back on his heels. "You all right?"

"Yes. Thanks. I'm fine. Not sure about Amy's filing, though…" I wave at the stairs, and nearly lose another folder. He slaps his hand on top of the pile, holding them all together. And his other hand is still resting on my arm – just *resting*. As though he's waiting for me to move away.

I don't.

Another wodge of papers slides down the stairs.

"I should probably get those."

And when he takes his hand from my arm, it feels like a cloud has covered the sun.

"You get the top ones," he says, hopping up. "I'll take the ones at the bottom."

"It's fine. Really." I point at the rolled-up paper in the back pocket of his jeans. "Another script?" (Because obviously, *that's* what I'm staring at.)

"*Sea Wall*. A monologue I'm trying to learn – it's for college," he adds. "My tutor says that keeping up with assignments while I'm working is good preparation for the future. He says it's what we train for."

"I wish my maths teacher had been so supportive when I talked to him about the classes I'd be missing."

Luke shuffles the papers from the bottom steps. "You didn't think I was going for another job or something, did you? I wouldn't give this up. I loved Lancelot when I read *Piecekeepers* – getting to be him is pretty cool."

He slides the sheets he's collected into my hands and somehow now he's kneeling on the step below mine, and his eyes are so close to me, I feel myself sinking into them so deeply that I don't even hear what he says – I might as well be underwater.

"You know, if you need someone to help you with your lines…?"

I look around for the person who said that.

We're alone in the stairwell, and it definitely wasn't him.

Which means it must have been me.

Oh, wow.

Having only talked to him a grand total of two or three times – one of which was him actually asking for help with this very thing, and me being no use whatsoever – I'm now blurting this stuff out. Why would he even take that as anything other than crazy? Besides, someone like Luke will have plenty of people to help him learn his lines, won't he? People on his course. His friends. His girlfriend, his boyfriend…I don't even know if he's with somebody. I don't even know if I care. Do I care? Why should I care? I just…I…

His cheeks – even in this light – flush a little.

"Only if you promise to be gentle. I'm not sure I'm made of stern enough stuff to cope with the kind of prompting you gave Tommy in the rehearsal room. I still haven't forgotten the look on his face."

"Well, I guess you'll have to make sure you don't screw up your lines, then."

Again: *wow*. It was meant to be light – a bit flirty maybe, a bit carefree – and instead it's just come out a bit…well, mean.

Something in his eyes flickers. He's studying me, I can

feel it. Just like I can feel the faint buzzing under the surface of my skin…and then he smiles. "I guess I will," he says, and something behind my ribs twists, squeezing the breath out of me.

He hands me the papers he's collected as I try to shuffle the stack into a more manageable bundle, and we head towards the stalls bar.

"I like the waistcoat." Again, me. For no reason other than never knowingly being too intelligent.

He tilts his head to one side, obviously trying to decide whether or not I'm kidding, then his smile widens. "Most of the front-of-house staff are off, but obviously I'm still around. Seeing as I'm not rehearsing today, they asked me if I'd do an extra shift and cover the press reception, and a job's a job." He works his tie looser at his unbuttoned collar, and just for a second his shirt twists with it and I catch a glimpse of his collarbone, pale in the harsh light. I glance back up at his face and his eyes are on *me* as he rolls his tie into a ball and vanishes it into a pocket.

"It doesn't get in the way? Working front-of-house when you're…*working*-working here?"

"*Working*-working?" His unscarred eyebrow twitches. "It's all work, really, and I'll take whatever I can get. It's just –" his voice drops to a conspiratorial whisper – "that I like some parts of it better than others."

I barely even notice when we reach the stalls bar, only

to find it deserted. A handful of chairs are scattered about, but the rest are still stacked on top of the small round tables. Three large platters sit in a neat row along the bar; empty except for a handful of crumbs, half a crust and a dozen strands of cress. It's not just deserted, it's barren.

Luke whistles. "The locusts have been through here, haven't they?"

"They have. I'll have to go and get something from outside."

He drums his fingers on the bar. "Can you wait five minutes?"

I grin and pat my paperwork. "This is going to take more than five minutes."

"Okay. Stay put. I'll be back."

And without another word, he disappears, leaving me alone with my paperwork and my non-existent sandwiches.

I help myself to a glass of reddish juice from the only pitcher on the bar that seems to have survived the onslaught, and shift the platters to one side, swiping the worst of the crumbs away. If nothing else, at least it's a big flat surface I can sort all the jumbled papers on, and undo the mess I've made of Amy's filing…

I've re-sorted the worst of it and am halfway through pre-filling lighting crew timesheets to leave at the stage door, when Luke reappears carrying a matching pair of bags from the sandwich place around the corner.

He holds one out to me. "Here. For you."

He got me lunch.

He actually went out and got me lunch.

"Sorry, I realized I had no idea what you ate, or even liked, so it's the safest one I could think of. Which means it's the most boring. Here." He hands the bag over a little apologetically. "Cheese and tomato. Sorry."

"No! Don't be sorry! That's brilliant. I love cheese. And tomato. Love them *both*! Together!"

Never in the history of sandwiches has anyone ever been this excited about one. I'm not sure whether to eat it or hug it. Or hug him. Which I don't. Obviously.

He pulls up a chair next to mine and unwraps his sandwich, carefully smoothing the paper out on the table. Without looking up, he says: "What about you? How come you're here?"

"Me?"

"No – I was talking to my sandwich." He sounds so serious that for a second I almost think he means it – and then he tilts his head and looks at me and I see he was kidding. Because obviously he is.

"Oh. Right. I've just always wanted to do this, you know?"

"Stage management's a pretty specific thing to want to do. I'm not even sure I know what half of it *is*."

"Well, I'm a pretty specific kind of girl."

What does that even mean, Hope? Stop talking.

Even this latest attack of stupid doesn't seem to bother him. All he does is laugh.

I try again. "I mean, I kind of grew up around theatre stuff, and this is the bit I liked best."

"I see." But then his face clouds – just slightly – and I can read the words forming on his lips before he gives them a voice. "Have...have you got family in the theatre then?"

I freeze. And panic. Simultaneously.

And somewhere in that moment, I decide the best thing to do is to take an enormous bite of sandwich and start chewing it, all the while beaming at him.

Wow, Hope.

As it happens, it's not the sandwich that saves me from having to answer. Someone in the room clears their throat loudly – someone who isn't Luke and definitely isn't me.

I snap back to the room, to the theatre...and see Roly leaning on the bar and grinning at me.

"Sorry to interrupt, loves. Luke – Rick's after you. Something to do with Tommy."

Luke stares down at his flattened sandwich paper.

"I've...got to go. Sorry." His voice is quiet and somehow it feels like he's slipping away, retreating from me. His eyes are flicking around the room and down again like always: the walls, the floor. So much the floor. I wish he'd look up, look at me.

I gulp down the mouthful. I don't want him to go –

not yet. "So, maybe I'll see you later – or tomorrow?"

He finally looks up at me; he shrugs and smiles and his eyes flash and I can't feel my fingers any more, and the whole room falls away.

"You'll see me," he says – and I believe him.

The moment shattered, Luke slips out of the bar, away through the doors into the foyer…but as he does, through the dimpled glass pane, I'm sure I see his blurred outline stop and look back towards me.

Did he look back, or was it a trick of the light; just another theatre illusion?

Roly watches me watching him go and purses her lips. "Tommy's looking for you."

"What for?"

"If I knew, love, I'd have said."

I didn't even know he was here. Uh-oh.

Roly fluffs her hair up with a hand. "What do you make of him then?"

"Who?" Although there's only one person she could possibly be talking about, my fingers automatically touch the sandwich wrapper on the table – because in my mind "he" means flashing blue eyes and an enigmatically-scarred eyebrow (I've decided he got it while rescuing a puppy – I'm not sure how yet, but it was definitely something heroic). But that isn't who Roly means.

"Tommy, obviously."

"Oh. Right. He's…umm…"

He's what? A demanding, stroppy, self-centred, rude pain in the arse – Hollywood star or not? Because if that's what she's asking, I definitely, definitely agree.

But I don't think that's what she's asking. Not if the half-smile when she says his name is anything to go by.

She finishes fluffing her hair. "Who'd have thought we'd have someone like Tommy Knight somewhere like this? Not one of the big London theatres – not even one of the little ones – but all this way out west?"

I can't decide whether she's prouder of the fact an A-lister has chosen to make his stage debut at the Earl's, or whether she's as crazy about said A-lister as all the fans who turn out for his premieres. Maybe it's a bit of both.

"He's okay." I shrug. "I didn't really get to spend much time with him in the rehearsal room." *Because I was running his errands or making his tea…* "And I've not seen him here yet."

Roly's face softens. "Well, I think he's *lovely*." She stares past me at a spot in the middle of the bar, and her eyes mist over.

"Where is he?"

"Hmmm?"

"Tommy. Where is he?"

"Well, he was over at my desk – but I doubt he's there now. If he's trying to find you, maybe he's gone to the production office."

"When did you speak to him?"

"Ooh. Maybe ten minutes ago?"

"*Ten minutes?*" In Tommy-world, ten minutes is almost a month. He's not exactly the patient type – as far as I can tell, if he has to wait for things, he gets bored…and that's when the trouble starts. "Why didn't you tell me sooner?"

"I was on my break, petal."

I leave the papers and Roly in the bar and hurry back through the theatre to the production office – which is deserted. I stick my head back out into the corridor. Nope. No sign of him there either. Maybe he's in his dressing room? Trying not to break into a run, I pass wardrobe. The door is ajar; warm white light and a cloud of hairspray seep out, along with the sound of George and Nathalie talking seriously about skin primers.

The door to dressing room number one is firmly shut, its gold foil star glittering away to itself, and when I knock there's no answer. I try knocking again.

Still no answer.

Maybe he changed his mind about needing me and he's busy now anyway?

I wait as long as I possibly can…and heave a sigh of relief. He's not there.

My relief evaporates as I turn away from the door – and there, striding towards me with a scowl, is Tommy.

He greets me more or less exactly as I'd expect. "There

you are. I've been all over the building looking for you."

Nice to see you too.

"Here I am. Roly said you were looking for me?"

He runs a hand back through his hair, which overnight has gone from being long and dark to shockingly short and blond. "Is it too much to ask that you're there when I need you?"

Which I would clearly know because I'm psychic.

I bite my tongue and give him a friendly smile.

Well. Friendly-ish.

I'm not sure he even notices, because he carries on in exactly the same weary tone as before, pulling a carrier bag out from behind his back. "I need this taken care of."

And because I can hear Amy's voice in my head, telling me I need to keep Tommy happy, I hold out my hands and let him hand me the bag. I don't even argue. Maybe it's fan mail he needs sorting, or replies he needs me to post, or…

I peer into the bag and what looks like a sweaty T-shirt and the cuff of a shirt sleeve peer back out at me.

He's given me his *laundry*.

"I…umm…?" I look from Tommy to his laundry and back again.

"The gym kit can be washed normally, but I'll need the shirt and the suit back for an event tomorrow night."

There's a suit under that lot too? What kind of state is *that* going to be in? I picture my mother's face if she heard about this. "I could probably use the washing machine down in wardrobe if…"

One eyebrow slowly, so slowly creeps up to an arch. "You don't put Givenchy tailoring in the *washing machine*." Every syllable is sharp and has spikes all over it.

"Sure. Okay. Right." Pretty sure you shouldn't scrunch it into a ball underneath your workout gear either, but there you go.

And without another word – not a hello, not a please and most definitely not a thank you – he stalks off, leaving me clutching the bag of Hollywood-worn dirty dry-cleaning to add to the timesheets waiting in the bar.

Welcome to the theatre. Like I said: how hard can it be?

ACT THREE, SCENE THREE

Not wanting to risk leaving Tommy's laundry (god help me) with the dry-cleaner, I take it with me when I head off at the end of the day – ducking out earlier than I really should to make sure I'm in time for the last express service slot. Amy will understand, especially after I waded through the timesheets and a stack of other admin and paperwork that needed to be done before we get into the full company rehearsals on the stage. Like any show, time spent rehearsing in the actual theatre is short and precious. We can't afford to waste any of it, which means everything from now on has to run like clockwork. Super-efficient, accurate clockwork. With one week till we open, every second counts.

I sit on the uncomfortable metal bench in the dry-cleaner's shop while they perform their super-expensive magic on Tommy's Givenchy. And his gym kit. With nothing better to do, and my brain still spinning from the day, I flick through my phone. Someone in the Earl's marketing department has set up a rehearsal blog and a *Piecekeepers* "countdown", posting a couple of carefully chosen pictures from the rehearsals every day. If Priya somehow hasn't figured out what I'm doing by now, this should fix it, and all without me having to say a word. Maybe that's part of the reason for the NDAs too: it's about protecting the show's image, not sharing too much and blowing the mystery. There's Tommy and Juliet studying the script; Rick looking thoughtful... and there he is. Luke, the photo obviously taken that first day I met him. I can tell from the T-shirt, from the way he's leaning over his book, but with his face turned up towards the camera as though someone's just called his name. They probably did. His eyes blaze through the screen at me, and I hold their gaze until my phone decides that's quite enough of that, and switches off.

Waking it up, I flick some more – and find an entire fan account on Instagram dedicated to pictures of What Tommy Might Look Like As Jamie In *Piecekeepers*. There's some amazing fan art and some slightly less-amazing Photoshop... as well as a series of pictures reposted from an account called TommyKFanGirl. She seems to be a local – or has at least followed Tommy around a lot during rehearsals – because as well as snaps of the outside of the theatre, there's pictures of him leaving his hotel, posing for a photo with another fan and smiling, and one of him parking his bike outside the rehearsal room, pulling off his helmet and combing down his longer hair.

"Parker?" The receptionist comes to the counter holding a ticket and a large stiff carrier bag with plaited paper handles and crisp white tissue paper peeking out of the top.

"Not for your mum then?" she asks as I take the bag.

"No, this one's..." I'm about to say "work", but Mum comes in here all the time and I can't risk it. "...something else."

"That's a lovely suit in there. Tailored."

"Shame its owner's a little *less* than lovely," I mutter, waving goodbye.

Tommy's hotel is just around the corner from here. If I drop his stuff off with the concierge (who will doubtless be overjoyed to see me again) then maybe he'll actually thank me tomorrow for getting it done so quickly.

Or not.

I mean – Tommy, thank me? Not likely.

I pretend not to notice the concierge's eye-roll as I stroll up to the desk.

"Yes?" He folds his hands in front of him.

"It's okay. I'm dropping off today, not collecting."

Nothing. Not even a flicker of warmth or humanity.

I give him my brightest smile.

Still nothing.

"Yes?"

"Mr Knight asked me to get this back to him. Could it go up to his room this evening?"

He peers at the bag and there goes the eyebrow. "Laundry."

"It's clean, in case you're worried...?" *Why would he be worried? Stop talking, Parker.*

"Mr Knight does know that *we* are happy to take care of anything he needs, at his request?"

"I guess he..." *Would prefer to dump it all on me?* "...didn't want to bother you."

"Mmm." He scowls at the bag and leans around the desk to hold out a hand.

And then I stand there like an idiot, waiting to be dismissed.

The concierge barely glances up from the luggage tag he's attaching to the bag's handle. "You can go now."

"Hello?" I close the front door a little harder than I need to when I get home. "It's me! I'm home!"

Obviously. I mean, of course it's me. I might as well go full info-dump and stand in the hall shouting that, goodness, I've had *such* a hard day at my *office internship*, dealing with the summer season brochures from the *community theatre* (all the while winking at an imaginary audience).

Nothing.

So I follow the sounds coming from the kitchen – and to my surprise find Dad stirring a cup of tea. Which reminds me – I haven't actually made a cup of tea for anyone today. I must be moving up in the world. He drops the spoon into the sink and takes a sip. "You're back late."

"And you're early – how come you're home?"

"We finished the finance project, so I thought I'd slip out. Good day?"

"Oh, you know. Did more paperwork." Which isn't even a lie.

"But you're enjoying it?"

I open my mouth – and close it again. Discretion. "I'm learning a lot – does that count?"

Suddenly, Mum appears from behind the fridge, holding the calendar. "Well, I still don't know why you're doing marketing. I didn't think that was what you wanted."

"I don't *know* what I want." Okay, that *is* a lie.

"Honestly, Hope…"

"Muuuuum…"

"I'm only saying. The last thing I knew, you wanted to work *in* theatre, not *for* one."

Only my mother would make that distinction. But then, why wouldn't she? She's about as theatre as it gets – just take all those statues and plaques she's won, the list of people who want her to dress them because anything touched by Miriam Parker brings that touch of stardust and glamour…

Except me, of course.

THEATRICAL

All Miriam Parker's glittering theatre fairy dust has brought me is doubt.

Nobody wearing one of her costumes onstage at the National or the Royal Opera House or in the Royal Exchange, or any of the other places she's designed for, has ever been told they'd be nothing without the outfit she made them. None of the journalists stopping the stars who wear her dresses on the red carpet has ever opened their interview with: "And of course, you know the only reason you're here is because of Miriam Parker?"

It's only me who has to listen to that kind of whispering.

"It's fine – it'll be…" What was it Luke said? "Good preparation. It'll be useful to know how that side of the business works."

Mum screws up her mouth the way she does when she's threading a needle. "I've told you before I'm more than happy to—"

"No! Thanks. But no. I'm good. Really." I nod at the calendar, wanting very much to be talking about something else. "What's that down for?"

"Your sisters. They're coming home!"

"Fantastic." I drop my rucksack on the nearest chair. I should be grateful really – between work and my wonderful perfect sisters being home from their wonderful perfect lives and their wonderful perfect jobs, Mum will definitely be too busy to take much of an interest in me. "When?"

Dad peers over the top of his mug. "Next weekend. Your mother's asked them back for a family dinner."

From the wall by the kitchen window, Faith and Grace stare out of their picture frames. Even their photos are perfect. Mine, by contrast, are always blurry because I was trying to avoid having my photo taken – or I've got my eyes shut because I blinked. Sometimes both.

Mum makes a dismissive sound. "*We. We've* asked them back for a family dinner – honestly, you make it sound like you don't want to see your children. You love having the girls home, all of us together. Besides, this is the best season the business has had since I went freelance, and I think we should celebrate that. And this is how I want to do it. They'll be here for the whole weekend."

He makes a harrumphing sound from behind his tea, but she's right. She should celebrate. There hasn't been a single red carpet in London for months without her work on it – and last month she got her first call from New York about a dress for the Tony awards.

But *next* weekend? Of all weekends, it has to be that weekend.

This time in a week, we'll be running though our dress rehearsal – and the day after that, it's opening night. *How* can they be home then?

The most important weekend of my entire life?

"So, Hope, can you make sure you're home early on

Friday, please?" Mum suddenly locks onto me as I'm about to go up to my room. "And don't try and fob me off with any excuses – marketing can wait. I want you here and *being nice*." She raises an eyebrow at me pointedly. There's three silver sequins stuck in her fringe, and they sparkle as she opens the fridge door…and takes out a box full of beading. "Ah. I wondered where that had gone. Now, never mind Friday. What can we have for dinner tonight?" She puts the box on the worktop and peers back into the fridge, poking at bowls of leftovers.

"I'm always nice. It's not *me* you need to tell." Which is true.

"Yes, I know, darling – but you do let your sisters provoke you sometimes…" Which is also true.

"Then maybe you should tell *them* to be nice?"

"Are you really going to make my dinner about the three of you again?" She takes a box of eggs from the fridge and balances a handful of tomatoes on top of it, blinking at me… and the sequins blink in time with her. I can't take anyone seriously with sequins in their hair.

"Fine. I'll be a joy, I promise. But these have got to go." I gently pick the sequins out of her fringe and hand them to her.

"Too young for me, do you think?" she asks, smiling.

"Mmm?" I make the best vague, non-committal sound I can, and grab my bag before I get roped into helping with whatever she's got in mind for the bead box. "Got stuff to do, got to go now, bye…"

"Hope…?" Her voice follows me out of the kitchen and into the hall, chasing me up the stairs and into my room – but I don't let it catch me.

ACT THREE, SCENE FOUR

It may only be Monday morning, but Tommy's fans have already formed a tight knot right outside the stage door, huddled down into their coats against the chilly drizzle; most of them holding postcards or autograph books, their phones always out in case he dashes past. Watching them from the corner of the Earl's, at the end of the alley, I wonder if TommyKFanGirl is among them – whether she's one of the excited ones chatting in the middle of the group, or one of the outliers, leaning against the theatre wall and reading.

Footsteps stop behind me. "There's a lot of them, isn't there?" Luke steps up beside me, eyeing the crowd and pushing his grey beanie hat back with one finger.

"I guess something about Tommy makes people crazy," I mutter. I didn't really mean for him to hear me, but to my embarrassment, he laughs.

"Don't like him much, do you?"

"I'm not sure. I love watching him onstage – who doesn't?"

"You just don't love him so much in person?"

"You could say that. Nice hat, by the way."

Luke laughs and pulls it off, running his hand through his hair. He jerks his head towards the front of the Earl's, to the main entrance and box office.

"I'm going in the front today – the foyer doors are unlocked. You coming?"

"But…" I look towards the stage door, and the group who have now noticed us and are trying to be subtle about watching us watching them. One of them holds up a phone – probably taking a picture. One way or another, Tommy's just as much of a pain even when he's not around.

"Excuse me…?" It's one of the fans – the one who was standing furthest from the door. She's maybe a year or two younger than me, holding what looks like a headshot of Tommy from his last film – and she's frozen. Her fingers are a deathly white colour and her fingernails have gone pale blue. Easter holidays or not, it's still not the weather to be standing around outside waiting for hours. "Do you work here?" She nods at the stage door.

"We do," I say – before it dawns on me that there is no "we". Luke's already disappeared off to the main entrance. "I do, I mean."

"Do you know if Tommy's around?"

How long has she been standing here? The tip of her nose has also gone white.

I have no idea whether I'm supposed to comment on Tommy's rehearsal schedule. Amy would probably hit me with one of her folders for even considering the question. Discretion, discretion, discretion. Non. Disclosure. Agreement. But the way I see it, if someone's prepared to stand out in the freezing cold and the wet hoping for just a glimpse of him, a smile, in return for helping make Tommy into "Tommy Knight", then they deserve something. Without people like her, Tommy wouldn't be *anyone*.

She's not so different from me, hiding around the corner from the Bristol Old Vic and watching Rick Hillier walking away down the street.

"He's due in this afternoon," I whisper, checking over my shoulder just in case Amy has suddenly strolled into earshot. "If I were you, I'd go warm up for a bit and come back later."

"When?" she whispers back, but I shake my head.

"I can't. I'll get in trouble. But later."

"Thank you!" Her face lights up as she tucks the picture into her pocket, wraps her coat more tightly around her and vanishes round the corner. I go the other way.

"You took your time." Luke is holding one of the main foyer doors open, waiting for me. Waiting for *me*. "What was that about?"

I duck through into the entrance. "Nothing."

"You shouldn't talk to them, you know. If too many of

them come, they'll cause problems. Roly won't like it – and when it comes to the stage door, Roly's word is law."

"They only want the chance to say hello to him. And anyway, without them, there's no show – remember?"

That isn't just true in Tommy's case – it's true for any show. No audience means it's just actors wandering about on the stage, talking to one another. It's why nobody ever says the last line in a dress rehearsal, and nobody ever, *ever* bows to an empty auditorium. No audience means the show doesn't exist.

And while a production like *Piecekeepers*, one based on a book that sold *so* many copies, one that so many people have already read and loved, will do fine on its own, there's no denying that having the face of a star like Tommy gazing moodily out of the posters pushes it into "unmissable" territory. A *Piecekeepers* production is intriguing. A *Piecekeepers* production with Tommy Knight playing lead character Jamie is an *event*.

Inside, the foyer is partway through its transformation: one side of it looks exactly the same as it always has, its scarlet carpet emblazoned with the swirling golden ET monogram, the smart gilt-covered mouldings surrounding the box office window…and then, on the other side, there's a stack of cardboard boxes taller than me, and a row of rolled-up *Piecekeepers* banners propped against the wall ready to be unfurled and hung around the theatre.

It makes me think of the ceiling of the auditorium when you look up from the stage – half of one thing, half another.

"You know why I like coming in this way sometimes?" He doesn't wait for an answer. "Come on. I'll show you." Luke bounces down the half-flight of stairs to the door into the back of the stalls, leaving me to follow.

Rows A – M
Ticket holders only beyond this point

I push open the door.

Inside the auditorium, the house lights are down but the decorated iron safety curtain is up, the black-painted back wall of the theatre on show and the stage lit. Not perfectly, but nothing's finished yet – that's what the next few days are for – focusing the lights, spiking out the layout of the stage with rolls of coloured tape to mark where *this* chair goes or *that* candlestick. This is the skeleton of it, the bare bones. The technical rehearsals that are coming are the few days we have left where it's fleshed out; where the muscle and sinew is added. People always think that rehearsals go on for ever, all of us going through everything from beginning to end, over and over and over…but that's not how it works. Not even here. Being under-rehearsed, sure, that's not great – but being *over-rehearsed* is worse. It's the fastest way to kill a production's soul. The trick is finding a happy medium. But right now, that doesn't matter. To me, this – the way it looks now – is perfect. Everything begins and ends with this.

The rows of red seats march away towards the stage. In the middle of the stalls, there's Rick's working desk, already stacked up with his notes and script. Nina's sit next to them, and at the other end is Amy's bag. And beside that, looking completely out of place sitting in the middle of the scarlet and gilt: the prompt desk with its switches and monitors, wheeled out from its usual spot backstage to sit next to the main creative desk, a basket full of headsets plonked beside it.

The entire auditorium seems to be waiting. It's filled with the most perfect, expectant silence – as though the whole building is holding its breath. All it needs is for someone to step onto the stage.

I can almost feel the quiet seeping into my skin like a dye, a drug. I will always be chasing this; this exact silence, because this is the only place I can find it.

"Beautiful, isn't she?"

Luke's voice cuts through the calm, shattering it. I was so lost in the space that I'd forgotten he was here – but there he is, sitting on the front of the stage and swinging his legs over the edge. Has he been watching me all this time? I head for the temporary steps up to the stage from the centre aisle of the stalls and the wood creaks under my feet.

THEATRICAL

"I like to come in when it's quiet. She always makes me think of an old ship." He says it like he's inside my head, inside my body and breathing this place in too. "Ready to sail away. You know she moves, don't you?" he adds, pointing to the row of pillars underneath the balcony. "These – they've measured them, and they twist. The original structure's built on marshland and reed beds, and when the water level rises, the whole auditorium shifts a little. Like she's getting ready to catch the tide and sail off and take all of us with her."

"Or like she's alive." I've fallen into calling her, well… *her*. It makes sense. The theatre may be called the Earl's Theatre, but she's really a grand old lady. You can tell.

"She is. Can't you feel it?" He lays one hand on the stage, palm down, and the way he does it is so gentle, so careful, that my skin burns. What would it feel like to have him touch *me* the way he touches the stage? Like something precious. Something – someone – loved.

He leans back and looks up, propping himself up on his elbows. One of the lights catches his face, and it makes him shine, illuminating him from the inside, and the play of light and shadow across his face accentuates his eyelashes, his cheekbones and the hollows of his cheeks; the line of his brow, his jaw, the curve of his mouth… He looks different under the spotlight. More relaxed, more confident. More…himself.

"Did you get the lines down?" I have to say something, and that seems as good as anything.

He tilts his head ever so slightly to one side, his eyebrow raised. "Lines?"

"*Sea Wall*. For college?"

"Ah." His face clouds. "Yeah. Bombed that one."

"Oh. Sorry."

I wish I'd thought about asking him sooner – maybe got his number and messaged him, rather than managing to crash the moment. But then I'd have been *messaging* him and would that be weird? I don't know. I feel like it would be weird…

"Apparently I was trying too hard. I've got to take another crack at it next week, and try…"

"Softer?"

"Try softer? You ever thought about becoming a drama teacher?" He laughs, but he's acting, and I can see him doing it.

He's laughing because it stung, whatever feedback he got – and I can read those lines, read between them.

"I don't know how you do it. Any of you." I wave a hand around the stage, the auditorium, and I plonk myself down at the front beside him and let my feet drop.

"Do what?" He shuffles back upright again.

"This. The being onstage. The standing in front of people, *acting*. How you all just…turn into somebody else for a couple of hours, and then you turn right back again at the end of it."

"Sometimes I wonder if the real me doesn't get a bit lost," he says quietly, then shakes his head. "Sometimes, I kind of wonder if that's the idea. Why I need it, you know? It's like I can just forget about everything else for a while. And anyway, I can't remember ever wanting to do anything else. My parents were both actors – did you know that?"

"I didn't. That's so cool."

His eyes are faraway and the part of my brain that loves to take a script apart, looking for cues and clues as to what's *not* being said, circles the "were". They *were* actors. So they retired…or…?

But he's already moving on. "My gran says I was always trying to put on shows for her…" He tails off and bites his lip as though he's let something slip, something I'm not meant to have heard.

Were.

"Anyway," he says, changing direction, "they say at college that the trick to acting is *not* acting."

"And that makes sense, does it?"

"I think so. Sometimes." He wrinkles his nose. "Or maybe it's just not getting caught doing it?"

I jerk my thumb at the wings. "I think I'll stick to back there."

"Talking of mysteries," he says, and leans back on his

elbows, "I don't know how you do *that*. All the cues – I looked at Amy's cue prompts and they might as well have been written in Greek. And the props…"

"The props are the easy bit. Anyone touching a prop that isn't theirs loses a finger." It was my best serious stage-management voice, but somehow it doesn't sound as convincing as it does when Amy says it. "And speaking of which…" Hauling myself up to my feet, I brush my hands off. "I'd better get going – I'm supposed to be checking them ready for the prop review."

I'm barely a couple of steps towards the wings when he calls my name. My heart somersaults inside my ribs, like it's trying to turn all of me around just by flinging itself at the inside of my chest.

"Are you around later? When I'm on, I mean. On the stage?"

"Your scene? Sure." Like I'd be anywhere else.

"My scene. Yes. That's the word I was looking for there. Another thing about acting – I'm not so great with words. Always better with other people's – I really do work better with a script."

I try not to smile – until he smiles too, and then I can't help it, and I don't want to anyway. "I'll be there – unless… you don't want me to be?"

"Not want you? With notes like 'try softer'? I don't think I can manage without you!" He laughs a little too loudly; it's acting again…until it isn't. "What I mean is that if you're there, and you're not too busy with Amy, if you've got time to watch, I'd…" He sighs and fidgets with the edge of his hat, turning it between his fingers and the rest of his words come out in a rush. "I'dlovetoknowwhatyouthinkofmeI meanof*it*."

He's given me a cue, so I follow it.

"And I'd love to tell you."

The air between us shimmers under the lights…

"Hope!"

Someone is calling me.

"Hope!"

What if I'm dreaming; this whole thing is a dream and Mum's shouting upstairs to wake me up because I'm asleep and I'm late for school…

"Jesus, Hope, what are you *doing*?"

That's not Mum.

That's George.

I come back to the world, only to see him peering out of the wings, hissing at me.

"When you're done doing…this –" he flaps a hand at Luke, at me, at us – "Rick and Amy are heading this way. They've been *waiting* for you – we all have. You're late! *Again*."

"Oh." No. No, no, no…I didn't sign in! "Right. Okay." I scramble to my feet, casting one last look at Luke, who smiles back over his shoulder at me and slips away into the shadows at the very moment Rick flings open the stalls door.

"Here she is!" He strides straight down the aisle, followed by Amy.

"Sorry. I came in this way and I got a little...distracted. I was here, though!"

None of this seems to matter much to Rick, who has his arms wrapped around a Manila folder, pressing it close to his chest.

"There's a last-minute addition to the props list, I'm afraid."

I don't miss the look Amy gives him.

"You'll be responsible for it, along with the other props."

As he hands me the new folder, Amy gives him another look – and I don't miss that one either. It doesn't make sense until I open the folder.

"Are you *kidding* me?"

I clamp my hand over my mouth. You don't talk to Rick Hillier like that. *Nobody* does. But before I can grovel, he shakes his head.

"Sometimes it isn't our decision to make. This is one of those times."

"But...but that's real. We can't use a *real* one!"

Rick holds up a hand. "I know this isn't usual, but it's a financial decision. It comes with a rather large sponsorship fee, and this is an expensive show."

"It will be if it gets lost," I hiss at George, who is peering over my shoulder at the folder. Unfortunately, I have massively underestimated how good Rick's hearing is, because he glares straight at me.

"Fortunately, we don't have to worry about that, do we?"

"No." My voice belongs to a very small child. Or possibly a small, wet kitten. But I know I'm right – I can tell by the way Amy's nodding, and even by the way Rick lowers his chin when he says it. They aren't happy about this either.

A *real* necklace, with *real* gemstones in it. It's not right. It is, in fact, so many different kinds of wrong. You never use real jewellery onstage; *never*. It's one of the unwritten rules of the theatre, and *literally* the reason costume jewellery exists. Maybe it started because of worrying about someone nicking it from the prop table, but now? Now it's as much a part of theatre lore as anything – if we're going to put a real necklace on the stage, we might as well all run around shouting "Macbeth!" and whistling in the dressing rooms. Mum might not believe in the old superstitions, but even she'd have a fit about this one.

Rick is already on the move, but Amy stops in front of us. I hold out the folder and give her my best helpless look.

She's still nodding. "I know. Not my decision – not Rick's either. But money's money. It's not the kind of thing producers can turn down easily." She pushes the folder I'm holding out back towards me. "We'll keep it in the production office safe, not on the table or with the personals, and it'll be fine. It's just a superstition," she adds, with her usual mind-reading powers. "Anyway, can I speak to you for a minute, Hope? Alone?" She gives George a firm stare, which it takes him a second or two to register.

Eventually, he gets the idea. "Oh. You want me to go, don't you? Okay. I've got…um…things to do. Sort hairpins…eyelashes. Baby wipes!" he babbles, and hurries off.

Uh-oh. This is like school, when your teacher asks you to stay behind for a moment, isn't it?

"Not a big thing," she starts, which is enough to make me feel sick. Anything that opens with "not a big thing" is usually A Big Thing. I arrange my face appropriately. "But I need to talk to you about your punctuality."

"I was here!" It comes out before I can stop it.

"You weren't in the office, and you didn't sign in – but I'll take your word for it this once. I need to know I can rely on you to be here and be ready to start on time. Any stage management job needs you to be on top of things right from the start – how can you avoid problems and get ahead of them if you're always running to catch up?" She pauses. There's more coming – I can see it in her eyes.

"Which brings me to my next point. I've noticed you seem to be getting friendly with Luke, and while it's none of my business what you do in your free time…"

THEATRICAL

Uh-oh.

"…I need to be sure that when you're here, your mind's on the job. On the theatre. This is a big production for us, and I need to know that everyone is fully focused during working hours. That goes for both cast *and* crew. You do understand what I'm saying, don't you?"

I nod enthusiastically out of sheer relief. If she was going to yell at me, she would have done it by now. "Absolutely. You're saying you don't want anybody getting distracted." I smile so hard it feels like my lips are never going to go back to their normal shape. "I understand completely."

"Good." Her face relaxes. "I'm glad. I wanted to make sure I was clear. We've had…past issues with people mixing personal and professional relationships. You have to be able to keep them separate in this job, or it can be a little like working in a powder keg. Friction causes sparks, and one thing theatres don't like is fire." She looks at the folder. "Besides, I think we've got quite enough to worry about already, don't you?" Amy doesn't wait for my reply. "Well, come on. I'd better show you the safe, hadn't I?"

Following her backstage, along the corridors, I don't see the breeze blocks or the bricks or the ducting on the way. I just keep hearing Amy's voice in my head. Maybe it's just as well I didn't get his number after all.

As we pass wardrobe, there's a shriek from behind the door, then a crash, then muttered swearing, then laughter.

When we get through the office door, Amy pushes her chair sideways along the floor and unlocks the little safe under her desk. There, sitting snugly inside, is a leather jewellery case.

"We'll keep the necklace in here. I'll print a sign-out sheet for it and you need to make sure we keep it filled out. In an ideal world, you should be the only person who touches it when it's not onstage, but that's not going to be practical, I don't think. Let's see. Jamie has to give it to Lizzie, doesn't he, and then she takes it off in the next scene...and that's it. The best solution is probably to put it in Tommy's dressing room right before kick-off, and then he'll have it, and he can give it directly back to you when it's finished with onstage." She nudges the door shut again and the box disappears from view. We both stare at the safe, and there's a long silence.

Leaning back against the desk, she looks me up and down.

"Now, where are we...oh, yes. We've got a couple of scenes Rick wants to run – they're on your schedule for today and tomorrow – and that illusion with the paintings is going to be the death of me. I think it might be the trapdoor that's doing it now – I'll take you down there with me so we can have a look. End of tomorrow is the prop and wardrobe parade. Most of the cast are working with their final props now, but we've still got a couple of temporary ones in play

– everything's in the blue crates in the wings, if you could set up the prop table?"

I smile and nod and I *think* I'm making my face look normal – but inside, every word she says is like a hammer hitting an enormous bell. I thought I was just about doing okay. I thought I had it…I thought I was making friends, getting along… But then she warns me off Luke, and now I have to keep track of a necklace…and what if I can't? It's so different from the Square Globe, where I could do everything with my eyes closed and one hand tied behind my back. Here, I feel like I need seventeen extra eyes and at least another twelve hands. What if I'm not as good as I thought, as good as I need to be?

My head feels too small to hold everything she's told me as I walk out of the office, so it takes me a minute and I'm already out in the corridor when I realize what I saw in there.

I need to go back.

I turn, and duck back inside; Amy's already on the phone to someone and barely acknowledges the fact I've walked in.

No, what I want is over there…

The black box theatre model is exactly where it was before, tucked back on the corner desk.

And it's different.

Someone has changed it.

Instead of the little throne and someone watching from

the wings, there are two little cardboard figures sitting at the very front of the stage. Just like…

I peer closer at them – they're rough and a bit scrappy, like they were made in a hurry and torn as much as they were cut out, but even so I can tell what I'm looking at. Two figures, side by side on the miniature stage. And one of them is wearing a beanie hat.

ACT FOUR

Tech

ACT FOUR, SCENE ONE

"No, it's still not right. Can we take it from the sound cue again, please?"

Rick runs his hands back and forth through his hair, like scratching at his scalp is going to fix the "vanishing painting" illusion happening onstage.

Or failing to happen.

I think everyone was hoping that when we got into the theatre and the actors were doing the trick on the stage with all the proper sight lines and the actual trapdoor underneath them (instead of a square of tape on the rehearsal room floor) it would all come together. But Tuesday's rolled around, opening night minus four, and it still hasn't, and it isn't, and no matter how hard everybody tries, the vanishing painting just *won't*. It is the least magical painting in the history of magic or paintings – and worse still, it seems to be not-vanishing in a completely new and exciting way every time the trick doesn't work. Either one of the actors moves at the wrong time, or the trapdoor sticks when it's opening (or closing or occasionally both), or – my personal favourite – they all somehow manage to drop the frame and the audience gets a perfect view of the painting still onstage and falling in slow-motion to land on its face with an almighty great bang.

Standing in the very front of the stalls and resting her arms on the apron of the stage, our stage magician Katie Khan frowns, then waves away the dust kicked up by the painting. Katie is to stage illusions what Miriam Parker is to wardrobe: the best. And she's come in specifically to make our stubbornly non-vanishing painting behave.

There's a long, thoughtful silence. Even the wings behind me are quiet – although that just makes it easier to hear when Amy, sitting with the creative team in the stalls, sighs and hisses, "I'm telling you, it's the trap!" into Nina's ear. Everyone else waits while Katie climbs up onto the stage and circles the scene; first going left, then right, then finally dropping to her knees behind Dom, smoothing her hands across the edges of the trapdoor and peering around the huddled knot of actors.

"I think it might be the trap, you know," she calls down to the stalls, and Amy makes a sort of growling noise.

"I knew it. But does anybody around here *listen*?" She's through the pass door between the auditorium and backstage and into the wings in an instant, rummaging through the toolbox under the props table and sending screwdrivers and pliers clattering onto the floor... And then she stops and turns her head to fix her gaze right on me.

"Hope."

Meep.

"Have you still got that hammer?"

Hammer?

Hammer!

"Yes! Yes! I do! I have the hammer!" I dig it out of my bag, where it has become a permanent part of my stage management kit, and brandish it with the kind of enthusiasm that usually gets people locked up.

"Great. With me."

In three strides, she's across the edge of the wings, onto the stage and has dropped through the trapdoor in the middle of the boards.

"Hope!" Her voice drifts up from somewhere under my feet.

"Yes. Right. Coming."

So I follow to the edge of the hole in the stage and peer down – only to see Amy and two of the stage crew looking right back up at me from the wooden platform below. It makes the drop a lot less than I thought, but still, it's a bit more than just a step down.

Seeing me hesitate, Amy holds up a hand, and I'm about to reach for it when she says, "You can just pass the hammer down to me if you prefer?"

Oh.

"No, no. I'm fine." I jump down onto the platform – and the trap slams shut after me. Muttering under her breath, Amy runs a hand across the mechanism, then pokes at the edge of the door a couple of times…and then takes an almighty great swing at it with the hammer. There's an ear-splitting CLANG, a crunch…and the sound of one piece of wood dropping into a slot in another.

"Try it now?" she calls, dropping her hand.

The trap slides silently, smoothly open and then glides shut again, sealing with barely a click.

Not that I care, because all of a sudden it feels like the air has been sucked out of the little room beneath the stage. Every sound above us is muffled now, and all of them are unimportant, except for one – the voice I can hear directly above me.

That's Luke.

Luke is on the stage right over my head.

"Are you coming?" Amy's words sound like they come from another room. And I know she's waiting for me and expecting me to follow her, and I should…but it's like my feet have been nailed in place.

A board above me creaks.

He's up there.

After Amy's warning yesterday morning, I've tried to stay away from Luke. Not "avoid" him, exactly – more "avoid being in the same space where we could potentially be alone together", which is harder than I expected. Not just because the back of the Earl's is a warren, full of tucked-away corners and sharp turns in corridors – but because it feels like he could pop out of any doorway, appear on any staircase at any time. This whole building feels like him. Or a part of him anyway. So being here but trying to keep my distance, keep my head down, keep focused like Amy said…it's like being pulled in two different directions at once. I even made a point of taking a bunch of schedules that needed updating down to the production office when I heard Rick say they were going to run through Luke's Lancelot scene.

"I'll be there – unless…you don't want me to be?"

That's what I said, wasn't it? That I'd be there.

And then I wasn't.

But now, he's up there. On the stage. And I'm here…

I can barely get my voice louder than a whisper. "I'll be right there. I just want to…"

I mumble something about wanting to wait and have another look at the trap, and a moment later I hear the main door shut behind Amy.

I stretch up my arm and place the flat of my palm on the boards above me, resting there. If I close my eyes and concentrate, I can feel the vibration of Luke's voice as he talks to someone up above, reverberating down through the stage; through the tips of my fingers.

I hold my breath, listening for footsteps in the corridor in case Amy doubles back to fetch me, but the only movement I hear is Luke's above. He's up there, almost so close I can touch him.

Through the boards his voice is strong and confident. It's so different from the quiet warmth of when he speaks to me – I wonder if Rick's got him running a line?

Nobody could tell me off for being in the wings to watch – after all, I've just *come* from there, haven't I?

I have to see – if I run, I might just catch it.

I jump down from the platform and head for the door, throwing it open and...

"Well, hello there!"

George is standing right outside the door. A small, high-pitched yelp forces its way out of me before I can clamp a hand over my mouth and stop it. All George does is grin. "Been busy, have we?"

"George, what the hell are you *doing*?"

He dodges the slap I aim at his arm and laughs. "Me? Hang on – I wasn't the one gazing adoringly at a ceiling."

"I was...checking the trapdoor. Obviously."

"Checking the trap. Of course. I saw Amy come out and thought I'd wait for you, but when you didn't come with her, I stuck my head around the door to check if you'd already gone." He winks at me, then adds: "You know if you want to *see* him, you stand a much better chance if you're in the actual auditorium, don't you?"

I snort a little too loudly. "That is *crazy talk*. I was... it's just..."

I have no script.

Help.

Just when I start to think he's enjoying this a little too much, George puts me out of my misery. "So, Luke. Going for the older man. Nice."

There are two options here: either I pretend I haven't the faintest idea what he's talking about, or I skip the denials and assume that George can see straight through me.

I've never been a very good actor.

"He's not *that* much older. He's only a first-year student, and it's not like he's...Tommy's age or something." I lower my voice to a stage-whisper. "But can you not make it into a thing – please? Amy's already given me a lecture about mixing personal and professional and getting distracted."

"Oh, please." George waves a hand at me as we turn the corner of the corridor ahead of wardrobe. "Like half the cast aren't busy mixing 'personal' and 'professional'. I tell you, the *things* you see when you work in wardrobe..." He stops mid-thought and grabs my elbow. "Oh my god, that reminds me. Did you hear?"

"Hear what?"

"Who's coming in to help with the costume parade later!

Only Miriam actual Parker! Miriam Parker! *I* get to work with Miriam Parker – well, not work *with* exactly, but…"

Everything else he says fades behind a high-pitched static howl. My ears feel like someone's let off a firework inside them, while somebody else pours a steady trickle of cold water over the top of my head.

"What's the matter with you?" George breaks off his monologue about how great Miriam Parker is and looks at me curiously. "You're really pale."

I open my mouth. Nothing comes out – not even a squeak.

I close my mouth.

My mother is coming *here*.

How the hell do I explain *this*?

I could tell her that the Earl's called the Square Globe and said they needed… No.

I could tell her that I was passing and happened to overhear… No.

I could tell her that I lied (repeatedly) about being in the office doing marketing and I've actually been here all along…

Definitely, absolutely, categorically no.

There's only one way out of this, short of changing my name and moving to Sweden immediately: I can't let her know I'm here, and I can't let her see me.

Which means I'm going to need help.

Checking the hallway, I push the door to wardrobe open and peer in. No sign of Nathalie or Jonna – or anyone else. Good. I haul George inside with me and close the door, leaning back against it.

"George."

"Hmm?" He looks over from the mirrored wall, where he's already been distracted by his reflection.

I might as well get it over with.

"Miriam Parker's my mother."

At first, I'm not sure he heard me – and I'm about to say it again, louder, when I realize George is staring at me. In fact, he's looking at me the way people always do when they find out. I recognize it. I can usually see the thoughts as they have them.

You? Glamorous Miriam Parker? Elegant Miriam Parker? Stylish, pulled-together, successful Miriam Parker? Your mother?

I wait, bracing myself for the comment – the "*I should have guessed you'd have a connection*" or "*I guess it's still who you know in theatre, not what you know.*"

But George doesn't say any of that. He doesn't actually say anything; he just keeps looking at me.

This might be worse than usual – but just as I'm starting to wonder if I've made a terrible mistake, he nods. "Sure she is."

"You think I'm kidding."

"Look, they got me once with the 'invisible concealer', so you go and tell Amy or Nina or whoever's trying to prank me this time that I'm not falling for it." He shakes his head. "Miriam Parker, your mother!"

"George."

"Mmm?"

"Do I look like I'm trying to prank you?"

He rolls his eyes and looks me up and down – and as his gaze moves from my shoes to my face and back again, his expression shifts. Just a little at first, then more and more as the impact of what I'm saying sinks in, until his mouth actually drops open. The next time he speaks, he sounds like someone who really has just seen a ghost. "You're not kidding."

"I'm not kidding. My mother is Miriam Parker, and she has no idea that I'm here."

"I can't...I...no." He puts both hands to his face and sinks into his make-up chair. Personally, I think it's a little overdramatic, but that's George.

I feel like I should say something.

"Sorry."

It's a good start, right?

"But...your *mother*." George gives me an anguished look.

"Like I said – sorry." I pick up one of the brushes from the counter, turn it round in my hands and put it back. "If it makes you feel any better, you're the only one I've told."

This does seem to make him feel better – at least a little, anyway – as he shuffles in his seat.

"Well, okay then. And you don't want anyone to know?"

"Correct. You *have* to keep this quiet – I mean it," I add, cutting him off before he can argue. "The second people find out, they…well, they *assume*. And they assume something wrong, okay?"

"What?"

This takes me so completely by surprise that all I can do is stare at him, while he stares back at me. Because he genuinely doesn't seem to realize – *or perhaps*, says a small voice in the back of my head, *perhaps it would never occur to George that anyone would think you didn't deserve to be here…*

So I take a deep breath and tell him.

"Okay. So, you know how I've spent all this time at the Square Globe, and then I applied for the internship here?"

"Yeah?"

"And you remember how when we went to the cinema, everyone was saying they missed me?"

"Get you, Little Miss Popular."

"George? Focus."

"All right. Yes."

"I left. I left the Square – or I *was* leaving, anyway. I said I'd help them out until they finished their next production, and then I got the internship here, so…"

"You'd already left? But I thought you loved it there. You keep saying…"

"I did love it there. I do. *But.*"

He fidgets in his chair, trying to rest his arm on the side and failing. Eventually, he gives up and folds his hands in his lap. "I'm listening."

And because he is, and because he's easy to tell, I do. I tell him about the director who spoiled it all with his little comments, the jokes about how they could have had someone else, someone maybe better, but Miriam Parker must have called in a favour. How it never seemed to matter that I was good on the prompt book and never missed a cue – he would always whisper behind my back when I passed.

It wasn't everyone – not by a long way, it was just one guy – but it was enough…because I started to wonder whether he was right.

"I don't want the same thing happening here – or anywhere else. You understand, right?"

Shifting some more in his seat, George frowns. He sighs; he pouts. He runs the full range of George-emotions. And yes, I *know* he's annoyed I didn't tell him until now, but all I can do is hope he understands why.

This is the longest George has been quiet since we met – even in the cinema, he was constantly whispering at me. But now? Nothing.

After a long, long silence, right when I'm beginning to

think he's forgotten how to speak, he makes a grunting sort of acknowledgement. "Okay."

"Okay?" Is that all I get after such a dramatic pause?

"I forgive you."

"You what?"

"I forgive you for not telling me."

I open my mouth to ask what that's supposed to mean – and then I stop. This is George telling me he understands.

"You promise you'll keep it to yourself?"

"Hope. Who am I going to tell?" He presses a hand flat on his chest, a picture of innocence – and that's too much.

"*Everyone*," I laugh.

He tries to look wounded; he almost manages.

"Hope Parker. Anyone would think I'm a gossip from what you say." But he breaks into a smile as he says it. "Out of interest, where *does* she think you are?"

I sigh. "The back office of the Square Globe, helping with the marketing mail-out."

"Doing mail-outs? And she believed that? She *has* met you, hasn't she?" His tone of utter disbelief makes me laugh; it almost makes me forget the predicament I'm in.

"You don't think it's weird?"

"Secret theatre *and* an older man. What a dark horse you are." But his voice dips as he adds, "Sometimes, people keep secrets even from their parents. *Especially* from their parents. Yours is safe with me." And then he's bright and grinning and George again, leaning in to the mirror to wipe a smudge off the glass. "So, how do we keep you and your mother apart?"

I think for a minute.

"You know, I might actually have a plan…"

Amy gives me a pointed look when I finally get back up to the wings, but I mumble something about helping George and she nods and hands me a roll of white electrical tape.

"Can you mark up the props table while I go down to the furniture store? We need to swap out a table."

I practically snatch the tape from her hand – not only does she believe my excuse, but I *love* prop work.

Laying out a grid of tape on the props table, I hear the door into the wings whisper shut, and look up to see Luke picking his way through the gloom at the side of the stage. "That looks fun."

I rip off another strip of electrical tape and add it to the grid. "It's actually more fun than you'd think. Very satisfying."

"Need a hand?" He hops up to sit on the end of the table. There's no avoiding him now…

"I'm almost finished – although unless you're a prop, you don't belong on there."

"If I was?"

"I'd have to label you." I wave a Sharpie at him.

"And what label would you give me?"

My stomach jolts like I'm on the first drop of a rollercoaster. "How about…*in my way*?"

I can *feel* him watching me; feel the warmth of his gaze washing over me like a tide, threatening to sweep me away.

I shouldn't have said that. It sounded too sharp; too grumpy. I try to soften it with a smile, show him I was only joking – but he's looking the other way now so instead I plonk the book I've rummaged out of the crate into its little space on the grid, labelling it with another strip of tape. The awkward silence stretches on and on. I think he's waiting for me to say something about yesterday's rehearsal, or why I wasn't there, or why he's not seen me around much in the last day or so…or just *something*. And what do I say about any of it?

Finally, he whips round to face me. "Are you around for the costume parade later?" He's so casual about it, but as he leans on the edge of the table the whole thing lurches forwards.

"Careful!" I grab the front of the table and level it, pushing the sliding props back into line. "I'm the stage management intern. Of course I'm here for the parade. I'm here for *everything*."

I imagine Luke in his Lancelot costume with the red

218

shirt I've seen in George's sketches, or in Jamie's costume out under the lights, but then I blink the mental pictures away. Today's turning out to be quite complicated enough already, thanks. That thought itself is a distraction, and yet again my mouth's off on its own mission. "And besides, with my mother coming in later…" I regain control and my mouth snaps shut. Nope. Not going there.

"Your mother? What's she got to…?" His eyes flicker, and I can see the thought behind them lighting up like flashbulbs, even as I *pray* I'm wrong. "Your surname's Parker, isn't it?"

"Yes?"

"Not Parker as in…?"

Great. Thanks to my stupid mouth and my stupid brain, I gave him enough to figure that one out on his own. I really need to be more careful. He's just so…*distracting*.

"You are not to tell a soul. I mean it." I put on my best warning voice. He grins and tips his head to one side, like he knows something. Like he knows *me*.

"Huh."

This is not how I wanted this to go. Not even a little bit.

"What does 'huh' mean?" I put the tape down and glare at him, folding my arms.

He frowns, taken aback. "It doesn't mean anything. I was just surprised. Miriam Parker's your mother, right? How come nobody's mentioned it?"

"Because…because I haven't told anybody. That's why. Because everyone does exactly what you just did when they find out who she is."

"And you don't want anybody doing you any favours because of it – or assuming somebody else already has."

"I…well, yes, actually." That was easy. Almost too easy. I'm used to people constantly thinking they know what I'm capable of – who I am – because they know her. But it doesn't seem to even cross his mind to think that – or if it does, he hides it better than the others. "So," I add, "if you could…maybe keep it to yourself?"

He shrugs. "If that's what you want. None of my business, is it?" But he gives me a look I don't quite understand. Something that's one part confusion to one part – what? Pity? Envy? I can't tell, and to be honest I'm still slightly thrown by how unshocked he was about Mum. Maybe I was expecting George Part II.

Suddenly he runs a hand back through his hair and sighs. "I'd better get down to wardrobe. Final fittings call."

And without even a goodbye, he slips away into the shadows again and it's me who's at a loss.

Luke's a puzzle. How can someone who wants to go onstage – and do that their whole life – be so closed in on themselves? All the actors we've had through the Square Globe have been the exact definition of "extrovert", all flinging doors open and booming voices, and Luke's just…

not. Like he's so uncomfortable in his own skin that he wants nothing more than to take it off, switch it for somebody else's.

I shake my head and rip off another strip of tape for the table.

"Can we have Lizzie's second costume, please?"

Rick's voice buzzes into my ear through my headphones on the shared crew channel, but there's no time to think. Instead, I flap at Juliet, who is standing in the middle of the quick-change area that wardrobe have set up at the side of the stage with everyone's costumes and a basic make-up station. George is finishing tucking her wig cap under the waist-length dark artificial hair that completes her transformation. He heard Rick as well as I did – that call was really meant for him – but he's ignoring it.

"We need Lizzie two," I try, but George hisses at me.

"Do you want her now, or do you want her right?"

"Both, ideally…"

He mutters something rude under his breath as he steps back and shoos her past me out onto the stage. We watch from the wings as she moves across the boards, while out in the stalls Rick, Amy, Nathalie and Jonna the wardrobe mistress check they're satisfied with the way the costume looks under the lights, before turning to my mother for her opinion.

THEATRICAL

From the safety of the shadows I can just make her out, sitting at the end of the creative desks with her notebook. I heard her come in, heard her telling Rick about what she's doing at the moment as he walked her to her seat; I listened to the two of them chat away about people they both know, shows they've got mutual friends in. As she sat down, she looked straight over to the edge of the flats where I was standing and I panicked – but she can't see me from out there. I know she can't. She was just getting a feel for the stage. Either way, I still took a step further back. George has told Rick and Amy that I'm doing something to help Roly, so might be a while. I'm not sure what he said I was supposed to be doing, but at least it means I can stay out of sight in the wings and help the wardrobe team (by which I mean George) get the cast and their costumes ready. As far as Amy's concerned, I'm busy being useful elsewhere – and everyone else is too busy to care *where* I am. I've even de-tuned my headset mic so they can't hear me out in the stalls. Now all I have to do is keep out of sight until Mum's gone. Should be a walk in the park.

Tommy's next up, and George scuttles off to the men's quick-change area on the other side of the stage. I scan the list pinned to the wall of the cubicle, checking off the cast names and pulling out the next costume. We're about three-quarters of the way through now, and any minute Luke should—

"Hope!" It's George in my ear this time – on a private channel, and far too loud for my liking. Loud, and panicky.

Uh-oh. I look across the stage, past Juliet working through the dips and twirls of one of her choreographed magic fight scenes, making sure her coat moves and she can stretch enough, and see George staring at me, wearing his headset.

"What?"

"Just…get over here."

I edge past the organized chaos of one quick-change area and dart across the rear of the stage. Thankfully, one of the backcloths has been brought in as a better setting for the costumes, and nobody except George sees me run through the crossover to the other wings.

"What?"

Tommy is standing in the quick-change area in his second Jamie costume: dark trousers, a loose shirt and a long overcoat and…

"Where's the bag?"

"That's the problem."

"The bag. He has to have the bag – it's a personal prop. It's in the dressing room…right? Tommy, you had it in your dressing room?" There's no point being polite about it – there isn't time, for a start. I look Tommy in the eye – or try to, because he fixes his eyes straight on his shoes.

"What have you done with it? Seriously, Tommy. Where's

the bag?" I know he knows which bag I'm talking about: it's a small brown pouch, worn on a long cross-body strap. I know he knows, because I handed it to him half an hour ago in his dressing room, just like he asked. And when I handed it to him, I reminded him that it's a really important part of this costume because he has to *use* it.

My headset buzzes into life, and there's Rick again. "We need to speed things up a little here, guys – can you send Jamie two out, please?"

"Where's the bloody bag, Tommy?" I hiss at him. If we don't get him onstage – and soon – someone's going to have the brilliant idea of sending for "our intern, Hope" to fetch the bag, and then I'm toast.

"I don't know," he hisses back at me. He blinks several times, fast – and yes, that really is panic. Tommy Knight is panicking. Star or not, name on the poster or not, he's slipped up. It's not catastrophic, losing a bit of a costume, and it's bound to turn up somewhere, but time is tight and everyone's tired and stressed and grumpy. Not least Rick.

"Just…go. We're running close to overtime."

On autopilot, I put my hands on Tommy Knight's shoulders and shove him out onto the stage.

It takes a minute and a half.

And then:

Jonna's voice, clear in the quiet of the auditorium. "George? Could you step out here for a sec, please?"

He flashes me a panicked look as he walks out onto the stage, shielding his eyes from the glare of the lights with his hand and pulling his headset down to rest around his neck like a giant collar.

Jonna speaks again. "We seem to be missing a personal? Jamie's bag. Do we know where it is?"

I can see George fidgeting.

Of course they spotted it. Why did they have to? Or why didn't we switch the bag over from the first costume and buy ourselves time to fix this later? I wince at the thought of Rick's face if he realizes that Tommy managed to lose it somewhere between his dressing room and here – never mind the extra overtime sheets I'll have to fill in if we don't get this sorted fast.

I flap at George. "Pssst. *Psssssssst!*"

As he turns to look at me, he does the worst, least-subtle job in the whole history of theatre of pretending he's remembering something, and from my safe spot in the wings I throw my arms around, extravagantly miming in his general direction.

"Oh." His eyes widen. "Sorry, yes…I was just taking it over to Tommy and I noticed there's a problem with it – a hole in the seam. It needs mending, or it'll completely open up. I'm so sorry…"

Out of the corner of my eye I see Tommy twist ever so slightly towards me, frowning at first – then blinking in surprise when he sees me pantomiming sewing something with a giant needle.

I stop.

He stares.

It's fun times all round.

"Right. Okay." Rick claps his hands together and the sound echoes around the stage. "If you can arrange for that to be mended first thing – and can we borrow Lizzie's for the purpose of the parade? We can? Marvellous."

I scurry back behind the crossover and snatch the bag off the *Lizzie 2* hanger, throwing it out at Tommy. He catches it obediently and loops it over his neck and arm, turning back to the auditorium with his coat swirling around him.

When I turn away from one Jamie, there's another one right behind me. Shirt, trousers, coat…but it's a different Jamie. The collar of his coat is slightly raised, giving him an altogether different air. His ruffled blond hair isn't white-blond from a bottle, but a softer golden sand. His face is in shadow, but I know he's watching me, waiting for me to say something.

And I can't.

It's like standing inside a mirror, looking from one to the other of them, and yet it's not. In the same costume, as the same person, they look so alike…but they're different. Perhaps because the insides are so different and it shows on the surface; even through the costume and the make-up and the lines…

"Last but not least – can we have the *other* Jamie two, please?"

"Not bad," I whisper as he slips past me, out onto the stage – and hearing me, he spins round with a grin, so his coat swirls out around him.

"It's not, is it?" he says, stepping out into the lights.

But I wasn't talking about the costume.

On the other side of the stage, Tommy escapes back into the wings – but as he does, he gives me a look I've haven't seen before: it's uncertain, and definitely un-Tommy. It's almost a question; asking me why I just covered for him. A question I can't actually answer.

Maybe I did it because I didn't want anyone to summon me out onto the stage to fix the problem – and blow my cover. Maybe it's because, somehow, it felt like the right thing to do. Maybe, just maybe, it was both.

I wait until I'm sure she's left the building, just to be on the safe side. The last thing I want, after skulking around the corridors and hiding in the office for ages, is to walk straight into Mum outside the stage door. So I make myself useful sorting paperwork…and only glance over at the model theatre across the room with its pair of little figures a couple of times.

It was him, wasn't it? It has to be Luke. Nobody else

would have done it. But he hasn't mentioned it. Without thinking, I pick up the tiny cardboard people and fold them together, sliding them into my pocket as…what? A touchstone? A talisman?

Maybe.

You can never have too much luck in the theatre.

When I've done everything that I can possibly do, I loiter just outside the stage door and watch the fans again. They're a lot more friendly than I imagined, smiling and chatting to one another, to anyone who comes out of the building. It's like they've adopted the whole company, the whole *show*, because of the connection with Tommy.

Some of the cast and crew say goodnight, some of them don't; some of them smile as they walk out through the stage door and agree to photos, some of them put their heads down and their earphones in. With no previews before opening night, we're still days from opening…but there they are. And they aren't going anywhere.

"Hey."

Luke has turned back into Luke, all the way down to his torn jeans. I pretend not to notice the approving murmur from the crowd around the stage door as he walks out. He shifts his bag on his shoulder. "You heading out?"

"I think so."

"Not going back with your mum?" He arches an eyebrow and I feel my face burning.

"Look, about that…"

"It's okay, you know. I won't say anything – you asked me not to, so I won't. And even if you hadn't, it's not my secret to tell."

He says it lightly, as though it's nothing, but I can feel the question in there like a box waiting to spring open.

"It's complicated. That's all."

"It's none of my business."

"I'd just prefer to keep it quiet. I don't want anyone thinking…"

Suddenly there's an explosion of chatter and laughter, and that can only mean one thing – and sure enough, there's Tommy. He's gone total film-star tonight: head-to-toe in black, topped off with an expensively swishy coat and dark glasses with round tortoiseshell rims.

He smiles, he poses for photos, he hugs, he signs things. He's the full Tommy, and it looks completely natural.

He's about to breeze past me, the way he usually does, when he pauses and peers over his sunglasses.

I give Tommy a half-smile, all the while praying that he's not going to ask me to do something *else*.

"Goodnight, Hope," is all he says – and then he's gone, just like that, to the collective sighs of his fans.

What's it like, living with that kind of devotion? Having to perform every time you step outside, any time you're where anyone might see you? Acting, but *always*; your life becoming the performance and the performance becoming your life…

Not that that excuses him from giving me his laundry.

In the middle of the frenzy around Tommy, Luke and I are simply ghosts. Nobody even glances at us as we walk away from the Earl's into the fog that has come up from the river. At least when it's foggy, it stops raining. Besides, I've always liked the fog. It makes the old buildings around here look like they're a stage set – almost as though the doors and windows are painted on and there's nothing behind them. You half-expect to turn a corner and find a couple of guys running a fog machine.

Side by side, we have fallen into step like it's the most natural thing in the world – and then he stops. "You were saying about your mum?" Luke points back at the door.

"Forget it. It's fine – and sorry for snapping at you. It's my own fault – I've been trying to keep it quiet, then I had to tell George and then I let it slip with you, and it all felt a bit much." I tail off feebly, and the fog billows around us. I can't seem to find the right words, the right way to explain it to make him understand instantly; to make him understand *me*. Even though, deep down, I can't help wondering whether he already does. I mean, it really did feel easy earlier. It never feels easy.

No. He doesn't know me – how can he? We've barely spent any time together, and he's an *actor*. It's what he does, making people feel a certain way, right?

And yet...

He walks beside me, still in step; waiting for me to say something else.

Say something, Parker. Actually out loud, not just in your head. He can't hear interior monologue.

I clear my throat. "I guess it's because I've only ever wanted to work in theatre, but as me. On my own terms, my way, even if that means I mess up sometimes. Does that make sense? It's...when your mum's good at something – and she is, I know she is – and you want to do something-that's-a-bit-like-what-she-does-but-not-quite, it feels like everyone's judging you. If you do well, it's because you had help. And if you don't, you're...I don't know, a disappointment or trashing her reputation or something. You can't win."

"That's not what she'd think though, is it? That you were a disappointment?" He raises an eyebrow as he says it and I instantly feel disloyal.

"No! Mum would never say that... Well," I correct myself, "unless we're talking about a *me versus my sisters* situation, in which case I'm *always* a disappointment." I snort.

"How come?"

"Mostly because I'm not Faith and I'm not Grace," I say flatly.

"No," he says – and as we pass through the pool of light below a street lamp, he glows in the fog. "You're Hope."

Which is the nicest thing anyone's said to me in ages, even if it is only my name. Because the way he says it makes it sound special – like it should be up in lights. Nobody ever makes it sound like that.

I'm not even sure what to say back: I suppose I could say "thank you", but then I'd be thanking him for saying my name, and that's starting to get weird – even by my standards. So I don't.

"But you must get the same thing, right? With your parents and acting?"

"Not exactly."

"What, you don't feel any pressure doing what they…"

And then I remember. *Were.*

My parents were…

I stop. It's not subtle, and he reads my panic like a script in his hand.

"It's okay," he says, and he nudges me to show he means it. "It was a long time ago. I was just a kid when they died."

"Sorry. And sorry for being a colossal idiot, talking like that. I should have thought…"

"Thought what? It's not as if I'd told you my life story, is it? 'Hey, Hope – just to let you know, my parents died when I was three and my gran brought me up, so make sure you don't ever mention them'?" He pulls his jacket closer and smiles a little sadly. "How *did* you know, by the way?"

"You said they *were* actors, and it was the way you said 'were'. Then you started talking about your gran looking after you and stuff, and I sort of filled in the blanks."

"You paid attention," he says, and when we walk under the next street lamp he's looking at me with an entirely new expression on his face; like I'm someone he's known *for ever* and we're meeting again for the first time in years. It's another little splinter of Luke that I didn't expect, another splinter of him that slides under my skin…and all I want to do is stop, right here in the middle of the street, in this warm pool of light, as the mist wraps around us like a blanket and the sky overhead slips from silver grey to orange to black. I want to stop time, stop the world. Pause the clock, reset the sun. Just stop.

Because I can't see past how his eyes widen right before he smiles, or the way the muscles in his arm moved *just so* when he reached down the stairs for all those sheets of paper, and there hasn't been a day that I haven't thought about him since I met him, however hard I try not to – first thing in the morning when I open my eyes, or last thing at night, slipping into the hazy drifts of my dreams.

"Which way are you going?"

"Whuh?"

He points up the street, then down it. "Which way?"

I've been too wrapped up in my own head again. All the

thoughts I haven't had time for today have ambushed me, not caring that the person they're actually about is *right here*.

"Oh. Bus stop. It's just there…somewhere." I wave in the direction of where the bus stop usually is. Not that either of us can actually see it through the fog, which is even thicker here. It feels like a chunk of the March sky just fell down and landed on us; thick white swirls of vapour cloud around our feet. Everything is velvet and soft grey.

"I'll wait with you," he says. "As long as you don't…?"

Don't mind? Are you kidding?

"No. That would be nice."

Nice. *Nice?*

His hand brushes against me, and it's so quick and so gentle that at first I think it's an accident. But then the backs of our hands touch again, and I don't want it to be just an accident, a move at the wrong time; I can feel the glow of the heat from his skin against mine, and I don't want it to be a mistake.

With the curtain of the fog swirling around us, I risk a glance down at our hands.

He's looking down at them too – and then he looks up and catches me watching him, and our eyes lock, and he smiles, and I smile, and we are perfect mirrors of each other and we could so easily be the only people in the world, lost in our own little fog bank.

His thumb moves, slowly at first – hesitant, then more certain – to graze the back of my hand. It traces a line across my knuckles and I will him to slip his fingers through mine, to take my hand in his…and right as I think he's about to do it, a rumbling sound tears through the fog as a bright yellow-eyed dragon comes snarling out of the mist.

"My bus!"

It roars past, heading for the bus stop. I have to go.

I don't want to go.

But I have to, because Mum's home by now and I've already blown one secret today. I don't want to blow another.

"I have to…I…"

"Go! I'll see you tomorrow, right?"

His hand drifts further from mine. But his eyes are still with me.

I don't want to go, but I have to go and I don't want to and I don't want to…

And before I even realize I'm going to do it, I lean forward and brush my lips against his cheek.

It's a goodbye, and a hello; an I know you and I don't and I want to know you – and almost before it's even begun, it's over and I'm running for the bus. I make it just before the driver shuts the doors and fling myself up the steps, waving my pass, making for the empty seats at the back and pressing my face to the window.

He's there, and the glow of the street lamp through the

fog circles him like a spotlight. And as he grows smaller and smaller, and the bus turns a corner and he's lost from view, I can feel it. I can.

That a moment ago, in the quiet of the fog – so like the velvety silence of the auditorium and yet so unlike it – there was definitely something there.

ACT FOUR, SCENE TWO

"Late. Late late late."

"You can't be late again, surely?" Mum rolls her eyes at me over the rim of her teacup. "You've been up an hour – how can you possibly be late?"

"Dunno." I stuff a banana from the fruit bowl into my pocket. I'm not exactly going to own up to the fact that I've spent the last hour emptying my entire wardrobe onto my bed and trying to pick out the right outfit for today. Not the dungarees – they make me look like a playschool teacher. Or possibly a playschool *pupil*.

My goodbye to Luke replays and rewinds in my head over and over and over again.

Oh god. Why did I do that? Why? *Why?*

I mean, it was only a kiss on the cheek, if you can even call it a kiss and not me sort of…gently headbutting his face. And it's not like I planned it. But then, standing there in the fog…

Not the blue skirt either. And not the dress with the cherries on.

Grey jeans, the white T-shirt with the charcoal stripes and a yellow cardigan. Green trainers.

Done.

Still late, though.

And – oh, look, what a surprise – it's raining. Just as well I didn't have time to do anything exciting with my hair…

The bus crawls through the traffic in the middle of town, and every minute we spend sitting, sitting, sitting makes me later. I'm dry, yes, but I'm now about to push into *chronically late* – and I can't be late. Not today. Not on the first day of…

Ah.

The first day of technical rehearsals.

I look down at myself.

The first day of technical rehearsals, for which – like the rest of the crew – I should be wearing black.

Bollocks. Bollocks bollocks bollocks.

There's nothing I can do – no time to go home and change. I'm already so late that I'll be miracle-level lucky if Amy doesn't freak out at me. Or worse. And I need this. I need a reference from her, or I'll never get onto a course, especially now I've not got the Square Globe to fall back on. I can't really ask them for a reference again, can I? And there's no way I'm asking Mum for one. Because if I don't get onto a course on my own merit, that's it – I'll never get to do the job I want without Mum's shadow hanging over me. What I need is to get on a good course, get a good result and get some good work experience – if I can do that, nobody will look at me and think *Miriam Parker's daughter, only here because of her mother's name.* They'll see me, not her.

But only if I get that far.

My bus finally pulls up at my stop, and I sprint for the portico of the big hotel at the bottom of the road – only for my bag to sabotage me by coming undone and spilling notes all over the (thankfully dry) pavement under the canopy. Sheltered from the rain, I try to stuff everything back in when there's a loud, piercing whistle. I look up and groan, because there, standing at the other end of the portico, just past the revolving glass door into the hotel, is a depressingly familiar figure in an expensive coat and – even in the rain – sunglasses. Having caught my attention, Tommy waves a lazy hand and rests what must be the biggest umbrella I've ever seen against his shoulder. It's enormous – you could probably fit half a dozen people under there.

With his other hand, he slides his sunglasses down his nose and peers at me over the top of them. "Are you coming, or do you want to spend the whole day soaking wet?"

I take a moment to ponder which option is less appealing:

running for the theatre in this monsoon and getting drenched, or walking with Tommy under his massive umbrella. Of course, if I walk in with Tommy, I might be able to somehow imply it's *his* fault I was late...

I make up my mind.

"Good morning, Tommy."

"Morning. Shall we?" He nods at the rain, and together we walk out from the shelter of the portico.

This is the most awkward umbrella I have ever shared. "You're late this morning." I'm actually close enough to be able to smell him. He smells *expensive*.

He makes a sound a little like a laugh, but not quite. "So are you."

"I...the bus. Traffic."

"Mmm." Tommy sniffs. "Always so cagey, aren't you? What's the matter – afraid of getting into trouble?"

"Ididn'tthinkthatwhateverwouldgiveyouthatideawhat everwouldmakeyousaythat?" It all comes out in a big rush. I'm not that transparent, am I?

This time, he really does laugh. "Look. My job, when you get down to the heart of it, is to pay attention to people. I admit I might not be the greatest actor, but you'll be pushed to find someone who's as good at reading *people* as I am – yes, even including my brother, before you say it."

"I wasn't going to say anything."

(This is a lie. I totally was.)

"Of course. So let me give you a piece of advice – professional, personal…take this how you want, but do take it: *stop it.*"

"Stop what?"

"This. This thing you do. You walk around with your head down like you're terrified someone's going to find you out. It's…disingenuous."

I let that last part slide on past me into the rain. I'm too shocked to do anything else – and Tommy sees it.

"You're afraid you're an impostor. You feel like one, don't you? Like you're a fraud, and someone's going to discover you."

"No?"

(Yes.)

"Let me tell you a secret. Everybody feels like that. Amy, Nathalie, Jonna, your little friend Luke…even my big brother. All impostors. All waiting for someone to unmask them. I can't imagine there's a single person in this business who doesn't know the feeling."

"Not you, though?"

"Oh, especially me."

"Sure. Even though you're 'Tommy Knight'?" I put little air quotes around his name – and it's almost like I'm talking to a normal person.

"But I'm not, am I?" he says calmly. "I'm just Thomas Hillier, Richard's little brother. That's who *I* am, and the rest of it's just…" He holds a hand out into the rain and catches a handful of drops, letting them pool in the bowl of his palm and then tipping them away in a tiny river. "You know why he's so irritated with me at the moment?"

This feels like it's supposed to be a dramatic pause, so I wait.

"I'm sure he's already told you – he seems to have told everybody else. It's the producers. They insisted on casting me, and they took the whole process out of Rick's hands. I didn't even have to audition. My name *was* my audition, whether I earned the part or not." He stops and, because I've got to quite like not getting rained on, I stop too. But then he turns to face me and pulls his sunglasses off, tucking them into the breast pocket of his coat. He has dark circles under his eyes, circles I've not noticed before, and already the stubble is standing out dark against his pale cheeks. "You can't outrun your name, Hope *Parker*, so there's no point hoping you can. Believe me, I've tried. So show them you own *it*, not the other way around."

An anxious ball rolls around in my stomach. Is he talking about my mother? How would he know that?

I can see the stage door from here, with its collection of umbrellas waiting outside. Any second, one of his fans will turn around and spot him…

"Show who?"

Tommy grins, and it's not his Hollywood smile – it's a

real one, for the first time. He raises an eyebrow and leans closer, resting his free hand lightly on my shoulder. There's a muffled shriek and as one, the fans turn and huddle more tightly together. Safety in numbers.

"Everyone," he whispers, and then he straightens up... And before I can even think, let alone answer, he's striding towards the door and the Tommy I've sworn at under my breath is back in the building.

And I'm still late.

"George! George!" I open the door to wardrobe and stick my head through the gap. "Are you here?"

"Where've you been? Amy was looking for..." George appears from behind a rack of old-fashioned dresses, wearing a neat black shirt and black jeans. Even his trainers are black. He looks me up and down slowly; measuring me carefully. "Isn't it tech today?"

"I forgot. Please help?"

"Help you?" Again, another look up and down. "I don't think *anyone* can help you."

"I meant help me find something black – there must be..." I stop. "Hang on, did you just diss my outfit?"

"Outfit? You mean you planned that? I thought you'd just shut your eyes and picked up the first things you touched."

"I...well, that's just rude."

243

"You want my help or not?"

"Yes!"

"Then get in here and we'll find you some blacks. There's bound to be something somewhere."

"Thank you!"

"That cardigan, though…?"

"This happens to be my favourite cardigan."

"You have a *favourite cardigan*? My god. I was right the first time. You're beyond any help."

I follow him into the depths of wardrobe and shut the door behind me.

For a theatre nut, the wardrobe department is its own Narnia. Any theatre gets through hundreds of costumes a year; if a piece can't be bought, it's made by whoever can work a sewing machine, or it's hired. The Earl's isn't that different from any other theatre – unless there are suitable pieces from past productions, most of it is made by Jonna and her team for each show. And most of it is here, through a door at the back of the wardrobe and make-up room.

"Wow." It's the world's most insane walk-in wardrobe. Four neat columns of rolling clothes racks stretch all the way down to the far end of the storage room, stuffed with every imaginable costume from First World War soldiers' uniforms to Regency ballgowns and what I'm pretty sure is a coronation robe. There's a leotard covered in bright coloured silk flowers (all hand-stitched) and a green silk

Grecian dress and a whole rack of 1970s suits with wide lapels and weird ties looped over the hangers. George disappears through a gap in the rails, then pops back out in front of me.

"I got you these from the lost-and-found buckets," he says, holding out what looks like a collection of black rags.

"Do I look that desperate?" I lift the end of a dangling sleeve, which – judging by the pattern of little holes around the cuff – has been part of a mouse's lunch. Roly's cat clearly doesn't come to this end of the building very often. I let it drop again.

"Yes. Go." George shoves the bundle at me, then pushes me behind another rack to change.

It could be worse, I guess. What he's found in the piles of clothes abandoned or forgotten by actors coming through the Earl's over the last six months are a cropped yoga jumper, a vest top and a pair of leggings, all in slightly grey-edged shades of tatty black. But they *are* black, and that should keep me out of trouble…as long as Amy ignores my green trainers, and does not kick me straight out of the building for being as late as I am.

"Thanks – you're a lifesaver." I stuff my own clothes into my rucksack and scramble for the corridor.

Slipping into the auditorium through the pass door from backstage into the stalls, I do my best to act like I've been there for *ages* and am not even slightly late. Rick and Nina glance up when they hear the door, but they're too busily immersed in their notes for anything else. Amy, though? Amy's eyes lock on me, laser-like, and she waves me over.

"Do we need to have another conversation about your timekeeping?"

It's said warmly, but I know a warning when I hear one. I roll through the list of excuses I could give…and stop. Because that's all they are. Excuses.

"I'm so sorry. It won't happen again. I promise."

"Great. Okay, so." She claps her hands together, and for a second it reminds me of Rick's *moving on* gesture. I guess when you work so closely with someone, over and over again, you start catching each other's mannerisms. Another week or two and I'd probably start to as well. "We're almost ready to get started on the tech – can you use the PA system to call all the actors to the green room, then pop up to the stage door and pick up the sign-in sheets?" She hands me a large plastic box with a lid, along with a roll of clear plastic bags and a Sharpie. "When they're all there, check everyone's happy and give them each a bag for their valuables – phone, wallet, jewellery, that kind of thing. We'll keep the whole lot here where there's someone around to keep an eye on it. I don't like the thought of things lying about with no one to watch over them. It's not how I run my shows." She closes her eyes, running through an imaginary list. "I'll do the furniture checks with Nina, and I'll hand out the personal props when you bring the company through from the green room. Then we'll crack through the risk assessments and we're away. All set?"

I nod.

Amy slaps the seat back enthusiastically, and we both pretend we didn't see the little puff of dust that floats up into the light. "Great. Let's see how far we can get before we need to stop for a tea break."

The company, when they finally make it to the wings with a lot of chattering, laughing, gossiping and general racket, fall silent as they all step onto the stage together for the first time and look out at the auditorium. Each of them scans it; measuring it, getting a feel for the weight of it, the scope of it; mentally adjusting the performances they had laid out in their heads. Not that Amy gives them long before she bounds up the temporary stairs and races through the list of things they need to not trip over, walk into or get in the way of.

The prompt desk is sitting there, waiting; a wireless headset all ready. As expectant as the auditorium. I fish my copy of the script out of my bag and open it to the first page. It feels both heavy and weightless as I set it down on the prompt desk, as though it wants to take off and fly.

It does. It wants to soar – I can *feel* it.

Now I've had time to process it, Amy's warning about

professional behaviour makes sense – especially when I hear her giving exactly the same talk to the company…and spot a couple of the ensemble edge ever so slightly apart from each other. So *that's* who George was talking about. I actually feel a little embarrassed for assuming it was only my behaviour that mattered: a little childish, a little self-centred. Because it's not about me. It's not personal – it's professional. This is my chance to show that I get it.

Her chat with the actors finished, Amy pulls out a camera. "All right, you lot. Company photo – say cheese!" They smile and laugh as she takes a snap, looking just like the pictures on the walls backstage, and then Amy turns to face the auditorium and gives Rick a thumbs up. "Ready when you are."

Settled down at his desk, he nods…and then he looks straight at me.

"When you're ready, Hope. And if you could bring in the curtain so we can take a look at that lighting cue right off the bat?"

I pull on the headset. It's heavier than the wireless one I've been using up to now, and the microphone takes some adjusting – but once it's settled it feels like it's always been a part of me. I flick a blue switch on the prompt desk and there's a crackle.

"Company to clear the stage, please. Tabs in."

The curtain slowly falls.

ACT FOUR, SCENE TWO

* * *

When we stop for a tea break an hour later, I'm ready to sleep for a week – but it's not even lunchtime yet. We only have two days of tech before our dress rehearsal day…and so far it doesn't look promising. So instead of collapsing, I push the headset down to sit around the back of my neck and fold my arms on the desk and rest my head on top of them. An hour, and we've covered precisely one and a half scenes. The crew have reset the stage again and again and again and again while Rick debates whether the light is too pink or too orange, and reruns the scene time and again with a different gel filter on the lights – which means that every time, the right bar has got to be lowered from the grid so the lights can be changed. I've made so many calls that my throat feels dry and prickly and the handwriting all over my script looks like it might actually belong to someone else. Someone writing in Cyrillic, or possibly ancient Sumerian. I can't read it, anyway. And that's without counting the way I miscued the first three lighting changes *four* times. After that, even Amy rolled her eyes – and I told myself that the fourth time would be the last time. She must be wondering what I'm doing here, why she picked me – whether she made a mistake. I'm certainly wondering that.

"I need my phone," says a disembodied voice outside the safe circle of my arms, ignoring the fact that – like everyone else – I'm supposed to be on a break.

"Hi, Tommy. Give me a minute. Why don't you head over to the green room and grab a cup of tea – I'll bring it through to you."

"No, I need it now."

"Of course you do," I growl into my elbows, and reluctantly haul myself up from the desk to rummage in the box next to me, pulling out his plastic bag with a flourish. "Ta-da."

He takes the bag and flounces off.

"Thank you?" I mutter at his departing back.

Nothing.

What else did I expect?

I push through the doors out to the foyer, where everything is hushed and still – unlike the green room, where they're all probably bickering about who got their blocking wrong and the fact we had to rerun the second section between Jamie and Lizzie seven times. I need time and space to clear my head right now, to tell myself I *can* do this, so I go straight to the deserted stalls bar, pick the nearest of the bench seats and lie down with my arms crossed over my face. Even here, I keep thinking I can hear my headset buzzing, or Rick calling my name, and I sit up twice to check before I realize it's only one of the fridges humming.

And then someone bangs a crate of bottles down on the bar, and I jump so hard that I almost fall off the bench.

"What the hell...?" Heart pounding, I sit up and glare at the bar.

"Sorry." Luke wrinkles his nose as he says it. "I didn't know you were here."

If anything, this makes my heart beat even faster. "It's you."

Because nothing says hi, how are you this morning, than stating the incredibly obvious, does it? I wait for him to say something about last night in the fog – but he doesn't. Not at all.

"Well spotted." He hefts another crate of bottles up onto the bar, then brushes his hands together and comes over to sit beside me.

Maybe he's forgotten? Or maybe I imagined it? Or maybe he thought it was an accident? I nod at the crates. "Bar work too? What about tech?"

"I'm not needed until this afternoon. To be honest, I take pretty much any work I can get as long as it fits around college. They're flexible here, so I help out with the bars when there's shifts going."

I think about my own stack of unwritten assignments and unread notes building up in my inbox. I keep meaning to look at them when I get home in the evenings, but I'm just too tired. I'll get to them. Eventually. But I've only got to juggle everything for a few weeks – how does somebody do it all the time? "Bar work, acting, ushering...and studying? That's a *lot*."

Luke snorts. "Acting's not likely to pay the bills any time soon – even this job. Maybe one day, but not yet. And college won't exactly pay for itself, and there's textbooks and voice lessons and *food*, so…"

He's not going to mention last night, is he? He probably wants to pretend the whole thing didn't happen.

Okay.

Fine.

"I guess you'd rather be doing more of *that* than *this*, though – right?" I jerk my thumb back towards the auditorium, then at the bar. For a second his face blanks. I can't read him at all; not until he speaks again.

"I'd love to be doing *that*. *That's* the dream. But in the real world, I have to do *this* too. We can't all…" He stops suddenly and sighs. There's a long silence, then finally he says, "I can't ask Gran to pay for everything, you know? It's not fair." He fidgets on the bench and the whole cushion bounces slightly under his weight. "How's the tech going?"

I give him a look and he nods seriously.

"That well?"

I slump forward and drop my head into my hands. "We're halfway through the second scene," I mumble into my palms. "It's never going to be ready."

"Yeah, we will be."

We.

As if I'd echoed him out loud, he carries on.

"Theatre's a team game. Everyone here knows it and they're all bringing their best. Besides, with Rick and Amy in charge and Nina backing them up, there's no way it can't be ready. They'll make it ready."

"They're always a team, are they?"

"Pretty much. You know what directors are like. They build a creative crew and bring them onto every project. Same designers, same stage management, same lighting... the people who can see what they've got in their head without them needing to spell it out. Besides, Rick would be crazy to let Amy go – I heard she's one of the best DSMs in the country."

I can certainly believe that, just from watching Amy this morning: while she's left me to call the lighting and sound cues, she's been taking notes; sometimes sitting back and studying the stage, sometimes jumping up and running through the pass door to adjust something backstage, or disappearing off to the balcony or the back of the stalls to check a sight line. It's like there are twelve of her, and they're all in motion, all the time. I can't decide whether that's inspirational or depressing, because no matter how much I try, I can't see how I'm ever going to be able to do what she does. And I'm pretty sure she wouldn't be impressed by me right now. After everything Amy has said about the personal and the professional and "not getting distracted", even sitting here talking to Luke feels somehow dangerous. So why then has dangerous never felt so safe?

He shifts on the seat. He smells like ginger and fresh coffee and sunshine, and I want to lean my head back against his chest to listen for his heartbeat, like the sound of waves in a shell you press to your ear. I want to know if it's going as fast as mine is.

I could sit here beside him for ever; listening to the fridges click on and off, the clock over the bar tick-tick-ticking the day away.

I blink at the clock.

Timekeeping.

Nuts.

"That's my break! Got to run…"

Back in the stalls, I pass Tommy by the door, whispering urgently into his phone, and despite my best efforts to hear what he's saying, all I pick up is a name: Emery.

Emery Greenway, singer, Tommy's on-off-on-off-again girlfriend, and just as famous in her own right as he is. From the way he's huddled over his phone, they're on again…and I'm willing to bet she's not too happy about something.

"Tommy – time…" I whisper, hoping he'll get the hint. He waves me away.

Fine. Let him get yelled at by Rick…

Except it's my job to keep things running to time, isn't it?

Crap.

I turn around and march back up the aisle.

"Tommy."

He turns his back to me and carries on.

"Tommy!"

Nope.

I put on my best announcement voice. "Mr Knight, we're starting again. If you could please take your place for scene three?"

He turns around, mutters something into the phone and hangs up, meekly handing it to me and trotting off down the aisle.

I look at the phone in my hand, and then at Tommy's rapidly retreating back.

"Huh."

Today is turning out to be *full* of surprises…

ACT FOUR, SCENE THREE

I escape the house for the second day of tech rehearsals with a promise that, yes, I will definitely help Mum get the latest of the premiere dresses she's made all packed up to be couriered off to its lovely owner. On the way to the theatre, I count up how long I spent sitting at the prompt desk yesterday, leaning over the script. Even with breaks, it's a long time. A *long* time. So long, in fact, that I have to pull out my phone and check my maths on the calculator. Still A Long Time. I've never sat in the same place for so long without moving. Never. Not even for exams. Not even for the *Angels in America* marathon double-broadcast at the cinema (although it was definitely Priya and not me who ran out to the loos a grand total of eight times – I *told* her the "mammoth" drink cup was a bad idea).

Even so, I can't wait to do it again. But when I get to the Earl's, the group around the stage door aren't acting quite… normally.

Usually when someone comes along, a few of them turn around to check who it is – and by now, when it isn't Tommy, or occasionally one of the other cast members, they smile politely then lose interest pretty quickly. Their initial enthusiasm for all of us has faded a bit – having seen me run in and out a few times, a couple of them say hi to me now, but mostly I'm part of the scenery.

But today, having seen it's me, a couple of them point, and then say something to the others…and they *all* turn round.

They all turn round and stare at me.

Maybe it's my hair? I check I've got matching trainers on; that I've remembered to actually put my (black) jeans on. (Mum even made a pointed comment about the fact I was wearing all black as I headed out this morning, so I had to pretend I hadn't even noticed. I *think* she believed it. Maybe I can act after all…)

Hair, clothes, all fine.

So what are they looking at?

I try a smile as I reach them, but my "Morning!" is only answered with complete silence.

They are *all* staring at me. No, not staring. Glaring.

And judging by the looks on their collective faces, they are *mightily pissed off*.

What did I do?

As I pass, they start whispering – and when I reach the

step up to the stage door, I hear it. Quiet, but clear: someone is booing. It's very quiet – almost too quiet to hear – but hear it I do.

Someone in the group is booing *me*.

I almost stop – but the sound is already getting louder. It's not just a whisper now, I can hear it clearly. And so can everyone else.

My face on fire, I half-turn to ask them what the hell's going on…but seeing me hesitate, another voice joins in. And then another. And another. Suddenly, they're all booing me and shouting at me and the noise is deafening and I don't understand – so I dive through the door and run up the stairs, stopping only when I get to Roly's desk.

Roly herself is peering out of the little window that overlooks the side of the theatre, watching the show outside.

"Did you hear that? What the hell?"

"Mmm-hmmm." She turns around slowly and folds her arms.

"What?"

"Not seen it, have we?"

"Seen what?"

"Mmm-hmmm." Roly picks her phone up from the desk and fiddles with it, then drops it on the sign-in book in front of me.

On the screen is the front page of the *SixGuns* gossip

section – and the first thing on it is a screamingly red header, and a tabloid-style photo of two people under an umbrella in the rain.

The caption?

KNIGHT IN SHINING ARDOUR?

And the photo?

Tommy, holding his giant umbrella over my head, leaning towards me with his eyes fixed on my face…

Oh god.

Oh god, oh god, oh god.

"*What…?*" All the blood that had rushed to my cheeks immediately drains all the way down to my feet and I scroll through the story, not really reading it. The words sort of… glance off my eyeballs and bounce around the desk.

Hollywood heart-throb Tommy Knight…

Cosying up to a mystery brunette…

Outside his hotel…

Walk in the rain…

Very close…

There are other photos: me coming out of his hotel, looking around. Me walking into his hotel…

The phone. The laundry. The guy on the pavement.

Oh god.

My voice, when I finally manage to get it to work again, doesn't even sound like mine. "What is this?"

"That?" Roly holds her hand out for her phone, and I

pass it back – almost dropping it, I'm shaking so hard. I think I might be sick. Or I might pass out. I'm not sure. Maybe both? She studies me as she puts her phone away. "Lead story on *SixGuns*. But there's been photos up on fan sites since late last night."

"I…I don't…I…" I look at her. "What do I do?"

She narrows her eyes at me, and there's a long, long silence. Eventually, she asks it almost casually. "Not true, is it?"

"Are you *kidding* me? *Seriously?*"

Faces flash through my mind so fast they blur: Mum. Dad. Priya. Amy. Luke!

Panic. That's what this is.

Has anyone seen it? How do I stop them?

Roly is oblivious to my complete terror. "That's not really an answer, though, is it?"

"Me and Tommy. Really. You think that's a thing that would *ever* happen? In this world or any other? You know I've been running all his stupid errands. Amy told me I have to keep him happy!"

"And you've been doing that, have you? *Keeping him happy?*"

Roly's question is so heavy with innuendo that it practically clangs down on the desk between us.

"What? You think…"

Somewhere at the bottom of my bag, my phone rings.

Maybe it's just a coincidence. Maybe I left my…my shoe at home, and Mum's ringing to ask me how I can be walking around with one bare foot. It could absolutely be that.

I look down.

Both shoes.

My phone rings one…two…three times. And keeps going.

Okay. That's not good.

I scrabble it out and watch as messages from Priya, Orson, Amelie, Priya again, Priya, Priya, Priya, Priya, half my class at school and – yes – Priya whizz across the screen so fast I can't even read them.

I guess my friends are all waking up and checking the *SixGuns* site.

Oh god, oh god, oh god.

I'm dreaming. I must be – it's all a bad dream and all I have to do is wake up to make it go away.

I close my eyes and try to clear my mind.

Luke. What's Luke going to say? What if he doesn't say anything at all? Maybe he won't care – I mean, he's not said anything about me kissing his face (oh god), hasn't asked for my number, or given me his. Maybe…

Maybe that would be worse.

And what if Mum sees it? How am I going to… No. That's ridiculous. No way is *Mum* going to read *SixGuns*.

Okay. Okay. Breathe.

It's just a stupid photo. A stupid, bad photo. And there's a perfectly ordinary, innocent explanation anyway. It's fine. It's. All. Fine.

I open my eyes to see Roly leaning over the sign-in book, resting her chin on her hands.

"So…no?"

"Obviously it's a no!" I rub my hands over my face. Just keep breathing; say what really happened. "He came out of his hotel as I was getting off the bus. He had an umbrella. We were literally walking down the same street at the same time to the same place and he decided to be an actual human for once and save me from getting soaking wet. Maybe it was a thank you for taking care of all the sodding laundry? Maybe it was just because he felt…I don't know, kind."

"Maybe he thought it would be good PR…" Roly mutters. I glare at her.

"You don't think he did this on *purpose*, do you?"

Would he?

Could he?

Whatever Roly thinks, she doesn't get to answer because George comes barrelling up the stairs.

"Did you—" Seeing me, he stops whatever it was he was about to say. "You've seen it, then?"

I nod mutely.

"Okay. Okay." He puts a hand on each of my shoulders. "I need you to tell me *everything*."

"George!"

"I don't mean like *that*." He rolls his eyes. "I mean I need you to tell me what really happened so we can—"

"What? Fix it? How do you fix *this*?" I wave my hand at the stage door. I wish I *could* fix it, but I don't even know where to start. Not when I'm still not one hundred per cent sure what's happening. What I am sure of, though, is what I need to do next, and it feels like I'm swallowing rocks. "I need to go find Amy."

"Okay. Let's go." Keeping his hands on my shoulders, and with my phone still going berserk, George spins me around and steers me towards the production office. As we reach the first door, he leans in and whispers from behind me: "Seriously, though. It's not true, is it?"

Amy is already sitting at her desk in the production office; her back to the door, her head bent over one of her folders.

George shoves me at her and makes a break for it; a couple of seconds later, I hear the door to wardrobe slam.

"Ummm…"

Amy looks up – and when she sees me, her face clouds.

This is not good. Actually, no. The being-late stuff was not good. The stuffing-up-the-cues was marginally more not-good. This is much, much worse. This is playing-hopscotch-on-a-minefield levels of not-good.

"Good morning, Hope. I think you'd better close the door, don't you?"

This is so very, very, very not-good, but I do it anyway and perch on the edge of the desk next to hers. She closes her folder and drops it on top of the pile to her right with one hand, opening her laptop with the other. The screen flares into life.

"Would you like to tell me about this?"

This is as not-good as it could possibly be.

There, on the screen, is a series of photos. Not just that single picture that made it onto the gossip site, but five or six taken one after another, zoomed in until they start to dissolve into pixels…but nowhere near grainy enough to cause any doubt about who's in the frame.

"It was raining," is all that comes out of my mouth.

"Yes?"

I can't put the words together. I just can't, it's too ridiculous, because who – even for a second – could really believe there could be anything between me and Tommy. A hot fist of anger clenches in the pit of my stomach, raking its nails along my insides.

"My bus was stuck in that traffic yesterday morning, so I got off at the top of the hill, outside the Grand, and Tommy was there, and he had an umbrella, and he offered to walk down to the theatre with me. So I didn't get wet?"

Amy studies me for what feels like for ever, her eyes

moving slowly across every part of my face.

"Okay, just let me say something. I know you don't believe me, and I know you think I didn't listen to your personal-professional talk, but I'm telling the truth. This is…it's not…it's…" I wave my hands, hoping they'll miraculously bring me the right word. "Made-up," I finish. It'll do.

And when I think this is it, this is the moment she fires me (can she fire me for this? I've got no idea, but she can definitely give me a bad reference…or none at all) she nods and closes the laptop with a *clunk*.

"I know."

"You…you do?"

"I wasn't born yesterday, Hope – unlike the people who read this nonsense." She waves a hand at the laptop and sighs. "Tommy's girlfriend included." She catches my involuntary twitch and nods. "I think we'll need to work around Tommy for a while this morning – he's a little… preoccupied."

I suppose at least this proves he didn't set it up as a PR stunt, though.

"I'm sorry." My voice trembles but it doesn't break. I won't let it. *I* won't break.

Amy shakes her head, and then leans forward and takes hold of both my hands, folding them into hers – and that's very nearly enough to tip me over the edge on its own.

"You have done *nothing* wrong. If anything, this is my fault. I should have expected something like this might happen, especially when they started camping out at the stage door – I'm just sorry you got caught up in it. It isn't personal – if it hadn't been you, it would have been somebody else from the theatre. It could have been anyone. We should have anticipated photos being taken at *some* point."

I force my lips together as hard as I can, focusing on that; trying not to think about how grateful, how *relieved* I am that Amy not only believes I haven't done anything stupid (not this time, anyway) but that she understands. Not that that helps me in the bigger picture – it wasn't just *anyone* getting booed on their way in this morning, was it? And it isn't just *anyone* who has to hope their parents don't see this. It isn't just *anyone* who has to face Luke – because he'll be here somewhere – never mind Emery-actual-Greenway when she arrives on opening night. How would that even go? *"Hi, I'm Hope – remember me? I'm the girl from the tabloids. The one they said was sleeping with your boyfriend? Welcome to the Earl's!"*

"…naturally. The box-office phones have been ringing for the last hour, and the lines aren't even open yet."

"Sorry?" I was so busy thinking about the terrible things Emery Greenway is going to do to me that I completely missed what Amy said.

"I said, marketing are over the moon. We were already ninety-three per cent sold out across the run, and now they're desperately trying to scrape together more tickets to release."

"What?" This time, I hear her, but it still doesn't make a lot of sense.

"You can't buy coverage like this," she says, shaking her head. "Believe me – they've tried. But the way things are looking this morning, we're going to completely sell out the full run within five minutes of opening those lines, and then it'll be returns only."

"Oh."

Right. Well. That makes it okay then, does it?

My face must show everything that's going through my mind, because when Amy glances up at me she smiles.

"I know it doesn't help, but in a day or two everyone will have realized it's nonsense – Tommy's people are apparently trying to get a follow-up for an interview he gave a couple of weeks ago. It's due to go in one of the weekend papers, so he'll clear everything up there." She pulls a sympathetic face. "And it *is* good for the show."

"Mmm."

She's right about that, at least. I've paid enough attention over the years to know that any publicity is good publicity when it comes to theatre.

"So. Shall we get started?" Already moving on, Amy

shuffles together a handful of folders. "We've got a long day to get through, and while Tommy's dealing with –" she waves a hand in the air – "everything, Luke's agreed to act as a stand-in for him so we can press on. We'll run Tommy through any changes later."

The thought of facing Luke right now, in front of everyone and before I've had the chance to explain all this, makes my stomach drop again. He knows it's all rubbish, right? Of course he does. He'll *know*. How can he not?

I follow Amy out of the production office and head for the side of the stage, glancing at the theatre model box as I pass – but the miniature stage is empty.

Amy calls the actors together, running through the same talk as yesterday for the benefit of the cast who weren't in before. In the middle of the knot of people, I spot Luke – or rather, the back of his head; tilted to one side as he listens, nodding occasionally – and the inside of my skin fizzes like someone's letting off fireworks in my veins. I will him to turn around, to see me standing in the wings and to smile at me…but he doesn't. Amy winds up, and I take a step forward as Luke nods one more time, then turns…

He looks over and sees me and I smile, wait for his eyes to meet mine…

And he looks right past me as though I'm not even there.

Maybe he doesn't see me in the darkness of the wings? That must be it. The lights are all set up for the first scene this morning and I can feel how hot they are, how bright they are, even from here.

I take another step forward, call his name…

He walks towards me…

And he walks right past.

"Luke?"

But he's already gone. I guess that tells me everything I need to know.

Holding my head up high and blinking fast, I step out of the shadows and onto centre stage, hurry down the steps and make straight for the prompt desk.

Jamie isn't in the first scene we cover – which means I don't have to deal with seeing him there, on the stage, almost within reach. But I still manage to miscue another lighting effect, making Rick sigh. And then there's a problem with the grid above the stage and everything grinds to a halt for ten agonizing minutes, during which I hear my name and "in for a long wait", followed by a hearty chuckle, drifting down from the fly-floor.

I flick a switch on the prompt desk and shove my headset back on. "I can *hear* you, you know."

My own voice rings uncomfortably in my head, awash

with feedback. It's followed by a mumble that might just be an apology – or might not. I rip off the headset before I have time to decide which it is – I'm not in the mood.

By the time we're up and running again, Rick has had a chance to rearrange the entire scene in his head, leaving actors, the techs and me scrambling to catch up with the lightning speed of his hand movements as he describes the new blocking.

We run it.

Rick doesn't like it.

Of course he doesn't.

I rub a hole in my page trying to erase the new blocking I'd sketched out, and when I look up…there's Luke.

Bollocks.

He's standing alone in the centre of the stage and I know – I *know* – I'm meant to be cueing something, someone, but I can't look away. However hard I try, somehow my gaze is pulled right back to him. It's just like the first time I watched him stand in for Tommy in the rehearsal room. Then I thought it was talent or charisma or whatever it is that actors have when you can't stop watching them…and maybe for everyone else, it was. Maybe to begin with it was even that for me, but not now.

Now, it's because I can still feel the brush of his hand against mine; the warmth of his skin, the softness of his cheek beneath my lips. I know I didn't imagine it – not in the fog the other evening, not when he bought me a sandwich. And all I've been able to think about at night when I close my bedroom door and turn out the lights is how I want to run my hands through his hair the way he does, to feel it slip like silk through my fingers. I want to lean in so close to him that I can feel his heart beating against *my* ribs, feel the rise and fall of his breathing in my bones. I want to slide my hand around the back of his neck and pull him closer to me, closer, closer and—

"Hope!"

It's so loud that I drop my pencil.

"Sorry…"

Rick is leaning forward in his chair, resting his folded arms on the desk. "Any time today…?"

I flip my prompt script over to the next page and pull the mic of my headset closer to my mouth, hoping nobody else can see quite how scarlet-hot my cheeks are. "Cue elec fifty-three."

The lights shift; the faintest hint of colour shimmering across the stage. It makes me think of sunsets thrown against stone buildings, of late summer afternoons…

…*of walking hand in hand along the river with Luke, my head resting on his shoulder*…

And *he's* right there. Almost within touching distance. Larger than life and smaller all at once. Both completely Luke and utterly not; his face, but with a stranger's mannerisms and movements and tone of voice.

How can he be up there, so near and so far away?

It's the strangest thing, because I feel like I *know* him – but how can I? How could I tell if he was just…acting? Because I don't understand how, if he feels even a *little* the way I do, the way I thought he must when we were out in the fog, he could look at me the way he did earlier. No, not at me. *Through* me.

Acting. Is it all acting? When does it stop?

My head is still in the auditorium, still following the script, still cueing. My heart is somewhere else. My heart is at the top of the staircase leading down to the foyer. My heart is dangling by the thinnest golden thread alongside the chandelier of cages.

My heart is falling.

Falling, falling, falling.

And from the top, it doesn't look it, but it's such a very long way down.

Luke manages not to make eye contact with me – or even to glance in the direction of the prompt desk – through the whole scene. All four runs at it. And short of climbing on top of a nearby seat, waving my arms in the air and shouting at him, there's nothing I can do. If this was happening in a play, it would be almost funny – you know, kind of like the bit where the couple fall out over a misunderstanding and maybe they won't get together after all…but by the time the curtain comes down at the end of the show, everything has been made right and everyone's with the person they're meant to be with. But it's not, is it? That's all just playing, all pretending – once they've taken their curtain calls, the loving couple let go of one another's hands and walk off in different directions to wipe off the make-up and the declarations of undying love.

He *seemed* to like me…but what do I know?

And then he's gone. The stage is empty.

Rick and Nina beam, nodding and adding notes to their scripts, and a seat behind me creaks as someone shifts their weight.

"He's not bad at all, is he?" says Tommy. "I'm going to have to watch out for him."

It no longer surprises me when people appear from nowhere around here.

"How do you mean?"

"He's ambitious, too, from what I hear. One day, I might be standing at the top of the stairs and feel a hand in the middle of my back and…" He mimes falling. "Can't go on with a broken leg now, can I?"

"You're being a dick."

"My, aren't we snappy this morning? And to think, we were getting along so well."

"That was before…" I close my eyes and clench my jaw. There's no use getting into a fight with Tommy about this, is there? Much as I'd love to be able to blame him, it wasn't actually his fault.

"Well, I'm sure it'll make you feel better that Emery has practically chewed my ear off about the whole thing – and she sounded just a little too happy to be able to tell me I didn't get the award nomination I was after this year *either*, so no doubt that will brighten your day." He curls his fingers in over his palm and studies his fingernails, and I almost feel sorry for him…but I recognize that voice. He's being "Tommy Knight". Like the last piece of a jigsaw slotting into place, the last tumbler in the dial of a safe's door dropping into sequence, I get it. I get him. And I can see right through him.

I flip over a couple of pages of the prompt book and draw a series of small and completely unnecessary circles in an empty space on one of the pages. Anything to look like I'm not paying too much attention to him. "Sorry about the nomination. That was the big TV drama last year, right?"

Out of the corner of my eye, I can see him watching me but pretending he's not. He flicks his hair back – forgetting it's short now, so all he's doing is tossing his head around like a demented horse…and little by little, the facade cracks. The mask slips, and sitting there is the same man – more or less – who offered me an umbrella in the rain. Just a guy whose girlfriend is pissed off with him and who's disappointed something at work didn't go the way he was hoping. Work he'd put his heart and soul into, all because it's what he loves to do, and because he can never outrun his name.

I see you, Tommy Knight.

And for the first time, I think I understand you.

With Tommy back in the room, we slog through the next handful of scenes; Rick pushes lunch break to the absolute limit of our working time, and I can hear the crew muttering darkly about Equity union rulings over my headset a full five minutes before we stop. After the constant noise of the morning's rehearsals, actors going through their lines, Rick calling out instructions, or scenery sliding in and out on its track, the sudden silence when it stops is overwhelming. I need to talk to someone, somebody who isn't just in my headset, and won't tell me I didn't give them enough of a standby warning for that last cue.

"George?"

The door to wardrobe is open, and I can see Nathalie and Jonna at the back of the room between two racks of costumes, their heads bent forward together over a sketchbook – but no George.

"In here!" The next door along – the laundry – is ajar.

I nudge the door open and peer round to find George leaning heavily on the ironing board, pressing what looks like a velvet jacket.

"Cavan decided that putting his jacket back on the hanger was just too much of an effort, and now it looks like garbage." He holds up the sad, crumpled jacket. It does, indeed, look like garbage. "I'm going to accidentally-on-purpose poke him in the eye with his eyeliner first chance I get – but before that, I've got to sort this. Jonna will kill me if she sees it."

"Well, I'm no expert," I say, peering at the iron he's picked up from the board, "but I'm pretty sure you've actually got to switch the iron *on* if you want it to do anything?"

He does a double-take, looking at the socket on the wall. "Oh, *what*?"

I lean around him and flick the switch on. The iron clicks as it starts to heat up. "Give it here."

"Are you *telling* me to let you take over the ironing? What would my mother say? What would *your* mother say?"

I elbow him out of the way, laughing. "My mother would say that you're about to press the velvet on the wrong side and you're going to totally crush the pile." I flip the jacket inside out and smooth it across the board.

"Jesus, today is just not my day." He stands at the end of the board, pretending to supervise. "You never thought about going into costumes too then?"

"God, no. Very, very no – would you? Can you imagine

how much that would suck? Bad enough wanting to work in theatre on my own terms, but if I wanted to do exactly the same thing as my *mother*?"

"And the rest of your family?"

"Dad's not into theatre, really. And then there's my sisters – Grace is a lawyer, Faith's an accountant."

George blinks at me three times. "That's not what I expected you to say. At all."

"I know. But that's my sisters for you. We couldn't be more different if we tried. They don't like me very much actually." Which is fine, because most of the time the feeling's mutual.

He snorts. "I think that's a bit of an exaggeration – I'm sure they love you." He leans his elbows on the other end of the ironing board and the whole thing creaks alarmingly. George moves his elbows. "It's just…well, family, isn't it?"

I shake my head. "No. It's Faith and Grace. And that's fine. We don't get on, and that's how it is. You don't have to like somebody just because you happen to be related. I mean, if it wasn't for Mum, I'd wonder if I was swapped at birth or something…" I rest the iron on the stand at the end of the ironing board. "You don't think *they* were swapped at birth, do you?"

I whip the jacket off the board and turn it right way round. It's not perfect, but at least it resembles the Magister's jacket again, rather than the crumpled rag it had become.

"That's not a bad job," George mutters, slipping it onto its labelled hanger.

"By which you mean 'Thank you, Hope, I am eternally grateful. Call on me in your hour of need and I will repay—'"

"Yes, yes. All of that."

"I…umm, don't suppose you've seen Luke back here recently, have you?" I pretend I'm very interested in the ball of lint on the floor under the ironing board, letting the question slip out casually.

Or perhaps not as casually as I thought, because George tips his head to one side and looks very hard at me.

"You want to talk to him about the Tommy thing?"

"There *is* no Tommy thing. Christ, George. Calling it 'the Tommy thing' doesn't exactly help, does it?"

"You know what I mean."

"Yes, I do. And yes. I do. But I haven't seen him since he was in tech earlier, and I don't know where he's gone, or even if he—"

George cuts across me. "You two are a thing, then?"

"What? No!"

"Really. Because – and fine, what do I know? – you certainly look like you want to be. You're going all gooey-eyed…"

"Eeew."

"Shut up. You know what I mean – every time he walks into the room, or heaven help us, he gets on the stage. And he—"

"He what?" I say it just a little too quickly, and George pounces.

"Why do you care? I thought you weren't a thing."

"We're not. He's not. I don't know. Okay? I don't know. Just…tell me."

"About him? Put it this way – if that's how a guy who *isn't* interested reacts to a story about you and Tommy, I'd love to know how it'd go if he *was*."

I stare at him. "Can you maybe use small words?"

"I did. But fine. You blatantly, *shamelessly* like him – so what are you doing standing around chatting with me for, instead of going to find out if the feeling's mutual?" He waits, then sighs theatrically. "And as I'm apparently going to have to do *all* the work here, if you *did* want to go find him, I heard him say he'd be running some lines for college up top in the Heffernan Room…"

The Heffernan Room, on the highest floor of the main building, is shut; the door closed. But when I peer through the little glass porthole set into the wood, I can see Luke silhouetted against the floor-to-ceiling windows that look over the surrounding roofs.

"Hey." I push through the door, letting it swing shut behind me, and I wait for him to turn around.

It feels like I'm waiting for ever – but eventually, he does, folding a copy of *Misterman* into his back pocket. It's become such a familiar gesture to me, him tucking a script away, that it almost makes everything better. Until I really see the look on his face. He doesn't look at me like we've somehow known each other for years any more – or even like we've ever met. He looks at me like I'm a total stranger, and it stings.

No. More than that.

It *hurts*.

"Hope."

"Good rehearsal this morning. Rick and Nina were really happy."

"Were they?" Is that a thaw in his voice? Maybe if I keep talking, he'll warm up.

"They were. Definitely. And even Tommy…"

I realize that was the very, most absolutely wrongest of all wrong things I could have said a fraction of a second too late – but there's nothing I can do except watch him turn his back on me again.

"*Tommy*." He says it to the window, not me. There's real venom in the name.

I stare at his back.

Outside, the sun moves behind a thick cloud and the room darkens and cools.

I didn't ask for this. Is isn't fair.

It really isn't fair…and I've had enough. Everything

that's been boiling up inside me since I got in this morning suddenly rises to the surface – and overflows.

"What's your problem, Luke? You've obviously got one, and it's obviously with me – so you can at least grow up and tell me what the hell it is, seeing as we've got to spend the immediate future in the same building."

"My problem?" All the warmth and softness has gone. He could carve words into the windows with that voice. "Clearly it isn't that *obvious* after all."

"No. It's not. Because I'm not psychic, am I? However much everyone round here seems to want me to be, and I…" This isn't where I wanted to go with this. "And all I know is that you were fine – *we* were fine, *more* than fine – and now suddenly you won't even turn round and look at me."

"You don't get it, do you?" he snaps, and now he whips around to face me and he's across the room and standing right in front of me in a heartbeat. "You're my problem. *You.*"

"Me? A *problem*? Oh, great. Thanks for that."

He ruffles his hands through his hair – again, it's so familiar and yet not. So close and so far away.

"Do you really not get it?"

"Yeah, sure. I'm a problem. I think I got it this time."

"No. You don't. I like you, okay? I like you, and I've liked you from the first time you spoke to me. And I don't like many people – not like this. I don't…" He stops and growls with exasperation, fumbling for the right words. "I don't exactly open up to people. It's not who I am, so I don't. Ever. Until…until you came along. I felt…I don't know, that I could trust you because you'd understand. That you *did* understand. And then Juliet showed me those photos of you and Tommy and…"

I stare at him. This is a lot. A *lot*.

"You like me?"

Really, brain? That's what we're taking from this?

But I've lost control and my heart and my mouth are doing their own thing. I'm just along for the ride.

"Yes, Hope. I like you. I thought you'd have worked that out by now."

"Well…"

No, actually.

Maybe.

I *hoped*…

I don't know; I guess I was so busy thinking about *me*, the fact I like *him*, that I wasn't really paying attention to how this might make him feel.

He sighs. "Look, I'm sorry. Maybe I should have said something, but that's not who I am. I thought I'd put the figures in the office to try and – I don't know – *show* you, and then I was worried it was weird. That I was making things weird…"

"You didn't want to make things weird, so you left little cardboard versions of us on the little cardboard stage for me to find? Yeah. That's not weird." I try to make it sound cool, but inside my heart is tying itself into a knot.

"I told you, I'm not so great with words. I know what I want to say, but half the time it comes out wrong – or it takes twice as long as anyone wants to listen. I don't always *get* people, you know? They usually take me a while, and I'm always second-guessing everything I say and do and..." He bites his lip and frowns. "But then you...and I thought... and then there's those pictures of you and Tommy..."

"You know it's not true, right?"

"Do I? I don't know anything – I barely know *you*!"

That stings some more, and the insides of my eyelids prickle. But I *will not* break.

I wait for him to carry on, and he does. "I didn't want to put any pressure on you. We're working together and...and I'm older than you, and even if that doesn't matter to you, it matters to me." He sighs. "But maybe I'm the only one, because there you are, arm in arm with Tommy."

"*Woah*. Just stop." I hold up my hands. How can I be this happy AND this furious at the same time? "First of all, if you care so much, did it not even cross your mind to *ask* me about Tommy? Did it not occur to you that I might not actually be desperately into him? Just *maybe*?"

Luke stares at the floor.

"And do you not think that maybe, maybe if you like someone – and you like them enough to get all like –" I flap my hand at him – "*this*, then you might actually want to *let them know how you feel*?"

"I did," he mumbles. "I am."

"Yeah, well. It's not exactly a Shakespearean declaration of love, is it?"

I've run out of anger, of indignation, of breath – and all I can think about now is the tiny little spark I've found in the middle of the fog inside my head.

He definitely likes me.

He said so.

Luke Withakay likes me.

"I'm sorry," he says quietly. "You're right."

"Of course I'm right. I'm stage management. We're always right. You should know that."

The corner of his mouth twitches, and I know that's a smile.

I know, because I've been paying attention.

I could annotate his gestures the same way he does his scripts. I could draw his face from memory the same way he draws out his lines... But even knowing that, and even after seeing the way he analyzes the smallest pause or shortest word in all those scripts he reads, somehow we both managed to miss this.

Until now.

And now it's up in lights and flashing on and off in giant letters, and suddenly I don't know how we're going to keep everybody else in the dark.

It feels like I fly across the floor to him, until there's no space between us. No space for weirdness or misunderstandings or whatever it is we've tried to put in the way. Now he really is close enough to touch.

Without a word I lift my hands and slowly, slowly, I bring them up to rest on his shoulders. His eyes are locked on mine and I can see him looking out at me. I see him and I *know* he's him and he's real. He's not acting; not pretending, not hiding.

And as I lean in to him and press my lips to his, feeling him tense at first, then relax and give under my touch, neither am I.

I float back down the stairs and through the corridors, and all of them feel warmer and brighter than before – until I turn a corner and walk straight into Amy.

She blinks at me. "What are you doing back here? I thought you were out front?"

"I…thought I saw a mouse?" It's literally the first thing that comes into my head, but anything is better than letting her know what I've really been doing. This – as far as Amy is concerned – would definitely count as "a distraction".

"Remind me to speak to the team about getting some traps down here. We've had problems with mice before."

"What about the cat? Surely the point of a theatre cat is that they actually catch the mice?"

Amy laughs. "That cat couldn't catch a mouse if it was lying flat on its back in the middle of his food bowl. Whatever Roly says." She runs a practised eye over me, over the corridor, then jerks her head back in the direction of the stage. "You've not seen Luke, have you? Rick wants a quick word with him."

"Luke? Nope. No. Not seen him in ages." I shake my head, but in my pocket my hand closes around a pair of folded cardboard figures – tiny in scale, but to me they couldn't possibly feel any bigger.

ACT FOUR, SCENE FOUR

When I get back to the creative desks in the auditorium, an enormous sheet of paper has been unfolded on the floor of the main aisle, and Rick and Nina are staring at it. Rick's arms are folded across his chest and he's chewing gum again, while Nina is scribbling notes on the sheet in orange Sharpie, occasionally glancing over at the rigging bars, which have been lowered all the way down from the grid and have come to a stop about a metre above the stage. Chris and another of the flymen are sitting on the edge of the stage, swinging their feet back and forth, while a couple of the actors have started what looks like a game of poker in the front row of the stalls. The dress rehearsal may be tomorrow, but apparently this is one of those decisions that Rick won't rush. Everybody else just has to wait.

"You've got orange pen on your ear," I whisper at Nina as I edge past her. She shakes her head, glancing up at me from the page.

"I put it in my mouth earlier – and I can't remember

which way round it was. I'm too scared to go look in a mirror."

"No, you're good." I give her a thumbs up, and Rick – obviously happy with the new changes to the lighting – shouts to the flymen. They jump up surprisingly lightly, and head back to the fly-floor, while Amy jogs to the front row. "Two minutes, everyone!"

I lean back across to Nina, pulling my headset around my neck, and grab her as she goes by. "Everything okay?"

She rolls her eyes. "Yeah, it's fine – just the blue light gel being one shade too blue in the end. I think I wrote the wrong one down? Or maybe Clare from the lighting department did? I don't know. *Somebody* did, anyway. I don't even know how he spotted it. I wouldn't have."

Chatter from the fly-floor fills my ears as I slip the headset into place, and I flip on the microphone.

"Quiet on the channel, please, we're almost ready to start."

They carry on chatting as though they didn't hear me.

I know they heard me.

I try again, clearing my throat extravagantly beforehand into the bargain. "Quiet on the channel, please."

They just keep on babbling. Is this another test? It feels like everything is a test with these guys – checking that you're for real, making you earn every single drop of respect.

But then, isn't that what I wanted? To earn it, not just have it handed to me because of who I was?

I listen to them and I look at the row of switches on the desk. If I flip this one up, and that one down, and then I switch the mic on…

I slip the headset down to my neck as feedback howls across the system – and when I pull my cans back over my ears, everything is quiet.

"Are we finished chit-chatting?"

"Standing by," says the voice I recognize as Chris.

Amy settles back in her seat and nods at me.

"Take the lighting rig out, please?"

"Lighting rig going out."

Slowly, the lights rise from the stage and disappear into the gloom of the grid, high above the stage.

"Lighting rig out," says Chris.

I nod back at Amy.

And here we go again.

The afternoon flies by, broken only by a tea break. And nobody's particularly keen on dragging that out, either – everyone's too focused on getting the job done. The dress rehearsal looms, and with forty-eight hours until we're doing this for real – in front of actual people – the clock isn't ticking so much as spinning wildly out of control. The dinner break passes largely unnoticed – except for the appearance of Roly at the back of the auditorium. She crashes through the doors, her arms full of pizza boxes, the pile almost too high for her to see over.

"Somebody order pizza?"

There's a stampede of creatives, techs and actors to grab a box from the stack, and gradually her face appears from behind them.

"Animals, the lot of you. *Animals*." But she laughs and shakes her head as she turns back to the stage door.

Sometime around eight, my phone pings with a message. It's my mother. I ignore it.

Sometime around eight thirty, my phone pings with another message. It's still my mother. I still ignore it.

Sometime around nine, my phone pings with yet another message. She never gives up. I throw it in my bag without looking at it.

Sometime around nine thirty – although time no longer has any real meaning and it could already be next month for all I know – Rick calls it. We're finally done.

"That's it for tonight, everybody – thank you very much! We'll see you in the morning for a full dress, please. Get a good night's sleep – it'll be another long day tomorrow." Amy claps her hands as the remaining actors amble across the auditorium to collect their valuables from the storage box. Some of them mumble goodnight, some of them leave without so much as a thank you. All of them look tired and emotional.

"Creatives! Tech meeting and breakdown in five minutes, please."

Nina, slumped back in her seat, mutters something about having an *actual* breakdown. I drop the headset on my prompt desk and flick off all the lights and switches. My copy of the script is covered, margin to margin, with notes and scribbles, and – on the bottom corner of the last page – a slightly wonky heart with what could be the letters H and L in the middle. Maybe. If you looked at it the right way.

I rub it out before anyone has the chance to see it.

Especially George.

Even *more* especially Luke.

The creative meeting isn't as bad as I'd expected – it's only fifteen minutes, and mostly just Rick running through the changes he's made during the tech compared to Nina's and Amy's notes. There aren't many, not by this stage. Any last hiccups should show up in the dress tomorrow, and then? Then, it'll be opening night…and there's no going back.

I check off the list by the stage door. It looks like almost everyone has signed out; even Roly's putting her coat on.

"Are you off?" she asks, winding her scarf around her neck.

"More or less. I've just got to get some stuff from the production office."

...And check the theatre model.

I want to see whether it's changed; whether *he's* changed it. I haven't seen him since we talked in the Heffernan Room, and that already feels like an age ago. A part of me was hoping he'd be hanging around here, or send me a message or...

My phone.

I guess I can't hide from it for ever – and it's probably better if I at least know how much trouble I'm walking into when I get home.

There are a lot of messages on my phone when I pull it out of my pocket: my notifications fill the screen. It mostly reads *Priya, Priya, Priya, Priya, Priya...* but the most recent (all seven of them) are from Mum.

Call home.

Call me at home.

Call me at home, please.

Why aren't you replying?

Call me.

Are you coming home soon? I need to talk to you.

Call me. It's important.

Gulp.

I spent so long thinking about Luke today that I had sort of forgotten about what those photos could do *outside* the theatre. No. I didn't forget. I blanked it out. Stuck my head in the sand and went full ostrich about it. But the pictures are still out there, aren't they? I stare at the string of messages. No. Mum would never have even *heard* of *SixGuns*, let alone go on the site. And the thought of her on one of Tommy's fan sites is just silly…

But still…

I take a deep breath and dial.

"Hi. You wanted me to call?"

There's a frosty silence, then finally: "Hope Parker, what on earth do you think you're playing at?"

"Sorry?"

Keep calm, keep calm…

"I have left dozens of messages on your phone. I even called the theatre…"

"*WHAT?*"

"But Priya said you were busy with something urgent and she'd let you know I rang."

I raise my eyes in a silent prayer of thanks for Priya. I guess that explains why there's so many messages from her too.

"Ummm. Sorry. It's been really manic."

"So I gather." A deep sigh. "Well? What do you have to say for yourself?"

Okay. She's obviously expecting something – but I'm not stupid enough to own up to *anything* unless she says it first. Basically, I need to know how bad the damage is before I can figure out what I need to do to limit any more. So I go with something safe and, hopefully, neutral.

"Sorry?" I try.

"Sorry? *Sorry?*" She pauses, and I hold my breath because this is still my mother, and any second now…

I really don't have to wait long.

"I should think you're sorry. All day I've been trying to reach you, and *nothing*. You *knew* I needed your help getting this dress boxed up, and you promised you'd be back in time to give me a hand with packing the train…"

The premiere dress!

A wave of relief hits me – instantly followed by guilt. I did promise, didn't I? On my way out this morning, right after she told me that "wearing black drains you, darling".

"Getting the netting folded into the box without crushing it is a two-person job…"

"The courier's coming at eight…"

And right before I sailed out of the door, I said I'd definitely help. And I meant to. I would have. I didn't think, did I? I should have known tech would go on this late.

No wonder she's angry. I let her down.

"Oh, god. I completely forgot. Things here got…"

"Got what, exactly?"

"Out of hand."

"Out of hand? In the marketing department?" She makes a clicking sound with her tongue against her teeth.

"I *am* sorry." It sounds a bit pathetic, but it's all I can say.

"Hmmm."

More clicking. But it sounds like this was all she wanted; not even to be mad at me about the dress – not really – but to be mad that I wasn't replying to her messages.

Which can mean only one thing.

She doesn't know about the photos.

I'm safe.

I apologize, and I apologize, and just for good measure I apologize some more, and tell her I'll be home as soon as I've finished. When I hang up, my hands are clammy and shaking – I can't tell if it's from tiredness, or sheer relief.

"Just make sure the door shuts behind you, right?" Roly, still waiting behind the desk with her coat on, looks pointedly at the heavy fire-escape bar across the stage door. She pauses, then nods once, and with that, she disappears down the stairs and off into the night.

Down in the production office, the model box is, at first glance, still empty. But when I look closer, heart pounding with hope and fear muddled all together, there's a little square of fabric on the stage. That doesn't make any sense. I pick it up and turn it over, rubbing it between my fingers. There's no note, no message; it's just a bit of cloth.

I turn off the lights, tucking the big red rubber band-wrapped folder Amy asked me to pick up under my arm, and walk back through to the wings and the pass door to get my things from under the prompt desk, stepping out into the front of the stalls. The auditorium is dark.

Typical.

No, wait. There is a light, a dim one, coming from a single bulb in a wall socket at the side of the stage.

The ghost light.

Like actual ghosts and cats, every theatre has a ghost light. Some people believe the ghost light's there to give the theatre ghosts the chance to perform if they want to – they say it's there to light their way across the stage or the stalls.

Others will tell you it's so the cleaning staff (and crew like me, hanging back after hours) don't fall off the stage and break their non-metaphorical legs in the dark.

I guess which you believe depends on how romantic you think the theatre is…

Right now, it's so still and so silent that I really, really don't want to think about ghosts.

Either way, light or not, the auditorium is still pretty dark, and I've left my stuff scattered all over my desk and my bag underneath it. Picking everything up in this light is going to be a pain in the neck. I move back along the seat rows, my hands checking off the ends as I go.

Row A, B, C, D, E…cross-aisle…F, G…

I step into the row and start shuffling along, counting the seats in the gloom as I go. If I look ahead of me, I can just about make out the lump of the prompt desk looming over the seats around it.

Halfway along the aisle, there's a sound.

It could be a footstep…up on the stage.

No such thing as ghosts. No such thing as ghosts.

I shuffle along the row faster.

There it is again.

It's a footstep. It is.

Someone's on the stage – somewhere. The ghost light's too faint for me to see them, but there is, I think, the faintest outline of…something?

"Hello? Who's there?"

My heart has somehow climbed into my throat and is beating so hard against the inside of my neck that I'm amazed it isn't what I hear when I open my mouth to speak.

There's no answer, but there's another footstep – and something else. Something that sounds like…fabric moving?

"Seriously. You can't be here. Who's up there?"

I stand as tall as I can and peer into the dark.

There's a click, and something moves on the stage…

And then the whole auditorium is flooded with light.

It's so sudden that my eyes spasm in shock, and I want to put my hands up to shield them.

I blink away the dazzle, and there he is.

"You didn't reply to my message." Luke is leaning against

the temporary steps up to the stage. Behind him, the iron safety curtain is down, and despite myself I wonder who brought it in. It must have been Amy…

"You messaged me? I don't remember giving you my number."

"George did – although you know it's on every call sheet as the emergency contact number, don't you?"

"Oh." I hadn't thought of that. But I'll decide what to do with George later. Throttle him or thank him – it could go either way. Maybe both?

"Sorry. I've not really checked it today."

"Look, about earlier…I wanted…" He clears his throat, but then his eyes meet mine and instead of slipping away from me, this time his gaze stays with me. "I wanted to apologize. For how I was, and for not being clear, I guess. I wanted…I just wanted to do the right thing."

"And instead, we both ended up feeling crap about everything."

"I suppose at least we did it together?" He tips his head to one side and rubs the back of his neck. "Come on." He swings himself up onto the step and leans out to me, holding out a hand. The stage lights catch his hair and standing there, smiling and waiting, to me he looks like he might be Lancelot for real, or a fairy-tale prince. What can I do but take his hand, and fall into the fairy tale with him?

His fingers close around mine, gently pulling me up onto

the stage. The second my foot hits the boards, the lights change – I can see them shift from white to a pale golden pink. *Summer dusk filter* says the part of my brain that is all theatre, all the time. The rest of my brain tells it to shut up. I don't want to know how it's done, or see the wires and the cogs, just for once. I only want to be here, now, with him. From somewhere on the fly-floor I hear a voice shout "Iron going out!" There's the sound of feet on a ladder, and a door banging – then quiet, and slowly, slowly, the safety curtain rises up and away.

Behind it is a forest – or maybe less a forest than a glade in an enchanted woodland. Ancient trees crowd in before a blue sky, and moss-covered boulders lie in dappled shade. There's a picnic blanket laid out in a patch of sunlight, and a couple of cushions and a picnic basket, and I can hear birdsong and the quiet babbling of a stream, smell the moss of the forest floor. Somehow he's managed to transport us through time and space to somewhere altogether different.

"How…how did you…?"

"I called in a few favours to set things up. And then a few more to clear backstage. Oh, and raided the pantomime backcloths."

The imaginary leaves of the imaginary trees shift in an imaginary wind as the filters on the follow-spots rotate, but I can't help waiting for the cool of the breeze on my face. When it doesn't come, it feels wrong, somehow – and then

I look at him, and he's laughing at me.

I laugh at me too.

"This is *amazing*. I just…I mean, it's like magic."

He beams. "I'm glad you like it. I thought if I was going to apologize, I should do it properly."

"Properly means grovelling. I'm not getting grovelling from this. I'm getting…picnic."

"Concise. My acting tutor would like you. Does that mean you accept?"

"Not sure, really. Needs more grovelling. You need to really explore how sorry you are. Seriously," I add, lowering my voice.

"Ah. So close. Sorry – no picnic for you. Thanks for coming…" He lays his hands on my shoulders and steers me back to the steps, and I want to memorize the feel of every single one of his fingers…but I'm not letting him off so lightly. Not when I finally feel like I'm getting to see who Luke *is* underneath, in person and not just from notes on a script. I duck out from under his grip and sidestep him. "After you've gone to all this trouble? No way."

I mean it as a joke, of course I do – but he doesn't take it as one.

"I was serious. I really *am* sorry. I am." He's barely a step away from me; his eyes sweeping my face as though it's the only thing in the world. "I can be whatever you want me to be," he whispers…

"*That* –" I poke the middle of his forehead – "is the very definition of acting."

He laughs and swats at my finger. "My tutor would *definitely* love you." He nods at the blanket, which of course is exactly the same as the fabric square from the model, scaled up. Automatically, I rub the cloth in my pocket between my fingers. "Come on," he says. "I'm starving."

So am I. The pizza feels like a long time ago, and my stomach growls as he opens the basket.

He raises an eyebrow at me. "What was that?"

"Sound effect. Obviously. Distant thunder." Or something. "Which reminds me – is it my imagination, or does it really smell like a forest up here?"

"Does it matter?" He pulls out a giant packet of Hula Hoops and flourishes it at me.

"Wow. Nothing says sorry like barbecue beef flavour crisps… Wait a minute, you've got the air freshener going, haven't you? You have!" I peer around him into the wings – and there it is. A squat box with a couple of red lights and a large vent on the front: what everyone calls the "air freshener" because it's actual name is long and fiddly and – frankly – nobody has the time. It works a lot like a dry-ice machine, only for smells. Just drop in a cartridge, switch it on and – presto – instant atmosphere: everything from spring flowers to coal smoke. Instant *expensive* atmosphere – the cartridges cost more than the entire budget of most of the things I've worked on at the Square Globe.

He rolls his eyes and opens the crisps. "I bet you were always the kid who saw a magic trick and immediately started trying to figure out how it was done, weren't you?"

I pointedly look down at my black clothes. "Now, you see, *I* am the very definition of behind-the-curtain. Figuratively, literally, actually. I'm a vanishing act. Watch me put on my blacks and disappear." I wave my hands in front of my face in a semi-mystical manner.

He laughs quietly and crunches a crisp, then holds out the packet to me. "Don't you ever wish you could switch it off? The needing to see how it's done?"

Apart from now? That's a big question, isn't it? Because if I didn't see how it was all done – if I didn't see the rigging and the wires, and the actors learning (and forgetting) their lines and blocking, trying out the different ways the parts all fit together to make a whole; see all the props and the scenery and the make-up and the rest of it – if I only saw the illusion…I wouldn't be me, would I? I'd be one of the people in the audience, the people wanting to be swept away – not one of the people waiting to do the sweeping.

Luke. This. Now. It's the first time I've felt this way. What does that even mean?

Theatre, Mum always says, is life. Infinitely finite, here for the shortest time and then gone. Barely a flicker on the needle of the universe, hardly more than a single wave out on the ocean.

But it *is* here.

Whatever it is that I'm feeling now, it's *here*. I can't pin it down, can't annotate it or block it out on the stage, but it still exists. It's still happening.

I'm not going to tell him all this. Inside my head, it's fine – but the second I try to say it, it would turn into a hopelessly jumbled, pretentious pile of crap. So I go with the next-best option and look him in the eye.

"Do you?"

"What, wish I could switch it off?" His brow creases as he thinks about it, and he flops back on one of the cushions, staring up at the grid above us. "I don't know. I guess it probably isn't the same for me."

"How come?"

It's a long time before he answers – although I can see he almost does at least twice before he finally speaks, changing his mind each time. At last, he makes a sound a little like a laugh, but sad. So sad it makes the inside of my chest ache.

"Because I think my whole life's been about trying on someone else's skin. It's the only thing I know how to do."

"Acting, you mean?"

"No. Not just acting. Not like that." He peers into the crisp packet as though the answer is at the bottom of it. "You remember I told you about my parents?"

I nod, wanting to give him the space to speak.

"They were both actors. They met when they were both in different productions and my dad's friend knew someone in my mum's show. The two of them went to watch it on their night off, and he saw her and that was it. And then they had me." His eyes shift from one thing to another, skimming across the stage, the lights, the whole theatre. Never quite settling on anything, let alone me. He scratches his nose as though it's been bothering him, and if I can see the acting happen, I can see what's below it too. I know why he does it. "I always wondered when I was a kid whether I'd be someone different if they were still around."

The silence of the auditorium listens to him, taking in each of his words.

"I never knew," he says – and without realizing it, he's slipped into his stage voice, the one with polished edges, the one that cuts through everything else – "whether I wanted to be an actor because it's somehow in my blood, or whether I'm just looking for the person I was meant to be. Whether the next script will show me what I'm supposed to do. Whether that's where the answers are."

"I don't believe any of us are *supposed* to be or do anything – we're just…us." It sounds less confident than it would if I didn't have a mouthful of crisps, but I mean it.

"You reckon? You think you'd have wanted to work in the theatre if your mother hadn't?"

"I don't know. I don't think any of us can know that, because it's not like we can see the other versions of ourselves, is it?" I play with the cap of a bottle of water. "How did…I mean, do you want to talk about it?"

He shakes his head. "I honestly don't remember much about them. I was just a kid. They died in a car crash, on their way to a rehearsal."

"I'm sorry."

"There's nothing to be sorry for. I barely knew them, when you think about it, and they never got the chance to know me. Like you said, we never get to see the other versions of ourselves, and Gran's been all the family I've needed – it's why I've always wanted to take care of her. She's taken care of me, and I feel like I owe it to her. Although she'd be *mortified* if she heard me say that."

"That's why you take all those jobs here? The bar, the front of house – all of it?"

He shrugs, but the corner of his mouth twists into a smile of recognition. "Gran freaked out when I told her I wanted to go to drama school. Completely, totally lost it. I'd never seen her like that – and the worst thing was that she wouldn't tell me why."

"Because of your parents?"

"I guess that was it. Maybe she thought if I did the same thing as them, one way or another she'd lose me too. I didn't think to ask. I just got angry about it. It felt like she was telling me she thought I'd fail, that there was no point in trying. The one thing that felt natural, that felt real and easy…and from where I was standing, she didn't think I could do it. I thought she was trying to protect me. That's what grans – grandparents, parents, whoever – do, right?"

"Maybe she was trying to protect herself?"

"I think maybe she was. Which makes me feel even worse."

"Why?"

He closes his eyes and takes a breath, then looks up at me through half-lowered lashes. "Because I auditioned anyway, and I didn't tell her until I got in."

Something curls around my heart; something that wasn't there before.

We're the same.

Two figures standing on the stage of a model box: one in the spotlight, one in the shadow, but each holding onto the other.

And because we're the same – and I know that now, as much as I know anything – I can tell him. I can tell him all of it, and trust that he'll understand.

"I think…I think I wanted to be part of the theatre *despite* my mother. She was always talking about theatre, and half the time we had other people coming in and out of the house to talk about plays or costumes or whatever – but that's just it." I stop, because this, more than anything, needs the right words. I try again. "My sisters, both of them, they're smart. Smarter than I am. They knew that only an insane person would follow Mum into the theatre, because everywhere you go, everyone you speak to, all you hear is 'She's Miriam Parker's *daughter*' and suddenly you have no idea whether things would be different if you weren't. And nobody else does either. There's always this nagging little doubt in the back of their minds – did you earn this, or did your name? Are you there because of what you can do, or who you know? And it goes on and on, until that little doubt that everybody else feels? You feel it too." The Hula Hoop I've been rolling around my palm breaks apart. "But the thing is, it was always just this for me. Theatre or nothing."

I drop what's left of the crisp into my mouth, and when I look over at him I can *see* that he gets it. Gets me. Gets this whole ridiculous thing I'm trying to do. "I've only told you and George about Mum. I haven't told anyone else, and I didn't tell my parents that I was applying for this. I didn't tell them when I got it, either. They think I'm working in the back office of the Square Globe, and I've convinced my best friend there to basically lie for me. For this."

"Why?"

"Because I wanted to do it on my own. And just for once, I wanted to be sure that it was all on me."

The lights glitter on the wires hanging from the grid, and from where I am – lying back on the blanket, my head resting on a cushion – if I close one eye and squint, they look a little like stars. In the stillness of the empty theatre it feels as if we could really be in the woods. If only there was a sky above us and not a fly-tower; if only the birdsong wasn't on a fifteen-minute loop, the same bird call repeating and repeating and repeating…

I know I should tell him this is a bad idea – that someone, anyone, *Amy*, might come back, might see us – but this feels right. Like it's where we're both meant to be and here is the place we're both most ourselves. I felt it the moment I saw him standing at the bottom of the staircase, looking up at me. Maybe even before that.

How could I get to know him anywhere else?

How could *he* get to know me?

We're the only people here. The theatre feels like it belongs to us.

He said he's cleared backstage – and he has. I heard the door…so how's he going to shut down the lights?

And the sound loop?

I look round at Luke, stretched out alongside me on the blanket, with his arms folded behind his head. He opens an eye and squints at me.

"What?"

"Are we on our own here?"

"Of course we are! What kind of question's that?"

"The lights, the sound…everything's still *on*."

"I told you, I called in a couple of favours and got it all

set up. The only thing we've got to do is turn off the master switch and it'll take out everything but the ghost light and the usual emergency lighting." He grins. "You should know that, though – right?"

I should. Whoops. "But how do *you* know about it?"

"Ah, you know. You pick stuff up…"

What this means slowly dawns on me. "You've even worked backstage, haven't you?"

He clears his throat awkwardly. "Work's work."

"Is there anything here you *haven't* done?"

He considers this, pursing his lips. Eventually he says, "I haven't done anything in finance."

I don't know whether to laugh or take him seriously. "Always here? Your jobs?"

Like I don't already know the answer. It's because he *has* to be here. It's where he's meant to be. Just like me.

He fidgets again, rubbing at the neck of his T-shirt, and shrugs. "Got to pay the bills somehow, right? Everyone here knows me – knows about Gran and my mum and dad too – and when there's work they ask me first."

"Oh." That wasn't quite the answer I was expecting and he knows it.

"You were hoping I'd say it's where I belong. Sure it is, but I'm just lucky it's worked out that way so far. I can't afford to be picky. There's dream jobs and just-jobs – and people here look out for each other." He keeps on rubbing at the neck of his shirt, like something there itches. "Unless you're someone like Tommy, acting's not exactly the best-paid job in the world, and neither Mum nor Dad left a lot of money. And Gran…" He tails off. "What?"

"What what?"

"What are you looking at me like that for?"

"Like what?" I blink at him, hard and fast enough to make myself dizzy.

"Like *that*."

"Nothing. It's just…" *It's just I didn't see that coming. I didn't see you coming.* "…just that I'm trying not to be worried you're going to have a crack at my job too. Seeing as you know all this stuff." I shrug.

He opens his mouth, then closes it again, as though I've surprised him. And then he smiles at me. "Okay. I see what you're saying." He puts a hand flat against his chest, tipping his face back towards the lights. "You feel threatened by my talent." He flicks at his hair – and I get what he's doing. It's a pretty good impersonation of Tommy. More than pretty good – it's uncanny.

"Don't." I'm half-laughing, but it still feels like what he's doing is a little mean.

"Fine." He eyes me, and something in the set of his jaw shifts; the way he holds his shoulders…and suddenly I'm looking at Rick, only with Luke's face. Which is very confusing indeed.

"Enough! Seriously." I throw a cushion from the hamper at him and it bounces harmlessly into the stalls. Luke laughs and turns back into himself. "Are all actors such tremendous show-offs?"

"I couldn't say. I can only answer for me." He laughs again, and takes a swig from the water bottle. "And I'm not, by the way. Not really."

I raise both my eyebrows at him. "That little performance wasn't showing off?"

"No." His smile fades, and suddenly he's serious again. "I just wanted to make you laugh."

The whole theatre twists around me; the pillars shifting in their places.

"The only thing that would make me laugh right now is the thought of you backstage, doing a crew job. Sorry, but I refuse to believe you've done that – no way are you the type."

"You don't think I could? Or *have*?"

"Nope."

"You're wrong."

"Prove it." I fold my arms across my chest.

"I don't have to prove anything." He shakes his head, laughing again. But this feels so real, so easy that I can't let it slip away. I can't let him slip away into one of those other faces he wears.

"You sound pretty confident about that." I pause for effect.

"Or maybe you just know you'd lose."

"Try me." His voice is half-laugh, half-growl, and almost enough to make me fall straight into him.

Almost.

"Okay, then – seeing as you're sure. A challenge. First one to the Heffernan Room wins."

"Wins what?" He sits upright. Obviously I have his full attention now.

"Bragging rights to a full and complete knowledge of the Earl's Theatre."

He snorts. "You know I'll win this. Easily. You're sure you even want to try?"

"If you're so confident, how about this? You can only use the backstage areas. No foyer, no stalls, *only* backstage."

"You can't get to the Heffernan from backstage. That's a trick and you know it," he says, and I pretend I wasn't hoping he'd forget that in his enthusiasm to prove me wrong.

"Okay, you can use the main staircase – but only from the dress circle upwards. Fair?"

"Fair. But…" He leans forward and his voice is almost a whisper, drawing me in, beckoning me…

I flash him a knowing smile, half-lean towards him…

And then I run.

It catches him off-guard, and I'm almost at the door to the backstage corridor before he reacts – but when he does, he *explodes*. I see him making for the other side of the stage – he's heading for the fly-floor, and suddenly my head start doesn't seem quite so big any more.

I map the theatre in my head as I run, plotting each staircase, every corridor, just the same as blocking out movements onstage. Just the same as memorizing the layout of the wings, of the prop table, the quick-change sections. I can see it all, the whole labyrinth. If I take *this* set of stairs, *that* corridor; cut through this room…

I crash out of the door into the darkened Scott Bar – deserted. But as I reach the stairs up to the Heffernan Room, feeling the soft carpet tugging on my feet with every step, I hear the same door flung open again.

I make the bottom of the final flight of stairs, swinging myself around the curve of the banister, and take the steps two, three at a time, up and up past the glittering chandelier – still lit, even at night, its caged bulbs like captive stars shining with all their might.

Halfway up, I see him across the turn of the stairs, laughing between the cords and the lights.

He spots me looking back at him and stops; leans on the banister and raises an eyebrow at me. "There's still time to admit defeat, you know," he calls across the gap. "You're not going to beat me in a flat-out race to the top."

"Really? Watch me!" And I'm running again, racing up the last flight…

Behind me, so close, I hear his laugh, warm and open – even now, I want to step inside it.

I reach the very top, and both my feet hit the floor a second before I feel his fingertips brush against the small of my back.

Underneath the fabric of my T-shirt, my skin blazes where his fingers touched and I turn around to look at him, standing on the top stair like he's been waiting there all day.

"You lose," I manage to pant with the very last of my breath.

"Do I? You've not made it to the door yet…"

And I'm not going to. Neither of us are.

When I step back to make room for him on the floor, his lips curl into a smile and his arm curls around my back. And then he draws me closer, his fingers tilting my chin up towards him as he leans down to me. I can feel his heart pounding in his chest, and even though he's barely out of breath, its beat perfectly matches mine.

ACT FOUR, SCENE FIVE

I keep my head down walking towards the stage door on dress rehearsal day. To say Mum was annoyed when I got in last night would be like saying that musicals have "a bit of singing" in them. But then I saw the good morning message from Luke on my phone, and my feet have barely touched the pavement the whole way from my house to here – despite the fact Mum has now moved onto full sister-preparation mode. I got up this morning to find a whole load of my stuff dumped out of the bathroom cabinet to "make some space" for Faith and Grace. They're literally going to be here for two days. It's not like they're moving back in, is it? Although I guess at least I should be grateful Grace won't be able to use all my conditioner like she did last time.

But the minute I turn the corner to the theatre, I come back down to earth pretty hard. It's not just nerves, either – it's the crowd. One or two of the perpetual group spot me and actually *hiss* as I walk past – which is friendly. But then

I recognize the girl I spoke to before – the one who asked me about Tommy – and give her a weak smile. She smiles back, so that's something.

Roly's desk is empty, and there is nobody there to see me sign in a full, triumphant five minutes early. I wait there for a minute, just in case, but no. So I head into the auditorium (before waiting to tell someone I was early actually makes me late) sling my bag under the prompt desk and look over at the stage.

Rick is standing centre stage, chewing.

Arms crossed.

Uh-oh.

The actors stroll on, expecting Amy's usual morning walk-through…and seeing Rick, stop dead. There's some scuffling in the wings as someone obviously walks straight into the back of somebody else who has stopped, and a fair amount of shuffling and muttering.

And then he starts.

His voice seems to project from somewhere underneath his feet, never mind his chest or his diaphragm. It comes from a deeper place than that – like he's part of the building, rooted in it; pulling something out of it…or maybe giving it a voice of its own. That's what Rick does when he's up there, and it's a shock. I've got used to "Rick Hillier" just being "Rick", sitting there in his chair, making notes or giving them, rubbing his hands over his cropped hair when he's thinking, and I completely forgot what it's like seeing him on a stage. It's like watching a bird of prey in the air: they look intimidating enough on the ground but to see one circling above you, wings outspread, is to know where it belongs.

"I know you're all keen to get on with the dress this morning, and we've got a lot to do – but one thing before we start."

Everyone blinks at him, waiting.

"It's come to my attention – the theatre's attention – that someone was here after hours."

Silence.

"And while this wouldn't be too much of a concern on most productions, well…obviously, there's a lot riding on this one and there's the question of spoilers and insurance and…"

No. No no no no no.

How does he know? Oh, god. We left stuff at the side of the stage, didn't we? I shoved it over into the wings and I meant to clear it away and then…*Luke*…and I completely forgot. This is it, isn't it? This is me done. This will be the final, final thing, won't it?

"It was me."

Everyone turns and looks towards the stall doors, where Tommy is leaning against the end seat of the last row.

"Sorry," he adds. He doesn't sound remotely sorry.

Rick folds his arms again, his toes almost on the very edge of the stage.

"You?"

Just like Tommy doesn't sound sorry, Rick doesn't sound convinced.

"I came back to work on a scene. By myself."

"You signed out..."

"Yes, I know. I came back. Later." He raises an eyebrow at his brother. "And yes, I forgot to sign back in. Sue me."

"The producers might," mutters Rick – just loudly enough to be sure he's heard – then pins Tommy with a hard stare. All Tommy does is study his nails. It's possibly the most Tommy thing I've ever seen, and Rick has absolutely no answer.

"Well, then. If that's all cleared up, I'll hand over to Amy, and then we'll get started. There's one or two odd scenes I know she wants to go over one more time, but once we kick off the main rehearsal, we'll be running straight through. Any concerns or questions, save them for the end. Have a good dress, everyone."

Amy takes over, running through all the usual health and safety warnings, a couple of points about some scenery that's been brought up from the workshop...but none of it sticks. It flies in through one ear and out of the other, because all I have room for in my head is *why*? Why did Tommy lie – and why did he lie to cover for us? For *me*?

I scramble past the desks to the end of the row, but before I can grab him, Amy calls my name. Reluctantly, I let Tommy go and watch as the door to backstage closes behind him.

"Hope?"

"Yes, coming. Sorry, Amy." As I clamber onto the apron of the stage, I try not to look back over at the wings. I should have put everything away...

"Did you get all that?" Amy's voice cuts through my thoughts like a buzzsaw. I blink at her – and to my surprise, she laughs. "You're tired, I know. This is how it feels at the end of every technical rehearsal period – it's the same for everyone."

I nod. This is all she's looking for, because she continues.

"I've got something nice and straightforward for you this morning before we start the full dress. Tommy and George are working on that final quick-change – you know the one? In the crossover downstairs." She holds out a stopwatch. "Tommy only has ninety seconds to get offstage after the blackout, get downstairs, change and then come back out onto the other side before the lights come up. Ninety seconds. That's the longest we've got for the scene change. Thirty seconds each way up and down the stairs and to get clear of the wings, which means he's got to do the complete change and the crossover in what's left – and he's got two fire doors to get through on the way. Can you take this down and time them?"

"Time Tommy changing?"

"God knows he needs the help."

As I kick the backstage door open, I wonder what all Tommy's adoring fans outside would make of *this*…

Neither Tommy nor George are particularly pleased to see me when I walk through the door downstairs to find George holding a bundle of clothes and Tommy standing shirtless in the middle of the corridor, with a shoe in one hand. "Faaaabulous," he mutters sarcastically – but that's nothing compared to what he says when he sees Amy's stopwatch in my hand. Normally, this whole situation might be pretty cool (seriously: shirtless superstar) but right now all I can think about is getting this done. The faster this goes, the sooner we can get to the rehearsal, and the quicker that's done, the sooner I can get home – hopefully before anyone (namely my sisters) has a chance to start talking about me behind my back, like they usually do. The only bright point is that at least if *they'd* seen the photos of me online, one or both of them would have been straight on the phone to Mum and as nobody's called me to yell at me – not about that anyway – I must still be okay. Even so, I can do without all the predictable niggling little comments, especially right before opening night. Either way, today is going to be *all* about timing.

"Sorry." I shrug, trying not to actually look at him. "But you've only got thirty seconds to get from here…" I walk straight past him, right along the corridor to the far end, "to here *and* do a full change. And you've not done it in under forty-five so far."

"Well, I can't. It's ludicrous," Tommy snaps, dropping the shoe and shoving his foot into it so hard that the elastic laces make a loud *twang*. "Why can't I just use the crossover behind the backcloth instead of all this sprinting up and down stairs?"

"Because the crew will be using it at that point. You've seen how much set there is to clear, and you know how long there is to do it. The best way is just to push everything back…"

"Even if that means I have to do this?" He flaps a shirt at me so hard that the sleeve snaps out through the air like a whip.

"Over and over and over. Ready?" I hold up the watch as he wriggles back into the shirt. "Ready, George?"

Both of them roll their eyes, and I ignore them both.

"Reset… And three, two, one…"

"This is ridiculous!" Tommy's howl of frustration bounces off the bare concrete of the corridor as he kicks the wall. Hard.

"That time was better – it really was. You got it down to…" I check the watch and decide it's probably best not to be too specific. Not since Tommy is now resting his forehead against the wall and muttering a long soliloquy of swear words at it, like it's somehow the wall's fault. I almost feel sorry for him.

"Look, we haven't got time to do another run right now. Rick wants to get the dress rehearsal started in a couple of minutes, so you'll get another chance at the end of that anyway." Nothing I say seems to be making any difference, good or bad. Tommy's not listening.

Now's my chance. I take a step closer, and even if he didn't hear me before, he obviously hears that, because he opens one eye and half-turns his head towards me.

"What now?"

"Tommy…"

"Spit it out, will you?"

"Earlier. When Rick said about someone being here last night…"

Was that the smallest glimmer of a smile? Or a flicker of triumph? It's gone too fast for me to be sure. I lower my voice. "You know, don't you? You know that I was here with…"

"With lover boy?"

Everything going through my head must be visible on my face, because he laughs quietly – but not unkindly. "Oh, yes.

I saw you. I *did* come back to work on a scene, funnily enough. I felt like I needed to clear my mind after...well, you know. That tabloid nonsense. So I thought I might as well do that. And I found the stage...shall we say, *occupied*?"

From the inside, my face feels hot enough to fry eggs on. I want the concrete to swallow me up and close over my head. Bury me under the theatre and have done with it. Tommy grins and shakes his head, pushing himself away from the wall. "You covered for me at the costume parade, didn't you? George told me that was all you. So look at this as my repaying the favour."

And with a flick of his head, he scoops up his shoes and pads away barefoot down the corridor without another word.

I didn't realize I'd done *him* a favour – I was just trying to do my job and keep everything and everyone running to schedule. Either way, though, I suppose it's worked out okay.

"What was all that?" George folds the second costume over his arm, ready to take it away for pressing.

"Just Tommy being Tommy, I think."

George nods as though he's listening, but he isn't really. He's *nervous*: nervous about the dress rehearsal, about the quick changes, about all his work finally needing to be on show, and he babbles away at me as we walk back over to wardrobe. Nathalie's already busy with someone in the make-up chair, and the radio's playing quietly in the background.

"Looks like I'd better give these to Jonna and get to work," George says, lifting his armful of clothes. I've got to know him well enough by now, even in this short time, to understand what the look on his face means, and I reach for his hand under the bundle, taking it in mine and squeezing it.

"You'll be ace. It's only the dress rehearsal – that means for you too. And they're only wigs. You're not fitting…I don't know, pacemakers or something. It's not life and death."

He blinks at me, then sniffs. "You know as well as anyone that theatre is *much* more important that *that*."

But as he says it, he squeezes my hand right back.

While Amy and Chris run through the fly cues one last time, I duck into a seat at the back of the auditorium. Sliding as far down into it as I can and resting my feet on the back of the seat in front, I call Priya.

"Hello, stranger."

"Funny."

"No, no. I don't know who this is. I mean, I thought it was my mate, but that was before she neglected to tell me she was hanging out with TOMMY KNIGHT. I had to find out like everybody else."

Ah.

"Look, I thought we'd sorted that…" It certainly felt like it after an hour messaging back and forth about Tommygate last night. The plus side is that because it's on *SixGuns* (which neither of them would ever *dream* of reading) at least it seems to have passed my parents by – which means that hopefully I don't ever have to have that particular conversation.

"And like I said, I get that you couldn't *tell* me it was *Piecekeepers*…"

"I knew you'd figure it out…"

"But you *could* have told me that you and Tommy were friends now."

"That wouldn't exactly be true."

"Seriously?"

I shuffle in my seat. "I'm sorry – they had me sign a confidentiality thing. I couldn't tell anybody. It wasn't just you, honest."

There's a long silence, then a sigh. However pissed off at me she may be, I know Priya will understand *that*.

"Fine. So how's it going at your secret theatre on your secret show with your secret star-slash-new best friend?"

I'm forgiven. For now… "Remind me what it's like to be outside? People keep talking about this thing called 'daylight', but I think that's a lie and it's all just another lighting filter."

THEATRICAL

There's a crash from somewhere behind the stage backcloth, but when I peer across the auditorium, nobody else is moving so I decide to ignore it.

"Don't pretend you're not loving every minute of it, Parker. And if you're not, I'm more than happy to trade places with you."

"Why? What are you doing?"

"Guess who – seeing as she *apparently* has nothing better to do during her Easter break – is helping her grandparents clean out their attic?" She shifts her phone, and something in the background crackles. "You have no idea what this place is like. There are spiders *everywhere*, and I just found a pile of magazines from 1982. Actual magazines that are older than I am. In the attic. And from the way my grandfather freaked out when I threw them down the ladder, they're apparently more precious than I am, too."

"You're taking them for the Square Globe props store, aren't you?"

She just laughs – of course she is. It's what we do. We scavenge, we borrow, we liberate.

I think back to my clunky old ex-Earl's headset at the Square Globe, and instinctively, I touch my ear where my current one should sit.

"Listen, Pree…I need a favour."

"Uh-oh."

"I *might* need one, anyway. I don't know yet…but can

you cover for me again?" I can practically hear her rolling her eyes, so I add: "Because you've done such a good job of it so far, and I'll owe you for ever?"

The crackling sound in the background stops. "Does this have anything to do with a certain leading man…?"

Seeing as I've been keeping her up-to-date about Luke in our messages, this conversation could go either way.

Not that I told her much, just his name. And what he looks like. And sounds like. And smells like. And how he acts. And…

I pretty much told her everything.

And then, of course, I remember that I'm talking to Priya, so she almost certainly meant Tommy.

"It's the dress rehearsal today, but Mum's ordered me home early to help her with dinner."

"They're definitely coming then?"

"Yep."

"You could always fake your own death. Get George to help you."

"It'll be fine. It's just…not a good time, you know? My head's full of stuff and…" I rub a hand over my face. I didn't realize how much I'd miss having Priya in the theatre with me, but suddenly the fact she's not there makes me feel overwhelmingly alone.

"Hey. Hey!" I can hear the boards of the attic floor creaking down the phone. "Don't you flake out on me.

No way. You're doing this – you're at the Earl's. Just like you always wanted."

"Yeah, but you're not here."

"And if I were in your place, I guarantee I wouldn't be chatting down the phone to you. I'd be living my actual best life in a professional theatre, just like you're going to do when you get off the line. Right after you get Tommy Knight's number for your oldest friend." She coughs pointedly.

"So if the rehearsal goes long, I can say I'm with you?"

"Sure. Or…and here's a revolutionary thought – are you ready? You could tell your mum what you're doing and make everything easier? She'd probably love it, you know."

"That's the problem. She would, and then she'd want to help, and I've had to dodge her once already when she turned up here…"

"You what? You didn't tell me that! She'll be so upset when she finds out!"

I hadn't actually thought about it like that.

But right now, with Amy striding across the stage and giving a thumbs up to Rick, it's not the time to think about it either.

"Pree, I've got to go, okay? I owe you – I'll make sure there's a ticket for you – I'll message you."

She shouts goodbye just before I hang up, and I stuff my phone into my pocket and slip back into the aisle.

ACT FOUR, SCENE FIVE

I drop into a seat behind the prompt desk. Amy's cueing the dress rehearsal, so just for once all I have to do is sit here and watch.

The lights go down, and the stage is dark…and it *starts*, and oh, my heart. Suddenly, everyone knows the steps, the notes. All the pieces have dropped into place and you can't see the hours, the weeks and months that have gone into it. It looks like everyone up there is saying the first thing that comes into their heads – not lines they've spent for ever learning, practising, trying with first one inflection and then another. Every time Jamie and Lizzie touch, it's like they can't not. Luke, *my* Luke, is not Luke at all, but Lancelot, pacing the floor of the Piecekeepers' tower and full of doubt and rage and despair… And even though I know he's under there, buried beneath someone else's soul, I feel almost guilty for the flutter in the pit of my stomach when he comes right to the front of the stage and stares into the auditorium. I can feel his voice echoing through every layer of my skin.

It takes me until the second half to realize I've stopped seeing Tommy and Juliet up there. I've stopped knowing that when Jamie runs a hand through Lizzie's hair, that pause – that tiny, tiny pause that lasts less than a single breath – isn't hesitation, it's Tommy keeping his hand from catching in Juliet's long wig. It doesn't look anything other than real.

THEATRICAL

And when it comes to an end, and they stop – that last line left hanging unsaid for luck – everyone else feels it too. It's like the building has come alive, like it's somehow smiling. Like the air's full of sparks or snow or…something magical.

When Rick stands and asks for the house lights, people trickle back onto the stage. He's smiling, and one by one, I see that same smile spread across every face up there; every face out in the auditorium.

Amy shuffles her notes together and sits back in her chair.

"We're there," she says.

I wish I could tell Luke how good he was, how good he is; I wish I could be waiting for him when he comes back up from the dressing rooms, but there isn't time. So I type a quick message to him, which is basically just a long string of exclamation marks and a heart…then I delete the heart. Then I put it back again, and add another one for good measure, before hitting *send* and stuffing my phone into my bag. Then I scoot from one side of the wings to the other, sweeping up bags, hats and assorted other bits of abandoned costume and throwing them all into a laundry basket from the quick-change area. All I've got to do is deliver this to George, pick up a folder from the office and I'm gone. And I'm not even *that* late. Sort of.

Wedging the basket under my arm, I shove the production office door open – and stop. All of the lights are off except one, right over in the corner – the one over the model box. Two little figures stand in the middle again, holding hands like before…but now they are turned to face one another, and above them is a tangle of thick red threads and tiny little golden globes.

Even when he isn't here, he is.

I smile and grab my folder, then flick off the light, leaving them alone together.

"You want to come hang out in the laundry?" George swings back and forth in the open doorway. "I've got some trousers to age with a cheese grater." He waves it at me to prove he's not making it up.

"Mmm. Tempting, but I've got to run." I shake my head and toss the basket of bags, hats and other bits of abandoned costume to him, checking my watch. "My mum's invited both my sisters home for a few days, so I've got an evening of family fun ahead of me and I'm already late." I stop wriggling into my coat and peer around him at the rack of costumes that need attention before tomorrow night. "Actually, do you want to swap? I'll take an entire night of ironing and trouser-grating if you'll go deal with my sisters…"

"Trouser-grating?"

"It's been a long day, George. Let it go."

"Mmm. Anyway, no deal. I've got enough sisters of my own, thanks, so a quiet night in an empty theatre is my idea of a good time."

"You have sisters?"

"Four." He holds up a hand, wiggling his fingers pointedly. "And a brother. But he's only eighteen months old, so he's not exactly much help."

"Wow. Four sisters?" I wince.

George closes his eyes and puts on a martyred expression. "Four."

"Are any of them coming to the show?"

"God, no. If I was doing the make-up for *Corrie*, they'd be well into it. Theatre, not so much. They think it's weird." He shrugs. "Are yours?" And then he catches himself and nods. "No. Of course not, because you've got your little secret thing going on, haven't you?"

"Look, I—"

"No, no." He interrupts me. "You need to get going, and it's none of my business. It's your life and everything – but have you maybe thought that you should just tell your mum? She seems really lovely, and even if you don't tell her, she's going to find out sooner or later…"

"And I've made it this far without her knowing, so let's cross our fingers it's later, shall we?"

"Like I say, your life. But it was good, wasn't it?"

"Today? It was *amazing*. And they all looked incredible."

"And you don't think that thing about dress rehearsals is true, right?"

"What thing?"

"A good dress means a bad first show?"

As soon as he says it I realize it's been scratching away at me all afternoon. A good dress rehearsal means a bad show. Always. If you believe in theatre superstitions, that is…

I squeeze his shoulder. "Don't overthink it. We're good. They were good, we were good. It's going to be fine. Everyone's worked so hard. We'll *make* it good. Like you said, we can't afford not to, right?"

"That's what I'm worried about."

ACT FOUR, SCENE SIX

Every single traffic light is red.

All of them, on every single road along my bus route.

We crawl, crawl, crawl along, stuck in the middle of an endless stream of cars, vans, lorries and other buses – none of them going anywhere fast. All the while, the second hand of my watch keeps ticking around. Ticking the time away.

I should have thought about this. I should have remembered that any bus takes twice as long in Friday night traffic. I should. I'm supposed to be good at the timing thing: I *have* to be. How can I keep everyone in a production running on schedule – how can I give *Tommy Knight* a hard time about taking an extra five seconds to change a shirt – if I'm always hopelessly late for everything?

I stare at my watch as though looking at it will slow down the flow of minutes, and promise the universe that if it lets me get home in time for dinner, I will never ever ever be late again.

Or at least not as often.

The universe answers with a phone call.

Of course it does.

"Hope, this is very disappointing…"

"I know, I know. I'm *sorry*. I'm on the bus, but the traffic…"

"I don't want apologies. I want you here, at home, where I asked you to be."

"I'll be there soon. I'm only five minutes away…"

In the background I can hear Faith's voice and Dad's too, low, and Grace laughing. A door shuts and the sound of the rest of my family vanishes.

"Why are you even on the bus? Why didn't you just walk like you usually do?"

Ah.

There *is* no bus from the Square Globe to home.

"I had to…there was…" My brain scrambles to come up with something – anything – and goes emphatically, *majestically* blank. "It's a long story, but I'm just down the road."

"How long did you say you're going to be? We're all waiting for you."

"I know, I know." I stand up and peer down the bus, down the road ahead. The traffic goes on for ever. "I'll try and get off – it'll be quicker." I squeeze my way down to the front of the packed bus, edging between other passengers – most of whom look at me with irritation – and tap on the driver's partition, pointing at the bus stop just ahead. It's meant to be for a different route number, but it's not like stopping here to let me off is going to delay everybody else. He nods and flicks on the indicator to pull in.

My mum's voice, still on the line, is far away yet oh-so-sharp as the bus doors creak open and I step down onto the pavement.

"Just get home, Hope. Now."

The house takes on a slightly different feel when my sisters are home, even from the street. There's a sort of Gracey-ness about the whole place, and Faith's car is parked right outside the gate. It's just as neat and prissy as she is.

The thing is, I love my sisters. I do. But I love them more when they're not actually around. As soon as they're here, I'm the baby again; a kid who doesn't know anything. And what makes it worse is that somehow, even though I don't mean to, I fall right into that. It's a role I'm destined to play every single time they come back for the weekend, and it *sucks*.

I kick the door shut behind me and drop my bag on the floor. There's Grace's overnight bag at the bottom of the stairs – the same old rucksack she's had for years, and the two tote bags she always has to bring with it because only half her stuff actually fits inside. And there's Faith's bag, although it's not really a bag, but some kind of complicated contraption made out of leather and brass and quite possibly the tears of small children. It's probably puppy leather, come to think of it.

The whole house smells like Mum's Proper Cooking, which is unusual at this time of year, when she's busy with award-show fittings and being whisked off to posh hotels to go over designs with stylists and stars, and dinner's more likely to be whatever we've got hanging around in the fridge and needs to be eaten before it goes off. When I was little and she was still working on theatre productions, she and Dad used to give these dinner parties for the theatre company at the end of a run, and I remember sitting on the stairs and listening to them talking and laughing as they ate, always trying to catch a glimpse of them all through the half-open door. My sisters always shut their doors and complained about the noise, but I wanted those evenings to last for ever. They made me feel like I was sitting on the edge of something special.

I'm not sure Faith and Grace are quite in the same league, but at least dinner still smells good – and I am *not* going to get into a fight with my sisters.

Not even Faith.

"Hope? Is that you?" Mum leans out of the kitchen door into the hall.

"Yeah, it's me."

THEATRICAL

"You promised you wouldn't be late. You promised me you'd be here."

"I'm sorry!"

"I just expected better from you, that's all. I don't know what's got into you lately – you come in at all hours of the evening, you don't reply to messages, you don't answer your phone, you dress differently… Is everything all right?"

"What? Yes! No, I'm fine. Everything's fine."

She isn't just annoyed that I've let her down – she's *worried* about me. A spike of guilt stabs my insides, but it fades quickly enough. Right now, I just need to be *normal*.

"I got home as soon as I could – I really did try to get back earlier." I kick my shoes under the chair by the front door and, taking a deep, calming breath, walk through to the kitchen.

It's like walking right back into a set – everything that made it our kitchen when I left this morning seems to have been swept away and replaced. The fruit bowl in the middle of the table no longer contains three wrinkled apples and a banana that's so overripe it's almost an entirely new shade of brown, a spool of white cotton thread, a grey button and two bits of junk mail about UPVC windows. No, now it contains an artfully-arranged pile of apricots and three pomegranates – and it's surrounded by candlesticks. Two of which I've not seen before.

Be. Normal.

"Those are nice – where are they from?"

"Oh, I saw them the other day in town. Your sister picked them up on her way – didn't you, Faith?"

Tucked away in the corner, sitting on the end of the old church pew where Mum likes to pile up her fabrics (which, like everything else in here, has been miraculously cleared and cleaned), my older sister raises a half-empty wine glass and smiles at me ironically.

I smile back, equally ironically. "Thanks for the offer of a lift, by the way. Really appreciate it."

The corners of her mouth twitch.

Be normal. Don't get in a fight. Normal normal normal normal.

"Do you need a hand with anything?" I look at the pristine table, already laid and set with dishes of rapidly cooling food. Mum follows my gaze and sighs dramatically. I'll take that as a no. "Okay, give me two minutes to change. I'll be right back…"

From the hall, I hear Mum calling after me. "Tell Grace to get out of the shower while you're there. You were so long, she thought she might as well go and have one now."

I make a run for it up the stairs. I need a shower too, and clothes that don't smell like the floor of the production office (damp and Wotsits, with a hint of stale biscuit and the faintest top note of oil), but it looks like getting clean isn't really an option now. A quick-change of my own, and I'll be ready to face an evening with my family. After all, I've managed a whole day of actors…

The bathroom door is firmly shut. Steam creeps out from underneath it, and I can hear someone singing over the noise of the shower.

"Graaaaaaaace!" I bang on the door. She stops singing… then carries on as though nothing has changed since she moved out.

Staring at the firmly locked bathroom door, I guess nothing really has.

"How's it going with your little work experience thing, then?" Faith makes a delicate circle in the air with her fork, jabbing it into a piece of chicken and then popping it into her mouth with a smirk. I'm almost disappointed she doesn't miss and stick it in her eye, particularly when she pulls a face at the fact it's gone cold. She could at least make *some* effort – like I am. "What is it you're doing again? Marketing?"

"Hope?" Mum taps the edge of her plate with her knife. "Your sister asked you a question."

"Hmm? Oh. Sorry. I wasn't listening." I ignore Mum's warning look and poke at a couple of peas. My fork misses, making a horrible scraping sound against my plate.

"Faith was asking about the office at the Square Globe," says Grace, heaping tepid mashed potato onto her plate.

"Except she wasn't asking. She was, as usual, being a bitch." Glancing up at the rest of the table and seeing the dagger-looks Mum, Dad and Faith are giving her, she rolls her eyes and adds, "Jesus, I was *kidding*?"

Right back to how we always were.

At least Grace is trying, though. Which is more than I can say for our sister.

"It's okay. I'm learning a lot, and—"

But that's not what Faith wants to talk about, is it? Only I don't see it coming until a fraction of a second too late...

"Mmm. Interesting. Great. Sure. And tell us about what you and Tommy Knight did to get in the papers?"

There's that smile again, the one I remember so well from years sitting across this table from her. The one she'd deploy right before she let some bombshell drop – how she knew I'd failed a test at school, or said or done *something*. She'd wait and wait...and then? Boom.

Just like now.

Boom.

There's Dad's sudden, emphatic coughing; the kind he always does when he's startled (usually it's when Mum announces just *how* much she paid per metre for a roll of fancy fabric). There's Grace sighing and sitting back in her seat, clearly thinking that she should have told Mum she was busy and couldn't come home this weekend. And then there's Mum, looking vaguely confused by all of it.

"Tommy Knight? Isn't he…?"

"It's nothing. Ignore her." I glare at Faith over the table, but it's too late.

"What's this about the papers?"

I go cold, then hot.

Then cold again.

Then hot *and* cold all at the same time.

What do I do? What do I do? What do I do?

I breathe, because breathing seems like a solid place to start.

I've got this. I have. I can fix this.

"I'm not in the papers. Tommy Knight's in the new show at the Earl's, and there was some stupid photo of him taken on the street and apparently I'm in the background. Like I said – nothing."

"Doesn't look like nothing to me…" And Faith plays her trump card, dropping today's paper on the table, folded open to the celebrity gossip pages. She clears her throat. "Hollywood hotshot Tommy Knight, spotted leaving his hotel earlier this week with a mystery brunette. Knight may be preparing to make his stage debut in the hotly-anticipated production of hit book *Piecekeepers*, but it looks like he's still found time to make friends. With his long-term girlfriend Emery Greenway rumoured to be flying over from the States for the opening night gala, it remains to be seen whether his most challenging performance will be to convince *her* that nothing happened…" She drops the newspaper with a look of triumph.

Oh. My. God.

I'm dead.

No, *she's* dead. Sister or not, I'm going to kill her. I really, very am.

The kitchen has gone completely quiet, and four pairs of eyes are looking right at me. There is nowhere to go. No amount of black clothing is going to hide me from this particular spotlight.

"Okay, so first – I was not coming out of his hotel. I was walking down the street with him. Secondly, it's *Tommy Knight*. Tommy Knight. And me? Hello? Do you think that's even likely?" I make a grab for the paper, but Faith is too quick and whips it back under the table.

Mum is staring at me, and Dad…well, he's gone into full Dad-mode, I can see it in his face. It's never far away at the best of times, but he falls into the trap of reverting to his Standard Assigned Family Role just like the rest of us, and now his "protective father" gene has been activated. If only he could be convinced to deploy that against his other daughters…or one of them, at least.

I give it one more try.

"Seriously, it's garbage. It's just somebody taking a photo and putting it online because *oooooh, Tommy Knight*. It doesn't mean anything. Nobody believes any of it, anyway."

"Faith?" Mum's voice is very calm and even. "May I see that, please?"

"The papers obviously believed it – enough to print it," Faith says as she passes the paper across the table and Mum unfolds it carefully, absorbing every word. Absorbing that photo – in which I very, very clearly not only know Tommy Knight but am having a conversation with him.

It's over.

After what feels like hours, and with every single second of the wait pressing down on me, Mum folds the paper again and smooths her fingers along the creases.

"Hope. Would you mind telling us what's going on, please?"

I open my mouth – but she holds up a warning hand.

"The truth this time, please. I think it's clear you've not been telling us that for a while – don't you agree?"

In my head, I hear a silent chorus of everyone who told me I should just come clean.

Well, I hope you're all pleased with yourselves.

Here goes.

"Okay, fine. So. The truth is that I *do* know Tommy – but that's it. We've been working together and that's all there is to it. I promise."

Mum rests her hands on the table in front of her. "Is it? Tommy Knight, at the Square Globe?"

I know, from her tone, from her eyes, from everything

about her, that she's caught me. She just wants me to admit it.

"No." I shake my head and dig my fingernails into my palms. "Not there. At the Earl's. I've…I've been working at the Earl's."

I see every one of their faces when I say it. Dad's frown, Faith's look of satisfaction. Grace's surprise…

And Mum.

Her face doesn't change – not at all, not even a flicker. Which only makes it worse.

"You're working at the Earl's." Her voice is low and desperately calm. "Doing what? Not, I presume, marketing mail-outs?"

"No." My own voice, now I hear it, sounds pathetically small and young; like a kid who's been caught out.

Which I guess is what I am now, isn't it? That's how I've always seen myself – as just a kid, pretending, hoping nobody finds out she doesn't know what the hell she's really doing… And look – it finally happened.

I just wasn't expecting it to be my family who discovered it.

"I've been working on the new show. The *Piecekeepers* one. As a stage management intern."

Mum's face still doesn't move. "And you've been lying to us. To me. All this time."

She'll find out sooner or later.

THEATRICAL

There's no room for excuses, no way I can ask Priya to cover for me – to *lie* for me – this time.

I take a deep breath. "Yes."

Nobody moves. Even the air in the room is completely still – as though none of us are even breathing. We are a tableau: a scene of a family dinner gone wrong. Secrets exposed, cracks opened...we're an actual theatre cliché.

"I think I'm going to go upstairs," I say to the silence, and push my chair back. I don't care that the legs scrape against the floor and squeal loudly. I don't even care that as I step away from it, the whole thing tips over and falls back with a crash. I walk out and up the stairs and I make it to my room. I close my door, sit on the edge of my bed and look at the posters, the photos of theatres, the model box, the piles of notes from this production sticking out from under the bed where I hid them.

I look at them, and then I calmly pick up my pillow, hold it over my face and scream into it until I can't scream any more.

When my door opens, I pretend I'm asleep. What I'm actually doing, of course, is lying on my bed in the dark, staring towards my ceiling and wondering how the hell I got myself into this mess. Because it really is a mess. Every time I blink, I see my parents' faces again: Mum's disappointment and hurt, Dad's disbelief and anger. I blink harder and the darkness blurs and smudges over itself. The floorboard next to my desk creaks and my light flicks on...and there's Mum, a mug of tea in each hand. She sets both mugs on the edge of my desk and studies me for a minute, like I'm one of her dressmaking mannequins.

"We need to talk," she says, and gently but firmly, she shuts the door. "Your father has insisted on grounding you – and to be honest, I agree with him. You lied – and you know you did."

All I hear is the word *grounded*. "But the show!"

"Hope Parker, I may be angry, but one thing I'm not is *unprofessional*. You'll finish the internship...then you're grounded. In the meantime, I think you've got some explaining to do, don't you?"

She settles on the end of my bed, the mattress shifting beneath her – and in a funny way it's a relief. I don't have to pretend any more, I don't have to pretend that I've spent the day being someone I'm not, doing something I haven't.

"There was an advert in *The Stage* for places at the Earl's. Student places, shadowing the crew and helping out. Stuff you need, experience and a reference and everything, if you want to apply for theatre school. Or if you want to have a chance of getting in, anyway."

"So you applied."

I nod. "I had to. It was like I didn't have a choice."

She makes a sound a lot like a sigh – but she doesn't actually seem angry. She said she is, but she isn't. Why isn't she angry? I would be, if I were her.

"I didn't think I'd actually get it. Not in a million years, not *me*. I thought somebody smarter or just…*better* would. And then I did, and then…" The words dry up and all I can do is look helplessly at her.

Mum passes me one of the mugs, taking a sip from the other.

"Is that why you didn't say anything to begin with? Because you didn't think you'd get it?"

The tea burns the back of my throat, but the hurt in her voice burns *all* of me.

"I didn't want you to be disappointed when I didn't get it. Mostly."

"Mostly?" Another sip. "And when you did?"

It takes me a long time to answer. I almost say a dozen different things, but in the end I know I have to tell the truth.

"I didn't say anything because of you."

"Me? But I could have helped you – I want to help…"

"And that's just it. You would have."

Bad start. I can actually see her prickle at this – but I need to go on now I've begun to talk.

"I know the theatre is your thing. I know it's where you come from and you love it. It's always been your place…and

I love that, I do. I love that you care about all the costumes and the dresses and the people. I love that other people see how amazing your stuff is and think it's amazing too. But do you have any idea how hard it is to walk into a theatre – the only place I've ever wanted to belong – and be…just me? Everybody *knows* you already. They know who you are and they know what you can do, and everyone respects you for it. But they don't know *me*. And all I want is to show them what I *can* do – show them that *I* can belong there. That I *do* belong there. Not because I'm your daughter, not because of you or your name, or you calling in a favour, or someone wanting to impress you…but because of me. Nobody else. Just me."

Everything fades to a whisper, and I rub my hands over my eyes to stop the room from blurring. How can I make her see – my mum, with her awards and her reputation – that I'm not rejecting her or everything she wants for me? I just have to earn it for myself – otherwise how would I know it was really mine? If I'm ever going to stop worrying about people whispering behind my back, I have to do this on my own.

But then I see it, and suddenly it's so clear that I don't know why I didn't sooner.

The only way to make them all stop doubting I really can do this job, have this life, is to stop doubting it myself.

Mum looks down at the quilt cover and – ever the seamstress – picks up a loose thread, snapping it off and neatly balling it into her hand.

"I've never told you what your grandfather said, have I? When I told him I wasn't going to work in the shop, cutting suits from patterns and turning up hems. That I'd been offered an apprenticeship at the Opera House." She pauses meaningfully, then adds: "One I'd applied for without telling a *soul*. He was furious, I think – but he didn't really show it. All he did was look me in the eye, and say, 'Well, if you think you can do it, then good luck to you.'" When she looks up, she's paler than I've ever seen her. "So I understand. I know what it takes, and I know how it feels. And I know what it means."

It honestly looks like there are tears in her eyes.

"Oh, Hope," she says softly, and her voice is rough, like there's a knot in her throat. "I'm so very proud of you."

She puts her mug on the floor and she reaches over and pulls both my hands into hers, pressing them tightly.

"If anyone can do this – and I mean anyone – *you* can," she says.

And as soon as she says it, I start to think that maybe she's right.

Now I'm not running around trying to hide what I'm doing from everyone, now everything I am and want is out in the open and I can just get on with it…I think I might believe it too.

I can – and I will.

Watch me.

ACT FIVE
Beginners,
Please

ACT FIVE, SCENE ONE

The crowd of fans I've got so used to seeing – for good or bad – outside the stage door every day has moved. For a heart-stopping moment I wonder whether all this nonsense about "me and Tommy" has made them, I don't know, abandon him. And then, of course, I see the queue snaking around the front of the building from the box-office doors and I kick myself for being such an idiot – they're all trying to get one of the last tickets for tonight and it's nothing at all to do with me. Tommy's ego is obviously contagious.

Because tonight? Tonight, we get to show *Piecekeepers* to the world for the very first time.

Tonight, we open.

I thought it would be weird going straight to an opening night with no previews. Most new shows have a least a couple of nights in front of an audience paying lower prices, fine-tuning and tweaking before they officially open. But not us. I'm not sure if that's a Rick thing – he had a notorious run-in with a critic after they broke tradition *and* an embargo and reviewed the first preview of a show he was in a while back. *SixGuns* – where else? – reported him saying that if it ever happened again, an embargo wouldn't be the only thing that got broken.

The stage door itself is shut, which means I've got no choice but to go in through the front. Taking a deep breath, I start edging my way cautiously through the queue, my head down in case they start with the hissing and booing again. Luckily, I arrive at exactly the same time the box office opens, and they're so excited that they don't even notice me, camouflaged in one of Grace's old hoodies over my standard backstage blacks, along with a pair of sunglasses.

The queue isn't the only change – the foyer is transformed. The *Piecekeepers* banners hang from every wall, along with posters of Tommy in costume and character, reaching forward as though to pull you into the picture with him. A couple of the fans are taking turns to duck out of the queue and take selfies with them. I take a quick photo of it all and send it over to Priya. She pings back a photoshopped picture of a cat giving a thumbs up. I guess that's a good thing? Across from Tommy's poster, the one of Juliet as Lizzie, her arms folded and her hair blowing out behind her, is getting almost as much attention. There's chatter and laughter and excitement filling the foyer like sunlight.

The Earl's is awake and breathing.

The Earl's is *alive*.

* * *

George is already in wardrobe, brushing the main Lizzie wig, when I walk up to the open door. He does a double-take when he sees me.

"This is a new look." He scrunches up his mouth. "Not sure about the sunglasses. They might be a bit much."

"There's no cardigan, though."

"We talked about that," he says sternly.

"At least the glasses got me past the queue." I pull them off and shove them into the pocket of Grace's hoodie.

"I don't know why you're so worried about it – I know it's a bit annoying, but it'll all blow over. Especially when people start talking about Tommy onstage."

"It's just…why did it have to be *me*, you know? And you were right, by the way. My mum found out."

George puts the brush down. "You're kidding me?" He sounds as Geordie as I have ever heard him.

"My beloved older sister told my parents about the photos. And then it all kind of…unravelled from there."

"So? What did she say?"

"My sister?"

"Like I give a monkey's about your sister. No, your *mother* – what did *she* say?"

Luckily, I know better than to take personally the fact that he's making this all about Miriam Parker.

At least, I'm starting to.

"It was…okay, actually. It really was. I mean, I'm pretty sure I'm grounded until I'm at least thirty, but they're going to let me finish things here first, so that's a relief."

"And you're okay?"

"I'm okay." I reach out to straighten a stray strand of the wig – and whip my hand away again before George gets the chance to slap it. "And like you say, it *will* go away, won't it? The stuff in the papers?"

"It will. Like they say about reviews – today's front-page story is tomorrow's chip wrapping. And even if it wasn't, Tommy's promo interview should sort it out when it's printed. Has he done the follow-up yet?" He starts brushing again. "Pass that hairspray, will you?" The gold can he's pointing to is almost as big as I am.

"I hope so. I think he did it over the phone last night. Not that it'll matter to him either way – why would it?"

"One word." George has disappeared behind a cloud of setting spray, but his voice is as clear as ever. "Emery."

Tommy's girlfriend. Right. She doesn't exactly seem the type to let something like this slide.

"Is she really coming tonight?"

"That's what I heard. She's not staying for the actual *show*, though – just to see Tommy beforehand or something. If you want to know, you'll have to ask Lucinda up in the theatre office. She's got a list of the VIPs coming. I've been hassling her for a few clues, but she's not budging."

I shouldn't even have to be thinking about this. There's so much to do before we open, and however casual George is being, I can see he's as nervous, as excited, as *everything* about tonight as I am. I don't have time to be worrying about Emery Greenway. What I need to do is get back to being totally invisible again – which is just how I like it.

"By the way," he says through the comb he's holding between his teeth. "Amy was looking for you two minutes before you got in. She's nipped out to run a couple of errands and she'll be back in half an hour or so – she wants you to check on Tommy. Apparently he wants something."

"Doesn't he always? Right. Okay. It'll be fine. It'll be just fine. I can handle that."

George spits the comb into the palm of his hand and looks right at me. "You know one of the best things about you, Hope?"

"My good looks. My sense of humour. Both of the above?" I toss my hair back in what, I realize immediately after, is a horrifyingly Tommy-ish manner.

"No." He pauses just a little too long for my liking. "It's that you're a terrible liar."

Everyone keeps saying that. I guess it must be true. Still, it's probably better being known as a terrible liar than as someone who called themselves a wizard-ninja wannabe, I think as I leave George to his combing and his spraying and head for the production office... Only to find my way blocked by someone in the usual off-duty actor/student uniform of ripped jeans and a faded black T-shirt.

"Hi," says Luke.

"Hi."

"I got your message after the dress rehearsal. Sixteen exclamation marks, huh?"

"Well, you know, I thought it was more descriptive than 'try softer'?" I shrug, and he laughs.

"How're you feeling this morning? Nervous?"

Not nervous, no. That's not why I can feel my heart pounding and my pulse racing. It's not nerves. "No. You?"

He's standing so close, so very close that it would be nothing to shrink the distance between us completely; to lean forward, lean into him. Rest my forehead against his shoulder...

Here in the quiet of the Earl's basement, hundreds of people have walked these halls before us – thousands. Actors and directors and stage managers and crew; wardrobe mistresses, stagehands, techs...and none of them matter as Luke's arm circles my waist and pulls me closer to him. The corners of his eyes crease into a smile, and he draws me to him...and then we both freeze at the sound of footsteps coming down the concrete stairs at the end of the corridor and someone whistling tunelessly.

Rick.

In the kind of sideways lunge I've only seen in musicals,

Luke dives into the laundry room and pushes the door shut, just as Rick rounds the corner. He looks remarkably calm and cheerful – more so than I've seen him this entire time.

"Morning, morning." It's halfway between a song and a chant.

"Morning," I mumble, trying to manoeuvre myself in between him and the laundry-room door while looking completely casual. And alone, and definitely not mixing personal and professional, or distracting the cast or getting distracted myself on the day of our first night. Not me. "You were whistling."

There's the briefest flash of panic across his face. "Bollocks. I was." He turns around quickly, three times on the spot, then nods. And to think Priya makes fun of me for being superstitious. Rick clears his throat. "You haven't seen Tommy, have you?"

"Uh, no. Is he signed in?"

"Signed in half an hour ago. He's probably in his dressing room."

"I could check? Amy said he wanted me for something."

"Did she?" He looks puzzled, then his expression clears. "Ah, I know what that is. Yes. There's something Tommy needs back at his hotel…" He rummages through the bundle of paperwork he's carrying and I groan inwardly.

Rick gives me a look.

Apparently I groaned outwardly too. "Sorry. But I think

the concierge at the hotel has probably had enough of me by now," I say weakly.

Rick grins and holds out a folded sheet of paper covered in Amy's handwriting. I open it in the middle of the corridor as he walks off towards Tommy's dressing room, humming loudly.

There's only the slightest pause in the humming when he hears the sound I make reading the note...and then he's gone, vanished around the corner.

ACT FIVE, SCENE TWO

Stage management, they say, is about being prepared. Being prepared for the next cue, the next show, the next crisis.

That, I get. But I'll admit that I was not prepared for *this*.

The day of our opening night, our press night…and I am stuck in traffic, sitting in a taxi full of roses.

It's not as romantic as I might have imagined, mostly because there are several thorns from one bunch wedged into my side (oh, *irony*) and something with too many skinny legs that is probably an incredibly poisonous spider climbing out of one of the flowers by my knee. A five-minute cab ride has never taken so long.

We finally pull up at the side of the road and the door opens and Luke peers in from where he's been waiting on the pavement. I look at him helplessly.

"Get me out."

I can see he's about to make a joke – but one look at my face tells him that won't go down well. Much like the look on my face when I read Tommy's note meant that he immediately volunteered to come and help, rather than running straight back into the laundry room.

"Please?" I add.

I mean, he had to walk here. Maybe I should have asked *him* to get in the taxi with the flowers...

He starts unloading bouquet after bouquet of roses from the car onto the hotel trolley the concierge has wheeled out onto the pavement. Red roses, white roses, pink roses, peach roses, roses that are apparently "gold" (although they look like plain old yellow to me), white roses with green streaks down the petals.

A *lot* of roses.

Enough to fill a room before Emery walks into it, exactly as Tommy requested.

And because I can still hear Amy's voice telling me we need to support the cast, support Tommy – and despite the fact this is nothing to do with the theatre, or a stage, or managing it – I am here to make sure the roses arrive safely. *Exactly as Tommy requested.*

Luke folds his arms, watching the trolley-load disappear through the doors of the hotel. "It's pretty impressive, you've got to give him that."

"I don't have to give him anything. I bought them. Me."

By which I mean I walked out of the theatre, hired a taxi and drove round every florist in town, begging, asking, bribing – sweeping up armfuls of flowers and putting them on the theatre account.

All this so Emery can arrive to a load of roses ahead of Tommy's opening night.

Between us, we gather up the last few bouquets and follow the trolley.

In the hotel lobby, people nudge each other as we pass, a couple, their arms full of flowers.

A couple under a chandelier, lights in their hair.

A couple lying on a rug in the woods.

A couple under a street light in the fog.

A couple.

The lift pings and the doors open. Luke nudges me forward. "Come on. I think something just crawled down the back of my neck." He rubs his chin against his shoulder, which is the closest he's going to be able to get to scratching with his hands full of flowers.

"Probably one of the poisonous spiders," I mutter. The lift is *tiny* – we barely fit in there along with all the roses that have been unloaded from the trolley onto the floor because it's the concierge's trolley, and one look told me that no, taking it in the lift was *not* an option. My hands are too full to press the button, so I try and knock it with my hip.

Spectacularly, I manage to press just about every button *except* the one I want. I guess I could try leaning forward and using my nose…?

Luke laughs, squeezing in among the bundles and bouquets as the door slides shut, and we start our slow progress up the building.

"You missed."

"I know."

"Let me try."

He half-turns, and edges around me on tiptoe, trying not to crush any of the delicate petals and pressing up against the door as I shuffle back. The noise of the tissue paper wrapping the bouquets is unbearably loud, and all the oxygen in the air has been replaced by eau-de-billions-of-roses. Something squashes under the sole of my trainer.

"Uh, I think I just trod on one."

"Nobody's going to notice one less flower in all this lot."

"It's not bad, is it?" I look around. There really are a lot of them. "I did that."

"Best bit of DSMing I ever saw."

Thinking on your feet, getting the thing done. No second-guessing, just finding whatever it is you need as fast as possible...

Maybe he's right. It might not be for the stage, technically, but it still counts. Kind of.

Thinking like a stage manager.

Outside, there's a whirr...and a clonk...and with a jolt that rustles all the flowers, we stop.

"What happened?"

"Ah. I think I pressed the stop button." Luke looks embarrassed. He cranes his neck around to check the panel. "Yep. I did. It's fine."

"It's fine? Why did you do that?"

"I didn't mean to, did I? There's not exactly a lot of room to manoeuvre." To demonstrate, he sticks out both his elbows. One rests against my ribs, the other against the door.

"So…unpress it?"

"I'm not sure I can." He twists around properly and peers over the top of three bouquets at the panel of buttons. Everything that was lit on there has gone dark. "I must've caught it with my elbow."

"You're sure it was you? Because I don't know how long I want to be stuck in here with all this…"

If it was just him and me, without the flowers (and whatever passengers they might be carrying), it would be a different story. But I'd still prefer it not to be in a tiny, tiny lift.

"Maybe?"

"You either did or you didn't."

"Look, just…hold this." He holds out his bouquets.

"With *what*? What am I supposed to hold them *with*? My other arms?"

"Fine." He settles the flowers he's holding on top of all the others – and without another word, he reaches forward and lifts the bouquets out of my arms, putting those down too.

And then he straightens back up and he looks at me and the light is dancing in his eyes and suddenly the lift can never be too small.

A couple in a stopped lift, surrounded by roses.

"Now. Want me to unpress it?"

I look right back at him, and then I look past him at the panel – and I shake my head. "No."

And I don't know whether it's him reaching for me first this time, turning his face towards me, the touch of his fingers dancing across my cheeks – or whether it's me, pulling him closer as his hand runs through my hair, brushing it back from my face…

All I know is that his lips against mine feel softer than any flower petal…and that close up, the scent of his skin is better than any rose. That his touch is warm and sure of itself – and that when he kisses me, he means it.

When the lift clatters open with a happy chime only a *little* while later, we're on the top floor of the hotel. The door to Tommy's room is open, and two of the housekeeping staff are waiting right outside. Luke passes the flowers out and between us we form a floral chain, passing bunches from hand to hand until we fill the whole room. There are flowers everywhere – on every table, in every corner, by the bed, on the desk…even in a huge glass vase in the bathroom. It's beautiful, like an enchanted garden. Maybe I thought it was stupid when I was stuck in a taxi with them and their leaves were trying to get up my nose…but the roses are definitely growing on me.

We don't speak as the lift rattles back down, not stopping until it reaches reception, but I can *feel* him standing beside me. When he takes my hand and links his fingers through mine, I feel it all the way down to my toes. But when I step out onto the marble floor of the lobby, Luke hangs back. He says my name and I turn…and there he is, holding out a single rose to me – a pink so dark, so deep that it's almost impossible to name it.

"Because nobody'll notice one missing, right?" I say lightly, twirling it between my fingers.

"Because sometimes, it's the things that nobody notices which *deserve* noticing," he says.

ACT FIVE, SCENE THREE

"And you're sure?"

"Yes, Dad. Your tickets will be on the door. There's a drinks reception in the stalls bar afterwards. I'll meet you there. Priya's coming too."

After everything came out about the Earl's on Friday – and by the time Mum and Dad had had several conversations behind several very closed doors – Mum announced that *of course* the whole family would be coming (with a pointed look at Faith) and would enjoy being there to support me. And then it turned out that she'd actually been invited to opening night anyway – because, naturally, she's Miriam Parker...

"And we should get to the main entrance...?"

"After seven, but before seven thirty," I shout back through the bathroom door, trying to wrap the towel around my wet hair. When I managed to run in here and get the door locked before Grace could get across the landing, I thought it was a minor personal triumph...right until Dad decided that now was the time to have a long conversation about tonight's logistics. I don't really have time for this now; not when I've got so much to do ahead of curtain-up, but when Amy suggested I take an hour or two this afternoon to have a break and freshen up, I wasn't going to say no.

"And what sort of thing should I wear? Should I be…you know, a bit smarter, seeing as it's opening night. I don't want to overdo it?"

Enough is enough.

I tuck the end of my towel in, and open the door to see him waiting patiently outside. Steam billows out onto the landing as the colder air outside the bathroom rushes in.

"Dad. It's an opening night. You've been to loads of them before."

"Yes – but not *yours*."

Oh.

"Okay. So, if you really want to know what to wear, maybe ask Mum. Clothes are…kind of her thing."

"She's out getting her hair done for this evening."

Of course she is.

"What will you be wearing?" he adds hopefully.

"Black. Because that's what we wear."

"Oh. Right."

He stands there in silence. I have so many things to do, and so much I need to get straight in my head, and I have to get to the theatre for five o'clock, but he's trying so hard.

I know how upset he was when the truth about the Earl's came out; hurt and angry and worried and, more than anything, disappointed. Although he's hiding it now, I think he might still be all of those things, and I hate it... But I also think he knows what this means to me – not just now but for my future too. And however upset he might be, he's not going to risk that – because whatever else he might be, he's my dad.

Who is still just standing there.

"What is it?"

"Nothing. I just thought I'd...check."

"Dad."

"Yes, love?"

"You've not come to any of the shows I've worked at the Square Globe."

"Well, that was different, wasn't it?"

"You won't be able to see me. You know that, right?"

"Nonsense." He lifts his hand...and for a second I think he's going to pat my head like he did when I was a kid. But he hesitates, and eventually he rests his palm against the door frame. "It's your night. Whoever might be on the stage, it's *your* night."

Sitting on the bottom stair, trying to get my (black) trainers on with one hand and shoving everything and anything I think I might need into my bag with the other, I don't even notice my sisters looming: Grace in the door of the living room, Faith eyeing me from the pew in the kitchen.

Grace smiles at me. "Are you going over already?"

"Amy asked me to come back for five. Everyone else will be off on their dinner break, so…" I jump up and grab my bag. It weighs more than any bag has ever weighed, and I could probably live out of it for the next fifteen years, so I think I've got everything – including, right at the bottom, a couple of cardboard figures that have been folded and refolded so many times they're practically crumbling. Touchstones; talismans. Because it is opening night, after all.

I'm ready.

"See you later."

"Break both legs…" Faith's voice is almost sing-song… and I can't decide whether she's kidding or not. I stop, my hand on the porch door.

"It's one leg. Break *a* leg. It's to do with how actors only used to get paid if they got out onto the stage, crossing the—"

"Leg line." She cuts me off. "I know."

"If I get hit by a bus on the way and actually break both legs, you'll never forgive yourself for that."

"Meh. I'll live." Faith shrugs…and then winks at me.

Grace gives me a goofy smile and her ridiculous thumbs up, and I'm out of the door.

* * *

On the bus, I go over and over the things I need to do, counting them off on my fingers as I whisper them to myself. The middle-aged woman sitting on the seat next to me moves further away.

Be like that then.

I take the bus one stop further than usual, all the way down to the station. This way, I get to walk up to the theatre past every bus shelter and bollard and display unit with our *Piecekeepers* poster on. And then I round the corner and it's straight ahead of me. The Earl's Theatre. In the slowly dimming daylight, it – *she* – shines, and my heart swells because that's *me*.

I'm the Earl's Theatre. So is George. So is Rick and Amy and Nina. Chris and Jonna and Lucinda the PR and Nathalie; Roly and Rav...and Luke. Even Tommy.

We are the Earl's Theatre.

The foyer lights glow through the glass doors, the awning signs sparkle on the front of the building and there are *Piecekeepers* banners hanging from the upper windows, brightly spotlit. Down on the ground, the queue already winds around the side of the theatre, past the HOUSE FULL sign on the pavement – and I actually recognize most of the faces at the front, patiently waiting for the doors to open even though they won't for ages yet. They're the same faces I've passed for days, including the ones who've smiled at me and the ones who've booed me. But looking at them all standing there, leaning against the wall in the cold and stamping their feet to stay warm...it's enough to make me shiver.

"It's not bad, is it?"

I didn't even know he was there. Luke's words come from behind me, so close that I can feel them on the back of my neck as his arms slip around my waist and pull me back against him. Even through my coat, I can feel the warmth of his body – although the moment is *kind* of spoiled when I realize that the strong arms wrapped around me are also, in fact, carrying two enormous plastic containers of milk.

"Thirsty, are we?" I step away from him and eye the giant bottles. "Here – gimme."

He hands one over, laughing. "It's not for me. It's a favour for the front-of-house guys – Sarwat went to get the stalls bar up and running and realized they're out of milk. I was going out anyway, so..." He brandishes his bottle. "How are you doing? Nervous?"

"Me? Nervous? No. No, no. Nope. Ummm. Ha." I follow him through the stage door and up the steps, past the desk where Roly is almost invisible behind a mountain of flowers, cuddly toys and cellophane-wrapped baskets of biscuits. Peering over the top of a bouquet of roses, she spots us.

"Don't suppose you fancy taking some of this lot through to the dressing rooms, do you?"

"Sorry, Roly." I shake my head. "I've done all my flower-arranging today." And I thought I'd emptied the whole town of roses already. As we head past, I hear her muttering, "Don't eat that," at Domino the cat.

Even indoors, it's still cold. I can't imagine how miserable it must be outside in the queue – especially as I'm pretty sure some of them have been there since this morning, with only the promise of Tommy Knight to keep them warm.

I stop and look down at the milk in my hand.

"Luke…"

"Mmm?" He turns towards me.

"Do you think they're going to need *all* of this in the bar?"

Ten minutes later, we head back out through the foyer doors carrying trays loaded with cardboard cups (found in the back of a cupboard in the production office) full of tea.

"Hi there!" I walk up to the girl at the front of the queue. Her hair is tucked behind her ears and under the long stripy scarf she's wrapped round and round her shoulders to keep the chill out. She eyes me suspiciously, so I nod at my tray. "It's a little while until the house opens, so we thought maybe you could do with a cup of tea?" She eyes me even more suspiciously, and it looks like she's about to turn away…but then I have a brainwave. "He's needed in wardrobe right now, but Mr Knight asked us to let all of you out here know how much he appreciates your support. He can't wait for you to see the show."

"Tommy Knight knows we're here?" Her eyes light up almost as brightly as the awning above us.

"He does, and he's so grateful to all of you. But he thought you might be getting a bit cold waiting." I lift the tray hopefully…and that's all it takes. She beams and takes a cup, turning to the person behind her – the girl I've spoken to before, from waiting for Tommy – who smiles in recognition.

"He sent us tea!"

It ripples down the line as we make our way along it: Tommy Knight sent them tea. Tommy Knight knows they're there.

Tommy Knight knows they exist.

All the times he's driven me crazy and I've wondered what the *actual point* of him was… It's this.

It was never about him. It's about *them*.

It's the simplest thing, and the best.

The last cup taken, we tuck our trays under our arms and follow the line of people around the side of the theatre.

"Why'd you say it was from Tommy?" Luke nods back to the queue.

"Because as far as they're concerned, it is. Besides, I'm invisible, remember?"

"Not to me, you're not." He reaches a hand towards me as though he's about to brush a strand of hair away from my face…and stops. "Oh, wow."

He's not talking about me, is he?

I follow the line of his gaze to the stage door.

Oh, wow indeed.

Not only is there another crowd around the steps, there's a guy who looks like someone squished two heavyweight boxers into the same suit standing at the bottom.

"Hi, yep, coming through – excuse me…yeah, mind your backs…"

I step around a couple of fans staring at a phone between them – uploading a picture, by the look of it. It's not till we make it to the steps that Luke whispers in my ear, making me strain to hear him through the sea of excited chatter around us. "It's Emery Greenway. She's here."

I snap my head round to face him so quickly that I almost lose my balance. "She's backstage? Right now?"

"I heard someone say she just went in."

My heart sinks. So much for my quiet hour before everyone gets back from dinner and things start getting serious. If Emery really is here, it's going to be bedlam, isn't it?

The suit blocks my way as I try and walk up the steps, holding out a hand the size of a dinner plate. "Sorry, no." His voice is so deep that I don't hear it so much as feel it vibrating through my ribs.

"Sorry, yes." I stand my ground. "I'm part of the theatre crew, and I need to get to work."

"Miss Greenway…"

"Miss Greenway will understand that as part of the technical team for the production in which Mr Knight is, in fact, starring, I *need to get inside*."

The hand drops.

"Thank you." And I sweep up the steps, through the door – and walk straight into Roly, who is peering around the edge of the frame, having apparently clambered out from behind the gift mountain.

"Big lad, isn't he?" She dusts herself down.

"Is she really backstage?"

Roly gives me a look.

Well, it explains the security.

"I need to check the props and personals."

"Well, then, you'll most likely meet her. She's holed up in number one with half the cast, as far as I can tell. Some people have nothing better to do." Roly tosses her hair back as she says it.

I raise my eyebrows at her. "You couldn't get through the door, could you?"

She shakes her head crossly. "It's *rammed* in there."

I put on my most serious voice. "It's about to get… unrammed."

"Unrammed?" She blinks at me. It's not the most eloquent thing I've ever said.

I give Luke a knowing glance. "I work better with a script."

Roly wasn't kidding about the crowd: most of the crew, and what actually looks like the *entire* cast, are loitering outside dressing room number one, its door open and the sound of laughter spilling out. At the far end of the corridor, through the crush, Luke gives me a wave and vanishes through another door to start his own prep for tonight. As the door closes behind him, I realize that I didn't ask him if *he's* nervous – not that he should be. He's knocked every rehearsal out of the park, and I can't wait to watch him from the wings; to watch everyone else watching him and seeing just how good he is.

I edge my way through the tightly packed bodies standing outside Tommy's room. "Come on, guys…it's gone five. If you want to eat, you need to *go!*"

Fragments of conversations drift past me: "smaller than I thought", "lucky Tommy, though", "just off a plane", "that voice"… I shoo away as many of the crew as I can and squeeze my way into the dressing room to check over Tommy's personal props and costume rack.

I've seen pictures of Emery Greenway before. I've seen videos of her singing onstage. I've heard her songs plenty of times…but nothing quite compares to actually seeing her there, in person.

She's folded onto the sofa in the dressing room, her shoes kicked off and her feet tucked under her; a bright red headscarf wrapped around her hair and knotted behind her head and a gorgeous shimmering yellow dress pooling around her. Her voice is like honey poured over silk, quiet and soft and liquid – but there's so much strength there that you can feel it. She looks up at me, and her eyes are the most incredible warm brown shot through with gold…and rimmed with *perfect* winged eyeliner. No wonder everybody loves her – she lights up the room just by being in it. She gives me an enormous smile, and raises an eyebrow as though she's waiting for me to say something…

"Miss Greenway? Five minutes."

My spine rattles, and I risk a quick look over my shoulder to see that the corridor is entirely filled by suit.

As she looks past me, I realize this is my chance to clear up everything about those photos with Tommy. What better way to make sure she knows that nothing happened than to *tell* her, face to face and in person.

I feel her gaze slide back onto me as she uncurls herself, scooping her shoes up off the floor with one hand – and I'm just about to open my mouth to speak when I spot Tommy, standing just out of her eyeline, shaking his head vigorously. I case I didn't get the message, he's also mouthing the word

"No!" over and over again, crossing and uncrossing his hands in front of his chest.

I guess he doesn't want me to say anything at all to Emery. Maybe it's a sore point between them…maybe *I'm* a sore point between them?

Yikes.

My mouth stays shut, and now I'm standing in the middle of Tommy's dressing room, staring at Emery Greenway like an idiot.

And she's still looking at me, still waiting.

I glare pointedly at Tommy – who stops flapping and takes Emery by the hand.

"Well, if you want to squeeze in a quick meet-and-greet we'd better get a move on. Don't want to keep them all waiting, do we? Oh, don't worry – we'll pick your things up from here…"

And with a dazzling smile (and only the quickest of glances back at me) he sweeps her out of the room to say hello to the fans at the stage door.

Right.

Okay.

I may as well just go and get the necklace and come back in a minute: it'll be easier when everyone's gone. I squeeze back out again, and decide against trying to pass the slab of walking muscle, still blocking the hallway, instead making straight for the production office. I drop my bag and punch the combination into the safe for the necklace, running through my list of personal props one more time as I fill in Amy's sign-out sheet for the jewellery. There's a whole row of premium seats in the stalls tonight for assorted sponsors and prop-lenders all keen to see their support onstage, including, right in the middle of the best row, the guy who's actually loaned us the necklace. I'm not quite sure who he is, but everyone seems to be very keen that he's happy – although that probably has less to do with the jewellery loan and the massive advert he's taken out in the programme than the big sponsorship cheque he gave us. Nobody's mentioned just how big it was, but from the way Rick and Amy talked about it, I'm guessing it was *big*-big – the kind of sum a show like this, with all its costumes and special effects, needs before it can even open. Hopefully Tommy will actually manage to put the necklace on Juliet the right way round tonight – unlike at the dress rehearsal.

I fish a couple of the other more valuable props out of the back of the safe and scoop them into my arms, and when I get to the prop table in the wings, George is already bouncing around beside it.

"Have you got the glasses? I need the glasses to go with Magister costume three."

I hand over his prop. "Here you go – calm down. And it's not a pair of glasses, it's an antique pince-nez. Says so on my props sheet. And why aren't you on your dinner break?"

"Was busy helping Jonna iron the shirt for Lancelot two. You know, for your lo-verrrrr... How's that going, by the way?"

"Not. Now. George. And go and eat something."

Book, pipe, candle, matches. Glass, bottle – refilled...

I touch every marked-out section of the table, the way I've done before every run-through, the way I've practised – reading out the name of the prop and putting my hand on it.

We're all good. Just the necklace to deliver to Tommy's dressing room.

Chris's voice shouts down from the fly-floor above us. I can barely hear him over the sound of the vacuum cleaners sweeping the auditorium. "Hope? Do you know where Amy is?"

I peer up into the darkness, and finally make him out, leaning over the railing. "I think she's on her break! What do you need her for?"

"Question about one of the cues."

"Now?"

"It's from last night."

I look at George. "What do I do?"

"Get up there – you know the answer as much as Amy does, right?"

"Do I?"

He folds his arms and scowls at me.

I look back up at Chris. "I'm coming up – hold on."

THEATRICAL

I haven't been up to the fly-floor since my first day in the theatre. The ladder is no less terrifying, and the gantry is still alarmingly narrow, with its wall full of ropes on one side and its drop down to the stage on the other. But Chris, gloves still tucked into his belt, dressed in his blacks just like I am, doesn't seem anywhere near as intimidating as he did then. Now, he's leaning over the narrow workbench bolted to the safety rail, peering at a script with a pencil in his hand. I pick my way over to the bench through the counterweights he's been sorting.

"What's up?"

He points at a scribble next to a line – which has also been scribbled over – with the tip of his pencil.

"This."

"Yes."

"Can you read it?"

"I…can't. No. Whose writing is it?"

"Whose d'you think?" he says wryly.

"Rick's. Okay." That explains it – the only people who can read Rick's handwriting are Amy and Nina. Both of whom are still out on their dinner break.

"I just need to know whether to change the weight."

I study the lines.

Everything on the grid – all the backdrops and curtains, anything that has to move up and down from the fly-tower – has to be counterweighted. And the lead flyman has to work out that counterweighting precisely. Too much, and he'll struggle to keep control of the rope. Too little and it'll go zooming up and crash into the grid.

I remember this conversation. I know I do.

"Give me a minute."

Chris opens his mouth, but I shush him. I need to think. Rick was standing there, and he said…what?

Something about…

I close my eyes – and then open them, grabbing Chris's pencil, scribbling alongside all the other scribbles. "Three. It says three."

He tilts his head to one side, pointing to the squiggle through the line. "And that?"

"He was taking it out, so he crossed it through – but then they put it back again later, so he's uncrossed the crossing out."

"Huh."

"I'll ask Amy to double-check when I see her, but is that okay for now?"

He looks over the line one more time and nods. "Yeah, that'll do it. Thanks."

"No problem."

I'm halfway down the ladder when he calls me back, and at first I wonder whether maybe he's going to do something like wink and tell me he misjudged me that first day; that actually, I'm all right… But when I stick my head back over the top, he's holding up the necklace in its case. I put it down on the workbench, didn't I?

"Lose something, did we?"

"Thanks. Don't tell Amy."

I can still hear him chuckling when I get to the bottom of the ladder.

Thankfully, the crush outside the dressing room has broken up. There's no sign of Tommy, but as there's a coat and expensive-looking handbag folded into the corner of the sofa, he must still be outside with Emery…and something tells me I probably shouldn't be here when they come back in to collect her things. I leave the necklace in the middle of his dressing table, clearing a space for it among all the not-good-luck-because-you-can't-wish-an-actor-good-luck cards, flowers and gifts. Roly's been collecting presents from the stage door all day. (The big pile of cuddly toys have, however, been relegated to a corner of the production office since he announced they gave him "the creeps".) Tommy's dressing room, in short, looks just like a star's dressing room on their opening night. His costumes are all there on the rack, personal props all ready…

Dressing room number one? Done. Now all he's got to do is get himself onstage on time, and we're away.

* * *

ACT FIVE, SCENE THREE

People filter back from their break, actors heading off to the still-dark studio theatre for their warm-ups (cue a chorus of "Haaaaaaaaaaaaah"s echoing through the building) and everyone gets back to the serious business of running last-minute checks. I spot Luke at the far side of the stage, checking one of the marks he has to hit during Lancelot's monologue. Behind him, Lucinda – in full head-of-PR mode – counts off seats against a list on her phone. Amy's walking the side of the stage with Rick, when Charlie, the head of front-of-house, appears at the pass door – smarter than usual in his opening night bow tie.

"You heard who's in tonight?"

Amy raises an eyebrow. "Who?"

"Haydn Swift – the guy who wrote the *Piecekeepers* book."

"You're kidding? He's in?"

"And his girlfriend, apparently. Lexi something. No pressure." With a grin, he disappears back into the auditorium – and very quietly, I hear Amy say, "It'll be fine," to Rick.

From a distance, you wouldn't know. You couldn't. But what I'm seeing on the stage is a team who've put everything they have, everything they *are* into this…and who are nervous. Even Amy.

"What if he hates it?" Rick's usually booming voice is no more than a whisper.

"He won't.""But what if he does? What if he thinks I've ruined it?"

"Well, for a start, it wouldn't be you, would it? It would be *us*. All of us."

She winks at me as she hurries past the prompt desk, and beams at Tommy coming the other way.

Why is Tommy coming the other way? Why isn't he in his dressing room, or warming up, or, frankly, anywhere other than here, with just over two hours to go before curtain-up? He needs to be *preparing*.

He grabs me by the arm and pulls me into the darkest corner of the wings, right behind the proscenium arch.

"I think we might have a bit of a problem," he hisses into my ear.

"Talk. Now. Fast."

"Emery."

"Talk faster?"

"I think she's taken the necklace."

ACT FIVE, SCENE FOUR

"She *WHAT?!*"

"I think she might have accidentally taken the necklace."

"How…I just…*what*?"

He keeps saying it, but somehow I can't quite make myself understand it.

Emery. Has. Taken. The. Necklace.

What?

"She had some jewellery sent over to her on loan for tonight, and I was given some at the same time."

"Oh no. It was in your dressing room, wasn't it?"

"Ah. Yes."

"She thought the necklace was part of the loan."

"Yes?"

"Okay. Okay. No harm done. It's fine. We'll just call her…"

"On this, you mean?" He sheepishly holds up a phone.

"She forgot it."

He nods.

We both look at the phone.

"Where's she going?" I ask.

"London."

"Back to the hotel first?"

"I think so. She has to go back to collect her make-up artist and then she's performing at some awards show later tonight. But by the time you get there…"

"Does her driver have a phone?"

"I don't have that number – he's an agency driver." Tommy frowns. "I've tried her agent, but she's not picking up – and neither's her assistant. I can't get hold of any of them, Hope, I've tried, I swear."

I feel sick.

The necklace was my responsibility. Props are *my* responsibility. Mine, and only mine.

And I've lost it. The ridiculous, stupidly expensive necklace whose actual owner is – even as we speak – heading for the theatre, looking forward to seeing his jewellery onstage tonight. And who will raise all hell if he doesn't see it and demand not only his sponsorship money back, but my head with it…

I *knew* that thing would be unlucky.

Tommy is pacing back and forth unhappily. "This is *just* what I need. Just what I need tonight. As if I don't have enough to think about already with *him* here…"

His grumbling is irritating enough to cut through my panic, and – finally – I lose my temper.

"You? What the hell's it got to do with you? What have you got to lose? If this doesn't work out for you, you get to run back to your shiny film career, don't you? Everyone makes a couple of jokes, and then you can just go back to earning *insane* amounts of money for waving your arms around in front of a green screen!"

He stares at me, taken aback. "*Excuse* me?"

"What about the rest of us? Stuck here in the real world? I need the reference from this. I need it. And losing a valuable prop means I think we can safely say I lose the reference too, don't you?"

"Oh, stop whining. Like dropping your mother's name in an interview wouldn't open every damn door you wanted." He flaps a hand at me, and it's the closest I've ever come to actually slapping someone. Everything else, I could take. The snitty comments, the attitude, the ridiculous errands – all of it. I can even let the question of exactly *how* he knows about Mum go... But *this* attitude? Now? This is over the line.

"Okay, stop. Just *stop*. You think you're so much better than me? Well, you're not. You've got no idea, have you? You sail through life, not giving a toss about *anyone* else."

He blinks at me. "I think that's a little uncalled-for. It's only a necklace."

"Maybe to you! But this placement – and therefore that necklace – is *everything* to me. I have done whatever I've been asked to do – and not just the stuff in the theatre. 'Keep Tommy happy,' Amy said, and I've done literally everything you've asked me to do. Even when it's ended up with me being booed in the street, having people photograph…me…"

I stop and grab Tommy's arm. He looks like I just wiped something awful on his sleeve, but I don't let go.

"Photographs. In the street. Outside the stage door. Social media. They put their photos on social media."

His expression shifts, changes…softens. And then he understands what it is I'm saying.

"Emery's fans. She's always stopping to talk to them – and we're always late because she does. It drives me insane…"

I cut him off with a look.

He clears his throat. "But she replies to their messages – and when she can't, she gets someone on her team to do it. If her account's suddenly flooded with notifications, or better, a hashtag, *someone* will notice. *They* might be able to reach her. And nobody loves a hashtag like Emery does. What about –" he purses his lips – "Stop Emy?"

"Yes! Okay. So we try and contact her that way…and if I can get to the hotel before she leaves for London, we can get the necklace back before anyone knows it's gone. Okay. Nobody else needs to know what it's about. Maybe we can say I'm getting her phone back to her? You said she's got to pick up her make-up artist?"

"Yes, but he might be waiting and just get straight into the car. If they get to the motorway before you get to them…"

I pull my hands through my hair, trying to think. Can I actually do this? I'm not sure I've got a choice. "Call the hotel – tell them to hold her if they see her. I'm going *now*."

"What if Amy asks where you are?"

"You're an actor, aren't you? Act!" I shout back over my shoulder, slamming through the pass door into the auditorium.

"Luke!" I yell at the top of my voice. One of the ushers pokes his head through the stalls door.

"Is something wrong?"

"Yes. No. Probably. Have you seen Luke? Luke Withakay? He was out here a minute ago."

"I think I saw him heading for the foyer."

He says something else, but I'm already running for the main foyer…and screech to a halt as I round the corner and realize that the front-of-house is not only open but full of *people*. The audience. They're starting to come inside – even if the house isn't open, the bars are. I freeze as Rick and Lucinda walk right past me, but thankfully neither of them see me to ask what I'm doing – they're too busy ushering a tall man in wire-rimmed glasses and a dark suit towards the bar. I recognize *that* face. That's Marshal Arthur, the country's most influential theatre critic. I take half a step back, just in case…then I see *him*, underneath the chandelier. Of course.

Slowing to my quickest possible casual walk, I thread my way through the crowd, smiling and nodding until I reach him.

"Hey!"

It takes him a second to see me. "Hey!" His face tenses, then relaxes into a smile. "I was just taking a last look before I came back to get warmed up…" He tugs at the hem of a fresh white T-shirt. I'm going to assume that's one of his own personal actor-rituals – but I can't stop to ask him now.

"I need you. It's an emergency. Outside."

Without a word, he follows me down the steps and out through the foyer.

"What is it?"

"I need to find some of the fans who've been around the stage door."

"You what?"

"It's Emery. She took the necklace we've borrowed, and I need to get it back. Now."

"You what?"

"You heard me."

"Can't you call her?"

"No. She left her phone. The fans might be our best chance of reaching her in time. They like you – help me talk to them?"

"You what…?"

A group of girls walk past us, right up to the poster

of Tommy – and pull out their phones. Bingo.

Just for once, I need to be *not* invisible.

For one night only, a strictly limited run...it's time to step into the spotlight.

I bounce up to them. "Hi. So, weird question – do you recognize me? Tommy's 'mystery girl', right?" I wave my arms in a jazz-hands gesture.

They all glare at me.

Maybe the jazz-hands was too much.

"I'm going to take that as a yes."

They carry on glaring.

"You're all fans of Tommy's, right?" I point at the photo. "It's fine – it's just...we've got a small problem with tonight's show."

The glares fade, and they start looking worried. I have their attention. Good.

"I don't suppose you guys have seen Emery Greenway in, say, the last five minutes? I really need to find her. As in *right now*. If you can help us, Tommy will definitely, definitely be happy to come out and meet you after the show. I promise."

After this, he'll do it because I *tell him to*.

This seems to do the trick. Two of them shake their heads...but one frowns and pokes at her phone. "She was literally just tagged on Instagram...here."

She holds out her phone. On the screen is a photo posted

two minutes ago of the river weir just around the corner and, in front of it, a car. Sitting in the back with the window down, blurry but still clearly identifiable and talking to someone outside, is Emery Greenway. The photo before it is her smiling and waving in front of the theatre beside her giant security guard – posted a few minutes before that.

I look at each of them in turn. "You all talk to each other online, right?"

They nod.

"Are lots of people checking in tonight?" I don't really need to ask – it's Tommy's big night. Of course all his fans are online, watching. If they can't be *here* for him, they'll be *there* for each other.

They nod again.

"Can you do something for me? I need to find Emery for Tommy. Look, there's a hashtag…" I hold out my hand without even thinking what I'm doing, and she passes her phone across. That was easy. Obviously my inner-Amy is starting to show. I tap *#StopEmy* into the search box…and sigh. There, posted under the hashtag, is a single photo of me, scowling at the camera.

Tommy.

He must have taken it back in the rehearsal room – I had no idea. And now he's posted it on *his* Instagram.

A moment later, another picture follows it – tagged just like mine. Luke's.

Except…it's his official headshot from the programme, and it comes from another account.

LWithakay.

I glance up from the screen just in time to catch him sliding his own phone back into his pocket. He sees me looking and shrugs, his cheeks colouring.

"I figure it all helps, right?" he mumbles sheepishly.

I pass the phone back and pretend not to notice their eyes flick from the photos to me, and then to Luke. Where they stay.

"All right. I need to get Emery's attention – or the attention of somebody who can contact her before she leaves town – it's life and death. Tag her in, message her, hashtag – go wild. And if anyone sees her, tell her not to leave until I've spoken to her!" Spinning back to Luke, I jab a finger at the street. "Someone posted a picture of her in the car." I look at him. "And she's being driven past the weir. If she's gone that way, the traffic…"

He nods. "The hotel?"

"The hotel. I can beat her there if I run. There's no way she's going to get through that traffic fast." I put a hand on his chest. "You should go – you need to get changed – get ready."

"Are you kidding? Absolutely not."

"Luke! The *show*…"

"Listen to me – we've got time. I'm not even on for the first few scenes anyway. I'm coming with you." He looks at me. "What are we going to do?"

"Improvise."

I grab his hand, and we're running; him in his jeans and his white T-shirt, me in my backstage clothes. We're running, hand in hand, through the middle of the city.

Behind us, the crowd streams into the foyer and the rest of the cast are finishing their warm-up…and out in the street, the first drops of rain start to fall.

We're waiting for a van to pass when, out of the corner of my eye, I see a guy in a *Piecekeepers* T-shirt stop dead in his tracks, look at us and pull out his phone.

The van moves. We move.

Across the square, left under the arch…and with every footstep the drops are falling faster and faster, heavier and heavier.

We take shortcut after shortcut, side street after side street. The windows of a coffee shop flash by; a group sitting on the bench in the window watch us pass.

Our hands feel like they were always meant to fit together.

A turn left, a turn right…and suddenly we're crashing out onto the main road and barrelling into the middle of the rush-hour traffic jam. A bus sounds its horn, long and deafeningly loud and a bunch of kids bang on the windows from the inside, holding their phones up to the glass.

"What are they doing?" Luke squints up at the window,

but the rain's too heavy to see. One of the kids holds up a piece of paper with something scrawled on it.

#StopEmy.

We dart in front of the bus.

It's working.

A taxi driver winds down his window and starts yelling at us as we pass him – complete with some very specific hand gestures. I accidentally-on-purpose knock against his wing mirror on the way.

"Sorry! Sorry!" Luke holds a hand out in apology as we weave through near-stationary traffic. The brake lights paint his soaked T-shirt Lancelot-red as we duck between the cars and vans... The wet road shines and through the raindrops, the headlights become spotlights.

From somewhere behind us, over the hooting, it sounds like somebody's shouting. No. Not shouting, *cheering*.

I risk a look back, shaking the rain out of my eyes. They *are* cheering – on the pavement behind us, a knot of four or five people are waving and shouting "Stop Emy!" their phones glowing in the gloom.

Stop Emy.

Stop Emy.

Stop Emy.

They're doing it – they're helping us.

Please let it work. Please let her see.

Please. Please.

It feels like we have half the town on our side. We have to make it. We *have* to.

Up ahead, I can see the sign on the front of the hotel shining like a beacon – but my lungs are burning and my heart is beating so loud and fast that I'm sure it's going to explode… And he never lets go of my hand, not even when we tumble into the glass revolving door of the hotel and out the other side into the lobby. There's no sign of her car outside – only a couple of taxis and a minibus.

"Maybe we beat her," Luke pants, leaning forward to rest his hands on his knees and dripping gently onto the lobby floor.

"I'll find out." It takes every last reserve of energy I have to walk over to the desk, swiping a drop of water away from the end of my nose. Ever-friendly, the concierge watches me coming over, sighs, and raises an eyebrow. I don't blame him – my hair is hanging down my back in wet ribbons and I'm wheezing and soaked to the skin from running in the rain.

"Yes, hello. And how may I help you today, hmm?"

"Hello, yes. You remember me? Crème de menthe, right? I'm from the theatre – I think Mr Knight may have rung ahead? We're trying to catch Em…Miss Greenway before she leaves."

"Ah." He folds his hands on the desk in front of him. "I'm very sorry – but as I already told Mr Knight when he called a few moments ago, she's already gone."

"Gone?"

"Mmm. Is there anything else I can help you with?" His expression is carefully neutral as he watches the lobby over my shoulder.

"But we ran. How can she be gone? We *ran*. And I have to...I have to get it. I *have* to. It's all a mistake..."

"I'm very sorry, Miss. There's nothing I can do. Unless..." He pointedly clears his throat.

That's it. The necklace has gone with Emery – and sure, it'll come back with her, but in the meantime what am I going to tell Amy? I'll have to own up and tell her the truth. I screwed up.

Someone taps my shoulder. "Excuse me?"

"Sorry. Yes." I step aside, combing my hands through my hair. I feel sick, and I can't tell if it's panic or just *running*.

"No...*excuse* me."

I know that voice. Honey, poured over silk.

The concierge's eyebrows are now perfectly balanced on the top of his head as he beams at the person standing behind me.

Emery Greenway.

She's looking me up and down, holding a phone in one hand...and a necklace box in the other. She is gorgeous and glowing and...*Emery*.

And I am...*not*.

I am, in fact, *soaking wet*.

"You know, the funniest thing just happened. We were in the car and my PR gets a call from my assistant back home, telling her that my social media is blowing up. So she lends me her phone – and what do I see?" She smiles and slides her thumb across the screen to unlock it. "The girl from all those photos with Tommy. She's racing across town to find me – and she's got her boyfriend in tow." She hands over the phone – and on it, there's a stream of pictures. Me and Luke outside the theatre. One of the three fans must have posted it. It's got a caption:

These guys are from the Earl's Theatre: @EmyGreenway – they need you! Please help them! #StopEmy

The username is TommyKFangirl.

Of course it is.

There's a column of hashtags and comments and reposts…

More photos.

More captions.

A blurred shot of us passing through a pool of yellow light, his hand in mine and mine in his and looking like art as we run into the dark.

The two of us running hand in hand, dodging traffic. A video, looping, of us plunging across the road and slipping in between the cars.

Me, turning my head in the rain to look behind me.

Luke's shirt, dazzling white in the headlights.

The notifications keep coming.

@EmyGreenway: have you seen this?

@EmyGreenway has THE most devoted fans!

@EmyGreenway: Don't get in the car! These guys need your help!

@EmyGreenway: I <3 U!

@EmyGreenway: if you can find them, help them out! Save Tommy's show!

#StopEmy #StopEmy #StopEmy #StopEmy…

It goes on and on – and of course *this* is when I remember I'm meant to be giving her own phone back to her. The one I forgot, because I was so busy freaking out and yelling at Tommy. That phone. Whoops.

"You get the picture," Emery says with a smile, holding her hand out for her PR's phone. I give it back, and she lightly passes me the necklace box, placing my hands around it, one above and one below. "I don't think this is meant for me. It's nice to finally meet you, Hope. Tommy's told me all about you. You've been a good friend to him, looking out for him. Thank you – he's not as tough as he likes everyone to think." She lowers her voice, and if anything it sounds even more gorgeous. "A piece of advice, sweetie. Never use real jewellery onstage – it's bad luck."

And just like that, she turns and sweeps majestically out of the hotel lobby, the doormen leaping over themselves to open the side door for her, while I stand there, dripping and fumbling open the box. There it is, shining innocently green against its white suede cushion.

I look over my shoulder at Luke. "We got it."

His eyes are a little too wide to be normal. He's as dazed as I am. "I think we got more than that. I think we just got famous."

"Infamous." And busted, on every possible level. There's no way Amy won't find out about this.

But that's all going to have to wait because the show comes first. I try to swallow a laugh, but it keeps threatening to bubble back up. Luke steps into the revolving door (no doormen for us) and gives it a shove, taking my hand as I follow him out. We stop on the pavement as Emery, in a haze of flashbulbs, climbs back into her car – pausing to blow us a kiss before she slides into her seat. As one, the photographers swivel, their lenses searching for whoever it was Emery Greenway might acknowledge – but all they see are an actor and an intern, both soaking wet, their fingers entwined.

Nothing to see there. Nothing at all.

ACT FIVE, SCENE FIVE

We make it back to the Earl's with just over an hour before curtain-up, and as soon as we're through the stage door, I'm practically shoving Luke towards wardrobe.

"Go! Go!" I shout after him as he jogs down the corridor, passing Amy coming the other way.

"Hope?" I hide the necklace case behind my back and try to look as casual and together as possible. Amy's eyes slide from my feet all the way up to my soaking wet hair, and back down again. "I won't ask," she says. Because of course, here I am looking casual and together and completely professional, and all the while I'm dripping onto the floor, just like the first time we met. "You'd better go to wardrobe and ask George to find you some dry blacks, then if you could pop your head into Tommy's dressing room and make sure he's getting ready? Nobody's seen him since Emery left, and I want to make sure he's prepared."

"Really?" I try not to sound worried, even though this sets an alarm bell ringing in my head. Because I have *definitely* seen Tommy since Emery left...so why hasn't anyone else?

Tommy's dressing room is empty when I stick my head around the door. Everything is exactly as I left it...but there's no sign of Tommy. Maybe he's just lying low until he knows we've got the necklace safely back in the building?

"Tommy?"

No answer. And nobody's here. It's just the standard dressing-room furniture: the well-used blue sofa, and the little mini-fridge chugging away in a corner, which looks like it's mostly being used as a table for cards and gifts right now. There's the costume rail with hangers for Tommy's jacket and clothes, and his first Jamie costume, as well as the opening outfit for the second half, ready to change into during the interval. His personal props – including that bag he lost at the costume parade – are all hanging from the rail in labelled plastic covers, just like they were earlier. In the corner, there's the enormous potted plant that someone's given him, draped in tiny white fairy lights, and last but not least there's the dressing table: a big white plastic counter bolted to the wall underneath a brightly lit mirror. I sigh, and stare at my reflection standing in the middle of an alternate universe dressing room. I wonder if her night's going better than mine? Taped to the edge of the mirror are a couple of photos: one, slightly battered around the edges and creased in a couple of places from being unevenly folded, looks old. Two boys standing on what looks like a pebble beach – and it doesn't take a genius to see a young Rick and Tommy looking back out at you. The other photo is even more instantly recognizable: it's Emery Greenway. But she looks different to how I've seen her before – this isn't a shot from a premiere or an interview, or even a paparazzi picture from the gossip columns (although god knows I'll never read another one of those after all this). It's just her, on a balcony overlooking a city; she's not wearing a designer outfit or a glittering gown, but a T-shirt and jeans. She has bare feet, and she's smiling straight at the camera. It's the kind of photo someone might take of their girlfriend – you know, if they were people like Tommy Knight and Emery Greenway.

Even after meeting her, I feel like I've intruded. I've looked behind a door that wasn't meant for me; seen something that was always meant to be private.

The counter itself is scattered with gifts, stage make-up, headphones, a hotel key, dry-cleaning tickets (oh joy), receipts…and newspaper clippings.

Newspaper clippings all about Tommy.

Even the thought of it's enough to make me roll my eyes – but looking closer, they're all about the Earl's, about the show…about whether people think he's going to be any good. The one on the top makes it pretty clear that they don't.

"They" – specifically – being Marshal Arthur, whose most recent opinion column sits neatly on the top of the pile of clippings. I skim the first couple of lines and my stomach drops. Who the hell let Tommy see this, *especially* on opening night?

"This is just what I need. As if I don't have enough to think about already with him *here…"*

That's what he said, wasn't it? I was so freaked out about the necklace that I didn't even think to ask who "he" was – but reading the absolute hatchet job Marshal Arthur's done on Tommy in this article, it all makes perfect, horrible sense. The more of it I read, the angrier I get. It starts tamely enough: do Hollywood stars belong on the stage? Apparently not, according to this – and especially not the Hollywood star whose dressing room I happen to be standing in *right now*. Why not? Because, says the column, he's self-centred, narcissistic and – frankly, as far as Marshal's concerned – has no right to even call himself a "proper actor".

It's this bit, this last sting in the tail, that makes my blood boil – because yes, Tommy's self-centred and yes, he's absolutely the biggest narcissist I've ever met…but I've also seen him act. *Really* act. I've watched him stand on the stage and fade into the character he's meant to be. I've held my breath just like everyone else in the room, waiting for him to finish a line or make the move we all knew was coming but which looks so natural and so real when he does it…

And after reading all that, Tommy must have seen Marshal strolling up to the foyer doors. No wonder he's vanished. I never thought I'd feel angry on Tommy Knight's behalf. Angry *at* him, maybe – but *for* him? I didn't expect that. But how dare someone like Marshal Arthur, someone who should know better, dismiss him before he's seen what Tommy can do on a stage?

The little wall-mounted speaker in the corner of the room crackles and Amy's voice rings out in the Tommy-less space. "Ladies and gentlemen, this is an intercom test, just a test. One hour until showtime. Thank you."

Okay. An hour until the curtain goes up.

Where's Tommy?

He can't have left the building – someone would have seen him. That means he's here somewhere…

Sitting on the dressing table, in the middle of all the bits and pieces, the object that I laser in on is Tommy's phone. Of course it's his phone – that thing and I have a relationship now.

But it's *here*, right next to Emery's.

Which surely means he can't be far away.

That was easy.

Okay. So he came back in here. He closed the door behind him, took his phone out of his pocket, posted those photos and put it down... I rest my hand on top of his phone, just like I'm talking myself through a props table and figuring out the working order for everything on it.

He put his phone on the counter and...

Fun fact about dressing room number one: it's the only one with an en-suite bathroom. Not that it's a particularly glamorous one – it's basically a cupboard with a toilet, a tiny sink and a shower cubicle jammed in there – but it still counts.

The en-suite door is closed. It's been closed since I came in here.

It's not just closed – it's *locked*.

And because it's a bathroom, that door only locks from the inside.

"Tommy?"

Nobody answers – but is that the sound of somebody moving around, trying to be very, very quiet?

"Tommy! Are you in there?"

A long, long silence. But it's not an empty silence – it's more like the silence of the auditorium. Waiting.

"Everyone's been looking for you. We need to go through your personal props and get you ready." I lower my voice. "I got the necklace, by the way."

Still nothing.

"Look, you could at least say something so I know you're not *dead*."

At last, there's a muffled groan from inside – followed by some pretty exciting swear words – and the lock on the door turns with a click.

"Tommy?"

The bathroom door swings open, and Tommy steps out. And he looks *awful*.

He's so pale he's turned a shade of ash-grey and his eyes have disappeared into dark hollows. Everything about him is sort of…slumped.

"What happened to you?"

"Not what. *Who*." His voice sounds like he's swallowed a bucket of rocks. I can barely hear him, even from a metre away. This is not good.

"Marshal's column? He's an asshat, trying to get more people to talk about him. He's *trolling* you. Ignore him."

"Ignore him? Ignore that?" Tommy waves a slender hand at the newspaper.

"You heard me."

"Ignore Marshal Arthur, when he's going to be in tonight. When I've *already seen him out there*."

"Come on, Tommy. It's opening night…"

"You don't say."

I was almost feeling sorry for him – right up until the point where he tried to drown me in sarcasm. So I decide to ditch the sympathy and try a different approach; the one that worked before.

"Enough, okay? Enough. We've got time…just not much." First thing, you need to get into your starting costume. Secondly, we need to get you up to show speed, and fast."

I know what this is. It's stage fright – and it's *bad*. More than bad. Tommy Knight with stage fright on the night he leads the world premiere of the stage adaptation of *Piecekeepers* means we're pretty much all screwed.

Nobody on this show can afford to mess up.

Nobody.

Or we're all toast.

I raid the stores in the green room. There's nothing else for it – I don't think Tommy's usual almond-milk decaf coffee is going to cut it right now. It's Rick's melt-your-face-off special secret supply of extra-strong dark-roasted Tech Rehearsal coffee or nothing. He hides it in an anonymous-looking tin at the back of the snack cupboard, and it's so potent it can caffeinate your eyebrows from across the room. Which means it's exactly what Tommy needs to get him moving.

I speed-walk back to the dressing room with the biggest mug I can find full of steaming heavily-sugared coffee, trying not to spill any of it on the way (it would probably dissolve the floor anywhere it splashes) and hoping Rick is out of range. You can smell this stuff across the auditorium, so if he's prowling the halls, there's no way I'll be able to avoid explaining what I'm doing. Or why.

"Is that for Rick?" someone calls after me from the other side of an open door, but I don't stop until I'm back in dressing room number one. Tommy himself is pretty much exactly as I left him, slumped forward onto his dressing table, his head resting on his arms.

"Right. Drink this. Now." I bang the mug down next to where I think his face is.

"I'm not drinking that." He doesn't even look up.

"It's coffee."

"I know that. It's Rick's coffee. It's vile," says the top of Tommy's head.

"Then you'll know what it does – and you know you need it."

There's a low rumble from somewhere between his elbows that might be him telling me to piss off. I ignore it.

"I'm going to go and see George, and ask him to come and do your make-up in here. Then I'm going to go out and get you some food – which you are going to eat without question – before Rick sees –" I gesture at him – "*this* and explodes."

Another vague noise – but I'm sure that's the beginning of a hand reaching for the mug.

"Okay. Okay. You…drink the coffee." I head for the door – then stop. "And you'd better hope Rick doesn't find out, or he'll kill us both."

Nothing.

Okay.

The door to wardrobe is shut.

"George. George? George! Are you in?"

I can hear voices from the other side, and the door opens just enough for George to stick his head out and peer at me.

"What?"

"Are you busy?"

"Do I look busy?"

"Well, right now you look like a floating head, so…"

He rolls his eyes. "Yes, I'm busy – what d'you want? Now's not a good time."

"It's Tommy."

"What is it?" The door opens a fraction more and a couple of the cast, getting their latex special-effect make-up applied, wave at me from the other side. I wave back.

"Tommy needs you," I hiss at George, hoping nobody else can hear me over the nervous laughter and chatting in the room. "Can you go over to DR One in a minute and sort him out?"

"Sure." George tilts his head to one side. "I'll just check with Nathalie…"

"No!"

"What?"

"No...need. It'll only take two seconds."

"All right..." He eyes me curiously. "I'll go right over."

"Great. Good. Okay. Cool."

"You all right?"

"Me?" It comes out a little higher-pitched and a lot louder than I meant it to. "No, I'm fine. Completely fine."

His eyes narrow down so far I can barely even see them. "Mmm-hmm."

But all I give him is a smile and a hurried: "Got to run, see you later, bye!" as I make a break for it.

Just like fire, nerves spread – and both are just as dangerous in a theatre, rippling outwards in ever-increasing circles. If a theatre is the still, calm surface of a lake, then a really bad case of stage fright in the company is like dropping the Empire State Building into the middle of it.

I'm not having that, so I walk as calmly-but-quickly as I can to the stage door – where Amy is leaning against the desk, checking the sign-in sheet.

No. Nonononono.

"Hope?" She looks up, startled to see me. "All set? How's Tommy doing?"

"Oh, fine. Fine fine fine. He's in his dressing room, freshening up. He...uhhhh... I'm just running out, actually, to…ummm…fetch a couple of things for him. While he gets into character?"

Maybe she's too distracted to notice my massive internal wince there. Maybe.

There's the longest of all possible pauses…and finally she nods. "Great. Thanks. When you get back, can you let him know we're ready whenever he is?"

"Yep. Sure thing. Suresuresure."

I walk so fast down the steps to the street that I almost fly.

Stage fright.

Stage fright…

A memory of sitting on the stairs in my pyjamas, listening to the voices drifting up from the dinner party in the kitchen. The door's half-open and I've been straining to catch snippets of what they're saying, these impossibly glamorous people Mum works with. Both my sisters are asleep, their bedroom doors closed tightly against the laughter and noise. So it's only me, pressing my face against the banisters, who hears the producer Mum's invited tonight clear her throat and say, over everyone else: "Stage fright? The best cure for that I ever heard of was…"

It takes me ten minutes to round up everything I remember – but I'm *sure* I'm missing something. There's something else, isn't there? One item I've forgotten.

I stand there, juggling the burger box, the net bag full of lemons and the bottle of sauce, and wedge my phone under my chin. There is only one person I can trust right now – the person I should have trusted from the start.

"Mum? No, listen. I need your help. Yes. No, it's serious – what do I give an actor who's bottled it? I've got the burger, I've got the lemons and the hot sauce… What else?"

Ginger ale. Obviously.

I look at my watch.

I don't have time to go back to the shop – not if I'm going to deliver this lot to Tommy before he's called to the stage. So where on earth am I going to get a bottle of ginger ale from?

And then, of course, it hits me.

I run back to the theatre with my phone still wedged between my shoulder and my jaw, balancing everything else as I dart through the crowds filtering into the theatre – not even caring who sees me or what they think. This matters more.

My phone call connects. "Luke! I know you're getting ready, but can you do something for me? It's an emergency. Another one. Can you borrow a couple of mixer bottles of ginger ale from Sarwat in the bar, and meet me in the green room in two minutes? It's…"

No.

Luke is Tommy's understudy. If there's *anyone* I need to not tell about this, it's Luke.

Which sucks.

"…it's a prop thing. Thank you thank you thank you!"

I hurtle through the stage door, straight on down to the green room – and there he is, two small bottles of ginger ale from the bar in his hands. And in full Lancelot costume. My heart lurches, because he looks like he was made for it. The shirt, the coat… And he's already been through make-up too – his eyes are even bluer than usual, ringed with dark eyeliner to make them stand out under the bleaching stage lighting. It's a *good* look.

Not. Now. Parker.

He waves at my arms full of junk food and lemons, and at my general demeanour. "Do I even want to know?"

"Thank you so much – can you empty those into a jug and stick it in the microwave?"

"The microwave?"

"And stir it so it goes flat?" I yank open the cupboards, looking for a glass.

"What scene's this for? You said it was a prop…"

Oh god, I want to tell him. I want to tell him and ask his advice…but if he thinks Tommy's a mess…

No.

I can't tell him.

However much I hate the idea, right now my first loyalty has to be to Tommy. Even if I resent that so much it makes me feel a little bit queasy.

Luke studies me, waiting to see if I break into a smile –

waiting to see if I'm pranking him somehow, or trying to make him laugh. Eventually, I guess he realizes I'm not messing around because he shrugs.

"Sure – whatever you need."

"You're a star."

"One day." He grins, and suddenly he's the Luke I'm falling for, costume or not, and I could stay here for ever, just breathing him in.

I'm supposed to be doing something, aren't I?

I snatch the jug out of the microwave. "Got to go – break a leg! I'll be watching in the wings!" I shout over my shoulder as I run for the dressing rooms, leaving him smiling and shaking his head in my wake.

He's the Luke I'm falling for.

Falling for.

Falling. For.

I can feel my heart glowing that little bit brighter than it did, and suddenly I'm smiling, and as I turn the corner to dressing room number one it's the thought of him that lights my way through the dark.

When I put it in front of him, Tommy looks at the hot-sauce-smothered burger like I'm trying to feed him a severed foot on toast. Still, he is at least upright, made-up and half in costume – so that's progress.

"What…is that?" He slowly extends one of his super-manicured fingers and jabs it for extra drama.

"Your dinner."

"No." He purses his lips and shakes his head as he says it. Again: extra drama.

"Yes." And because I can be dramatic too, I put the glass of hot (freshly flattened) ginger ale mixed with the juice of two (freshly squeezed) lemons in front of him. And yes, there's a couple of pips floating around in there too, and sure, it looks a bit murky and weird, but we're on a schedule. "And this goes with it."

"No." He pushes both the plate – because I did actually go to the trouble of putting it on a plate, at least – and the glass away.

"Yes." I push them back.

Reluctantly, he lifts the top of the burger bun and peers under it. "What in god's name *is* this? Are you trying to poison me so your boyfriend can take over?"

"Hardly. And if I was going to do that, I can think of much more inventive ways of doing it than feeding you a dodgy burger." I knock his hand away from the bun. "This is Miriam Parker's fail-safe actor stage-fright fixer."

At the mention of my mother, he raises an eyebrow.

I nod. "Yes. Miriam Parker is my mother. And if anyone knows about theatre, it's her. So I called my mother. For you. And of all the people in this building, *you* know what that means. So you're going to eat the stupid burger and you're going to drink the disgusting drink and you're going to be grateful. And then you're going to pull yourself together and go do your job, and let me get on with doing mine, because there's a whole load of people down the hall right now who are counting on *both* of us."

Tommy looks remarkably smug (still slightly grey under his make-up, but smug) when I mention Mum. So he *did* know when he gave me that little speech about names. Interesting. And something I'll think about later, because the speaker hisses again – and there's Amy. "Ladies and gentlemen, this is your half-hour call. Half an hour, please. Thank you." I have no time.

Without another word of complaint, he picks up the glass and takes a sip, wincing as he swallows – then catching my eye over the top of the glass, he takes another mouthful.

Better.

After a few gulps of that (and I can't exactly say I envy him – but Mother knows best), he decides to brave the burger. Two bites in, he looks at me piteously.

I shake my head. "Sorry."

"You could at least try to sound like you mean it," he says around a scorching mouthful of food.

"I do mean it, but as you might have noticed, we're on the clock here. You told me there was no point trying to outrun my name, and you were right. I can't pretend I'm somebody I'm not and I can't hide who I am. I shouldn't have to, either. You told me to show everyone that I'd earned it, and you were right about that too. This is me, earning it." I look over his shoulder into the dressing-room mirror and meet his gaze and hold it. "Now it's your turn."

ACT FIVE, SCENE SIX

Amy's already at the prompt desk in the wings, her notes and folders neatly stacked either on it or underneath it. She's ticking something off in her notebook and glances up as I settle into my seat beside her.

"It's nearly time – everything okay? *You* okay?"

"Yep. All good. We are *all good*." My voice shakes even as I try to keep it steady. Seeing the front-of-house staff giving the auditorium one final check through the prompt-desk monitors doesn't help my nerves (which are already pretty knackered after this evening's drama – and just think, we've not even got to the actual *show* yet).

"Great. I thought you could write tonight's show report for Rick." She magics a sheet of paper out from beneath her folder and hands it to me with a flourish. "It's the usual sort of thing – here's my template."

I look at the page she's handed me. Start time, end time, approximate size of audience, notes and comments – all the things that make a theatre tick. And nowhere does it say I have to tell them about the lead actor's catastrophic wobble beforehand. Good.

Amy clears her throat quietly, and when I look up she's holding out a headset and pointing to a switch on the desk.

"I've called the half, so how about you get us ready to open the house."

And she may try to hide it, but I can see she's smiling as I press the button to switch on the backstage PA and pull the mic closer to my mouth.

"Preparing to open the house, please. Iron out."

In my mind's eye, I see everyone in the dressing rooms and the labyrinth of backstage corridors look up at the speakers. Up on the fly-floor, Chris and Rav the flymen are adjusting their gloves.

Time ticks by unspeakably fast. People are running from one side of the stage to the other, and there's a shout that echoes around the empty auditorium as well as through my headset.

"Iron going out!"

Slowly, the safety curtain rises – leaving the stage exposed. There's no stage curtain any more – not since Rick announced that it made him feel like we were putting on a production in the nineteenth century.

Amy passes me a laminated card with writing on it. "Right, then. Let's open the house."

"Sure."

I can't believe how much my fingers shake as I take the card from her – almost enough to drop it, or to miss the switch that opens the mic channel to all the front-of-house areas: the foyer, the bars, the corridors and stairs and bathrooms. But I don't.

"Good evening, ladies and gentlemen, and welcome to the Earl's Theatre. The house is now open for this evening's performance of *Piecekeepers*. The house is now open. Thank you."

I've barely even finished when Amy's reaching across me, flicking another switch and speaking into her own headset.

"Ladies and gentlemen, the house is now open. The house is now open, so please avoid crossing the stage and using the pass door into the auditorium, thank you." Another switch. "This is a crew call, please. Work lights off, ladies and gentlemen. Blues on."

Around us, the lights flicker off, leaving us with just the dull glow of the blue backstage lights and our tiny little prompt light. And as we sit there, hidden in the gloom at the side of the stage, I can hear them making their way into the auditorium. The audience. *Our* audience. It's barely more than a whisper at first, but gradually the sound of their voices grows as more and more people come in to take their seats.

We make the five-minute backstage call – the beginners'

call for everyone we need at the start of the show – and suddenly, Amy nods at the monitors. "You're opening the show too, by the way."

"Me? You're kidding. Actually cue the start of the show?"

She smiles, and looks me in the eye. "You've earned it, especially after your little adventure chasing jewellery across town."

Ah. "About that…"

"No. You don't need to."

"But I—"

"It's live theatre. Things go wrong. What matters is how you fix them – and that the show goes on. Besides, maybe some superstitions are right."

That was…not what I was expecting. But okay.

"So?" She looks at me expectantly. "Like I said – you've earned it." She pulls her headset mic a little closer to her mouth, cues the three- and two-minute front-of-house warning bells – then calmly calls beginners, presses a button and goes straight into a final front-of-house call.

The door – the one that I remember walking through for the first time like it was only five minutes ago – opens quietly and, one by one, they appear behind us. But it's not the actors filling the wings – not at all. It's their characters.

It's not Juliet standing behind me, tucking a strand of her wig behind her ear; it's Lizzie, smoothing down her long hair.

It's not Vicki from the ensemble rolling her shoulders beside the prop table; it's the gallery security guard who Lizzie saves.

Standing behind her, silhouetted by blue light against the door, it's not Tommy, but Jamie, completely unprepared for what's about to happen to him.

I adjust my headset, flicking the switch for my mic.

Everything builds and builds and builds to a white noise in my ears...and then Amy raises a hand and drops it, and everything is silent, waiting. Expectant.

"Stand by beginners. Stand by sound cues one, two." My voice is both too loud and too quiet at the same time.

"Standing by," says a voice in my ear.

"Stand by elecs cue one."

"Standing by."

"Beginners, places, please." Closing my eyes, I count to ten under my breath. "And...cue elec one."

I can see them through the monitors on the desk: the first few rows of the audience. I can see the girls from the queue and Haydn Swift and Marshal Arthur; their eyes fixed only on the stage and the people who step out onto it.

Because whatever happens back here, whatever drama and tragedy and comedy might be taking place around us all...out there? The show does go on. We make it.

* * *

It's the smallest thing. I bet nobody in the audience even notices it – I'm not even sure whether Amy, her eyes tracking every cue in the script, picks it up. But I do. Maybe I'm just so wired, so fixed on Tommy's performance after...well, everything, that every word, every gesture he gets through feels like a victory.

So I *do* catch it, and I tell myself it's nothing.

The briefest of all possible pauses, halfway through a line.

A place that, ever since I started this role, he has never put a pause.

Maybe it's just because he needed to take an extra breath. It doesn't *mean* anything.

And it doesn't...until the next one. A definite break in the middle of a line, a tremor in his voice...and then a desperate fast glance over at the prompt desk. His eyes lock onto mine and, very quietly, Amy leans in and whispers: "Get the prompt script to the right page." I look back at her, and she shakes her head. "Be ready to catch him if he needs you."

I flip ahead in the script, scanning the lines; the ground Tommy has to cover before he can retreat to the darkness of the wings. As I skim, I hear another pause where there shouldn't be one. Amy swears under her breath and already I can feel the atmosphere starting to turn. Looking straight out at the stage, I hold up the script book so that the next

time Tommy looks over, he'll see it and know we're there –
a safety net. That we – *I* – won't let him fall. All he has to do
is make it through the next three minutes.

Three minutes which must feel like a lifetime out there.

He makes it through the next line, and the next…then
stumbles again, getting a word wrong and having to rework
the rest of it. Another slip and people will start to notice,
and then he'll unravel from the heart down in front of
them all.

Ten lines to go.

Five.

Four, and then he's got to come to me for the necklace.

Three.

Come on, Tommy.

Two.

I slip out of my seat and pick my way past the back of the
flats to the prop table, picking up the necklace case, ready.

One more line…and suddenly he's striding towards me,
a little faster than he's done before, his eyes wide but vacant.
I can see the beads of sweat pricked out across his face;
the rivers of it running down under his collar. He's there,
but he's not. He's not Tommy and he's not Jamie – he's
stuck somewhere in between, and he's lost.

He barely even looks at me as he leans in to grab the
necklace, so when I close my hand around his wrist, he
jumps. Tommy Knight looks up and sees it's me, and his

other hand locks around my arm and holds it like I'm a lifebelt.

Luckily for him, that's *exactly* what I am.

I pull him as close to me as I can, until my lips are practically touching his ear, because neither of us can afford for anyone else to hear.

"Show them *you* own *it*. All of them."

He takes half a step back and something flickers across his face as we let go of each other – and then he's gone, back out into the blinding white lights.

The second we reach the interval, Rick swoops in to herd Tommy off to the dressing room, a protective arm around his shoulders. The door backstage swings shut behind them and Amy stretches, pulling off her headset. "Great job, Hope. I'm going to get some water – you want anything?"

I shake my head. I'm not sure I can actually manage words right now.

As the safety curtain comes down, I look across to the other side of the stage at George – still draped in all the bits of scarf and wig and bag he's removed from assorted actors as they rushed offstage. He looks back at me, and he's got the weirdest expression on his face; it's like he's about to cry, but because he's so happy and so relieved and so *everything* that he doesn't quite know what else to do. I guess

I must look the same, because he nods at me and blows me a kiss. I blow a kiss right back at him as he hurries off down to wardrobe.

Amy isn't gone long, and when she comes back, she's carrying a jug of water and two glasses.

"Well, we're doing all right so far. *He* seems to be enjoying himself, anyway." She taps the audience monitor, where a tiny black-and-white Marshal Arthur is writing thoughtfully in a little notebook. The screen is far too small to see what he's jotting down, but that doesn't stop us both from trying. Amy pours a glass of water and takes a swig. "I thought we were going to lose Tommy at one point, though. He really did worry me. I started thinking we should have pushed for previews, more rehearsal time, more tech time…"

"Oh, I don't think anyone noticed. I barely even did," I say. Possibly a little too quickly.

She eyes me over the top of her glass. "Mmm." Another swig. More eyeing. "He just suddenly seemed so much less…Tommy. He's never had to work in this kind of environment before, and I don't think he's used to being so exposed and vulnerable."

"But that's what acting *is*…right?" I shuffle closer to her seat. "It *is* being exposed and vulnerable – it's not about putting *on* extra layers of protection and pretending to be somebody else, it's about taking them off and pretending they're you…"

Oh.

That's why Luke wanted to act. It's not about hiding behind someone else's skin at all. It really is about fitting someone else's soul over your own, letting it creep inside every corner of you, and you into it, until you can't tell where the join is any more. And you can't just shrug that off when the lights go down – a piece of that character, that person, that soul, stays with you. You carry the memory of it around with you as part of who you've been. The way you might a family…the way – whether I like it or not – I carry fragments of my sisters, my father, my inescapable *mother* around with me.

Suddenly, more than anything, I want to find Luke and tell him that I get it. That I understand.

It's *family*.

Family is the key that unlocks us; the thing that makes us both different and both the same. I always felt I had too much, that I was always standing in somebody's shadow. For Luke, his family *were* shadows; shadows and ghosts… and now the spotlight is the only place he feels safe. Just like I only feel safe out of sight, in the dark.

Family is what opens us out…so it's family we seek. Family that matters more than anything in its own way; family who depend on you – working together, making things happen.

Which is why we both came to the theatre.

ACT FIVE, SCENE SIX

* * *

The second half floats past like some kind of dream. Tommy sweeps past me and back out onto the stage, and the instant the light hits him it's clear something has changed...because now, he really is owning it. The role, the stage, the *name*. And he's got the audience. Out of the corner of my eye, I even catch Amy smiling. When the vanishing painting actually *does* vanish, I hear her whisper "Yes!" under her breath, and as the whole audience gasps, it's all I can do not to cheer. On the far side of the stage, I watch George work: changing coats and costumes, adjusting wigs and pinning hair with only seconds to get everything done. He's a blur of motion, and looks like he's got fifteen hands all doing something different at once – but he's smiling and he doesn't miss a single cue.

When Luke steps out onto the darkened stage – walking forward until he hits that mark he was so careful to check – and the single spotlight at the very edge of the apron catches him and makes him shine, Amy nudges me; pushing me towards the very edge of the flats for a better view. Whatever I *thought* this would be like, however I thought I would feel listening to him, seeing him drop to his knees as Lancelot breaks...this is both a thousand times better and a thousand times harder. On the one hand, I want to run out, pull him to his feet and tell him that everything will be okay, because my heart is aching for him...and on the other, I never want him to stop.

In the shadows, I listen as his voice fades to a whisper, and I watch the spotlight die. When it comes back up, Lancelot is gone.

"Hope! Quick-change and crossover," Amy hisses. "Go!" She holds out her stopwatch.

I drop my headset on the prompt desk, grab the watch and run for the stairs.

"Where is he…where is he…?" I lean into the fire door at the end of the corridor, propping it open. We're so nearly there, so near the end that I can taste it. Just Tommy's big changeover scene – the last scene – and we're home free.

We've kept them since the interval, all of them. I've heard it – the kind of silence that only comes from an auditorium full of people so caught up in what they're seeing that they can barely breathe. And none of us want to lose them now.

George is pacing, his whole body tense. Ready to grab the first door and open it for Tommy to run through.

They've practised it every day, over and over, even without me and my stopwatch – but somehow, Tommy's never made good enough time to be back on that stage when the lights come up. He's always just a few seconds too slow.

"Come on, come on…"

ACT FIVE, SCENE SIX

There's the crack of the sound cue (number 307) and the echoing thump of feet on the stairs.

Here he comes, through the first doorway and along the corridor towards me, stripping off his shirt as he goes and dropping it on the floor, while George – keeping pace with him every step of the way – somehow manages to drape, wrap and throw his new costume over him, even tossing one shoe at a time ahead of him for him to step into.

Behind him, at the far end of the corridor the door swings open again – and there's Luke, still in his last Lancelot costume, still with a smear of stage blood across his cheek, watching.

I look at the stopwatch.

"Twenty seconds, Tommy…" I call down the corridor at him.

He nods to show he's heard me – and as he comes closer, he does the strangest thing. He raises his hand…and as I flatten myself against the door to let him pass, he gives me a high-five.

His eyes meet mine, just for an instant.

"Thank you. For everything."

And then he's gone, running for his exit – his entrance – utterly changed.

Quick-change managed, George flops against the wall and slides down it in a pile of discarded clothes. I walk over to him, picking up a shoe on the way, and reach down to help him up.

"Did you hear that?" I hand him the shoe.

"Hear what?"

"That's the first time he's said thank you to me."

"The theatre does funny things to people," he says with a shrug – and above us, the auditorium erupts into the loudest applause I've ever heard.

I shoot a last look down to the far end of the corridor... but the door's already closed. Luke's gone.

"Come on – if we run, we can make it back up for the curtain call." I grab George's hand, and together we sprint for it: back up the stairs and through the door marked STAGE and into the wings, packed with all the rest of the cast; with Rick in his suit and tie and Amy and her headset, and we wedge ourselves into the very side of the prompt desk at the exact moment the lights come back up.

Together, they all walk out onto the stage for their bows, and Amy leans in to Rick and taps the right-hand monitor on the prompt desk – the one looking out into the audience.

"Look," she whispers – and points to the front row, where Marshal Arthur is already standing, his notebook tucked under one arm so he can clap, and...

"Is he *crying*?" George squints at the monitor.

I don't know because I'm too busy watching the little group in the row behind, where my mother, Miriam Parker – yes, *that* Miriam Parker – is clasping my dad's hand and beaming. Next to them is an older woman, her open programme tucked under one arm as she applauds…and there's something about the way she holds herself, something about the way her expression slips between old grief and fierce pride as she gazes at the stage that tells me I'm looking at Luke's grandmother. And then they're lost to view as in front of them, a guy with untidy dark hair and the girl with long hair beside him are jumping to their feet and clapping and whooping.

"Doesn't look like Haydn Swift hated it to me…" Amy says quietly.

And without a word, Rick throws his arms around her and laughs – right before Tommy comes barrelling into the wings to haul him out onstage to take his own bow.

In the darkness of the wings, I look around me at all the people who made this happen, crowding in to hear the applause, their faces faint in the blue work lights and the ghosts of the spotlights. I hear the fly-floor creak quietly as Chris moves above us. Nobody out there can see us – half of them don't even know we exist – and that's exactly how it should be.

We are invisible, inaudible, intangible.

Theatre ghosts – that's all we are.

And looking around me, I can't think of anyone I'd rather be.

EPILOGUE

Get-out

CURTAIN CALL

The auditorium empties faster than it filled – especially tonight, with a reception in the bar and congratulations to be shared. *Piecekeepers* has opened, and tomorrow I'll have to write up the show report. Until then, the job's done. The crew have tidied up their areas and their kit and either changed into fresh clothes and headed to the bar to celebrate, or simply slipped away into the night.

But opening night or not, someone's always got to be the last to leave.

I turn off the switches on the prompt desk, one by one.

One by one, the monitors, the red lights, the blue and the green fade out.

I flick off the work light and the fluorescents, and the wings go dark. There's only the house lights in the auditorium now...and the ghost light, shining away in the gloom.

I walk out onto the stage, right out into the very middle... and I catch myself before I bow. Bad luck to bow to an empty auditorium.

"What if it isn't empty?" shouts a voice from the back... and I look up, all the way back to the stalls door.

There, a glass each in their hands, are my entire family.

Mum, Dad, Faith and Grace – and bouncing up and down beside them, Priya.

Mum shoves her glass at Dad, who almost drops it, and cups her hands around her mouth into a funnel, because apparently she's forgotten how acoustics work. "Go on! Take a bow!"

So I do. I bow, and they cheer.

Even Faith.

"I'll be out in a minute," I call back. "You shouldn't be in here – go through to the bar." And they do, laughing and talking too loud, just like they always do...and I don't miss the look back over her shoulder that Mum gives me, nor the little nod.

I could've done without the bow. That nod was all I needed.

The silence of the auditorium settles and I turn back to the wings...and there he is.

Luke, silhouetted against the glow of the ghost light; his hands in his pockets and already back in his own skin.

Waiting.

For me.

Because, just for once, it isn't my name that matters – and I don't have anything to prove.

I just have to be me.

ACKNOWLEDGEMENTS

Theatre is a team game…and so is publishing: you may not see them, but this book would not and could not exist without these people.

Rebecca Hill and Stephanie King, who gave Hope & the whole Earl's team wings and helped them to fly. Without their encouragement, their advice, support, enthusiasm and wisdom, Hope and company would still be stuck on the ground. Sarah Stewart, for making me look much smarter than I really am – and for pointing out that yes, we know his eyes are blue. Which was true. The whole team at Usborne who have taken a jumble of pages in Word and turned them into a beautiful book. It's an extraordinary kind of alchemy. Stevie Hopwood, publicist extraordinaire and all-round theatre kid: the theatre world's loss is my substantial gain.

Juliet Mushens at Caskie Mushens – agent, hero, icon – who understood Hope from the very first page, and who somehow always knows.

Jemma Edwards at the Bristol Old Vic, who answered all

my questions (even the stupid ones) with incredible good humour and showed me behind the curtain. Hope's world is built on those foundations – and they don't move.

Sharon Clark and Simon Stephens, whose theatre writing classes taught me not just about writing, but about trust and creativity and much, much more.

John East at the Theatre Royal Bath, who ran the theatre production summer school where this idea began. Although I still haven't quite forgiven him for making me not only act, but carry a tray full of borrowed glasses across a stage while trying to do it…

Clare Thornthwaite and Alex Knight, my partners in theatre crime, to whom this story is dedicated. Thank you for the adventures, the cocktails and the singing nuns. One day we'll make it to the Oliviers in person.

Lizzie Ryder, singing teacher and friend, who didn't even mind when I had a tantrum over Sondheim – or being turned into a character in an imaginary book. Thank you for opening the door to a whole new world. ("Deadface" and "just do less" are my new personal mottos.)

Katie Khan, who was remarkably calm about being transformed from author into stage magic supremo, and Lucinda Tomlinson – who suddenly finds herself in the Earl's PR department.

Bertie Carvel, whose advice about acting works just as well for writing, and who unlocked a whole section of the story in my head during a conversation in the Almeida foyer.

My friends who have told me their theatre stories – both true and apocryphal – and who will know who they are (and where the bodies are buried).

My family, as always, for putting up with me on a daily basis. Even when I'm in the middle of a first draft.

Lastly, the theatres and all those connected to them (backstage and front-of-house staff, companies, creatives and crews) who have in some way inspired this book. The Earl's Theatre is fictional – as is the Square Globe Community Theatre – but I wanted it to reflect my love for my favourite real theatres: the Bristol Old Vic, the London Old Vic, the Almeida, the Royal Court and the Theatre Royal Bath. They are remarkable places, doing brilliant work, and if you get the chance to visit one (or all) of them, and to support them, do. Theatre is for everyone.

MEET MAGGIE HARCOURT

Maggie Harcourt is the critically-acclaimed author of *The Last Summer Of Us* and *Unconventional*. She lives in Bath with her family, and can be found in the theatre stalls whenever possible.

What's the best thing about theatre, Maggie?

I love the magic of it: a stage is a glimpse into a whole other world, and theatres always feel like places where incredible things can happen.

What is the most romantic play you have ever seen?

The production of *Much Ado About Nothing* that I saw one summer when I was pretty young, performed by a touring company in the ruins of Llansteffan castle near where I grew up. It was the first Shakespeare I'd ever seen, and I can still remember watching it against the backdrop of the castle walls, and the light glittering on the sea as the sun started to set. After that, I went home and learned all Beatrice's lines from the play.

@maggieharcourt maggieharcourt maggiehaha.tumblr.com

IF YOU ENJOYED **THEATRICAL**, YOU'LL LOVE
UNCONVENTIONAL

"A gorgeous one-of-a-kind novel, perfect for fans of
Rainbow Rowell."
MAXIMUM POP!

"Breathlessly brilliant – spine-tinglingly romantic, unashamedly
geeky, smart and funny… It's a perfect meeting of worlds:
fantastic fandoms, books you want to live inside
and a completely gorgeous love story."
MIRANDA DICKINSON, SUNDAY TIMES BESTSELLING AUTHOR

"*Unconventional* is the ultimate love story for the age of fandom
and, much like a meeting with your favourite celebrity, it will
leave you breathless."
MEREDITH RUSSO, AUTHOR OF "IF I WAS YOUR GIRL"

"Maggie Harcourt is the UK's answer to Rainbow Rowell.
Unconventional is original, funny and I wish I could
transport myself into it, amongst all the characters
who stole my heart right from the beginning."
LUCY THE READER

"*Unconventional* is the swooniest swoonfest."
MELINDA SALISBURY, AUTHOR OF "THE SIN EATER'S DAUGHTER"

EVERYONE'S A FAN
OF SOMEONE

UNCONVENTIONAL

"A gorgeous one-of-a-kind novel, perfect
for fans of Rainbow Rowell"
Maximum Pop!

Maggie Harcourt

also by Maggie Harcourt

THE LAST SUMMER OF US

The air smells of hot, dry grass trampled underfoot.
It smells of diesel, of cider and cigarettes and burgers
and ice cream and the ends of things.
The end of the summer.
The end of us: of Steffan and Jared and me.

This is the story of a road trip.
The story of three best friends crammed into
a clapped-out car full of regrets and secrets,
on a journey that will change their lives for ever.

A story of love, lies, grief, friendship and growing up.
A story you'll never forget.

"Exquisitely sad and yet touchingly beautiful.
And so, so real."
HOLLY BOURNE, AUTHOR OF "AM I NORMAL YET?"

THE LAST SUMMER OF US

Where do we go from here?

MAGGIE HARCOURT

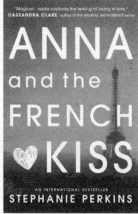

Love this book? Love Usborne YA

Follow us online and sign up to the Usborne YA
newsletter for the latest YA books,
news and competitions:

usborne.com/yanewsletter

 @UsborneYA

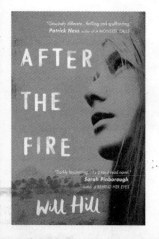